No Strings Attached

Read More Kate Angell

SWEET SPOT (Richmond Rogues)

NO TAN LINES (Barefoot William)

UNWRAPPED (anthology)

No Strings Attached

KATE ANGELL

KENSINGTON PUBLISHING CORP.

www.kensingtonbooks.com

KENSINGTON BOOKS are published by

Kensington Publishing Corp.
119 West 40th Street
New York, NY 10018

ISBN-13: 978-0-7582-6920-1
ISBN-10: 0-7582-6920-X

First Kensington Trade Paperback Printing: May 2013

10 9 8 7 6 5 4 3 2 1

Printed in the United States of America

ACKNOWLEDGMENTS

Alicia Condon, my editor. I appreciate you.

Hallie Flack, my friend since elementary school. You inspired Sophie Saunders.

My go-to ladies who support me when I'm writing: Sue-Ellen Welfonder, Jina Bacarr, Marion Brown, Debbie Roome, and Kelly Callahan. I thank you.

At the beach the rule is no shirt, no shoes . . .

NO STRINGS ATTACHED

One

"Blonde, metallic blue bikini, left side of the pier near the boogie board rental," Mac James said in a low voice as he handed Dune a twenty-ounce cup of black coffee from Brews Brothers. The scent of Bakehouse doughnuts rose from a bakery box. "I'm betting Brazilian wax. She's definitely a two-nighter."

Dune Cates raised an eyebrow. "Brazilian?"

Mac blew on his coffee to cool it. "Women discuss boxers, briefs, or commando on a man. I debate waxing."

Dune shook his head. Mac was his partner on the professional beach volleyball tour. On court, they were as close as brothers and in each other's heads. Off court, their lifestyles differed greatly. Mac was up for anything at any given time. Dune, on the other hand, was more conservative. He had foresight and weighed the pros and cons. He knew when and where to draw the line, whereas Mac had no boundaries. He saw life as a free-for-all.

Mac had dated more women than Dune could count. He'd recently parted ways with a waxing technician at VaDazzle Salon in Los Angeles. The salon was known for its pubic hair designs. Mac now played his V-games with the eye of an expert.

Dune had pretty much seen it all. His bed partners shaped their pubes into lightning bolts, hearts, and initials.

One female surfer dyed her pubic hair pink. Another was striped like a zebra. His most fascinating lover had been shaved and decorated with stick-on crystals. She'd sparkled like a disco ball.

His preference was, and always had been, a light bikini wax or totally natural. He didn't need creative techniques to turn him on.

He leaned his forearms against the bright blue pipe railing that separated the boardwalk from the beach. He took a deep sip of his coffee. It was midmorning and the sun warmed his back right between his shoulder blades. The heat never bothered him. He'd grown up at the beach. The sand and shoreline were home to him. It was where he earned his living.

He looked toward the boogie boards. The blonde stood out. She was definitely Mac's type. His partner loved long hair and legs that went from here to eternity. The woman's hair skimmed nearly to her waist and her legs were sleek and toned.

Dune read women well. He knew who liked him as a person and who only wanted a piece of his action. He recognized the blonde as a woman who enticed men and enjoyed their attention. She made a theatrical production of laying out her towel, then rubbing on suntan oil. She was soon slick. Her entire body glistened.

Beside him, Mac opened the bakery box and offered Dune first choice. He selected a glazed doughnut. Mac chose one with chocolate frosting and sprinkles.

"Sweet cheeks near the volleyball net," Mac said between bites. "Red one-piece, black hair, French wax. Nice walk. I'd follow her anywhere."

Sweet cheeks was tall and slender, Dune noted. She moved with the slow, sensuous grace of a woman who knew her body well and owned the moment. The lady was hot.

Mac squinted against the sun. "Tattooed chick in a fringed camo thong bikini, third in line at the concession stand," he said. "Is that a tat of a rattler coiled on her stomach?"

Dune checked her out. "Looks like one."

She was a walking advertisement for a tattoo parlor. He saw just how much she liked snakes when she widened her stance. A python wrapped her left leg; its split tongue darted out as if licking her inner thigh.

"Snakebite, Dude," Mac said. "Woman's got venom. I bet her pubes are shaved and tattooed with a cobra."

"She's definitely into reptiles."

Mac reached for a second doughnut topped with cinnamon sugar. "Sex and snakes don't mix. I'd go soft if I heard hissing or a rattle."

"Major mood killer," Dune agreed.

They drank their coffee and ate their doughnuts in companionable silence. All along the coastline, sunbathers sought their own private space. That space was limited. The expanding crowd was an improvement from the previous summer when the economy tanked and one person had the entire beach to himself. It felt good to see his hometown thrive.

Mac nudged him, pointed right. "Check out the desert nomad at water's edge."

The woman was easy to spot. She was short and overdressed for the beach. She wore all white. White reflected the sun. A Gilligan bucket hat covered her hair. Her sunglasses were enormous, hiding her face. A rain poncho capped her shoulders, and she wore waterproof pants tucked into rubber boots.

She walked slowly along the compact sand, only to retreat when a splash of foam chased her. It appeared she didn't want to get wet. She bent down once, touched the water, then quickly shook the drops from her hand.

She played tag with the Gulf for several minutes before

turning toward the boardwalk. She tripped over her feet and nearly fell near the lifeguard station. The guard on duty left his female admirers and took her by the arm. He smiled down at her. She dipped her head, embarrassed.

The lifeguard gave her an encouraging pat on her shoulder and sent her on her way. Her rubber boots seemed overly large, and she stumbled two more times on her way to the wooden ramp. Sunbathers scooted out of her way.

The closer the woman came, the slower Dune breathed.

His heart gave a surprising squeeze. *Sophie Saunders.* He was sure of it. No one else would dress so warmly on a summer day. And Sophie was naturally clumsy.

Ten months had passed since he'd last seen her, although he'd thought about her often. They'd come together for a worthy cause: to boost the Barefoot William economy.

His younger sister Shaye had organized a local pro/am volleyball tournament to keep their town alive. He'd provided the professional players. The pros were auctioned to amateur athletes. Sophie had bid ten thousand dollars to be his partner. She wasn't good at sports, but she had the heart of a champion.

Sophie, with her brown hair and evergreen eyes, had a high IQ but low self-esteem. She was a bookworm, shy and afraid of her own shadow. She feared crowds and the ocean, yet she'd powered through the sports event and made a decent showing. He wondered if she'd ever learned to swim.

Her image had stuck with him. He remembered things about her that he'd rather have forgotten. She had amazing skin, fair, smooth, and soft. Her scent was light and powdery: vanilla and innocence. Her hair smelled like baby shampoo. She hid her curves beneath layers of clothing, yet her body gave off a woman's heat.

She'd bought her very first swimsuit for the tournament. He could close his eyes and still picture her in the cobalt blue tankini. He could hear the male fans on the outdoor bleachers applaud and whistle their appreciation. Sweet Sophie had an amazing body.

Their team had fought hard during the event. He'd tried to shield her when they'd battled through the loser's bracket. His best attempts hadn't saved her, not by a long shot.

Sophie wasn't the least bit athletic and had taken a beating. Opponents nailed her with the ball time and again. She'd gotten sunburned, bruised her knees, and eaten sand. Yet she'd never complained. Not once.

To this day he regretted not telling her good-bye when the weekend ended. Instead he'd watched her walk away. It had been for the best. She was a Saunders, and he was a Cates. A century-old feud had separated the families back then.

The lines of hostility had blurred when Shaye married Sophie's brother Trace. Both sides had eventually accepted their marriage. Only his Grandfather Frank had yet to come around. He was old-Florida, opinionated and stubborn, and set in his ways.

Dune figured everyone would forgive and forget once Shaye became pregnant. She and Trace wanted to start a family. Dune anticipated her announcement any day now. No one would want to miss the birth of the couple's first child.

He absently rubbed his wrist. He'd played a big part in Barefoot William's financial recovery, only to suffer for it later. Tendonitis was a bitch. Freak accidents occurred in all sports. Some were career-ending.

He'd taken a dive at the South Beach Open and fallen on his outstretched hand prior to his hometown tournament. He'd suffered a scaphoid fracture.

His orthopedist put him in a short, supportive cast and recommended that he not take part in the event. Dune refused to let his family down. He managed to serve and spike with one hand as well as others could with two. He'd played through the pain.

In retrospect, he shouldn't have participated. He'd aggravated his fracture further. Despite additional surgery and extensive therapy, he never regained full strength in his fingers and wrist.

He was a man of quick decisions, yet the thought of retirement left him feeling restless, indecisive, and old.

Sophie was so young. She was twenty-five to his thirty-six. Their age difference concerned him. He'd dated sweet young things, all worldly and experienced. But Sophie was unlike any woman he'd ever met. She was sensitive and vulnerable, and made him want to protect her.

He preferred no strings attached.

Here she was now twenty feet from him, her head down, watching her steps so she didn't fall. She made it onto the boardwalk without mishap and visibly relaxed. Her sigh and small smile indicated she'd accomplished a great feat and was proud of herself.

Mac stared at her, too. "It's Sophie. Damn, she's cute. Let's go talk to her."

Dune hesitated. "Let's see where she's headed first."

He removed his Suncats, a brand of sunglasses he'd recently endorsed on the tour. The lenses were small and oval with a dark olive tint. The sporty frame never slipped down his nose, even when he sweat or wore sunscreen. He hooked the sunglasses at the neck of his white polo.

Sophie was slow to move. It took her several minutes to catch her breath. Once she had, she entered Crabby Abby's General Store. The cherry red door caught on her rubber boot heel. She shook her foot until it released.

"Let's follow her," Mac said, tossing his coffee cup and

the bakery box into a trash receptacle. "I need my Sophie fix."

Still Dune held back. "She's working."

Mac looked skeptical. "In that outfit?"

"She has a change of clothes inside," he said. "Abby's employees all wear shorts and a tank top."

"What's she doing on your boardwalk?" Mac asked. "Padding her trust fund?"

Dune shook his head. "She doesn't need the money. According to my sister, Sophie's trying to find her niche in the working world."

"Her niche wasn't Saunders Shores?"

"Not from what I understand." Dune then shared what Shaye had told him. "Sophie's shy and has struggled to fit in. She spent time at Trace's office, the Sandcastle Hotel, several boutiques and bistros, but nothing appealed to her. She's yet to settle on a career."

Shaye had further mentioned that the elite businesses overwhelmed Sophie, a fact Dune chose not to share with Mac. Sophie was quiet, reserved, and avoided crowds whenever possible. She was drawn to couture, but found it difficult to outfit upscale clientele.

Food service was not her strong suit, either. She'd messed up orders and dropped trays. She hadn't been fired, but the owners were relieved when her ventures took her elsewhere.

Dune ran a hand along the back of his neck, blew out a breath. "My sister's taken a special interest in Sophie," he said. "Shaye suggested she explore job opportunities on our boardwalk. Sophie refuses to be paid, so she's volunteering."

"She may like Barefoot William so much she decides to stay," said Mac.

Sophie as a permanent fixture on his boardwalk made Dune uneasy. He hoped that wasn't the case. He wasn't certain he wanted her here full-time. She was too nice, too naïve, and too in need of a keeper. She'd prove distracting.

He wasn't in town long enough to watch over her. Nor did he have anyone in mind to appoint to the task. No one he'd trust, anyway.

He could easily understand her fascination with his hometown. The Cates's northern cement boardwalk linked to a wooden pier that catered to fishermen, sun worshippers, water sport enthusiasts, and tourists who didn't wear a watch on vacation.

Amusement arcades and carnival rides drew large crowds. The specialty shops sold everything from Florida T-shirts to ice cream, sunglasses to sharks' teeth, and shells to Hula-Hoops.

A century-old carousel whirled within a weatherproof enclosure. Its walls of windows overlooked the Gulf. The whir of the Ferris wheel was soothing, while the swing ride that whipped out and over the waves sent pulses racing.

Neon lights flashed at night and music poured from many of the shops. People danced down the boardwalk, free and uninhibited. Many played blacklight volleyball on the beach. Glow-in-the-dark Frisbees were tossed along the shoreline. A few tourists skinny-dipped near the pier after midnight. Barefoot William was as honky-tonk as Saunders Shores was high-profile.

Waterfront mansions welcomed the rich and retired in Sophie's world. Yachts the size of cruise ships lined the waterways. Private airstrips replaced commercial travel. The wealthy were a community unto themselves. *Forbes* listed Saunders Shores as the wealthiest resort community in the country.

"So?" Max nudged Dune with his elbow. "Do we surprise Sophie or not?"

He shrugged, still reluctant.

Mac rolled his eyes.

Dune scanned the beach. A NO LITTERING sign caught his attention. He'd played Big Word, Little Words as a kid, a game where the player made shorter words out of the letters of the longer one. He did so now to distract himself from the matter at hand. Littering: *Let, get, ring, in, gin, it.*

"You never told her good-bye and you regretted it," Mac persisted, interrupting his game. "It might be nice to say hello. You're home for a month. You're bound to bump into her." He paused. "You know you want to see her."

Dune was conflicted. He and Mac could go together or Mac would go alone. A part of him didn't want his partner alone with her. Mac had a soft spot for Sophie. He used to tease her until her whole body blushed. She blushed more than any woman Dune had ever known. Mac could easily turn his teasing into hitting on her. That bothered Dune a lot.

"I'm in," he finally agreed.

Mac grinned.

"What are you smiling about?" asked Dune.

"You know what I'm smiling about."

Mac knew him as well as his own brothers. Dune had always considered Mac family. Mac was the bat-shit crazy cousin who pushed everyone's buttons. And got away with it.

Approaching Sophie now gave Dune the opportunity to establish boundaries. He didn't want hero worship or fan girl from her, only a friendship. Keeping her at arm's length worked best.

He braced himself as he walked the few feet to the general store. He hated the fact Sophie threw off his breathing. His chest hitched just as it always did right before the first serve in a volleyball game.

Anticipation wound him tight.

★   ★   ★

Sophie Saunders was on her hands and knees on the hardwood floor when Dune Cates and his partner Mac James pushed through the door. *Dune.* Her stomach dipped and her body went soft. The Windex spray bottle and cleaning cloth she was using to wipe down the glass shelves of the pharmacy counter slipped through her fingers. The bottle hit the floor and rolled just out of her reach.

She pushed her orange half-frame reading glasses higher on her nose, then peeked through the crack of the small wooden doors and watched the two men approach. She knew them both, but hadn't seen either one since the previous summer when she'd partnered with Dune for the pro/am volleyball tournament to raise money for Barefoot William.

It had been the best three days of her life. They'd scored the winner's trophy in the loser's bracket. She cherished the small trophy, designed with a silver volleyball on a block of polished wood. It sat in a place of honor on the top shelf of her antique glass-front barrister's bookcase between her clothbound first editions of Louisa May Alcott's *Little Women* and Augusta Jane Evann's *St. Elmo*.

The trophy was visible from all angles in her library. She would look up from reading, see the award, and smile. The trophy made her feel like a winner. It gave her strength and contentment.

Her inner peace vanished the moment she saw Dune. He made her jumpy and edgy and nervous. Gossip on the boardwalk had him coming home in June. But it was only the middle of May. Sophie hadn't expected him today.

Shaye had mentioned her older brother was taking a short break from the pro circuit. His thoughts were centered on retirement, although he'd yet to make the formal announcement. He and Mac were to play in the Huntington Beach Classic the first weekend in July. After that it was anyone's guess as to his future.

Sophie secretly hoped he'd be returning home. She'd had a crush on him ever since elementary school. Time had not diminished her feelings. She could still recall their long-ago first meeting.

She'd been on her bicycle riding home from school when her backpack had slipped off one shoulder and knocked her off balance. She was a chubby, uncoordinated seven-year-old, and when her bike tipped, she fell hard.

Her glasses had flown off and the zipper on her backpack split. Her books had skidded over the pavement.

She had so many books to gather. Her last stop of the day had been at the library. With the weekend ahead, she'd stocked up on reading material. As a child, she had found a great escape in fairy tales.

She remembered that a horn had honked and a car swerved around her. She'd looked up and noticed she'd stopped traffic. The more she hurried, the clumsier she became. Books dropped as fast as she picked them up.

Her classmates had passed her on their own bikes and snickered. She wasn't popular. She had one close friend whose mother picked her up every day.

Dune had come to her rescue. He'd ridden up on a motorcycle that roared so loud she covered her ears. He'd cut the engine, set the kickstand, and removed his helmet. She'd stared at him, this older boy with the mussed blond hair and Lion King–gold eyes.

He'd climbed off his bike and collected her books. In a very short time he'd fixed the zipper on her backpack, then doctored the cut on her chin with a Superman Band-Aid. She'd been good to go.

They'd exchanged first names, but back then neither had known they were sworn enemies. Cates and Saunders didn't mix, yet he'd been nice to her. She'd never forgotten his kindness. Her mended childhood backpack still hung in a storage room in her garage. He'd made a lifelong impression on her. She'd hero-worshipped him as a kid, then been awed by the man when she entered her twenties. Her biggest wish was to know him better.

She sighed softly. She'd hoped for the perfect moment to get reacquainted. Now was not good. She was stuck behind the counter on sore knees with the scent of Windex on her hands. She quietly rolled her shoulders and neck. She should've stood up the moment she saw Dune and Mac and made her presence known. As it was, she'd look like a jack-in-the-box should she pop up now.

She squinted down the aisle, studying both men. Mac was tall and rangy with shaggy dark hair, blue eyes, and an easy smile. He wore a gray tank top printed with *I Win, You Lose, Game Over* and black board shorts. He lived life on a dare and laughed easily. He charmed women out of their swimsuits with no more than a smile.

Then there was Dune. Sophie's breathing deepened. At six-foot-six he wore a white polo, worn jeans, and a lean masculinity. His hair was shorter than she remembered, which only sharpened his features. His shoulders were broad and his body toned. He was one fine-looking athlete.

He'd recently turned thirty-six, and photographs of his birthday celebration had surfaced in a dozen sports magazines. She'd purchased copies of each one. Those pages featuring his sexy grin were dog-eared.

Mac had thrown the bash on Huntington Beach in Dune's honor. The party was open to the public. Thousands had attended. Volleyball fans were loyal and loved to celebrate one of their own. Dune belonged to them.

Women surrounded him in the photos, standing twenty deep in their string bikinis, all trying to claim his attention. Dune stood among them in a tropical pair of his designer swim trunks and a disarming smile. He'd had to hire a tractor trailer to haul away his gifts.

Dune was a champion in his sport. He'd won every tournament on the professional beach volleyball tour. Media followed him as closely as the cheering crowd. He was accessible to the press and never declined an interview. There'd been no rise and fall to his career. He'd been a solid, dominant force from his first serve. His talent and sportsmanship were legendary. He'd received the coveted *Sports Illustrated* Sportsman of the Year Award, a top athletic honor.

Men wanted to be him and women wanted to do him. His female fans called him Beach Heat. He was that hot.

Sophie now watched as the two men approached the pharmacy. They walked slowly, as if they had all the time in the world. She imagined her heart was pounding hard enough to draw their attention. She held her breath, afraid to exhale.

She'd hoped when she next saw Dune she would look more presentable. She was uncomfortable in her own skin, and the more she covered up, the better. The employee dress code at Crabby Abby's was a red halter top and khaki shorts. She felt nearly naked.

Dune was used to women wearing next to nothing. The beach brought out their tanned, toned bodies in tiny bikinis. Sophie faced the sun in a hat, long tunic, loose slacks, and rain boots. She layered on so much sunscreen, she looked like a ghost.

She watched as the men stopped before the shelves stocked with toothpaste and deodorant. Each selected his favorite brands before moving down the aisle toward feminine products and male protection. Sophie swallowed hard when Dune reached for a neon blue box on the top shelf.

"Night Light Condoms," he read from the back of the

box. "No need to reach for the light switch. These condoms glow in the dark."

Mac rubbed his jaw. "Night Light fits tight, but I like Black Ice. Condom has a nice, easy slide."

The two men turned toward the pharmacy counter.

And Sophie curled into a tighter ball.

Dune leaned his hip against the edge and cleared his throat. "Should we get boxes of two-fifty or order cases of one thousand?" he asked Mac.

Sophie gaped and her eyes went wide. *One thousand condoms.* They were planning on having a lot of sex.

Mac set the items he held onto the countertop. "I'd say the latter, but let's ask Sophie."

Could a heart stop? Apparently she wasn't good at hiding. They'd known her location all along. She wished for a hole to open and swallow her. No such luck. She untucked just as Dune rounded the counter. She breathed him in. His scent was masculine and clean, hinting of lime and sunshine.

He offered his hand and she took it, pushing slowly to her feet. His grip was large, callused, and supportive. Her hand disappeared within the curve of his palm.

Having seen Dune through the cracks of the counter doors was one thing. Up close was quite another. He overwhelmed her. She held his hand until he loosened his grip. She would've loved to hold on a little longer, but that seemed inappropriate.

She faced him now, her eyes leveled on his heart. At five-two she was forced to look up. Way up. She did so, meeting his amber-brown gaze. Her composure slipped and kept on sliding. She blushed. She was as embarrassed by the heat in her cheeks as by her reaction to him.

She hated wearing her feelings on her sleeve while Dune wasn't the least bit affected. He stared at her, long, hard, assessing. His smile was slight, his expression unreadable.

He crossed his arms over his chest and widened his stance, but didn't say a word. Sophie couldn't have spoken if her life depended on it.

Mac, on the other hand, was a man of action and affection. He pulled her to him and kissed her full on the mouth. A quick kiss, soft and tasting of sugar.

"It's been a long time, babe," he said, still holding her close. "Have you missed us?"

Shyness overtook her and she dipped her head. She wasn't good at banter. Flirting eluded her completely. Honesty was her policy.

"You've crossed my mind on occasion," she admitted in a soft voice. Mac was easy to remember. He'd teased her throughout the volleyball tournament. His sexual exploits were as infamous as his spikes on the court.

Dune was an equally gifted athlete, yet he was far more serious in his outlook on life. He was definitely more distant. His departure the previous summer without so much as a good-bye had laid Sophie low.

She'd paid big bucks to be his partner. He hadn't owed her anything beyond a weekend of his time. That was all he'd given her.

The final image she had of him was him drinking a beer on the beach in the middle of the celebration while she stood alone on the boardwalk. Her heart had hurt for six months afterward.

"Hello, Sophie," Dune's deep voice rolled over her, more formal than friendly. He raised his hand and *ruffled* her hair, as if she were a child. Her jaw slipped, and the air in her lungs hitched like a hiccup.

Eleven years separated them. Age didn't matter to her, but it apparently did to him. To add to her embarrassment,

Mac burst out laughing, a gut-busting laugh that only confused Sophie further. Was she the butt of their joke?

Dune cut Mac a look so sharp that Mac stopped laughing. Mac went on to straighten the strands of her hair that
Dune had mussed. He then squeezed her shoulder, which
shored up her confidence.

"I'm surprised to see you guys," she finally managed.

"We saw you on the beach," said Mac. "You were
dressed for a trek across the desert."

"I didn't want to get sunburned."

"No chance of that," he assured her.

Dune stared at her. "You were at the water's edge, skim-
ming the waves with your fingertips."

She bit down on her bottom lip. "The Gulf scares me,"
she admitted. "I still don't swim, but I'd love to wade ankle deep someday."

"I was a lifeguard one summer," Mac said. "I'd be happy
to teach you how to swim. You won't earn an Olympic
medal, but most everyone can dog-paddle."

"Sophie isn't everyone," Dune said. "She'll conquer her
fear in her own good time."

"Maybe she'd like to skim board," Mac suggested.

"Or maybe not," said Dune.

Definitely not, Sophie thought, agreeing with Dune.
She didn't have the coordination to run along the shoreline, toss the rectangular board, then hop on and ride the
breaking waves. She'd fall flat on her face. She'd be buried
in the sand at high tide.

Mac wrapped his arm about her shoulders, tucked her
against his side. She didn't protest. She knew he liked
women; the closer they were the better. His body was
warm, his stance relaxed. "How long have you worked
here?" he asked.

"Two weeks," she said. "I volunteer part-time."

"Is Abby crabby?" asked Mac.

Sophie shook her head. "Not in the least."

"You're on *my* boardwalk." Dune drew a line in the sand between the Cates and the Saunders.

Teasing or a taunt? The neutral tone of his voice made it hard to tell. "Shaye issued me a work permit," she said.

He came back with, "My sister no longer runs Barefoot William Enterprises."

Sophie scrunched her nose. She wasn't about to argue the point. Dune's grandfather had removed Shaye from her duties when she married Trace. The older man went on to appoint Kai Cates as president.

Kai might be the overseer, but Shaye was the primary consultant. Her advice and direction kept the town in the black. Family and friends might not approve of her husband, but no one disputed her authority.

Sophie was certain that Frank was aware of Shaye's involvement, but he let it ride. He and Shaye had once been as close as father and daughter. Sophie hoped they would be close again someday, once Frank accepted a Cates had married a Saunders.

Until then, the century-old dispute still lingered. Sophie loved history and had researched both families. Shaye and Trace shared a stack of journals, dating back to the turn of the century. Each yellowed page spelled out the disagreements and distrust between the founding fathers of the Gulf community. Sophie found their lives fascinating.

For a heartbeat she turned back time and recalled the depth and insight of the entries, the long passages outlining the two writers' dissatisfaction and differences.

William Cates's documentation dated back to 1906. The very day he left Frostbite, Minnesota. He'd been a farmer broken by poor crops and a harsh, early winter. He'd sold his farm and equipment, then hand cranked his Model T and driven south. He had no destination in mind. He sought warmer weather and lots of land.

The trip was long and hard, yet he pushed on until the Florida sunshine thawed him out. On a long stretch of un-inhabited beach, William rolled up his pant legs and shucked his socks and work boots. He walked the shore-line with the egrets and horseshoe crabs at low tide. The salt water was crystal clear.

Once he experienced the warm sugar sand between his toes, he vowed never to wear shoes again. He put down roots, married, and named the fishing village Barefoot William.

Even after he was elected mayor, William walked bare-foot through city hall, as did the other town officials. Back then, life existed on a man's word and a solid handshake.

William's journal was a personal pledge to his family and longtime friends. He gave his word that expansion along the Gulf Coast would be slow and selective. There was no rush to build beyond the long pier and short board-walk.

For two decades, the fishing village remained small and laid-back. Welcoming. Until the day Sophie's great-great-great grandfather Evan Saunders disrupted the peace. It had been a sad day for the Cateses. Sophie's sympathy lay with William.

She knew from the journals that Evan was a capitalist with big-city blood. He wore three-piece suits, a bowler hat, and polished brown oxfords. She'd seen a black-and-white photograph of Evan. The man looked pretentious. It was rumored he defied the heat and never broke a sweat even in summer. He dared the sun to shine.

Evan set his sights on real estate. His journal was filled with predictions and diagrams for growth. He contacted Northern investors and, within six months, the Saunders

Group began to buy up land. Evan wanted to citify the small town. He sought to turn Barefoot William into a wealthy winter resort.

After reading the journals through 1950, Sophie discovered the sordid truth. Her ancestors had dominated, at times, through deception. By backstabbing and being underhanded, too.

She'd learned about Evan's payoffs and bribes.

Money was his mistress.

William Cates's wealth came through family. They were close-knit, and he protected his own. He fought for his town. He battled zoning and expansion. He believed in squatters' rights.

Evan was a developer and wanted the very best. He built his own boardwalk, yacht harbor, and extravagant beach house. He snubbed the barefoot mayor. Animosity flared between the men. They had sparred for sixty years.

On an overcast day with thunderheads rolling, the conservative and the capitalist had drawn a line in the sand, which neither had crossed during the remainder of their lifetimes. The line later became Center Street, the midpoint between Barefoot William and Saunders Shores.

On a sigh, Sophie mentally closed the journals. The two towns had historical roots that ran deep. She hoped the day would come when everyone stepped out of the past and got along.

She was a Saunders; there was no denying the fact. She was born to a life of privilege. She'd grown up quiet and content with a trust fund that would last her indefinitely.

Only recently had her soul stirred and she'd become restless. She wasn't the person she wanted to be. She needed to overcome her shyness and find her purpose, however small. She needed to move outside her comfort zone.

She'd gone to Trace and Shaye and sought their guidance. They suggested she work in several shops until she found a business that truly appealed to her. Crabby Abby's was her second venture.

The boardwalk stretched long and inviting. Each shop was filled with excitement. She'd find her niche. She was sure of it.

"Sophie, babe, you're drifting on us." Mac snapped his fingers before her eyes. "You've got two of the biggest names in volleyball offering to take you to lunch and you're lost in space," he teased.

She blinked, blushed, embarrassed by her attention lapse. "Sorry," she said.

The corners of Dune's eyes creased and his lips twitched. He was amused. "How soon are you free?" he asked.

She glanced at her watch. It was eleven forty-five. "I'm done with my shift at noon."

"You're volunteering," said Mac. "Can't you leave whenever you want?"

"I promised Abby four hours," Sophie said.

Respect lit Dune's gaze, fleeting yet discernible. "Some of us are more dedicated than others."

"I finish what I start," said Mac.

"No, you don't," said Dune. "You recently left a promotional shoot for volleyball a half-hour early."

Mac made a face. "How many times did the photographer want me to serve the freakin' ball?" he asked.

"More than once," returned Dune.

"The guy should've gotten the shot with my first spike," Mac argued.

"It wasn't a spike," Dune said. "You bounced on your toes like a girl, then underhanded the serve."

"Don't believe a word he says," Mac said to Sophie. "I was cooperative."

Dune ran a hand down his face. "You behaved badly."

"I gave you more camera time," said Mac.

"The shoot wasn't about me," Dune reminded him. "It was about partners in sports."

Mac cut him a hard look. "How long do you plan to be my partner?" he asked.

All fun and baiting subsided. The question hung in the air unanswered. Sophie watched as Dune rotated his wrist, flexed his fingers, then fisted his hand until his knuckles turned white. He unclenched his hand and shrugged, a man uncertain and subdued. "Time will tell," he said.

Mac's stomach growled. "Damn, I'm hungry. Let's head to Molly Malone's. Dune's buying lunch."

"I can afford—" she was about to offer.

"No, you can't," Dune said. "Mac eats for ten men. He's always starving."

Sophie liked Molly Malone's. The corner diner had the best food on the boardwalk, along with a spectacular view of the vintage carousel. Locals and tourists alike stood ten deep at the door, waiting to be seated. The restaurant was known for generous portions and homemade pie. Sophie's favorite flavor was chocolate chiffon.

Dune placed a tube of Crest, a small bottle of mouthwash, and his box of condoms on the glass countertop. "Ring me up," he said.

Sophie glanced at the Night Lights. She remembered his earlier comment. "Did you want to order a case?" she forced herself to ask.

Dune stared at her.

Mac grinned. "Sophie, babe," he said, lowering his voice. "Dune's active, but not *that* active."

"Enough on my sex life," Dune said sharply.

Mac ignored him. "Two cases would work nicely for me."

Sophie reached for a pen and paper.

"Don't write down his order." Dune placed his hand over hers, stopping her. "He's playing you."

His palm was warm and covered her entire hand. She wanted to turn her hand over and lace her fingers with his. Just for a second. That second ticked by.

Dune released her before she made a fool of herself. He hadn't shown any interest in her. It would be unwise to make the first move. He might reject her.

Her hands shook as she rang up and bagged his items. She was so nervous she gave him a dollar too much in change, which he returned.

Mac came next. She had his order ready to go in half the time. She then excused herself to change clothes.

She enjoyed working at the general store. Abby Cates had given her a small closet in the storeroom to hang several outfits. She had her nomad layered beachwear, two hats, a Windbreaker, several tops, and a pair of navy cropped slacks.

She kicked off her flip-flops, then slid off her red tank and khaki shorts, down to her gray lace bra and high-cut panties. She loved feminine, romantic underwear. Satin felt intimate and pleasurable against her skin.

She'd never been more excited. She was about to have lunch with Dune. Mac was the perfect buffer. He'd keep the conversation going. He talked enough for three people. Sophie never had much to say.

It took her only six minutes to dress. She felt comfortable in her pale pistachio silk blouse and cropped pants. On a whim she'd bought a pair of blue-and-green striped Keds. She found them fanciful. She wore them now.

She grabbed her brown leather hobo bag and left the storeroom. Her heart slowed along with her steps in the short hallway. What a difference a few minutes could make.

She'd left Dune and Mac alone by the counter; as she returned, she found the men surrounded by women near the magazine rack. Six to be exact.

All wore inviting smiles and string bikinis.

All touched and flirted and wanted more than autographs. The men didn't seem to mind. Not one bit.

Dune leaned against the wall. His smile came easily, warm and welcoming.

Mac openly loved the ladies. He curved his arms over the shoulders of the two closest to him, grafting them to his side.

"The Blue Coconut, tonight," she heard Mac say. "Bring your friends."

Sophie had heard of the peanut bar there, but had never been invited to party. Beer for a quarter brought in an early crowd. Customers ate unshelled peanuts and dropped the hulls on the floor. Darts, pool, and a jukebox rounded out the night. Fun for some, Sophie guessed. She, on the other hand, preferred a good book.

Her insecurities took hold and she felt suddenly out of place. Her clothes covered her from neck to knee, whereas the beach babes flashed cleavage and flossed their butt cheeks.

Sadness settled on her chest. Disappointment turned her toward the back door. She could sneak out and take to the alley. Dune and Mac wouldn't miss her. They had six willing women available for lunch and much more.

She tripped over her feet in her retreat, banging her shoulder against the wall. Another bruise, she sighed. She wished she were more coordinated.

Her hand was on the doorknob when the masculine scent of sunshine and lime warned of Dune's approach. "Running out on us, Sophie?" he asked, drawing out the words. "Mac won't be happy."

Mac wouldn't be pleased, which meant Dune didn't care one way or the other.

Sophie sighed and her shoulders slumped.

She decided she wasn't hungry after all.

Two

The doorknob clicked and sunlight lit the hallway. Dune Cates was so stunned he was slow to react. *Sophie leaving?* What the hell?

She had both feet out the door by the time he made his move. He grabbed her by the shoulders and pulled her back against him. He had big hands, even for a man. One hand could fully clutch a volleyball. His fingers were long; his palms were wide. His grip tightened as her body twisted and she lost her footing. He set her upright, but not before his fingertips grazed the outer softness of her right breast. She inhaled sharply. Stilled.

He sucked air as well when she slowly turned to face him. She was short and touched him low. Her shoulder brushed his upper abdomen and her hip swiped his thigh, just south of his balls. Her scent made his entire body flex. Vanilla, a hint of baby powder, and inexperienced woman blended with her body heat. Their tight space got very warm, very fast.

His cock stirred. He released her so quickly she hit her funny bone on an aluminum ladder standing nearby. She winced and rubbed her elbow. She frowned at him.

"Sorry," he muttered. He stared at a bottle of bleach on a high shelf, which took his mind off his erection. Big Word, Little Words. Clorox, he read the label on the bottle. *Or, ox, lox, loco.* He slowly got his body under control.

Sophie looked up just as he gazed down. Her eyes were wide; her full pink lips were slightly parted. Her expression was shy and unsure. Hopeful and wistful.

He grew uneasy. He'd been around enough women to know that look. Hers was the look of expectation. Expectation often came with a crush. A crush would make Sophie vulnerable.

He couldn't be absolutely certain she was into him, but he planned to be cautious. She was too sweet, too shy, to get caught up in his chaos. His life was unsettled and he needed to concentrate on his career and not another person.

He had the urge to take a giant step back. To give them both some breathing room. Unfortunately the hallway was cramped and the space was limited. He wore leather sandals and his bare toes now bumped the white rubber tips on her blue-and-green striped Keds. He jammed his hands in his jeans pockets, put on his game face, and forced a calm tone he didn't feel.

"You agreed to lunch," he said, watching her closely.

"I thought you'd changed your mind," she quietly returned.

"Why would you think that?"

"Those women."

"Which women?" he asked.

"The ones you were talking to."

"When?"

She looked as confused as he felt. "A few minutes ago."

"Where?"

"By the magazine rack."

He finally understood. He'd smiled at the sexy six, then tuned them out. He'd kept one eye on the hallway, on the lookout for Sophie. She was his priority.

The girls had come on strong, but Dune hadn't weakened. They had extra tickets for an afternoon booze cruise and were looking for hook-up buddies. They wanted to get down and dirty and drink.

Dune was familiar with *Tide One On,* the luxury ship docked north of Barefoot William. On sunny days the cruiser dropped anchor ten miles off the coast. Those onboard enjoyed food, drink, and music. A small swimming pool on the lower deck cooled and soothed sunburns. A hot tub bubbled and steamed on the upper deck. Swimsuits were optional.

What happened on the Gulf stayed on the Gulf.

It was a wild time.

Mac had shown some interest in the cruise but, in the end, he'd kept his word to Sophie. Mac could always take Dune's speedboat out to the party yacht later in the day.

He held her gaze now. "What about the women?" he asked.

"They're tan, beautiful, and"—her voice lowered a little—"fun."

"You're not fun?" he asked.

"Not that fun."

"There's something to be said for cute and shy," he said, right before he ruffled her hair.

Sophie blinked. Her face fell and her disappointment showed. His friendly gesture had somehow hurt her feelings. He wasn't certain what he'd done wrong. Neither did he know how to fix it.

She blew her bangs out of her eyes, then led him down the hallway. She dragged her feet. The rubber on her Keds scuffed the wooden floorboards.

He followed her, his gaze focused on her backside. Her brown hair brushed her shoulder blades, shiny and loose. Her spine was straight. Her ass was shapely. He liked her walk; he found the roll of her hips appealing.

He was slow to look up once they reached Mac. Mac cocked an eyebrow and Dune locked his jaw. Damn, his partner had caught him eyeing Sophie's butt. Mac's grin was knowingly evil.

Don't go there, Dune glared at him.

Mac's smile only got bigger.

Dune's neck grew warm.

Mac let him off the hook. He took Sophie by the hand. "I'm starving. Let's feed me." He led her down the aisle toward the front door.

The aisle was narrow and the two bumped against each other with each step. Their contact was minimal, yet Dune found it irritating and way too intimate.

Mac continued to hold her hand as they made their way to Molly Malone's. Dune frowned. They looked like a couple. Sunbathers came off the beach, ready for lunch, and jammed the boardwalk. The crowd forced Dune to fall in step behind Mac and Sophie when he would've preferred to walk by her side.

Mac loved women, that was a given. There were three of them going to lunch, yet Mac was turning it into a two-some. His interest in Sophie frustrated Dune, even if it was no more than friendly flirting. Dune couldn't hear their conversation, but Mac's easy grin and occasional wink drew Sophie's soft smile. She relaxed in his company.

A dozen people stopped Dune on his way to the diner, all requesting autographs. He never refused a fan. Sophie and Mac had disappeared by the time he signed baseball caps, volleyballs, and Frisbees.

He looked around when the crowd cleared. Where the hell was Mac? Dune wondered. Mac was a crowd-pleaser, yet today he'd split with Sophie instead of entertaining his fans. Dune didn't like him sneaking off.

He jogged the rest of the way to the diner. Customers clustered at the door, patiently waiting to be seated. The tables were filled, but three counter stools stood open. Dune watched as Mac guided Sophie to the counter. His hand pressed low on her spine as they wound around the four-tops.

Mac nudged Sophie to the far end, where she took the stool against the wall and he scooted in beside her. Dune crossed the diner and dropped down next to Mac.

"Hey, Dune, welcome home," his cousin Violet said as she filled water glasses and grabbed napkin-wrapped silverware for her customers. "Give me a sec. I'll be right with you."

Dune swiveled his stool and looked about. His Aunt Molly had remodeled. The colors reflected the beach, aqua and sand tones. Blue leather booths replaced the cracked and torn black seats. The light brown tiles were an improvement over the scuffed gray linoleum.

One wall was decorated with restored vintage photographs, each one depicting the growth of Barefoot William. One black-and-white photo showed the original fishing pier under construction. Another pictured the boardwalk with only three shops. In the largest of the photographs, ten big boats were scattered offshore. Commercial fishing had supported the town for fifty years.

Dune's favorite photo was one of his great-great-great grandfather William Cates, taken on the beach at twilight. A breeze lifted his gray hair off his face and fluttered his white shirt. His pant legs were rolled up as he stood ankle deep in the waves, fishing from the shoreline.

Dune's ancestors had kept a tight hold on the growth of the town. Family and relatives owned and operated every business and entertainment along the boardwalk and pier. Their roots ran deep.

Only Nicole Archer, owner of The Jewelry Box, wasn't immediate family. She was involved with his second cousin,

Kai. Everyone figured she was close to being a Cates. They would eventually marry.

A busboy cleared off a table near the counter and the clatter of dishes drew Dune back to Sophie and Mac. He noticed Mac leaned into her, conversing quietly so Dune couldn't quite hear.

Sophie listened, but said very little. Her responses came in a nod or small smile. Mac was charming, and she was being charmed. Son of a bitch.

Dune set his back teeth. It was time to break them up. She was his friend, too. He wanted some time with her. He nudged Mac with his elbow, kept his voice low. "Put Sophie in the middle."

Mac had the balls to smile. "Like a sandwich?"

Dune ignored him. "Just make the switch."

Mac shrugged. "She's not saying much."

"Maybe she'd rather talk to me."

"Feeling confident?" his partner challenged.

Not necessarily so. Sophie hadn't spoken to him since he'd ruffled her hair. "Talk to the wall for a while," he said.

Mac stood. "Musical stools," he said to Sophie. "It's time to switch."

Her eyes went wide. "You want me in the middle?"

"Kinky, babe." Mac took hold of her shoulders and slid her next to Dune. "If he bores you, we'll change back," he said.

Sophie swiveled toward Dune. One of her knees bumped his thigh. Her color rose. "You're frowning," she said, concerned. "Is something wrong?"

"Everything's fine now," said Mac as he settled on his stool. "That's his happy face."

Dune glared at Mac. For whatever reason, Mac was riding his ass. He held himself in check, not wanting to give himself away. He liked having Sophie next to him. The counter stools were close together and with each sideways shift of their bodies, his denim thigh brushed her silk slacks. They seemed almost attached in the small space.

He made the mistake of shifting too sharply just as she changed positions. It was a moment neither of them could've expected or predicted. Her short legs were parted and his knee pushed in. He accidentally kneed her.

Kneed her in the crotch.

The moment was imprinted in time. Jarred toward him, she shivered. Naïve awareness pressed her thighs together which only drew him deeper into her. Her softness held him tight.

His muscles flexed, bunched, knotted. His dick stiffened. He hadn't bothered with his boxer briefs that morning. The bulge in his jeans stretched long and hard. Zipper tracks now marked his cock.

He winced, and she panicked, nearly falling off her stool. He reached out and steadied her. Her skin felt hot beneath her silk blouse. He saw her nipples pucker.

She dipped her head, looking guilty, unsure, flushed. A woman turned on.

He released her and pulled back. He forced himself to breathe evenly.

They both swiveled their stools to face the counter.

He caught Mac's odd look over the top of Sophie's head before his smile broke.

"What are you smiling about?" Dune sharply asked.

"You know what I'm smiling about," said Mac.

"Wipe it off your face."

Mac's smile only got bigger. "Come talk to me and the wall," he said to Sophie. "We're more interesting than Dune's knee."

Her conversation with Mac didn't go well. Dune watched as she nervously played with her paper napkin.

Her palms were moist and the napkin shredded. She was having a hard time holding it together. Their contact had left her anxious and edgy. Her color was high. She was damn cute when she blushed.

He needed to calm her, as soon as he calmed himself. He ran one hand down his face, went on to stare at the *Welcome* sign that hung above the cook's station. *Me, we, meow, come,* he decoded smaller words from the bigger one.

He finally caught his breath and said, "Shaye mentioned you're playing volleyball."

Sophie managed a nod. "Your sister encouraged me to join an indoor league," she said. "I play for Serve-ivors, a six-woman team. We all have nicknames. Shaye's known as 'Spike.' Your cousin Jenna from the T-shirt shop is 'Threat.' Violet is 'Thumper.' Eden, who does the old-time photography, is 'Bam.' Nicole, the jewelry designer, is 'Glitz.' " She paused, sighed, added, "And I'm known as 'Knee pads.' "

Knee pads. She needed protection when diving for the ball. Dune had played alongside her. She had more heart than coordination.

Mac patted her shoulder. "A nickname shows you've arrived, Soph," he said. "Dune's been Beach Heat since he first set foot on the pro circuit. It's tough being so good-looking," he ribbed his partner.

"You're Ace-hole." The corners of her mouth curved slightly. "You have your own promotional T-shirts designed with *Kiss My Ace.*"

"Love me or hate me, I play to win," said Mac.

"So do I," she said with conviction. "I don't have much to offer my team, but Shaye said I'm improving. We play in the high school gym."

Dune understood. "No sunburn, no swimsuits." He'd

hate to see her flawless complexion weathered by the sun. She was self-conscious about her body. She preferred clothes to skin.

"I wear a team T-shirt and sweatpants," she said as she reached for the list of daily specials clipped to the counter-mounted menu holder. "We have a cheering section made up of family and close friends. Everyone offers encouragement no matter how poorly I play."

"How's your serve?" asked Mac.

She ran her finger along the laminated edge of the specials, pulled a face. "The ball goes into the net."

Mac coughed into his hand. "Same as Dune."

Dune leaned his elbows on the counter, cut Mac a sharp look. "You're to blame for my two bad serves at Hermosa Beach," he ground out. "You changed hand signals at the last second. I didn't have time to make the correction."

"Slow reaction time, old man."

"You flipped me the bird with the second signal," Dune said. "We were lucky to win the set."

"Won it in overtime," said Mac. "I hate overtime."

Violet arrived a moment later, her order pad in hand. "The diner's been packed all morning," she said. "Customers are chatty and slow to leave. Molly's still running the breakfast specials if you're interested."

"Go ahead, Sophie." Dune let her go first.

She glanced at the specials and was quick to decide. "Belgian waffle and apple juice," she said.

"Double cheese-bacon-chili burger," Mac said, preferring lunch. "Onion rings, slaw, macaroni salad, and a vanilla milk shake."

Violet wrote quickly. "You eat your weight in food."

"Be nice to me, Vi, and Dune will leave you a big tip."

Dune rolled his eyes. He always tipped big. His aunt owned the diner and Violet was his cousin. He'd tip the price of the meal, maybe more.

Dune went with his favorite. "Turkey sub, sweet potato fries, and a root beer."

Violet left to turn in their order. Dune searched for something to say. He needed a topic to draw Sophie out. "How's the job fair going?" he finally asked her. "Shaye mentioned you're working your way down our boardwalk."

She clasped her hands in her lap, then looked at him over the rim of her reading glasses. "I started out at Old Tyme Portraits," she said. "Photography wasn't my niche. Eden kept me around longer than I deserved. The job wasn't tough. I just didn't do well."

"What happened?" Dune wanted to know.

She released a soft breath. "Customers would stand behind life-size cardboard cutouts with only their faces showing above vintage swimwear and I'd take their picture. None of my photos were in focus. I cut off their heads."

"Better than cutting off their—" Mac began.

Dune glared and Mac swallowed his last word.

Sophie paused, thoughtful, "I've been at Crabby Abby's for two weeks and I'm ready to move on. Abby's been great, but—"

"You want to do more than wipe down shelves and ring up sales," Dune said, reading her mind. Shaye had revealed that Sophie was book smart, but had little life experience. She would excel in the right position.

"The boardwalk offers a lot of career choices." Sophie sounded hopeful. "Some are serious and others fun."

"What's next for you?" asked Mac.

"Either stilt walker, unicyclist, or pogo stick jumper."

Mac had no tact. He laughed so hard he choked. "You're kidding us, right?" He gasped for breath.

"Not a joke." She looked worried. "Should I pat him on the back?" she asked Dune.

Dune shook his head. "Let him choke."

"Sorry, Soph," Mac wheezed. "You surprised me, that's all. I didn't take you for a daredevil. Be sure to wear wrist and shin guards and knee and elbow pads."

"Already purchased," she assured him. "I may be clumsy, but I'm seeking adventure. While I don't plan to go near the ocean, I want the full boardwalk experience."

Mac patted his butt cheek, said, "The seat on a unicycle is really narrow and small. It will split your—"

Dune stopped him with a hard look.

Sophie dipped her head. "I'll manage."

"Stilts will make you taller than Dune," Mac added.

A whole lot taller, Dune thought. His palms began to sweat. Bold and daring would cause her a lot of bruises and possibly a broken bone.

"All three skills take a lot of practice," he said from experience.

The tourists enjoyed watching the stilt walkers, unicyclists, and pogo stick jumpers. The novelty performances drew big tips. He'd attempted and adapted quickly to all three skills as a teenager. Each talent required perfect timing and balance. Sophie had neither. Put her on a pogo stick and she'd be spring-loaded. Who knew where she'd bounce? Dune hated the thought of her taking chances.

"You could be a mime," Mac suggested. "You're shy and wouldn't have to talk."

"I want out of the box," said Sophie.

Dune rubbed his brow. He felt protective toward her. He needed to discourage her without hurting her feelings. "A Beach Branch of the Chamber of Commerce recently opened next to Goody Gumdrops," he said. "You could work Reception."

Stick her behind a desk. His suggestion didn't sit well with Sophie Saunders. She appreciated his concern, but refused to be discouraged. Pigeonholed in an office sharing travel tips and passing out promotional flyers wasn't as exciting as trying to unicycle, jump on a pogo stick, or walk on stilts.

This was her summer to step outside her shadow.

She hadn't told anyone that she had a training session scheduled with Rick Cates that very afternoon. He was the best unicyclist on the boardwalk. Rick was Dune's third cousin. They were to meet at a reserved employee parking lot south of the boardwalk for her first lesson.

Rick belonged to a uni-troupe of ten performers. He rode a six-foot high "giraffe." He knew numerous tricks and stunts. He was a crowd-pleaser. Sophie had watched him spin in circles, juggle orange tennis balls, and bounce the single tire three feet off the ground. He had circus talent.

She, on the other hand, would be lucky to ride a straight line on a much shorter cycle. She was tentative, yet up for the challenge. It would be new, exciting, fun.

Their lunches arrived a moment later. Violet set Sophie's plate down first. "Enjoy." Vi winked at her.

Dune and Mac both eyed her food.

Mac couldn't contain his grin.

"What are you smiling about?" asked Dune.

"You know what I'm smiling about," said Mac. "Our Sophie's into whipped cream."

She loved whipped cream. The homemade topping was her downfall. Vi had been generous. The sliced strawberries and bananas were special little extras. Violet took good care of her volleyball teammates.

Mac curved his arm about Sophie's shoulders, then said, "That's foreplay on your plate."

A magazine article she'd recently read agreed with Mac. According to "Finger Food for the Bedroom," whipped cream scored high for teasing and tasting. The thought of licking the topping off a lover made her blush.

Her cheeks grew as heated as Dune's gaze. She watched

him watching her. She swore he could read her mind. She self-consciously licked her lips.

He lowered his voice, then asked, "Taste good?"

She hadn't taken a bite.

Mac saved her from herself. "Want to make out?" he whispered near her ear. He dipped the tip of his finger in the whipped cream and traced her lips. He leaned in for a kiss, but she held him off with a hand to his chest. He laughed, snuck a strawberry, then eased back.

"Such a sweet mouth," he said ruefully. "If I tasted you, I'd like you. Way too much."

She didn't believe him for a second. Mac's relationships were short, hot, unemotional. He'd kiss her and walk away. She quickly wiped her mouth with a napkin.

Dune shifted beside her. He appeared tense. His gaze was dark and his frown deepened. He sprinkled sea salt on his sweet potato fries, then proceeded to eat in silence.

Sophie went still. What had just happened? Dune was ticked and Mac was trying not to smile. She shook her head. She didn't understand. Mac was incorrigible and she knew never to take him seriously. So why had Dune? She didn't know what to say to make things better, so she picked up her knife and fork and cut into her waffle.

"Back to the wall." Mac swiveled right. A short time later, he flagged down Violet and ordered a second burger with extra chili.

"Chew your food," Sophie told him as he polished off the last of his onion rings. "Your stomach doesn't have teeth."

"Parental advice," said Mac. "You don't look like my mother. You're more of a—"

"A friend," Dune said from the corner of his mouth.

"Could go further," said Mac.

"Not on my watch," said Dune.

Mac's grin was easy, as if he was quite pleased with himself. He let the conversation go.

Sophie was halfway through her waffle when Dune turned her way. She'd taken a bite of strawberry and whipped cream when his gaze settled on her lips. She slowly chewed, biting her tongue twice. She could barely swallow. The food settled like a lump in her stomach.

She went to wipe her mouth, only to have her napkin slip off her lap. Dune passed her another from the napkin holder. Their arms brushed; a reminder of his solidness and strength and her need to firm up. She didn't get much exercise beyond volleyball.

"What are you plans for the afternoon?" he asked her.

She didn't want to worry him or have him think poorly of her. He'd shot down her ideas, which she still planned to explore. "I'm going to visit store owners," she said, and meant it. She'd check out the shops after her session with Rick. "I need to invest my time wisely. I'm thinking Goody Gumdrops." Shaye's penny candy store. "Or Three Shirts to the Wind." A popular T-shirt shop.

"Don't forget the Chamber of Commerce," Dune added.

Last on her list. "I'll stop by." She would poke her head in the door. That way she could honestly say she'd been there. She gave him a small smile, then asked, "How about you, lots to do?"

"I need to stop at Pet Outfitters and buy some dog toys for Ghost."

She blinked. "Ghost?"

"My Weimaraner," he explained. "I have a beach house in Malibu, but I've yet to buy a home in Barefoot William. My mother's allergic to fur, so we stay with my grandfather when I'm in town. Mac snuck in the back door and claimed a guest room, too."

"Where does your grandfather live?" Sophie asked, curious.

"Frank lives in a stilt house on lots of acreage," Dune said. He grinned. "He has a long list of repairs lined up for me to do. Today I'll replace the broken boards on the porch."

Mac sucked the last of his vanilla shake through the straw. Sucked it loudly. "Beware of the nail gun, dude," he said. "I remember—"

"No, you don't." Dune stopped him short. "He has a lousy memory."

"I've got total recall," said Mac. "You shot yourself in the foot and required twelve stitches."

Dune shrugged. "Small scar."

"Should anyone care about my whereabouts," Mac continued, "I'm headed to Three Shirts to buy a change of clothes. Then I'll be borrowing Dune's speedboat to locate *Tide One On.* I'm going to play."

"You've got six willing playmates," said Dune.

Mac nodded. "Odds are good."

Violet brought his second burger. Mac dug in. Sophie nudged him, making sure he chewed. She was fond of Mac. She admired the way he lived life, always self-assured and at a dead run. His humor and arrogance would appeal to many women. Just not to her.

She preferred all that was Dune. He was mature, stable, and evaluated his next move. He had both feet on the ground. Levelheaded worked for her.

"Do you have room for dessert?" Violet offered once Mac finished his burger and she cleared away their dishes.

Mac stood up, stretched, rubbed his stomach, then dropped back on his stool. He went with Key Lime pie.

"One slice or two?" Vi knew him well.

"I'll start with one."

Dune and Sophie passed on dessert. They were both full. Sophie didn't want to weigh herself down. She was about to unicycle.

"You'll sink like an anchor if you swim this afternoon," she warned Mac.

"There'll be all kinds of floaties in the pool," he assured her.

She understood. Mac would never drown. The buoy-breasted women from Crabby Abby's would keep him afloat.

Mac finished his pie and the busboy removed his empty plate. The boy was young and in a hurry. He backed into Violet just as she set down a large glass of tomato juice before the customer seated on Dune's left. Vi jerked and the glass tipped. Tomato juice spilled on the counter.

Dune was quick. He leaned back, avoiding the spill. He made a grab for Sophie's arm, but he was a second too late.

She, unfortunately, bore the stain. Her forearms rested on the Formica and one sleeve of her silk blouse absorbed every last bit of the tomato juice.

"Ah, crap." The boy looked horrified.

Violet peeled off a handful of napkins from the holder, then went to the soda fountain and pressed club soda. Dampening the napkins, she dabbed the seltzer on Sophie's sleeve. The stain began to fade.

"We'll pay for the cleaning bill," Vi was quick to say. "Chuck is my older sister's son. Lisa is a single mom. I'm watching him while Lisa looks for work. Molly agreed to let him help out today. He's twelve, always in a rush, and needs to slow down."

Violet glanced toward the kitchen, kept her voice low. "Chuck started out in the back this morning, washing dishes. He broke so many plates that Molly was forced to order a new case. He got moved to the fryers and burned batches of french fries. Now in the dining room, he bumps into me and a glass of tomato juice spills, soaking your sleeve. He figures the faster he works, the quicker the day will pass. He plays Sandlot Softball and has a big tournament this weekend. He plays shortstop and is coordinated on the diamond, but in the diner, not so much."

"I'm clumsy, too," Sophie said softly. She shook her sleeve. The material was damp, but no real damage was done. Accidents happened. She'd had more than her fair share.

Chuck's shoulders slumped. "Here comes Molly," he said as the owner of the diner pushed through the kitchen door.

"Dune, Sophie, Mac," Molly greeted them warmly. "I heard you were here." Her short hair was frizzy and her cheeks were flushed from the heat of the stove. She was plump; a true testament to her home cooking and generous portions.

Molly glanced from the red-streaked counter to the pile of soggy napkins, then to Sophie's wet sleeve. "Do I dare ask?" she groaned.

Chuck shifted behind the counter, uneasy and expecting to be fired. Sophie couldn't allow that to happen. She felt bad for the boy. "I distracted Chuck," she said.

Dune eyed her with as much surprise as now showed on Violet's face. Mac's lips twitched. He was amused.

Molly looked skeptical. "How'd you distract him?" she asked.

"She was flirting with the boy," said Mac.

Sophie elbowed him in the side. "He's twelve."

"Sophie mentioned a job," Dune said casually.

"A job away from the diner?" Molly looked hopeful.

Sophie touched Dune lightly on his arm, appreciative of his thought. She ran with his idea. "My gardener could use an assistant for a week or two. Lawn maintenance is hard work. It's hot outside and I'd pay Chuck well."

"Pay me?" The boy's jaw dropped. "How much?"

She had no knowledge of pay scales. She took a guess. "Twenty dollars an hour."

Conversations stilled around them. Customers looked her way. She blushed. "Too low?" she asked, afraid she'd insulted Chuck.

"Too high by at least ten dollars," said Dune.

"When can I start?" Chuck sounded excited.

Sophie would discuss the boy with her gardener later in the day. "Tomorrow," she said, "nine to two."

"Do I get weekends off?" Chuck hesitantly asked.

"I wouldn't want you to miss your tournament," she said.

"I'll buy you a bag of popcorn anytime you attend a game," the boy told her.

Sophie liked popcorn. "We've got a deal then."

"Why don't you take the remainder of the day off," Molly suggested, "and rest up for work tomorrow?"

Violet glanced at her watch. "Your mom should be home in an hour. Clear the remainder of the tables; then you can cut out." She reached in her apron pocket, slipped him three dollars. "Stop for ice cream, two scoops max."

The boy turned to Molly. "Can I use you for a job reference?" he boldly asked.

"You've only been here five hours."

Chuck shrugged, then took off to bus the dirty tables.

"Thank you, Sophie." Molly patted her on the shoulder. "I owe you a free piece of pie."

"Way to go," Dune said to her when the counter area cleared. "You made both Chuck and Molly very happy."

She warmed to his compliment.

"Ready to go?" he asked.

She was ready for her unicycle lesson.

Dune paid the bill and left a sizeable tip. Violet walked them to the door. She went on tiptoe and kissed Dune on the cheek, then pushed Mac out the door. "I appreciate what you're doing for Chuck," she whispered to Sophie. "See you at volleyball practice."

Back on the boardwalk, Mac was quick to part ways. "I'm off." He dropped a kiss on Sophie's forehead. "I'll be at the Blue Coconut later tonight if you want to catch up," he told Dune. He left for the T-shirt shop; a change of clothes was his top priority.

Sophie wondered if Dune would show, and if so, who he would take home. With his looks and popularity, he would draw a lot of attention from the women. The thought depressed her just enough for him to notice.

"Something wrong?" he asked.

She shook her head. "I'm gathering my courage to meet with the shop owners," she said. Rick didn't own a store. He was considered boardwalk entertainment.

"You'll do fine," he encouraged her. "Don't be shy. Speak up for what you want."

She'd like Dune in her life. Even for a little while. She wanted to get to know him personally, not learn about him through his sister Shaye. But she couldn't bring herself to tell him so. Maybe someday.

"Take care, Sophie," he said.

She waited for him to ruffle her hair, but he didn't this time. Instead he gave her a friendly pat on the back and sent her on her way. She'd taken six steps before she turned slightly, in hopes of catching him walk away. She wanted to check out his backside. She squinted against the sun.

To her surprise she found him leaning against the bright blue pipe railing, his gaze on her. There was an intensity and thoroughness to his stare. Unnerved, she tripped and stumbled into the cinnamon churro cart. She'd never felt more awkward.

Collecting herself, she apologized for the mishap, then bought a bag of churros from the cart owner. She had no intention of eating the sugary fried dough sticks. She was full from lunch. Instead she'd give them to Rick. He was a teenager who burned a lot of calories.

She was afraid to look back a second time, so she took off for the employee parking lot. The boardwalk was long and crowded. She didn't do well around a lot of people.

Crowds made her nervous. She stuck close to the multi-colored storefronts. Her heart was pounding by the time she reached Rick.

She found him lounging on a beach chair at the base of a queen palm. A unicycle lay on the grass beside him. The lot was shaded and almost empty. She planned to avoid the three vehicles and the vintage Harley.

Rick rose and greeted her with a high five. He accepted the churros with a smile. He was younger than Sophie, but with the start of his beard, he looked her age easily. He wore a Tampa Bay Rays baseball cap, white T-shirt, sweatpants, and high-top sneakers. "You showed," he said.

"Did you doubt me?"

He shook his head. "You look delicate, but determined."

"I plan to go the distance."

"Let's do it," Rick said. He pulled a black nylon athletic bag from behind his chair and unzipped it. He shoved the churros in a side pocket, then passed Sophie the protective gear she'd purchased several days ago and left with him.

She dropped her purse by his athletic bag and he assisted her with her wrist and shin guards, then her knee and elbow pads. A pair of short leather gloves, too. Rick placed a small helmet on her head, then hefted the unicycle off the ground.

"This isn't hard," Rick assured her. "Don't be nervous and tense up on me. Exhale, Sophie."

She could barely breathe.

He started her lesson. Riding a unicycle was more complicated than she'd imagined. Once he finished his instructions, he held the cycle upright. She stood on tiptoe, gave a little hop, and scooted onto the seat. Only to slide right off.

The mounting took a good twenty minutes. Balance was not her friend. Her feet slipped on and off the platform pedals. She fell twice. The cement had no bounce. She'd be bruised tomorrow.

She finally settled on the very narrow, very uncomfortable seat and Rick moved to stand before her. He straddled the tire and she gripped his shoulders. Her fingers curled into his T-shirt in a death grip.

"A little hip action," he encouraged her. "Slowly rock back and forth. Think sex, Sophie. Feel the motion."

Sex was not a good reference for her. Her hips felt stiff and rusty. Like the Tin Man from the Wizard of Oz.

Rick gave her plenty of time. "Looking good, girl," he praised her. "You can let go of my shirt now."

She shook her head. She wasn't ready to release him.

He made the decision for her by rolling his shoulders. "Extend your arms to the side," he instructed.

Her arms went straight as airplane wings, while her knees knocked against the frame. Her body was shaking from the inside out.

"Don't be afraid," he said. "Remember what I've taught you. Lean your upper body toward me and pedal."

She bit down on her bottom lip as Rick eased back a step, just beyond her reach. "I can't do this." Her voice sounded shrill, even to her own ears.

"Yes, you can," Rick said. "Breathe, Sophie."

She inhaled so sharply that the sudden rise of her chest threw her shoulders back. The unicycle began to roll—

Backward.

"Whoa, wrong direction, babe," he called after her.

Panic seized her. She was pedaling away from him and she couldn't stop herself. Her legs were on automatic pilot. She was picking up speed, wobbly and swerving. Her reading glasses slipped down her nose.

"Hit the brakes," shouted Rick as he jogged after her.

She was afraid to stop pedaling. A sudden stop and she'd

wipe out. Falling was not to her liking. She had no idea what was behind her. Or what she was about to hit.

"What the hell?" Dune's deep angry voice rose from the sidewalk.

Sophie caught both the man and the motorcycle from the corner of her eye. She was circling toward them. The look on Dune's face could've flattened the tire on her unicycle. He was that mad.

Dune dropped the bag he was carrying and sprinted toward her. His long legs ate up the distance. He had almost reached her when Sophie tipped left. The pavement rose to meet her.

Dune grabbed her before she kissed the cement. He wrapped his arm about her waist and lifted her off the seat. The cycle rolled several feet and fell over.

Rick caught up to the two of them. "Riding backward is twice as hard as going forward." He applauded her. "You're a natural, Sophie."

Her talent was the last thing on her mind. What struck her first was how tight Dune held her. He was squeezing the life out of her. Her breasts pressed against his chest and their hip bones bumped. Her feet dangled six inches off the ground.

She flattened her hand over his heart and felt it race against her palm. The beat was far too fast for the short distance he'd run. She wiggled her toes, wanting to stand. He released her so quickly she staggered backward. Rick steadied her.

Anger narrowed Dune's eyes and his nostrils flared. "This isn't the Chamber of Commerce," he stated.

No, it was not, Sophie silently agreed.

"What were you thinking?" he asked her, only to turn on Rick before she could answer. "You put her in danger," he accused.

Sophie removed her helmet. Her hands shook as she slid her glasses up her nose. Her legs barely supported her. "Unicycling was my idea," she managed. "I asked Rick to teach me. It's all part of my boardwalk experience."

"The sport is safe if you take it slow," said Rick.

"Slow?" Dune crossed his arms over his chest, then looked down on them both. "She was riding a runaway unicycle in reverse."

"She didn't fall," Rick said, making his case.

"Because I got to her first."

Rick shot Dune an odd look. "What are you, her keeper?" he asked. "I would've caught her before she hit your Harley."

His motorcycle. Sophie now understood Dune's anger. His concern lay with his bike and not with her. She'd come within five feet of hitting his prized possession. She doubted Rick would've reached her in time, no matter his assurance.

"The lesson's over," Dune said to his cousin.

Rick was about to object, but the look in Dune's eyes moved him along. Rick retrieved the package Dune had dropped and tossed it to him. He then picked up the unicycle and walked Sophie back to his beach chair. She removed her protective pads and he packed it all up along with her helmet. She grabbed her shoulder bag.

"Later," Rick said as he set the chair, unicycle, and gear in the back of his pickup truck. He waved as he pulled out of the parking lot.

Sophie wasn't sure what to do or say next. The moment was awkward. Her shyness tied her stomach in knots. She hadn't meant to deceive Dune. She'd merely cut the corners off the truth. He was looking at her now as if she'd lost her mind.

"Don't be mad at me," she said softly.

His jaw worked. "I'm not mad, merely concerned. You made my heart race."

"You were afraid for me?" That surprised her. "I thought you were worried about your motorcycle."

"Harleys don't bleed when they fall over."

She hadn't meant to cause him alarm, but she liked the fact he'd agonized over her, even a little.

"I'm klutzy and chances are always good that I'll scrape a knee or twist my ankle." She gathered a breath. "Tomorrow I walk on stilts."

He frowned. "It's safer to join a corner street band and shake a tambourine. Maybe drive a pedal cab or draw caricature portraits."

"I don't want safe," she said, speaking from her heart. "I've always been quiet, fearful, invisible Sophie. This is *my* summer. I want adventure. It's time to discover me."

He turned introspective. His brow creased, then eventually smoothed. He stared at her for a full minute before asking, "Ever ridden a Harley?"

Excitement gripped her. "Never."

"It's a rush."

"Adrenaline is my middle name."

Dune smiled. "I have an extra helmet," he told her. "Hop on and I'll give you a ride home."

She went for it. "Twelve-thirteen Saunders Way."

Three

"We've gone as far as we can go," a man said.
A woman sighed heavily. "There's more to us than three months."

Mac James looked toward the back of the shop and listened. He'd entered Three Shirts to the Wind through the tangerine-colored door and found the place empty. Apparently there were two people in the storeroom. Jenna Cates and an unidentifiable man. Voices were raised. They were breaking up. He was getting an earful.

He looked around the shop. Three Shirts carried everything from plain white cotton tees to brightly colored polos. Some had caricatures while others had decorative designs. A few naughty slogans raised eyebrows. Most sayings were funny or silly. Overhead clotheslines stretched the width of the ceiling, displaying a line of Barefoot William attire.

Mac browsed the revolving circular racks as the ensuing argument grew even more heated.

"What about this weekend?" Jenna asked sharply. "We had plans."

"I'm out."

"But you know the Sneaker Ball is close to my heart."

The man snorted. "Parks and recreation means nothing to me."

"You told me you liked kids and sports."

"To get in your pants."

"Bastard."

"Whatever."

A door slammed and Mac assumed the dude had split. Whoever he was, he sounded like a douche. But then, Jen wasn't all that easy to get along with, either. Mac knew her from his trips home with Dune. She had short dark blond hair and a tight body, and wore round glasses. She had decent breasts. He hadn't given much thought to her waxing.

Over the years, he would've been nice to her had she been nice to him. But sarcasm was her second language. More often than not she took a sander to his balls for no apparent reason. They'd never gotten along. He preferred his women sweet and considerate.

Mac expected her to be angry when she returned to the shop. Instead he caught the hurt on her face, her bent shoulders, and slow step. He felt a split second of sympathy until she spotted him. Then her anger snapped back. Lady looked fierce.

He knew she needed to vent. She was Dune's cousin and, in deference to his partner, he allowed her to let loose on him rather than a paying customer. He planned to charge his clothes to Dune's account.

"Heard you got dumped," he said.

She walked toward him in cuffed jeans and a cropped white T-shirt with the motto *Tell Me Something Good*. A bit ironic, he thought. She wore Barefoot sandals, which didn't have a sole. Thin crystal chains connected a toe ring to an anklet. Her toenails were painted gold. He found her feet sexy.

"Eavesdropping?" she hissed. Her chin was high and her hands were clenched. She looked ready to punch him.

He shook his head. "Your voices traveled through the wall."

"You didn't make your presence known," she accused.

He shrugged. "You needed to finish your fight."

She flinched. "How much did you hear?"

"If I tell you I like sports, can we do it?"

Her cheeks heated. She crossed to a rack of T-shirts, selected one, and held it up. He read the slogan, *Not in this Lifetime.*

Two could play this game. He flipped through the hangers, found a shirt scripted with *I Want to Be Your Next Mistake.* He waved it at her.

She flashed him back. *Tool or Jackass. Hee-Haw.*

He came across the perfect one for her. *Bitchiness Becomes You.*

She responded with the shirt, *I See Dumb People.*

His next one had her rolling her eyes. *Never Be in Line for a Halo.*

She blew out a breath and said, "Enough T-shirt talk. What do you want?"

"Shirt, shorts, and a towel," he told her. "I need a change of clothes. I'm headed to *Tide One On.*"

"The party boat is clothing optional."

So he'd heard. "I can party naked."

"I'm sure you can."

"Do I get customer assistance or do I shop on my own?" he asked.

"You don't need me to pick out your clothes." She returned to the front counter.

He could've used her help. He had deuteranopia and was partially color blind. He had trouble discriminating between red and green hues. The colors appeared muted or faded. He compensated by purchasing his clothes in basic colors, so the mix and match came easily. Only a few close friends knew about his vision deficiency. He wanted to keep it that way.

He wound around the circular racks until he reached

the shelves of folded shorts. Size thirty-four. He read the inside label: dark brown. He could live with brown. Shorts down, a T-shirt to go.

The selection was enormous. He killed a little time going from rack to rack, spinning and reading, and keeping one eye on Jen. She didn't hide her feelings well. She wiped her eyes with a Kleenex and her lip trembled. She was still upset over the split.

"What's with the Sneaker Ball?" he asked from across the room.

"What's it to you?"

"It's a cause close to your heart."

"Why do you care what's important to me?"

Lady was snippy, difficult, irritating. But she'd just gone through a breakup. He took that into consideration and tried to be nice. "I'm in town for three weeks. The event sounds big."

She took overly long to respond, finally saying, "The affair is this weekend. Shaye and I are co-chairwomen. Black tie and sneakers. It's a night to raise money for outdoor activities. The dance is held on the pier. Barefoot William supports its youth. The entire town turns out."

"Everyone but you."

"Salt to my wound," she muttered as she collected a notebook from the counter and crossed to the nearest revolving rack. She cut him a look, then said, "No further disruption. I'm taking inventory." She held up a shirt. *You Have the Right to Remain Silent. So Please Shut up.*

He didn't want to be quiet. He looped around until he stood directly behind her. "Twelve, thirteen, fourteen," he disrupted her counting.

She elbowed him in the gut. "What's with you?"

He rubbed his abdomen. "I'm being sympathetic," he said.

"You're being an ass."

"Breaking up sucks."

"How would you know?" she challenged.

"I've been dumped." She glanced his way, sharp and disbelieving. He recalled his play date days. "I was young. It was summer in the park. The moms sat on wooden benches while the kids played. Missy Harris and I were both three. Enter Canyon Carter, the older man, age four. We shared toys in the sandbox. Canyon offered Missy a teddy bear he'd gotten wet while drinking at the water fountain. I went with a Tonka truck. She preferred the one-eyed soggy stuffed animal. Broke my heart."

"Scarred you for life, I see."

"For about a week," he said. "Until Libby Atwell went down the sliding board and flashed her floral panties."

She stepped around him. "Panties do it for you?"

"What are you wearing?"

"My Thursday cotton grannies."

He let his gaze drop. "I imagined silk bikini. Definitely a Brazilian wax."

"Stop staring at my crotch."

He looked up slowly. "Only if your tits stop staring at my eyes."

"Jerk." She turned her back on him. "Aren't you done shopping yet?"

"Never rush the customer."

"I want you gone. *Now.*"

He followed her to the sale rack. Shirts and shorts were half-price. "What caused your breakup?" he asked.

Pain and annoyance flickered across her face. "Why would you care?"

"Curiosity." He'd found over the years if a woman talked about her broken heart, the hurt didn't fester. He'd had women cry on his shoulder. Others had actually slapped him in their rage over another man. One had kneed him in the groin.

He glanced at his watch. He had a few extra minutes to spare. He'd listen if she wanted to talk. She was slow to come around.

"We split over sex," she finally told him.

"He needed it ten times a day and you could only go nine?"

She rolled her eyes at him.

He tried again. "You were the horny one?" Hard to believe, but he had to ask.

Her answer came through a T-shirt. She set down her notebook and located a step stool and a chrome pole garment hook. She stepped up, using the pole to straighten a T-shirt that had twisted on the hanger. *Earn It* was scripted on the front.

Mac's laugh was immediate and inappropriate, but he couldn't help it. "You made him *work* for sex."

She climbed down. "Stan thought so."

"No man likes to jump through hoops for nookie."

She turned on him. "I'm not easy."

He never thought she was.

"I made him wait."

For nearly three months from the sound of their breakup. "Your dude suffered blue balls, uncomfortable but curable," he said.

He hadn't been in Barefoot William long enough to turn blue. He'd hook up on *Tide One On*. He had his eye on the tall brunette from Crabby Abby's. Her white crocheted string bikini was so small she spilled from the top. He figured she was bare shaven. He thought about buying her a *Friction Club* T-shirt. He needed a good body rubbing.

"Did you care for the guy?" he asked Jenna. In his mind, knowing someone for three months was lust, not love.

"I thought we had more in common than we actually did."

"Deceiving bastard."

She tried not to smile, but he saw the slight curve of her lips. She showed him a T-shirt with the slogan *I Used to Have a Handle on Life, but It Broke.* She was ornery and standoffish, but still feeling vulnerable.

She went on to count a row of men's cargo shorts, jotted down the number, then hesitantly asked him, "How long do you stay in a relationship after you realize it's over?"

"A minute, maybe two." He'd broken a few hearts. Several of his lovers had begged him to stay. But if he wasn't feeling it, he was gone. He wasn't being mean, merely honest. "Leading a woman on is far worse than letting her go to find the right man."

"You're the wrong man in so many ways." She pointed to a shirt pinned to the wall. *Your Sole Purpose in Life is to Serve as a Warning to Others.*

"Do you always let your T-shirts speak for you?"

"The slogans say it all."

He wandered over to the men's shirt rack, sizes medium and large. He looked through the larges. He liked the slogan *Got Sex?* He would fit right in on the booze cruise.

His shorts were dark brown, but he couldn't distinguish the background color of the T-shirt. He raised both shorts and shirt and called to Jen. "How's this?"

She scrunched her nose. "Orange isn't your color."

He put back the shirt, tried again. This time he chose what appeared to be a tie-dye with *Try Me, You'll Like Me.* "Jen, does this work?" he asked.

She glanced over. "Only if you're a firecracker. Red-gold is too bright. More women than men buy tie-dyes."

Crap. He'd yet to nail the shirt. He hated to draw her into his decision, but he didn't have all afternoon to fool with the color. There was a beach babe on the party yacht with his name on her. "Pick one out for me?" he requested.

"Do I look like your mother?"

"A little bit around the eyes."

"I'm busy," she stated. "The inventory won't take itself."

Contrary woman. "Help me with my shirt and—" His heart skipped a beat. "I'll take you to the Sneaker Ball," he said in frustration.

She did the unexpected and laughed in his face. "Not a sincere invitation," she said. "What makes you think I'd go with you?"

"I'm a volleyball god."

"Believe what you will."

"Guess you'd rather go alone."

"Guess you're right."

What was her problem? Mac wondered. Women stood in line to date him, yet Jen hung back, reluctant and indecisive. She looked a little nauseous.

Several minutes passed before she set down her notepad and found him a shirt in a light color. Beige or white, he guessed. He smiled over the slogan: *You Say Psycho Like It's a Bad Thing.*

She handed it to him. "Tan goes well with your brown shorts."

He felt a mild sense of relief.

"Need help with a towel?" she asked next.

"I can manage." He headed toward the shelves of towels near the front of the store. The color didn't matter. He snagged the first one within his reach.

Jen came up behind him. "I didn't take you for a peach kind of guy."

He'd thought it looked deep gold. A rack of sunglasses on the checkout counter caught his attention. Very cool shades by Bandy West and Red Eye. He lost sunglasses as fast as he bought them. He tried on a narrow dark frame with even darker lenses. "What do you think?" he asked her.

"What does it matter?"

"I'll be wearing only my Bandys shortly."

"Buy a bigger frame."

"There's not a frame big enough—"

She held up her hand, stopped him. "Too much information."

"I have a lot to share."

She'd had enough of him. "Pay up so you can go pass out."

"I don't drink to pass out," he said. "But I still get hangovers."

"Hangovers are a waste of a morning."

"All depends on who you're spooning."

"I've never known sex to fix a hangover."

He grinned. "I have. It's all about blood transfer from the brain to the penis. Pain shifts to pleasure on climax. Headache's gone."

Jenna Cates stared at Mac James. There was something about him that irritated the hell out of her. He was too good-looking and he flipped off life. Chiseled and athletic were a dangerous combination. He seduced by breathing.

Sex was as much a sport to him as volleyball. Town gossip had him in and out of a relationship before a woman could pull up her panties. Commitment gave him hives.

He was an amazing volleyball player, according to her cousin Dune. When Mac was "on," he was unbeatable. He'd never played in Dune's shadow. Focused and honed, he had years of greatness ahead of him. Should Dune retire, Mac would be in demand as a partner.

Jen had watched countless games on television. The Cates clan followed Dune religiously. Beach Heat and

Ace-hole dominated. The moment a game ended, Mac embraced his fans before accepting his trophy. Men shook his hand and women grafted themselves to him. The beach babes consoled him when he lost. The night was one big party when he won.

His lifestyle went beyond what she'd ever known. He lived life large and, for some unidentifiable reason, that grated on her last nerve.

Perhaps she was a little jealous, she forced herself to admit. Men didn't flock to her. The few guys she dated lied to her without remorse. She'd become a spinster with four cats at twenty-eight. She told herself that didn't bother her overly much. She had the T-shirt shop to keep her busy.

She glanced at Mac. "Cash or plastic?" she asked as she rang up his sale.

"Put everything on Dune's account."

"Mooch."

"I don't carry money or credit cards with me."

"That's because you travel with Dune and he always pays."

"Eventually I pay him back."

She handed him the receipt to sign.

He wrote *Dune Cates.*

"You've got my cousin's signature down pat," she noted.

"Should have, I've forged it enough."

"What a good friend you are." She knew she sounded snarky.

His jaw shifted and he was suddenly serious. "Dune accepts my idiosyncrasies."

"Idiocy is more like it," she said as she slid his items in a plastic bag. She passed it to him.

He didn't immediately pick it up. Instead he flattened his palms on the counter and leaned in. His gaze was narrowed, deep blue and questioning. "Are you a man-hater or is it just me?" he asked.

"It's you and men like you." She was honest.

"What exactly am I like?" he pressed.

She didn't hold back. "You're irresponsible, unpredictable, into yourself—"

"You know this how?" he cut her off.

"Through my best friend."

"Which friend?" He appeared genuinely curious.

"You dated Bree Bennett a year ago. Dated her twice, then never called again."

"Bree?" His brow creased. It was obvious he didn't remember her.

She jarred his memory. "Redhead, dimples. She manages Petals on the boardwalk."

"The flower shop chick." He took it all in, then said, "She had issues. Gossip ruins reputations. Your conversation with Bree was preconceived and one-sided."

"I say she's right."

"I say she's wrong."

Her chin came up. "Prove it."

"Why should I accept a dare to prove I'm a nice guy when I don't much care what you think of me?" He shook his head. "No motivation, babe."

He shot her down and she sent him on his way. "The booze cruise waits," she said. "Go spread yourself around."

He eased back, scooped up his plastic bag. "I give good spread."

Her heart gave an odd little squeeze.

He walked toward the door, only to turn at the last minute. "Feel better?" he asked.

Surprisingly she did. Her breakup seemed ages ago. Mac had a way of moving time forward. "I'll live," she said.

"Then my work here is done." He was gone.

His departure left a gaping hole in her afternoon, one she didn't want to dwell on. Over the next four hours customers came and went. The UPS driver dropped off two big boxes. She unpacked the shirts, steamed the wrinkles, then hung them on the front racks.

A particular slogan fit her well: *No Outfit is Complete Without a Little Cat Fur.* The story of her life.

Another motto described Mac James: *On the Eighth Day, God Created Volleyball.* She knew Dune would like the shirt. She set one aside for her cousin.

She went on to choose a few items for the sale rack, items that hadn't moved for months. She then decided to rearrange the display of flip-flops. Her part-time sales associate would clock in at six to work the evening shift. Jen had two hours before she closed out her day.

She took a short break, returning to the storeroom to grab a Cherry Dr Pepper from the mini fridge. A café table, small desk, and narrow set of cabinets fought for space amid boxes of Barefoot William key chains, baseball caps, and waterproof wallets. Her ex-boyfriend's presence still lingered. Stan Caldwell had always worn too much cologne. She sprayed Lysol to remove his scent, then returned to the main shop. The man was dead to her.

She popped the tab on her soda, took a sip, and grew thoughtful. She wished she had a date for the Sneaker Ball. But there was no longer anyone special in her life. Stan had turned out to be a prick.

Her days revolved around T-shirts and shorts. Her work attire was casual as well. The Ball was her chance to feel glam and girly. She'd chosen a dress by Daze, a strapless black silk with a fitted bust and tapering pleats from the waist down. The designer's creations turned a man's head and made his jaw drop. Her sneakers were silver with gold ties.

She was co-chairwoman and had a couple's ticket for the event. She'd now rip the ticket in half. She knew Mac James's invitation rose from sympathy. She refused to be his pity date. They had nothing in common.

She finished off her soda, then swept the hardwood floors. Customers had tracked in sand. Dusting came next. Five-fifteen. Customers swarmed her shop. Beachgoers were headed home and wanted to buy last-minute souvenirs. T-shirts were always on their lists.

Jen assisted each one. She helped find the perfect shirt to keep Barefoot William alive in their hearts and minds for months to come.

Her skin suddenly prickled in warning. She glanced toward the door just as Mac James and his crocheted-bikini date walked in. The woman was sunburned from her day on the party yacht. Mac's tan had only darkened.

He found her in the crowd. His gaze was sharp and very blue. Too sharp for a man who'd partied on *Tide One On*. His hair was wind-blown. He wore the *Psycho* shirt she'd chosen for him earlier as well as the brown shorts. He was barefoot. He looked lean and masculine; his expression, smug. A man soon to get laid.

His date appeared a little tipsy. Mac's peach-colored towel wrapped her hips and the knot kept slipping. Her eyes were red-rimmed and she kept licking her lips. Jen figured her mouth was dry and she needed lip balm. She sold it in several flavors. Mac could pick out the one he'd like to kiss. Jen took him for a cherry or pineapple taste tester.

"Excuse me for just a minute," she said to a barrel-chested male tourist from Wisconsin who'd taken thirty minutes to choose between T-shirts that read *Body by Buddha* and *Beer is my Best Friend*. Jen suggested he take both.

She crossed to Mac. His arm draped the brunette's shoulders and they appeared joined at the hip. The woman clung to him as if she were afraid he'd wander off.

Jen faced him, raised one eyebrow. "Party over so soon?"

"I had Dune's speedboat so we left the yacht early," he said easily. "Kami liked my shirt so much that she wanted to check out your shop. Jen, Kami," he introduced them.

Jen forced a smile. "Look around. My store has the largest selection of shirts on the boardwalk."

Kami stroked Mac's chest. Her fingernails were painted licorice black. "Find me one," she said.

She couldn't make her own decision? Jen cringed inwardly. Mac was not a man to rely on. He didn't make great color choices.

Kami with the long hair and sunbather body drew Mac from rack to rack, holding up shirt after shirt. She giggled like a girl and her breasts jiggled. Mac's approval came when she held up the belly shirts. He liked a bare midriff on his woman.

"Mine!" Kami spotted a hot pink shirt with the motto, *Trace My Tan Lines with Your Tongue.* Mac grinned, then nodded. She threw her arms about his neck and kissed him.

Those still in the store turned and stared. The kiss lasted longer than what was appropriate. So long, in fact, that several parents herded their kids toward the door. Jen refused to lose business to their lip-lock.

She crossed to Mac and hissed near his ear, "Take it outside."

They broke apart and Kami sighed. "I'd rather take him to bed."

"Later, babe," said Mac. He passed Jen the shirt. "We got what we came for. One T-shirt. Unless there's something else that catches her eye."

"Do you like body jewelry?" Jen asked Kami. "I sell a lot of belly chains."

"I like body candy," Kami said. "SweeTart bras and panties are yummy, but Red Hots are my favorite. They heat a man's tongue and leave a warm trail—"

"No candy here," Jen stopped her. "The belly chains are on display at the front counter. Most have ornamentations."

Kami tried on every single one, twenty-five to be exact. She gave Mac a belly chain fashion show, which he seemed to enjoy. He stood with his arms crossed over his chest and his stance wide. He stared at Kami with absolute focus, as if she was the only person in the room.

Kami ate up his attention. She finally narrowed her choices down to two chains. She squinted at the dragonfly. "What color are the wings?" she asked Mac.

Mac bent toward her, eyeing the ornament that dangled near her navel. The corners of his mouth creased and he seemed to hesitate.

Jen gave him a moment to consider the color before she said, "The wings are pink quartz."

"I also like the tribal charm," Kami debated.

"Dragonflies are free," said Jen. "Tribal charms are—"

"Wicked." Kami giggled.

Definitely so. Jen was certain Kami would go tribal until Mac said, "The dragonfly looks best against your skin."

"You think?" Kami took a second look in the full-length mirror on the wall.

"I like the dangle."

His date hugged him. "I love shopping with a man who knows what looks good on a woman."

It was a belly chain, Jen inwardly groaned. Not a cocktail dress, business suit, or designer sportswear.

"We'll take it," Mac told Jen.

"Lip balm?" Jen suggested for Kami's dry lips.

Kami checked out the fruity flavors. She looked to Mac. "Cherry, mango, or pineapple?"

He went with pineapple.

"A charge to Dune's account?" Jen asked.

Mac nodded. "He'd approve of the purchases."

Men, Jen mused. A little dazzle near the navel and their eyes dilated.

"No need to wrap the chain," Kami said. "I'll wear it."

Mac signed the credit slip. It was a nice sale for Jen, her biggest of the day. She hoped Mac kept his word and paid Dune back.

Mac and his date were ready to leave when Kami noticed the poster hanging on the wall that listed all the upcoming boardwalk and beach events. She put her finger under each word as if she couldn't read and comprehend an entire sentence all at once.

She was still a little drunk, Jen guessed.

"Look at all these events to kick off summer," Kami slowly said. "Stand Up Paddle Races and the Boat Float. There's sandcastle building and a kite flying contest. The Sneaker Ball, how cool is that? It's this weekend. Let's do it. Tickets can be purchased at the Chamber of Commerce."

Jen's stomach squeezed just a little. She'd had the chance to go with him. She'd busted his balls instead.

To her surprise, Mac didn't jump on Kami's offer. He leveled his gaze on Jen instead. Her heart rate did the unthinkable. It quickened. Goose bumps skimmed her spine. Restlessness shifted her weight from one foot to the other. She looked away.

"You'd have a great time," she said to Kami. A ticket sale was a ticket sale. A couple's ticket went for two hundred dollars.

"Are you going?" Kami asked her.

"No date, but I'll be there," Jen said.

Kami frowned. "You can't go alone. Invite a guy buddy or a friend with benefits."

Jen had numerous male friends. But they already had dates.

"As far as relationships, Jen has her T-shirts and the boardwalk," Mac said. "They keep her happy."

"I prefer men," said Kami.

Mac was definitely a man. He was also an ass. Jen gave a wave, then hinted, "See you." Hoping they'd leave. They did, and neither one looked back.

At six p.m. sharp, Jen's part-time associate clocked in. Jamie Maye was a high school student, smart and dependable, while exploring her own sense of self. She'd recently added orange highlights to her brown hair. A new piercing placed a barbell above her left eyebrow. She ran track and was a star in the fifty-yard dash. She had a high metabolism and packed protein snacks for her three-hour shift.

Jen left Three Shirts in good hands. She met up with Bree Bennett at Brews Brothers, the boardwalk coffee shop. It was a weekly ritual between friends. They'd order caramel mocha iced cappuccinos, kick back, and discuss their day.

The scents of freshly brewed coffee, cinnamon scones, and peanut butter cookies teased Jen when she entered. Shades of green gave the shop a relaxing atmosphere. Philodendrons flourished in hanging brass planters. Booths, tables, and clusters of chairs invited customers to sit and savor their coffee of choice. Wi-Fi was available. There was no rush.

Bree was already seated when Jen arrived. She'd grabbed two comfortable leather chairs in the corner. She'd angled them to face each other for privacy. Their drinks sat on a side table. They took turns buying.

Bree was all smiles. "I booked the Abner-Jacobs wedding," she said. "After a month of my sending faxes and proposals to the bride, Genevieve Jacobs picked Petals over Saunders' Bouquets. I finally beat the competition."

Jen raised her plastic cup and the women toasted. "That's major money coming your way."

"I'm going to hire extra help," Bree said. "It's a society wedding, very classic and sophisticated. The church theme is lavender and ivory. The reception will showcase a deeper plum and dove white."

"Best news ever," Jen said, then added tongue-in-cheek. "Looks like Flower School paid off."

"I owe you a lot," said Bree. "The Floral Design Institute was your idea. Knowing how much I enjoyed pruning plants and arranging cut flowers, you pushed me toward a degree. You even filled out my application. And, once I was accepted, you drove me to Miami in time for the start of classes."

"And now look how successful you've become."

"I love working at Petals, but someday I want my own shop."

"Growth is good," Jen agreed. "You're going big-time."

"Speaking of big-time," Bree said, lowering her voice. "I heard Dune and Mac are in town."

Jen nodded. "They arrived on Tuesday." It was now Thursday. "Mac stopped in Three Shirts today. He was headed for *Tide One On* and bought a change of clothes."

Bree took a long sip of her Frappuccino, then made a face when she got brain freeze. "How's he doing?" she asked.

Jen shrugged. "Okay, I guess."

Bree shifted on her chair, looked uneasy. "I made a huge mistake with Mac," she slowly admitted.

"How so?" from Jen.

"We went out twice and, by our second date, I got ahead of myself. Three orgasms in an hour, and I told him I loved him."

"That was lust talking."

"It freaked Mac out. He was dressed and gone in under a minute."

"You were angry afterward."

"I regretted my actions," said Bree. "I went ballistic on the man and said some pretty mean things."

That she had. Words such as *irresponsible, unpredictable,* and *egotistical* crossed Jen's mind.

Bree finished her drink and said, "Every woman should experience a Mac James in her lifetime. Looking back, I can honestly say he's likeable, fun, and looks amazing naked."

Looks amazing naked. More than Jen needed to know.

"Henry's my world now," said Bree.

Henry was her man and soon-to-be fiancé. They'd dated a year and were comfortable, compatible, and inseparable. He'd be picking Bree up shortly. They'd have dinner together.

Jen would go home to her cats.

"I found a dress for the Sneaker Ball," Bree said. "It's pale blue, low cut with a swing skirt. My tennis shoes are bright orange."

Jen nodded, turned quiet, not wanting to discuss the Ball further. She had nothing to contribute.

Bree picked up on her mood. "You and Shaye put the event together. Tickets are nearly sold out. Where's your excitement?"

She couldn't hide much from her friend, so she came clean. "Stan broke up with me this morning. No date."

Bree's eyes went wide. "No way."

"Mac James was in the shop when it all went down."

Bree scrunched her nose. "How embarrassing."

"Definitely humiliating," Jen agreed. "He felt sorry for me and extended a pity invite."

"I hope you accepted."

Jen *almost* wished she had. She now had second thoughts. "I can have a good time without a date."

"Ah, sweetie, it just won't be the same."

Which Jen knew. She'd be alone, greeting the partygo-ers with a pasted-on smile. Men would be charitable and offer her a courtesy fast dance. It was the slow songs that made a woman want to press her body against the right man. The night was very romantic. There'd be no romance for her this year.

"Can you contact Mac and tell him you've changed your mind?" Bree asked.

"He's already moved on," Jen said. "He met Kami on the booze cruise. She's more his type."

Bree wasn't giving up. "What about Bill Landers, the new lifeguard?"

Jen shook her head. "He's into Violet. She packs him a sack lunch from the diner each day."

Bree went down a long list of men and Jen dismissed each one. She ended with, "How about Chase Wallace?"

"He's a senior in high school and madly in love with my assistant Jamie."

Bree had run out of options. "Looks like it's you and the man in the moon then."

Jen could do worse. "I'll survive."

Four

Twelve-thirteen Saunders Way. Sophie had survived the motorcycle ride. Dune Cates had given her a real opportunity to experience his customized Harley Sportster, taking the long way home. They'd ridden for three hours and covered Barefoot William and the surrounding county. She'd wrapped her arms about his waist and leaned into him. He liked the womanly press of her body. Her breasts were round and firm and her thighs had hugged his hips. She'd held on for dear life.

She hadn't screamed or jerked. She'd trusted him.

He set the kickstand on the driveway of crushed pale pink seashells. He removed his helmet and hung it on the handlebar risers, then dismounted and said, "You can get off now."

She twisted slightly toward him and winced. "No . . . I can't." Her voice was barely a whisper.

Dune understood. Her muscles ached from the big bike's vibration along with the jarring speed bumps and potholes. She'd been afraid to shift even the slightest bit, concerned that she would throw him off balance. She was probably too stiff to move.

He watched as she blinked the dryness from her eyes, then shook out her hands and rotated each ankle. He figured her fingers and feet had fallen asleep and now tingled as they wakened. Her helmet slanted over one eye. Her reading glasses were askew. The top two buttons on her blouse were undone. The curve of her breast and the lace on her bra were visible. He stared a little too long.

"Your Harley is fast," Sophie said in awe.

"I drove forty-five."

Her eyes went wide. "It seemed like seventy or eighty. The scenery just swept by. Cars looked like they were in slow motion and people were a total blur."

"Motorcycles have that effect," he said. Riders felt like they were flying when riding a Harley. It was a rush.

"I'm stuck," she finally admitted.

"Just swing your leg over the seat."

"I have no swing."

He helped her sit sideways. "Can you stand?" he asked.

"No feeling in my body," she said. "Even my bottom's numb."

Dune kicked himself. He hated the fact he'd caused her pain. He was used to cruising hours at a stretch. This was Sophie's first ride. He should've driven her straight home. "Wiggle your feet and get the blood circulating again," he suggested.

She did so and winced. "Prickles."

He dropped to one knee and began to massage her right calf, then moved to her left. She was small-boned. Delicate. He found he liked touching her, which left him wary. Sophie made him want to protect her. He prided himself on no strings attached. Ever.

He went on to rub both her knees and worked halfway up her thigh. He had long fingers and stopped himself before he touched her any higher. He was close to the danger zone. "Try standing," he said.

She stood, but was still shaky. He gripped her elbow and steadied her, then went on to unsnap her helmet and remove it. After brushing back her bangs and straightening her glasses, he tipped up her chin. "First time on a bike can leave you sore," he said. "You're clenching muscles you've never clenched before. Same with"—he was about to say sex, but changed his mind—"horseback riding."

She nodded. "Horseback riding left me tender."

"You've ridden?" That surprised him.

"I took lessons when I was seven, but I quickly gave up. I bounced and bruised a lot."

He felt her pain.

She next flexed her fingers and attempted to button her blouse. She was all thumbs. Another button popped open in the process. Her bra flashed. All gray, lacy and sheer. Her chest was flushed and her nipples puckered.

He stood over her and asked, "Need help?" He didn't want her flashing the gardener planting flowers near the front door.

She nodded. "Assistance would be nice."

He was on her in a heartbeat and focused fully on the task. She held her breath as he worked the buttons. The callused tips of his fingers skimmed the lace on her bra and brushed her breasts. He took his time with the button over her cleavage. His own breathing deepened.

"There's no need to fasten the top button," she choked a moment later. "I don't need the collar under my chin."

He let his hands drop. Still, his gaze held on her breasts for a considerable time. "Nice blouse," he said.

"Even with the stain?" she asked.

"It adds color."

"That's what I thought," she said, smiling.

She was being gracious, Dune thought. The busboy had lucked out. Most women would've flinched or berated the kid for his clumsiness. Not Sophie. She'd been quick to forgive Chuck, then taken Dune's suggestion and offered him a job.

Dune was impressed by her kindness.

A breeze picked up and the towering Florida pines cast shadows across the driveway. The scent of gardenias lay heavy on the air. "I appreciate the ride home," she said in a polite manner.

He glanced toward her three-car garage. "You don't drive. How do you get around?"

"I call our driver Roger."

"You chose my Harley over the family limo?"

"Roger is rather stoic," she said.

"So was the guard at the gate." The uniformed man had looked down his nose at Dune, his expression disapproving as hell.

"The family compound doesn't get much traffic," she said. "Gerald doesn't see many motorcycles."

"I've had my Harley since high school," he told her. She didn't look surprised. "It's the only way to travel."

She glanced at her watch. "I've taken up your entire afternoon," she said, alarmed. "What about the repairs to your grandfather's porch?"

"Schedules can be broken," he said easily.

She was visibly relieved.

Silence stood between them. Dune shifted his stance. *Now what?* he mused. He wasn't ready to leave. He liked Sophie's company, but there wasn't much more for them to do or say at that moment. He'd never struggled with inviting himself into a woman's home. Yet Sophie was different. He didn't want to intrude.

His words sounded stilted and unnatural when he asked, "Can I get a glass of water before I go?"

"How about red raspberry sun tea?" she offered.

"Sounds good."

Dune liked sun tea. He made it often at his home in California. All he had to do was fill a large glass jar with

cold water, then add four to six tea bags of his choice. After adding a lid, he'd set the jar on the railing of his back
deck. The tea brewed in the warmth of the sun. It was
worth the hour wait.

He retrieved her purse from his saddlebag and handed
it to her. The broken seashells crunched beneath their feet
as they walked toward her house. Sophie's steps were tentative. Her legs barely carried her to the front door. He
settled one arm about her shoulders to keep her close.
Their sides brushed and she stepped on his toes twice.

They made it to the columned entry. Her home was
contemporary in an old-Florida setting; the stucco was
painted antique white with a terra-cotta barrel roof. Trees
and shrubs grew naturally around the grounds. The gardener worked on his hands and knees beneath the big bay
window.

"What are you planting, Luis?" Sophie called to him.

"Mrs. Saunders wanted white roses across the front,"
said the older man with the weathered face and blue ban-
dana wrapped about his forehead. "I went with your
choices, Miss Sophie. Kaleidoscope and Firecrackers."

Sophie smiled. "Reds and yellows. The colors will come
alive."

"I trimmed the Calusa Grape on the bamboo arbor and
breezeway," Luis told her. "The vines were running wild."

"You have a lot to do," she said. "Would you mind if I
hired a young boy to work with you? His name is Chuck
Cates. He's twelve. He has lots of energy, but he won't
cause you any trouble."

Luis was thoughtful. "I fertilize tomorrow. Should he
make it through the day, we'll keep him."

"I appreciate all you do," Sophie told him.

"You like me because I listen to you and not your
mother." The man was wise.

"You know me well," Sophie said as she fished her door

key out of her purse. "I'm turning twenty-five soon. I don't need my family doing all my thinking for me."

So her birthday was coming up. Dune stored the information. He'd get the exact date from Shaye. If he wasn't in town, he'd send her a card, maybe even flowers.

The lock clicked and Sophie walked inside. Dune followed, only to stop in the entry to take it all in. Elegance met history in a fascinating amalgamation of past and present. The foyer was wide, long, and guarded by two medieval knights encased in glass. The sets of armor stood tall and polished, from the helmets and chain mail down to their boots.

A wicked-looking flail—a blackened steel ball with spikes—hung from one knight's gauntlet. The other held a battle-ax with a curved steel head pinned to a hardwood shaft. The knights looked ready for battle.

Sophie stood back and allowed him to look around. The overhead skylight splashed sunlight across aqua marble. The flooring appeared so pale and fluid, Dune felt he was walking on water.

Expansive arches opened to spacious rooms showcasing Italian leather furniture, oil paintings, and crystal vases with freshly cut flowers. He was quick to learn that her fascination ran to weaponry throughout the ages.

Sweet, innocent Sophie had bloodlust.

He entered the living room and slowly turned in a full circle. Her home was an exhibit. He read the plaques beneath the weapons. A medieval sword gallery fought for wall space with a Viking ax and a Hundred Years' War dagger. A samurai sword was mounted next to a seventeenth-century musket. A two-handed Danish sword looked sharp and dangerous.

He admired a 1713 Casque Normand or Norman helmet forged with a nasal guard displayed on the coffee table alongside a preserved medieval fiddle.

"You live in a museum," he finally said.

Her smile was small. "I'm a collector. Sometimes I feel I was born in the wrong era."

He surprised himself by saying, "I like the Wild West." He'd never shared his affinity for cowboys with anyone prior to Sophie. He figured she'd understand.

She did. "Outlaw or U.S. Marshal?" she asked.

"I'm law abiding," he said.

"I have a pearl-handled six-gun."

That he wanted to see. He followed her through another arch and down two steps into her sunken private library. Dune was surrounded by books on all three sides. There were floor-to-ceiling shelves and individual glass-front bookcases, too. He'd never seen so many novels outside a public library.

A three-tiered glass curio cabinet showcased the six-gun along with a 1760 single-shot flintlock and a set of dueling pistols. A pair of silver Celtic knot-work earrings appeared delicate and out of place amid the firearms.

"Impressive, Sophie," he said as he walked around the room. Two crescent-shaped couches faced each other to form a circle. An enormous ottoman sat in the middle. He could picture her sinking into the deep burgundy leather sofa, a book in hand, her orange reading glasses low on her nose.

An antique bookcase with a curved front caught his eye. Original clothbound first editions were kept under glass. On the top shelf sat her volleyball trophy from the previous summer. It was small, yet visible from all angles of the room.

Dune smiled to himself. She hadn't thrown the trophy away. She'd given it a place of honor instead. His own tiny prize could be viewed among his two hundred tournament trophies. He'd placed it front and center. Meeting Sophie was a good memory for him.

"The kitchen's at the back of the house," she said, stepping out into the hallway. "The tea's brewed."

He trailed behind her. Their height difference amused him. He liked watching her walk. Her hair swept her shoulders. Her posture was perfectly straight. Every few steps and the rubber sole on her Keds scuffed the marble floor. She pitched forward, but caught herself. Dune would've grabbed her from behind before he'd let her fall.

Her house went on forever. He glanced in several more archways and came across her office, a space decorated with a heavy oak refectory table darkened with age. A medieval laird's chair stood nearby, the wood smoothed by centuries of use and carved with a square-sailed galley. It was magnificent.

Historical banners and medieval clothing adorned the walls. He admired a Crusader's cape and Templar's tunic along with a long, but color-faded Celtic Dragon and Great Griffin banner.

He paused in the doorway of her TV and entertainment center. Jigsaw puzzles were one of her leisure activities, he noted as he stepped into the room. Several large, complicated puzzles were in progress simultaneously on different tables. He read one box top: twelve thousand pieces went into Michelangelo's *Creation of Man*. The puzzle was nearly completed. The *Dalmatian* jigsaw made his eyes cross. There were so many black spots on the dogs. They all looked alike. *The Earth from Space* had so many blue pieces, he'd never have the patience to match them.

He returned to the hallway and asked her, "Do you live here alone?"

She nodded. "I inherited the house from my grandparents on my mother's side of the family. They felt Florida was too hot and moved back up north. I remodeled and moved in."

A second wide hallway curved right toward the

kitchen. Dune figured the bedrooms were off to the left. He wondered about her bedroom. Would there be more books and weaponry? Would it be simple and elegant, or a lot of frills? Did Sophie sleep in a nightgown, cami and bottoms, or nude?

The thought of her nude had him nearly walking into a wall. He stopped just short and shook himself. He had no business thinking about her sleeping arrangements. His visualizing left him hard. Damn, he was uncomfortable.

He paused near the sliding glass doors that opened off the kitchen and into the backyard. Dune's jaw dropped when he saw a small Civil War cannon anchored beneath an arbor. Three iron cannonballs were placed by a wheel. The barrel was pointed right at him. It was so realistic he expected it to fire.

Beyond the cannon was a large swimming pool, oval in shape with a short diving board and a separate Jacuzzi at the shallow end. A cabana provided shade. Dark blue patio furniture surrounded the deck. A red air mattress floated on the crystal clear water.

"Has the pool ever been used?" he asked.

"Not by me," she said, "but my grandparents were strong swimmers."

"You need to learn to swim," he stated.

She shrugged her shoulders. "Maybe someday."

"Someday soon," he surprised himself by saying. "I'll teach you."

"I wouldn't make a good student," she said. "You know I'm afraid of water."

"I'll help you overcome your fear."

"We'll see."

Dune let her slide for the moment. The topic wasn't dead. He just didn't want to push her and have her panic.

The thought of her in a swimsuit, slick and sleek and

clinging to him, stiffened him further. He stuck his hands in his pockets and did some shifting.

With her back to him, she motioned toward the kitchen table. The legs were thick stainless steel and the top was pale gray glass. "Have a seat," she offered.

Dune slid onto a café chair, glad to be seated. He soon realized anyone looking through the glass top could see he'd pitched a tent beneath his zipper. He didn't want Sophie knowing she'd turned him on. He needed to calm himself.

Big word to shorter words. He looked around and found a plaque above a wooden shield that hung on the wall beside him. Richard the Lionhearted. He concentrated on Richard: rich, char, rid, chair, rad, chirr . . . *hard*. The game emphasized his erection. He sucked air. His dick was alive and stirring.

He watched as Sophie moved around the high-tech kitchen. The stove was touch-screen with a glass top. One side of the Sub-Zero PRO refrigerator was stainless steel; the other had a glass door. He could see the raspberry tea inside.

"Summer captured in a jar," she said as she removed the gallon container along with a tray of sliced fruit.

A brief knock on the sliding doors announced a woman in kitchen whites. "Miss Sophie, are you home?"

"I've just arrived," Sophie said from the counter. "I'm fixing tea."

The older lady quickly crossed to her. "Let me help you," she said.

Dune saw Sophie's shoulders stiffen slightly. She shook her head. "I can handle the tea." She made the introductions. "Marisole, this is Dune. Mari is our household chef. Dune is my friend."

Marisole looked him over. A woman in her late forties,

he guessed, dark-eyed and slender. Her hair was braided. Her expression was mother-hen. "A much older friend," she said, making it sound like he was robbing the cradle.

"Not that many years separate us," Sophie said. She set the jar of tea down on the gray slate countertop, then reached in a low cupboard for two tall cranberry glasses.

Marisole took the glasses from Sophie and crossed to the refrigerator. "Crushed, cubed, or ducks?" she asked Dune.

Ducks? Very expensive refrigerators froze designer ice. Sophie's fridge was one of them. "Ducks," he said.

Marisole gave Sophie ducks, too. The chef stood close by as Sophie poured the tea, as if she anticipated a spill. Dune frowned slightly. Marisole was overly protective. Sophie was twenty-four not four, and even if she made a mess, she was capable of cleaning it up. Both a sponge and paper towels were in arm's reach.

Sophie next squeezed slices of orange, pineapple, and lime into their tea. The final touch came when she added fresh blueberries. She found an iced-tea spoon in a drawer and stirred briskly, then passed him a glass.

The ducks seemed to paddle in his tea. He took a long sip. It was fruity and refreshing and the best red raspberry tea he'd ever tasted.

"You make good tea," he praised Sophie.

Her cheeks pinkened. "The sun did all the work." She brought her glass and sat down beside him.

Beside him, Dune noticed. Not across from him. Their shoulders bumped and she didn't seem to mind their closeness. He rather liked it, too. Her scent warmed from an afternoon in the sun, innocence beneath the heat of the woman.

The chef kept an eye on them as she puttered around the kitchen. She ran her hand over the buccaneer pirate musket preserved on a shelf between the stove and refrigerator. He was glad the antique could no longer be fired.

He looked at Sophie. "Do you have something you should be doing?" he asked.

"She requested an early dinner," Marisole answered for her. "She has volleyball tonight."

"Practice or a game?" Dune asked.

"Practice only," said Sophie. "Our team gets together two nights a week. The official games are Sunday afternoons."

"You said you were improving."

She gave him a self-deprecating smile. "Practice has not made me perfect."

"You have heart." He knew that to be true.

"But no height," she said. "I see more under the net than over."

"I'm glad you're sticking with it."

"Shaye's urged me to be more social."

"My sister knows everybody and their brother," he said ruefully. "She's never met a stranger."

"She's fortunate to have so many friends." Sophie sounded wistful.

"Who do you hang with?" he asked.

"Mostly with myself."

Sophie needed to get out more.

"She has Luis and me, too," said Marisole as she returned to the refrigerator and selected an assortment of vegetables. She laid them out on the butcher-block island. She selected a knife from the slotted cutlery block. She went on to chop lettuce. Rather aggressively, he noticed.

Dune was mildly amused. Apparently, the chef didn't like him much. He had no idea why. She remained as their chaperone.

Sophie was his primary concern. He focused on her.

"What's going on in your life besides your adventures?" he asked.

"Shaye recruited me to help decorate the pier for the Sneaker Ball," she said. "There are only two days before the event and lots to do."

Marisole glanced at them over her shoulder. "No need to string lights," she said. "There'll be a full moon on Saturday. The sky will sparkle."

Dune hadn't taken the chef for a romantic, yet her face softened when she looked at Sophie. He realized Marisole was quite fond of her. "Your brother Trace asked me to oversee the buffet," she said. "I think it will be delicious. I created the menu. The dishes will be catered by the Sandcastle Hotel."

"Lobster in sweet butter? Salmon steaks?" asked Sophie. Dune swore she moaned.

Marisole nodded. "I'll be sure to bring a plate home for you," she said. "Unless you have a date?"

Sophie shook her head. "I bought a ticket, but I have no plans to go."

Dune felt Marisole's stare and met her gaze. The chef leaned against the island counter, one hand on her hip. She raised one eyebrow, as if to challenge him.

What the hell? He clutched his glass and let the condensation cool his warm palms. Mari's initial welcome hadn't been friendly. Yet somewhere between adding duck ice cubes to his glass and chopping lettuce, her opinion of him had improved. She wasn't very subtle.

The chef was a matchmaker.

Dune's chest tightened. He was aware of the dance; it was an annual event. The Sneaker Ball kicked off summer. Shaye always twisted his arm and sold him a ticket whether he planned to attend or not.

"Black tie, fancy dresses, and sneakers," Marisole said as

she diced a green pepper and a stalk of celery. "A night to remember."

She reached for a carrot peeler and shredded a fat carrot. "Miss Sophie has three pairs of Keds and so many pretty dresses. Some still have the sales tags."

Dune ran one hand down his face. He'd received Marisole's message, loud and clear. Could the chef be any more obvious?

Sophie wasn't quite so quick. It took her several seconds to realize what Mari was suggesting. She looked horrified when it soaked in. She put her hands over her face and spoke through her fingers. "I apologize for Mari. She didn't mean to put you on the spot."

The chef's look said otherwise. She shrugged, selected a small, sharp knife and turned three turnips into tulips.

"It's fine," he said. "I haven't finalized my plans."

Marisole might have done him a favor. He'd received dozens of text messages from women seeking him out. Many dated him for his popularity, while others wanted him only for sex. All claimed they had sexy sneakers for the ball.

Then there was Sophie and her Keds. She was an entirely different story. She was cute, kind, considerate, and into weaponry. But friendship was one thing, dating her was quite another.

She reminded him of someone who decorated for the prom and volunteered to serve punch. She was the wallflower no one asked to dance. She'd be a bridesmaid twenty times over before taking her own walk down the aisle.

Perhaps it was her turn to be the center of someone's attention. *His* attention. He'd leave her memories to last a lifetime. He would make sure of it.

He gently circled one of her wrists with his fingers and lightly squeezed it. She lowered her hands. Still, she couldn't look at him. "The dance might be fun," he admitted.

"I'm sure you'll have a great time."

"I wasn't planning on going alone."

Dune would have his choice of any woman in Barefoot William, Sophie Saunders thought. Shaye had offered to set her up, but Sophie had declined. A special night deserved a special man. There was no one in her life who qualified for the gala.

Marisole tossed the salad ingredients in a wooden bowl. She placed Sophie's first course in the refrigerator, then quickly cleaned up. "Your parents wanted Feta Chicken for dinner. It's in the oven at the main house. I'll return shortly." She eyed Dune. "One plate or two?"

Dune finished off his iced tea, stood. "I need to get going. My grandfather's grilling steaks tonight. He's expecting Mac and me."

"I'll return in a moment," said Marisole. She disappeared through the sliding glass doors.

Sophie rose, too. "I'll walk you out."

"And I'll take you to the dance."

She was startled. He couldn't be serious. "I can't be your first choice."

"I'm asking you, Sophie."

"There has to be someone else."

He scratched his jaw. "Are you trying to talk me out of taking you?"

It sounded that way, even to her. She hadn't meant to be ungrateful. She gave him a small smile. "I'd like to go with you."

"Let's kick it then."

They parted ways in the foyer. He chucked her lightly under the chin, then ruffled her hair. "We'll have fun, buddy." And he was gone.

Buddy? She ran her fingers through the mussed strands. Some of her excitement left her. A man who patted a woman on the head saw her as a child. The Sneaker Ball was her big chance to make a major impression on him. She wanted Dune to see her as someone special.

She returned to the kitchen. Marisole was again present, arranging a single place setting at the table. The kitchen was informal, yet the chef insisted on a linen tablecloth, sterling silverware, a crystal goblet, and fine china.

Sophie sat down and started on her salad. Mari allowed her two bites before asking, "So, do you have a date for the Sneaker Ball?"

She couldn't help but grin. "Dune took your hint."

The chef sighed. "I'm so glad, little one." Marisole crossed to her and gave her a big hug. Her affection was genuine, warm, and crushing.

"He's nice and tall," Marisole said. "I like height on a man."

"So do I," Sophie admitted.

"He's good-looking, too."

"Fans call him Beach Heat."

"He's a little old for you."

Sophie silently disagreed.

"Talk to Mrs. Shaye," Marisole suggested. "She will help you select the right dress and sneakers."

Consulting her sister-in-law was a good idea. Sophie was clothes-conscious, but too short to pull off designer fashion. Shaye had once helped her pick out a swimsuit. Sophie would seek her advice after volleyball practice.

The chef replaced her salad plate with a warm dinner plate from the oven. Feta chicken breast and brown rice was one of Sophie's favorite meals. She ate half, then requested the rest be wrapped up and saved for a midnight snack. She loved to read late into the night and often found herself hungry.

She asked Mari to call for her driver, then took off for her bedroom. Her steps were light, but her thoughts were heavy. She had a lot of planning ahead of her.

She slipped out of her clothes and into gray sweatpants and her *Serve-ivors* T-shirt. She kept on her Keds. A Scrunchie secured her hair. She left her reading glasses on the dresser. She often got hit in the face. She didn't want her glasses to break. A navy blue leather athletic bag sat on her bed, packed with a towel and her elbow and knee pads. Shaye insisted she wear the protective gear.

The family driver was waiting for her out front. Roger assisted her into the limo. Shaye Cates would bring her home. It had become a ritual and gave the two women bonding time. They often stopped for ice cream.

"Barefoot William High School Gym," she told Roger. They were off.

"Awesome overhand serve! Way to go, Knee pads." Shaye cheered as Sophie stretched every muscle in her body to achieve her goal. She'd always served underhand, yet tonight she attempted the more difficult overhand serve and nailed it. The ball cleared the net by a full inch.

She had no idea where the power came from, only that she felt remarkably strong tonight. Dune's invitation to the Sneaker Ball exhilarated her. She felt she could handle anything, which included practicing hard with her teammates.

A short time later, Jenna from the T-shirt shop praised Sophie further. "Damn, girl, nice spike. You're on fire."

Sophie had jumped and thumped the ball hard. Another first for her. She bent at the waist and breathed deeply. She was improving. She was glad the women had the gym to themselves. She felt daring with no one watching.

The six players were split into three per side. They encouraged and pushed each other to hone their skills. Sophie didn't want to be the weakest link. She was out to prove herself tonight.

Ninety minutes later, the women kicked back on the high school bleachers. Sophie was hot, sweaty, and in need of a shower. Still, she felt marvelous.

Shaye opened a cooler and passed out lemon-lime Gatorade. They all drank deeply without speaking for a few moments before Nicole, owner of The Jewelry Box, caught her breath and said, "I'm worn out."

Sophie admired the jewelry designer in her T-shirt and white shorts. Nicole promoted her designs even at volleyball practice. Jade double-hoop earrings set off her green eyes. A silver chain necklace with a turquoise dolphin pendant dipped just below her cleavage. A wide gold ankle bracelet glittered above her blue-and-white Nikes.

Eden from the photography shop fanned herself with her hand. Sophie noticed the younger girl's nails were painted half orange, half red, with a streak of gold down the middle. They looked like a sunset. "Who needs Zumba or Pilates?" Eden wheezed. "Volleyball is a full-body workout."

Sophie agreed. Her muscles felt raw and stretched to the max. Her thighs had yet to fully recover from her motorcycle ride earlier. Now volleyball left her arms and shoulders sore. She'd take a bubble bath the moment she got home.

Shaye rubbed the back of her neck with a white towel. "Sophie, Jen, Violet, are you all still available to help decorate the pier tomorrow?"

Two of the three nodded. Violet shook her head. "Sorry, but I got called in to work. The diner's been so busy that Molly asked me to pull a double shift."

Shaye understood. "I'm glad business is good. I'll get

Trace to help if we get behind and need another set of hands." She turned to Jen. "How about Stan, would he give a couple of hours?"

"He wouldn't give a second," Jen was slow to say. "We broke up this morning."

The women sympathized. "So sorry," said Nicole.

"Son of a bitch," Violet ground out. "His timing sucks."

"Anything I can do?" asked Sophie.

"Not a thing, but thanks," said Jen. "I'll be at the event solo." She nudged Sophie. "Any chance I can talk you into a girls' night out?"

"Sounds perfect," Shaye said, encouraging Sophie. "You could dress up, then stand with Jenna, Trace, and me at the entrance to the pier as we greet the guests. Does that work for you?"

Sophie clutched her hands in her lap. Her date with Dune had yet to fully sink in. Sharing the fact with her friends made her a bit uneasy. She shifted nervously on the bleachers, bumping the bottle of Gatorade with her hip. She made a fast grab and only a few drops spilled. She dabbed the spot with her towel.

"Sophie?" Shaye prodded her. Her sister-in-law knew her better than most. "What's up?" she asked. "You look like you've got a secret."

"I have a date," Sophie confessed.

The five women stared at her, wide-eyed and surprised. Violet's jaw dropped and Eden nearly slid off the bleachers.

"With *who?*" Shaye was the first to ask.

"With Dune."

"My brother Dune?" came from Shaye.

Sophie nodded.

"Details," said Jen.

Sophie wasn't sure what to say. Girl talk was new to her.

She skimmed over running into Dune and Mac at Crabby Abby's, then their lunch together and her unicycle lesson. She ended with the motorcycle ride home and her inviting Dune inside for iced tea.

"I'm not sure he would've invited me on his own," she said, recalling Marisole nudging him. "Our chef hinted that he should take me. She put him on the spot."

Shaye pursed her lips. "My brother would never feel obligated to take anyone anywhere," she said. "You became friends last year at the volleyball tournament. There have been several women pressuring him to go to the dance. He feels comfortable with you."

Comfortable made her heart sink. She was excited and anxious. She wanted Dune to feel the same way.

He was experienced, that Sophie knew. Women approached him, wanted him, and boldly told him so. He might not be as sexually active as Mac James, but he never lacked female attention. He was desired.

Shaye sensed her concern. "Do you have a dress?" she asked.

"Several, but I'd like something new."

"New and special." Shaye understood. "Zsuzsy in Saunders Square is sophisticated and classy. We'll go shopping early tomorrow morning."

"How about jewelry?" Nicole asked. "I have the perfect necklace. Two long strands of crystals that sparkle like stars."

Sophie nodded. "Sounds lovely."

Violet grinned. "Sexy undies? Or nothing at all?"

Shaye narrowed her gaze on her cousin. "It's a first date, Vi," she said. "No one's jumping bones."

"Sneakers?" asked Eden. "You're short and Dune's tall."

Sophie shrugged. "I'd planned on wearing Keds."

Shaye snapped her fingers. "I have the perfect tennies.

Puma makes a black satin, high-heel sneaker. Very hot. You can order them online tonight and request next-day delivery."

Sophie sighed. "I can barely walk in flats."

Shaye patted her on the shoulder. "You'll be fine. Hold on to Dune's arm. He'll support you."

Sophie's heart warmed as she looked at her teammates. These women were her friends, a first for her. She could pull it all together and make it work.

Or so she hoped.

They called it a night shortly thereafter. Shaye drove her home. They stopped at The Dairy Godmother and enjoyed butterscotch sundaes. Afterward they agreed on a time to meet the next day. Ten o'clock worked for them both.

The ideal dress was out there somewhere.

A dress that would leave Dune speechless.

Five

Sophie had purchased the perfect dress. Shaye insisted the black satin strapless was made for her. The fan-pleated Empire bodice and tulle skirt were both feminine and formal. She'd purchased the two-strand crystal necklace from Nicole Archer. Her chest sparkled.

Her dress boosted her confidence, even if she was falling apart.

Dune Cates would arrive in six minutes.

Her back zipper was stuck.

She stood before the full-length mirror in her bedroom and fought with the tab. She worked the zipper to the middle of her back, then twisted her body like a pretzel to pull it higher. It wouldn't budge.

She crossed to the pale blue brocade fainting couch and sat down with a heavy sigh. She had so few friends. There was no one she could call. Her mother and father were out of town. Marisole was at the Sandcastle overseeing the buffet. Shaye was on her houseboat clear across town. The rest of her volleyball teammates were getting ready for the Sneaker Ball.

She sighed. Life challenged her on a daily basis, but to have a zipper take her down was the lowest of the low. She glanced for the fifteenth time at her bedside clock. She was running late.

She'd wanted to wow Dune, but there was no wowing him now, not with her dress unzipped and one shoelace on her black satin high-heeled sneakers tied in a knot. Her manicure suffered one broken nail.

The doorbell rang; a jarring sound. The night wasn't starting out well. She'd wanted to make a grand entrance, yet that wasn't to be. She knew Dune would help her, but she hated asking him. She wasn't as incompetent as she appeared.

Walking in four-inch heels was a trial by fire for her when she was used to wearing flats. Balance was not her friend. She grabbed her black beaded evening bag and somehow made it down the hallway without mishap. The front of her fan-pleated dress gaped slightly. She placed a hand over her heart to hold it in place. She didn't want to flash him.

She opened the door and he stole her breath. Dune was one hot body on the beach, but put him in a suit and the man was heart-stopping. He'd gotten a haircut and was clean shaven. He smiled and his eyes warmed. He appeared glad to see her.

"I was late in renting a tux and had to settle for a dark suit," he said ruefully.

There'd been no settling—the man was amazing. "You look nice," she managed. Phenomenal fit him better. His black suit looked as tailored as any tux. His burgundy tie set off his starched white shirt. His Nikes were black and gray. He appeared sharp, handsome, and stood out. A tall, athletic man among men.

"New dress?" he asked.

She blushed. "New and unzipped." She gave him her back. "Would you mind?"

The callused tip of his finger brushed her shoulder blade as he worked the zipper. Goose bumps rose on her arms.

She breathed easier when he turned her to face him. "Easy fix," he said.

He eyed her thoroughly and intently from the top of her hair, brushed two hundred strokes, to her bare shoulders, then down her dress. "You look pretty," he complimented her.

She would've preferred gorgeous, hot, or sexy, but she could live with pretty. At least he hadn't ruffled her hair.

He narrowed his gaze on her sneakers. "No offense, Sophie, but can you walk in those? They're like stilts."

She gave him a small smile. "My latest adventure. I'm hoping so." She crossed her fingers behind her back.

He offered his arm. "I've got you."

She figured if she made it across the crushed seashell driveway, she could walk the pier. Every piece of shell seemed determined to twist her ankle. Dune was her anchor.

"No Harley tonight. You don't want to arrive windblown," he said as he walked her to a dark blue SUV. "Mac took off with my grandfather's pickup truck, so I borrowed my parents' Tahoe. My mom has allergies and is feeling under the weather. They won't be attending the event."

He held the door open for her and she slid comfortably onto the leather seat. She fastened her seat belt, then sat quietly. Dune had said she looked pretty. She held his compliment close to her heart. It warmed her from the inside out.

Marisole may have twisted his arm to take her to the Sneaker Ball, but she'd make sure he didn't regret his decision. Dune was far more exciting than a night spent curled up on her couch reading; her date, a bowl of popcorn.

He settled in beside her and buckled up. "Ready?" he asked.

She nodded. She was as ready as she'd ever be.

Thirty minutes later, Dune parked the Tahoe on a side street near Molly Malone's diner. They walked a short distance and took their place in line at the entrance to the pier. Six men formed a barrier, each taking tickets as Shaye, Jenna, and Trace welcomed the couples.

It was a magical night, Sophie thought. Her decorating efforts the previous evening added to the enchantment. She'd worked alongside Shaye and numerous volunteers to breathe life into the Sneaker Ball.

The pier pulsed with excitement and anticipation as if the night had a secret up its sleeve. Sophie's heart quickened and she found herself smiling for no reason.

All around her the rides and amusements stood dark. The tiny white lights strung between poles twinkled against the fading twilight. She loved late spring when the days stretched toward summer and the sun stayed up late.

She glanced toward the Gulf and her stomach fluttered. She faced her fears tonight. She didn't do well around water. High tide cast waves against the wooden pilings. Frothy foam spread along the sand. The beach was empty. It was a night to be on the pier, to party, dance, and support a community cause.

Florists had supplied fragrant plants and flowers. The summer perfume of Heaven Scent gardenias, Angel Trumpets, and Night-blooming Jasmine wafted on the salt air. A slight breeze kept the humidity at bay.

Trace and his crew had rolled out a red carpet. Sophie looked down its length at the hundreds of people gathered. Smiling, happy people out to have a good time. The men's sneakers were either solid or two-tone colors while the women's were flirty and feminine. Their sneakers ranged from tiger stripes and pastel plaids to all that glittered.

Violet from the diner wore gold tennies sprinkled with

fairy dust. Nicole Archer from the jewelry store had slipped into a pair of pink satin ballerina-style sneakers. The ballet ties wrapped her calves.

Sophie's steps were tentative and her knees started to buckle. She clutched Dune's arm a little tighter. *You can do this* was her mantra for the night.

He let her take the lead, allowing her to focus on the fun and not her fears. He produced the couple's ticket and they entered easily. Her brother Trace came forward and smiled encouragingly. Shaye and Jenna embraced her.

"The bar's set up at the far end of the pier and the buffet is across from the bumper cars," Shaye told them. "Dance wherever there's space."

Dancing, another hurdle to clear.

"Ready?" Dune asked, looking concerned.

She didn't want him worrying about her. "Very ready," she assured him.

Mac James was the first person she recognized. He leaned against the pier railing, looking restless. He caught her eye and winked. She winked back. "Sophie, babe," he said on their approach. "You look hot, sweetheart."

"So I've told her," said Dune.

Sophie felt his arm tense beneath her fingers.

Surely he wasn't upset by Mac's compliment. The two men exchanged a look. Mac grinned and Dune's jaw tightened.

"You made it." Dune seemed surprised.

"Jen finally caved and accepted my second invitation," Mac told them. "The woman can debate an issue to death."

"She made you work for it," said Dune.

"Jen agreed to our date two hours before the event," said Mac. "She's last minute."

"So are you," Dune added.

"I thought I was doing her a favor until she set down rules." Mac didn't appear happy. "I had to park at the curb and honk. She didn't want me near her house. I was banned from the pier entrance. She refused to let me greet the guests. I'm a people person. I can shake hands and smile. I'm not out to embarrass her."

"Maybe your clothes put her off," said Dune.

Mac pulled a face. "I was forced to raid Frank's closet. We're talking 1940s. Grandpa needs to update," he said to Dune.

Sophie couldn't help but grin. She liked his look. "Your navy suit is very swing scene," she said. "Your hand-painted tie with the pin-up girl is classic."

The corner of Mac's eye twitched. "I thought my suit was dark brown." He snapped his black suspenders. "These pants have a permanent postwar crease." He scratched his thigh. "The fabric is itchy. They're so high cut at the waist, they restrict my blood flow." He adjusted himself.

"Hands out of your pockets," said Dune.

"Frank tossed me a fedora on my way out, which I left in his pickup," Mac added.

"Nice sneakers," said Sophie.

"Converse is my brand."

Mac pushed off the railing and glanced toward the buffet being set up just beyond the carousel. "Damn, I'm hungry. Maybe I could sneak a plate."

"You should wait until Jen wraps up her hostess duties," Dune said. "The buffet doesn't open for an hour."

Mac didn't heed Dune's advice. He eased around Sophie and headed toward the food. "No one will miss a chicken wing."

"Marisole will cut off his hands if he steals one bite," Sophie said. "Trace put her in charge. Our chef will guard the buffet with her life."

"I've seen her wield a kitchen knife," said Dune. "The snap of serving tongs can be just as dangerous."

The heat index rose as more guests arrived. Dune ran

his fingers beneath his collar and loosened his tie. "A man's got to breathe," he said.

"How about a beer?" she asked. She knew her brother Trace appreciated a cold one on a hot day. Dune looked warm.

"A good idea," he agreed. "Do you want to wait here or come with me?"

"Go with you." She didn't want to be left alone.

He took her by the hand and led her along the railing toward the makeshift bar. It took an hour for them to reach their destination.

Dune was home. He knew everyone and they slowed his progress. His popularity rolled on to Sophie. People were polite, but their full attention was on her date. She stood beside him, yet she felt a pier length behind him. She was glad he held her hand; otherwise she might've been pushed aside or possibly shoved over the railing. The Gulf looked dark and scary.

Dune sensed her unease. "Excuse us," he finally said.

The bamboo bar curved like a horseshoe. Six bartenders poured drinks. The line moved fast. "Wine, water, something iced and fruity?" Dune asked when it came time for them to order.

Sparkling water didn't sound like a party drink. She knew so little about alcohol. He came to her rescue, "Coors and a virgin piña colada," he ordered for her.

Drinks in hand, they strolled back down the pier. It was less crowded toward the entrance. That was where they chose to enjoy their drinks. Sophie ate the fruit from the cocktail spear, then twirled the tiny pink umbrella between her thumb and forefinger. The pink spun white to red beneath the twinkling lights.

She wasn't a big conversationalist, but Dune didn't seem to mind. He leaned back against the railing and sipped his beer. "My life has been crazy lately," he said. "It feels good to unwind. It's you and me tonight as far as I'm concerned. No one else matters."

No one else mattered. She liked the fact he could relax with her. He was so handsome that she'd never breathe easy around him. He gave her butterflies.

Raised voices and a sudden commotion turned their attention toward the six men taking tickets. People shifted, allowing Sophie a look at the gatecrasher.

She blinked over his size. He looked tough as nails with his square jaw and military haircut. He was built like a wrestler. He wore a black T-shirt, jeans, and athletic shoes. She bet he had tattoos and outstanding warrants.

The man pushed by the ticket takers. He didn't give Trace the time of day. Instead he faced off with Shaye. His scowl was dark, his fists clenched. "I want in." His voice was deep and angry.

Shaye didn't give an inch. Her stance was aggressive for a woman in a pale lavender slip dress and orange Adidas. "Sorry, pal, you can't enter without a ticket." She held her ground.

"Tickets sold out yesterday." The man's voice carried on the air. People openly stared. A few narrowed their eyes. One man appeared to swallow a smile, which shocked Sophie. There was no humor in this standoff. The new arrival was mad. She was afraid someone might get hurt.

"You had plenty of time to buy one," Shaye stated. "They've been on sale for months."

"I only arrived today."

Shaye squared her shoulders. "No forethought. It's not my fault you didn't plan ahead."

"I live day to day," he said harshly.

The argument made Sophie shiver. She leaned closer to Dune. She didn't do well with confrontation. Her stomach squeezed and she felt nauseous.

"You need to leave." Trace backed up his wife.

"Hell, no," said the man.

Dune stiffened beside her. "I'll move him along," he said to Sophie. "Wait here." He walked toward the entrance.

Sophie shook off her fear and followed at a safe distance. She watched as Dune edged between Jenna and Shaye. Dune was several inches taller than the man, yet the man was thicker in the chest. Their expressions were confrontational; their stances intimidating. The air rippled with testosterone.

"Leave now or I'll be forced to remove you," Dune told the man. He passed Shaye his empty bottle of Coors, then slipped off his suit jacket. Jen took it from him.

"Dial nine-one-one now," said the man. "Jackass is going to need an ambulance."

Sophie panicked. She couldn't bear for them to fight. The man wanted a ticket and she had an extra one in her evening bag. Dune had used his ticket to enter the dance. She had brought hers just in case he forgot his.

She drew a deep breath and pushed through the thickening crowd. The tension between the men was palpable. A mere foot separated them now. Both were close to throwing a punch.

Her knees were shaking so badly she was afraid she'd sprain an ankle. Yet she managed to make it to Dune's side. She gripped his arm. "Stop, both of you." Her voice was so soft she wasn't sure anyone heard her.

Dune did. He took a step back. He glanced down on her fingers and his brow creased. He looked as uncertain as she felt. "Trust me, Sophie, it's okay."

"No, it's not." Her courage was motivated by her fear of Dune getting hurt. "There's no need to fight. I have an extra ticket." She unsnapped the clasp on her bag and produced it. She passed it to the angry man. "Please, take it."

The man stared at her. His dark brown eyes were nearly black. His mouth twisted menacingly.

Her words ran together when she added, "You don't have a date and you're dressed inappropriately, but at least you're wearing sneakers. Shaye may make an exception for you."

Silence settled so heavily, Sophie couldn't breathe. Everyone stared at her. All appeared stunned. Most were speechless. No one could believe her actions. Dune seemed the most shocked.

"Damn, she's civilized," the man finally said.

"She's got more manners than you," said Jenna.

"She's also pale," the man noted.

"You frightened her," Shaye said, her tone disapproving. "She's shaking."

Fear had drained her. Sophie's heart still raced. She placed her hand on her chest and took a few deep breaths.

Jenna returned Dune's suit jacket. He immediately draped it over Sophie's shoulders. He then tucked her against his side. She found his body solid and comforting.

"You're safe for now," the man told Dune. "I won't mess up your pretty face tonight, but watch your back tomorrow. I'll catch you without your protector."

"I'll be waiting," Dune said.

"Knock it off, you two," Shaye scolded before she threw her arms around the big man with the bad attitude. She hugged him tightly. "Welcome home."

Dune slapped him on the back and the men bumped fists. "It's good to see you, bro."

Sophie's eyes went wide. *Home? Bro?*

The man grinned at her with a flash of white teeth and a single dimple. He relaxed his stance. "I didn't mean to scare you, sweetheart," he said. "My taunting is a ritual. It's who I am. I make a scene and blow off steam. I haven't seen my family in months."

"Eight months to be exact," said Shaye. "Zane is the worst of us all. He acts out."

Dune made the introductions. "Sophie Saunders, my date, meet Insane Zane, my younger brother."

"A Saunders, huh?" Zane asked.

"Insane?" His nickname left Sophie uneasy.

"She's Trace's sister," Dune responded first to his brother, then to Sophie. "Zane's a hurricane hunter with the 53rd Weather Reconnaissance Squadron. He's stationed at Keeslar Air Force Base in Biloxi, Mississippi. He flies into tropical storms and the eye of a hurricane. He's mental."

Zane stared at Sophie. "My job's a little more dangerous than playing volleyball."

"Not if you have Mac James as a partner," Dune said and everyone laughed.

Everyone but Sophie. She had yet to fully comprehend the Cates family *ritual*. One in which even Shaye played a part. They had an unusual way of greeting each other. She shouldn't have interfered, yet her fear for Dune had been real. She hoped she hadn't embarrassed him.

"Sophie," Zane said. "You are brave, babe. How long have you been Dune's bodyguard?"

She was anything but brave, yet boldness had stirred when she thought Dune was in trouble. "I don't protect," she said softly. "I find solutions. I had an extra ticket."

"Speaking of tickets," Zane said to Shaye. "You could've sent me one or set one aside."

"You should've called," she said. "I had no idea you were coming home."

"Pure spur of the moment trip."

Shaye frowned. "You never make plans."

"Whenever I do, they usually get canceled."

"No date?" Dune asked.

"I thought I'd steal yours."

"I go home with who I bring." Dune drew Sophie even

closer. Her cheek pressed the front pocket on his shirt. She wrapped her arm about his waist. They were a natural fit. His strength and warmth relaxed her.

"She's cute," Zane said.

"She's classic," said Mac James, coming to join them. "Stand in line, dude, I met her long before you did."

"What the hell does she see in Dune?" asked Zane.

"I have no idea," Mac said, tongue-in-cheek. "He's old and broken."

"I have a few good years left in me," Dune said.

"I have more than you," said Zane. He cocked his head. "The music's started. Go dance with your woman."

Sophie waited for Dune to deny she was his woman. He didn't. Instead he slipped on his sport jacket, then put his palm to her lower back and guided her toward the carousel. The ride was closed, but that didn't stop him from sneaking in. He raised the chain and they ducked under.

Sophie glanced around. It was as private a place as they'd find anywhere on the pier. She was glad to be alone with him.

The twinkling white lights reflected off the hand-carved purple and white horses with the jeweled amber eyes and gold saddles. Dune led her onto the polished wooden platform. They now stood between the horses, a man and a woman amid the shadows of the orange scalloped top.

The music reached them. The DJ favored slow songs, a mixture of past and present. Lonestar's "Amazed" followed "I Don't Wanna Miss a Thing" by Aerosmith. The music seduced them before they even started dancing.

Dune gazed down on her. "My protector," he said with a half smile. "What possessed you to step between me and the wild man?"

"I was afraid for you," she said softly, honestly.

He kept on staring at her, as if he were trying to figure her out. "You're five foot two, a total lightweight, yet you defended me. You had no idea Zane was my brother."

"I thought I could talk him down," she said. "The extra ticket worked."

"You were fearless."

"You didn't hear my knees knocking?"

"Fortunately, you didn't have any weaponry with you."

"My Viking ax would've come in handy."

Dune laughed, rich and deep. "You had my back, and I thank you." He then held out his hand. "Dance with me?"

She eased into his arms. There was nothing formal or conventional in the way he held her. He bent slightly and wrapped her against him. Her high-heeled sneakers gave her height. She slid her arms about his waist. Her cheek rested over his heart. Her stomach pressed his groin.

Grace eluded her. She'd taken ballet, but she hadn't gotten beyond the plié. Her rhythm was always off, yet she refused to miss an opportunity to dance with Dune even if she stepped on his feet.

This was the most romantic night of her life. Even so, she needed to keep the evening in perspective. They were just friends. He had his choice of women. Chances were good he would've chosen someone else besides her had Marisole not twisted his arm.

Someone prettier, someone sexier, someone taller.

She had a lot to overcome. One day at a time, she thought, sighing. The reflection of a star twinkled in the amber eye of a white wooden horse. Sophie swore the mount winked at her. She took it as a lucky omen.

They slow danced through several songs, even the fast ones. She felt the warmth of his breath on her brow, heard the steadiness of his heart beneath her ear. A hint of his cologne mixed with the starch of his shirt. She felt safe, protected, and unafraid.

★   ★   ★

Dune Cates rolled his shoulders. His back grew tight from hunching over. Sophie was the shortest woman he'd ever danced with. Looking down on her now, he ignored the ache between his shoulder blades. Instead, he recalled her facing off with Zane.

His brother could be a royal pain in the ass. Zane played people. For those who didn't know him, he appeared rough, angry, and confrontational. For those who knew him well, he was good-natured, loyal, and a positive role model. He loved kids and sports and was a hell of a mechanic. He'd flown home for this event.

Dune still couldn't believe Sophie had stood up to his brother. This slip of a woman with her silky hair, fancy dress, and high-heeled sneakers had dared to step between them. Each was a foot taller than she and twice her weight.

Sophie of the soft smile and sweet innocence was surprisingly daring. Her inner warrior woman had surfaced. He liked that side of her.

Pressed against him now, she kept her eyes closed, and her breathing was even. She was genuine and kind. She was an amazing woman and would be even more so when she came into her own.

He'd tucked a lot of life under his arm.

She was on the road of discovery.

He smiled to himself. He might suggest she take dance lessons. She'd stepped on his feet several times and he'd taken a heel to his instep. They swayed more than danced. He liked her scent, vanilla and female. Her body was soft, yet compact. He liked holding her.

He tried to ignore the press of her stomach against his groin and concentrated on the sign above the ticket booth. Carousel. Big word, shorter words. *Car, our, sour, are, rouse . . . arouse.* His game wasn't working.

He inched back fractionally only to have her lean forward. Her body sought his and he sucked air. Less space separated them now. He was about to pitch a tent. He needed a diversion.

Such a distraction came in the form of Mac James. "Mind if we share your dance floor?" his partner called from the chain by the ticket booth. Mac didn't wait for Dune's response. He lifted the metal links for Jenna to duck under and he followed.

Their peace was broken, Dune thought. It was just as well. Another minute with Sophie and he'd sport a boner. "We've got company," he told her.

Sophie turned in his arms and he sensed her reluctance to release him. He curved his hands over her shoulders, squeezed. She relaxed. Her bottom brushed the top of his thighs, just south of his balls. Heat circled his neck. He exhaled and fought his body for control.

Mac grinned, and Dune narrowed his gaze on him. "What are you smiling about?"

"You know what I'm smiling about."

"Knock it off."

"Are you surviving the night?" Jenna asked Sophie. "There are hundreds of people and lots of noise. I know you prefer it quieter."

Sophie nodded, then said, "It's very crowded, but Dune and I are off to the side. I'm enjoying myself."

Dune was having a good time, too, he realized. A better time than he'd expected. Sophie was quiet, yet easy to be around. He'd never imagined she'd be such a turn-on.

"What about you two?" Sophie asked Jen.

Jen pursed her lips. "We're okay for the moment."

"We hit the buffet," said Mac. "The food's great."

Dune noticed the stain on Mac's tie. "Food goes in your mouth, not on your clothes."

Jen rolled her eyes. "The man used his napkin as a bib and still made a mess. He went back for seconds. Marisole chased him off when he tried for thirds."

"Killer crab cakes with mango sauce," Mac defended. "I was hungry. There's no food at Frank's house."

"Because you ate it all," Dune said. "We're down to dog kibble."

Mac pulled a face. "Lamb and rice tastes bland," he said. "It's not my favorite flavor."

"Mac took the last Milk-Bone from Ghost," said Dune.

"Your dog growled at me."

"Could you blame him?" asked Dune.

"Dog breath," muttered Jen.

"I brushed my teeth," said Mac.

Dune shook his head. Mac was incorrigible. Jen chose the straight and narrow. They made an odd couple.

"We've Got Tonight" by Bob Seger began to play. Bodies would press against one another and couples would kiss. Dune stood back as his partner and cousin faced off.

Mac wanted to dance.

Jen did not.

"We agreed to no touching," said Jen.

"It's a slow song," argued Mac.

Jen crossed her arms over her chest. "An arm's length between us then."

"This isn't a cotillion."

"How do you know a cotillion?" she asked.

"I once rode a dirt bike on a public sidewalk in my hometown of San Diego," he told her. "The cops pulled me over and gave me a ticket. I faced a juvenile judge who court ordered ballroom dance lessons. His Honor thought to make me a gentleman."

"The judge was?" Dune already knew the answer.

Mac shot him a dirty look and said, "My dad."

They all laughed at Mac's expense.

"Mac was a hell-raiser," Dune said to Jen. "The stories from his childhood—"

"Wouldn't surprise me in the least," she cut him off. "I grew up alongside you and your brothers. Every one of you ran wild on the boardwalk. You were always bloodied, bandaged, and in trouble."

Jen winked at Sophie. "One time Dune tried to jump his dirt bike from the boardwalk onto the beach. Not a smart move. He flipped the bike midair and dislocated his shoulder on the landing." She sighed. "Shaye was the only one with common sense."

"Good times." Dune said as he and Mac bumped fists.

"How about you, Sophie?" asked Mac. "Ever been on crutches or have a cast?"

She stood quiet, her expression thoughtful. Dune was aware she'd grown up alone without a lot of playmates. Much of her life centered on her home. She read books and collected weaponry. She'd never had close friends until recently. Her volleyball team was drawing her out of her shell. Tonight she stood on the pier surrounded by people. A big step for her, he knew. He doubted she'd ever had an accident. She'd been protected by her family.

She surprised him by saying, "I fell off my bicycle once. I needed a Band-Aid."

A short pause before Mac said, "Babe, you're one of us."

Dune heard her soft sigh of relief. Acceptance was important to her. He blinked against the sudden image of a small girl on the side of the road. The impression faded as fast as it formed. In that moment he felt a strange connection to Sophie, even though he had nothing solid. He let it go for now. He'd figure it out later.

"Food or dance?" he asked her.

"Food," she said. "I skipped lunch."

Dune took her hand and they headed toward the buffet. The line was long and once again he was greeted by guests. He was good at small talk. He'd found over the years that once people complimented him, they felt free to chat about themselves and their own accomplishments. They wanted to prove to him that they were worthy of his time.

He saw them all as his equals. He'd been blessed with height and athleticism, yet everyone had skills to hone. It was all about making smart choices, along with fighting off volleyball rookies who wanted to take him down. There was only room for one top seed. He would hold on to his spot as long as he possibly could.

They finally reached the first-course table and each took a plate. Dune chose the short ribs in a raspberry glaze and Sophie went with salmon steak. They both added fresh vegetables to their plates. Dune picked chocolate-caramel mousse for dessert. Sophie debated between key lime pie and strawberry flan. Dune had big hands. He snagged both for her.

"Run before Marisole catches us," he said to her.

Sophie, burst out laughing. She laughed so hard she could barely keep up with him. He liked the fresh, free sound of her laughter. She needed to laugh more. She also needed to take off her high-heeled sneakers. She was wobbly.

They located a wooden bench where they could sit and eat. He picked up the ribs with his fingers, while Sophie ate with formal finesse. Plastic silverware in hand, she precisely cut each bite. He swore she chewed twenty times before swallowing. The ribs were messy and he used his napkin, then reached for hers. She didn't mind. He smiled when she finished her meal with two desserts.

Conversation circled around him. People stood before him, even while he ate. He didn't mind much. He was used to crowds. He nodded a lot, while keeping one eye on Sophie. Gone was her stiffness and apprehension. She openly stared at him, fascinated by his popularity and how he handled his fans.

She appeared to be taking mental notes and making her own adjustments amid the gathering. She even managed to speak to the mayor of Barefoot William, complimenting him on his recent Preservation Act to protect the nesting areas of the loggerhead sea turtles.

Mayor James Cates wanted to talk politics. He brought up a controversial topic. "How do you feel about my decision to limit construction to only five-story buildings along our shores?" he asked. He knew Sophie was a Saunders, but sought her opinion anyway. Dune waited to hear what she had to say.

She took a moment to collect her thoughts. "I think William Cates would agree with you," she said slowly. "I've read his journals. Honesty and integrity were important to him. He conducted business with a handshake. He was the barefoot mayor for more than forty years. He was a kind, logical man who believed life wasn't meant to be hurried. He wanted the area to develop at its own pace."

She fingered the clasp on her evening bag. "William was involved in every aspect of the town. He was laid-back and"—she smiled, then continued—"religiously took afternoon naps during the heat of the day on a canvas hammock between twin palms. He wrote that on waking, he often fell out of his hammock. He took long walks along the beach with his hound dog Buddy. He loved to fish."

Her expression was shy, but serious. "William built the original stores on the boardwalk. His fingerprints are on every plank of the pier. High-rise condos would take away from his memory. He was a man of intuition and vision. He was rich beyond what money could buy.

"Check the city records," she suggested. "The official bylaws allowed for expansion of the boardwalk and pier, but not much else. Go back in the archives and honor your founder's wishes."

The mayor eyed Sophie with respect. "You're quite the historian," he said. "I agree with you. Stop by the courthouse sometime. My office door is always open. I'd like to carry on our conversation. William was an interesting man."

Dune caught her surprise. She was an encyclopedia on Barefoot William history. People had stopped to listen as she spoke about their town. A significantly large group circled them now. He could tell that they hoped she'd continue, but she didn't. She seemed embarrassed to have drawn attention to herself.

A meeting with the mayor would boost her self-esteem. Dune wanted her to feel good about herself. He had yet to read William's journals. Perhaps it was time to meet his ancestor through the man's own words.

They mingled further and Sophie survived. He knew everyone from Barefoot William, which was nearly everybody present. He recognized a few people from Saunders Shores, but didn't know their names. They were Trace's business associates, who arrived late and left early. He imagined they wrote sizable checks to support parks and recreation.

"Full moon and I'm wanting to howl," Mac James said as he came up behind them.

"Howl and I'll muzzle you." Jenna joined them, too.

Mac took a long pull from his bottle of beer. "I have the urge to skinny-dip." He waggled his eyebrows at Sophie. "Are you with me?"

Sophie blushed. "I'm scared of the water."

Her fear didn't faze Mac. "No need to worry. I'll hold you tight."

"No, you won't," said Dune. Not tonight, not ever. The thought of Sophie naked with Mac tightened his gut.

The fact Mac even suggested it rattled his cage. "Shaye would kill you if you flashed her guests."

"I'd take him down before he shrugged off his suit jacket," Jenna warned.

"I'd drag you down with me." The look on his face was so suggestive, Jen punched him on the arm. He winced. "Lighten up. I'm out for some fun." He finished off his beer. "I'm ready for another."

"Three-beer limit, that was our deal," Jenna reminded him.

"Buzz killer."

Their exchange had Dune shaking his head. Mac was restless, bored, and about to do something stupid. He'd be a handful for Jen. Dune glanced at his watch, then took charge. "It's close to two a.m. and the crowd's thinning. Let's call it a night."

"What about sex?" Mac asked Jen.

"You have two perfectly good hands."

"Guess I'm going home to make balloon animals with my condoms."

"Blow softly. You don't want them to pop." Jen turned and walked down the boardwalk toward the parking lot.

"Worst date ever," said Mac as he took off after her.

"I heard that," Jen called over her shoulder.

"Worst, worst, worst," Mac repeated.

Sophie watched them leave. "Not the worst, but the best," she said. "Years from now their grandchildren will smile when they hear about their grandparents' first date."

"You've got to be kidding," said Dune. "They don't even like each other. They're acting like children."

"I say they like each other a lot. They just don't know it yet," she said. "They'll be engaged by the end of the summer."

He couldn't help himself. He laughed out loud. Sweet,

romantic Sophie was dreaming. "You don't know Mac like I know Mac. He'll drop Jen at her house, then peel out, leaving rubber. He won't think about her again."

"She'll be on his mind all night long."

His brow creased. "What makes you so sure?"

"Mac likes the chase and Jen won't be caught."

That was true. However, Mac never pursued a woman who made him work too hard. He liked his relationships easy. He and Jenna rubbed each other the wrong way.

"Care to wager?" he asked.

She thought it over. "I've never gambled, so this might be fun. For every move Mac makes on Jen, I win a prize," she said. "Something small, fun, nothing elaborate."

Sophie was competitive. Dune liked that side of her. "For every day he avoids her, you owe me. I'm betting Mac never looks at Jen again."

"I say he stops by the T-shirt shop on Monday."

"I say you're wrong."

"I've decided to volunteer at Three Shirts next week," Sophie told him. "I'll be at the store when Mac shows up."

"It's going to be a long day with you watching the door."

She yawned then and quickly covered her mouth. Dune saw she was tired. It had been an eventful evening. Sophie had outlasted most of the guests. She'd overcome several of her fears and lived to tell about it. He was proud of her.

"Shall we call it a night?" he asked. "The DJ and the bar have shut down and the clean-up crew just arrived."

She lifted one foot, rolled her ankle, then admitted to him, "My feet hurt."

He walked her toward a wooden bench. "Sit down and take off your sneakers."

"Go barefoot?"

"Your feet will thank you."

He helped her with a small knot in one of the laces and

off came her dressy tennis shoes. She stretched out her feet, small feet with red marks across her toes. Her toenails were painted red. Sexy, he thought.

Sexy? Not a word he usually associated with Sophie. There was something about her small, pale, shapely feet that made him want to start his hands low and work high, right up her body.

A jarring thought and one he dismissed as fast as it formed. It was time to drive her safely home, then walk her to the door and say good night.

Sophie stood up and sighed. He took her high-heeled sneakers and stuck them in the pockets of his sport jacket. She held out her hand, an unassuming gesture, but one that made her secure. He had no problem holding her hand. He rather liked it.

Neither spoke on the ride home. Anticipation settled between them. Dune felt it and wondered if Sophie did, too. A question weighed heavily on his mind: should he kiss her? He debated the kiss from every angle.

Pro: Her sweetness and innocence appealed to him. He'd always dated sun-bronzed beach babes who'd been around the block at least once and knew the score. He'd never take advantage of Sophie. He liked her. A lot.

Con: A solid friendship lasted longer than most lovers. Sophie had a romantic heart. Women often read more into a kiss than was actually there. He never led a woman on if he could help it.

A short time later he pulled the SUV into her driveway, then cut the lights and engine. The full moon turned the crushed pink seashells to gold. Dune helped her out and, being barefoot, she took to the grass as they walked to the door. Two outside lanterns lit the entrance. They stood beneath their amber cast.

"Thank you for a wonderful evening," she said. "It meant a lot to me."

"I had fun, too." And he meant it.

Neither moved, they only stared, for a very long time. Her gaze was wide, hopeful, expectant. Time seemed to stop, as if waiting for him to make his move. He'd yet to decide what move to make.

The Sneaker Ball was a big night for Sophie. Memories were important to her. Ruffling her hair was out of the question. A handshake seemed lame. He went with the kiss.

Slowly, gently, he framed her face with his hands. Her skin was pale and smooth. Youthful. The pulse in her throat quickened. She was fragile and feminine. Genuine, giving, and kind. She had a good heart. And a kissable mouth, sweet and generous. Inviting. He found himself studying every detail of her face, taking his time, making every second count.

He leaned toward her and she lifted slightly on her toes. They came together. The front of his starched shirt pressed her fan-pleated bodice. His knee sought space between her thighs. He supported her against him.

She gave an involuntary sigh.

His throat was suddenly tight.

The brief brush of their lips quickly complicated his life. She was a woman worth kissing. His chaste kiss soon deepened. She kissed him back, softly at first, fitting her mouth to his, responsive and seeking.

She clutched his forearms, a woman of trust and innocence. Their kiss was as perfect as any he'd ever known. Her inexperience excited him a little too much. Heat swelled between them. His body stirred. He'd lingered too long.

He eased back and released her. Her eyelids were heavy, her green gaze veiled. His after-midnight stubble had scratched her cheek. Their scents mingled: her vanilla, his lime, and their arousal.

She was Trace's sister, he reminded himself, a young woman with a lot of world to conquer. She would continue her summer adventures with or without him. He planned to keep an eye on her. It wouldn't be a hardship. He could teach her to swim, maybe even to drive, when she wasn't busy seeking her career.

He needed to leave now before his dick talked him into staying. " 'Night, Sophie," he managed to say.

She fished her key out of her purse, inserted it in the lock, and gave him a small smile. He then passed her the high-heeled sneakers he'd kept in his jacket pockets. She opened the door and stepped inside. The slide of the dead bolt and beep of her security system called it a night.

He took a solo walk back to the Tahoe.

Six

The front door to his grandfather's stilt house hit Dune in the ass when he entered. His granddad lived ten miles from the beach, preferring to distance himself from the tourist trade. He had an orange grove along with grapefruit, banana, and peach trees. He liked to pick fresh fruit.

Dune rubbed the back of his neck. He was tired and moving slow. Sophie lingered on his mind. All he wanted was a good night's sleep. It wasn't to be.

There was a two-man party in the living room. Mac James sprawled on a papasan chair. The chair was large and bowl-shaped with a gold cushion. Zane was stretched out on the couch. The men wore only their boxers.

Mac's boxers were white with big red lips down the fly. Most likely a gift from some woman he'd dated. His pin-up girl tie draped over one shoulder. A flex of his pec and she appeared to wiggle.

Mac's lower lip was cut and slightly swollen. Dune frowned. Surely his partner hadn't gotten into a fight after leaving the pier. He didn't want an explanation on what had happened. He'd save his questions for morning.

Empty LandShark Lager bottles littered the coffee table. The guys were tying one on. They played Best-Ever, he noted, a drinking game that drew heavy debate. Their raised voices drowned out the television infomercial for organic nuts and juices. The present topic centered on the best outfielder of all time. Their discussion was getting heated.

"Has to be the Phillies third baseman, Mike Schmidt," said Zane. "He hit four home runs against the Chicago Cubs in nineteen seventy-six. He earned ten Golden Gloves and was a three-time National League Most Valuable Player."

"Shortstop Cal Ripken was a member of the three-thousand-hit club," Mac shot back. "He hit more home runs than any other shortstop in the history of Major League Baseball."

"My vote is for Stan Musial," Dune said as he crossed the room. The stilt house was old, but never smelled musty. It had a lived-in feeling that took him back to his youth; back to family cookouts, games of hide-and-seek, and lazy afternoons on the porch swing.

There was hominess in the faded and frayed blue-and-green braided rugs that scattered the hardwood floor. The hutch in the corner had three good legs. Puppy teeth had gnawed an inch off the fourth. No one had scolded Ghost.

His grandmother's commemorative and collectible plates gathered a light film of dust on the shelves. Nineteen-fifties sheet music was propped on the upright piano. His Grandmother Emma had tried to teach Frank to play, but he'd gotten no further than "Chopsticks." "Our duet," he'd called it.

Stacks of newspapers and magazines crowded the La-Z-Boy recliner. His grandfather wasn't a pack rat or a hoarder. He got rid of items when he was darn good and ready and not before.

The man was eighty-six. He could do whatever the hell he wanted as far as Dune was concerned. He might suggest a cleaning woman come in once a week. Someone who'd keep up with Frank's laundry and chase dust bunnies. Someone who did windows.

He slipped off his sport jacket and tie, then shoved Zane's legs off one end of the couch and dropped down. He grabbed a beer, leaned back, and stretched his arms along the low back. He returned to the conversation at hand. "Musial had quick feet for a first baseman and was a strong base runner. He was an All-Star twenty-four times and hit twelve walk-off home runs for the Cardinals."

"You three don't know baseball," Grandfather Frank said as he joined them. He wore pajama bottoms and an old robe. He was a tall man and still carried himself well. His face was weathered and he had bed head.

"Mind if I join you?" he asked.

"Park it," said Mac.

Frank settled on the worn La-Z-Boy and reclined. He yawned widely. He was a widower of twenty years and still missed his wife. She'd been the love of his life. He slept only a few hours a night, claiming he hated sleeping alone. He was loyal to her memory.

Frank was both ally and friend to his grandsons. They often crashed at his place when they were in town. He didn't mind their noise and bickering. The cedar stilt house wasn't very big and, with three additional grown men, the wood stretched at the seams.

"You three are forgetting Mickey Mantle, Joe DiMaggio, and Ty Cobb," Frank stated. He expanded on their greatness. Zane and Mac went on to drink another beer while Dune's thoughts shifted to Sophie Saunders and their good night kiss.

The sweet kiss had him wondering if and when he could kiss her again and if the second kiss would be as good as the first. He was certain that it would be, maybe even better.

He'd see her again tomorrow. They'd made a bet, an

easy win for him. Mac wouldn't show up at Three Shirts. When he didn't, Dune would collect a winner's kiss. A good prize—

"Dude, you're drifting." Zane kicked Dune in the calf to get his attention, far harder than was necessary. "We're going to order pizza. Are you in?"

"Make mine with the works," he said. "Who delivers at this hour?"

"Zinotti's" said Zane. "We can order take-out until four a.m." He reached for the cordless phone on the coffee table, then looked to his grandfather, who gave him the number. Frank didn't cook much. He had a speed-dial memory for the local fast food restaurants that delivered.

"Isn't that Eddie Z's shop?" asked Dune.

"Same guy," said Zane.

Dune had gone to school with Eddie. Eddie's goal in their high school yearbook had been to be a millionaire by the age of thirty. He'd fallen short. Town gossip had Eddie spending money as fast as he earned it. Most times he was flat broke. He had loans up his ass. He often borrowed from his employees and there were weeks when he didn't make payroll.

"I'd hate to be dropping off pizzas at this hour," said Zane after he'd placed their order. "Suck-ass job."

There was nothing wrong with pizza delivery, Dune thought. It was the kind of job that paid the bills, but wasn't a permanent career. Sophie and her adventures came to mind. Unicyclist wasn't her calling in life. He was certain of that. Neither was stilt walking. Still, she tried what was new and different in order to experience life to its fullest. It was her summer.

Mac and Zane cleared their throats at the same time, drawing his attention. "What?" he asked.

"We're talking, you're tanking," said Zane. "What's the Best-Ever drinking hole? Mac wants to go back to Crazy

Kate's in Houston and I vote for Booze Camp outside the Air Force Academy in Colorado Springs."

"Nothing wrong with the Blue Coconut here in town," Dune said. "We've all gotten drunk and been bounced."

"Your local cocktail waitresses are as hot as any chick at Hooters," said Mac. "What about you, Frank?"

The older man scratched his chin. "I traveled to Chicago years ago before I got married." He smiled at the memory. "Wally's Back Alley served a strong rum and Coke."

Mac raised his beer. "A toast to Wally's."

The men all drank.

"Best-Ever car?" Mac asked next as he reached for another lager. "I'm going with Mustang."

Frank pursed his lips. "1947 DeSoto was well built."

"My 1967 Chevy Impala shits and gets," said Zane.

Mac grunted. "You pour your paychecks into repairs."

Zane shrugged. "It's all worth the howl and growl."

"I heard you coming down the road," said Frank. "You rattled the windows."

"I'll stick with my Harley," said Dune.

"Fast bike, faster women," said Mac. "You are the man."

Not *the* man, but a man, Dune thought. His reputation was larger than his actual lifestyle. He was selective. He'd been with fewer women than the men thought. Just because he was surrounded by hot chicks following a volleyball tournament didn't mean he took one home. Most nights he crashed with Ghost. His dog was good company.

He absently wondered if Sophie had ever had a pet. He figured she'd be good with animals if she didn't fear them. Perhaps something small like a hamster, rabbit, or turtle. Maybe a cat or pocket-sized dog. He'd suggest it to her. She had a big heart.

"Dune?" Mac threw one of Ghost's dog toys at him. "You're zoning again."

Dune caught the Nylabone Frisbee before it took out his eye. "What was the question?"

"Best-Ever date," Zane said.

"For me, any date I get laid," said Mac.

Grandfather Frank snorted. "You're young yet, boy. When the right woman comes along, it won't matter if you share a cup of coffee or take a walk, being together is what counts. Holding hands becomes special."

Mac pulled a face. "No disrespect, but sex tops coffee and a walk."

Frank closed his eyes. "All men get a wake-up call sooner or later. Just you wait."

Dune agreed with his grandfather. The right woman would knock Mac on his ass. Dune waited for that day.

Beside him on the couch, Zane had gone quiet. Dune knew the reason. Any discussion on women drew his brother to Tori Rollins. Zane had fallen hard for her in high school. They'd sneaked off and gotten married after their June graduation, only to divorce when Zane received last-minute acceptance to the Air Force Academy in August. It had been a whirlwind three months.

Zane wanted to fly and Tori wanted him grounded. The thought of him becoming a hurricane hunter only added fuel to their fire. Damn, they could fight. No other girl could go toe-to-toe with Zane and not start crying, yet Tori had. She had a temper to match Zane's own.

Zane stuffed a throw pillow behind his head and said, "I play and lay. I've been dating an exotic dancer from Naked Thighs for a few months. Ava has great hands. She flips me on like a light switch. Nothing serious, though."

Mac looked at Dune. His know-it-all expression was irksome. "You?" he asked. One corner of his mouth curved slightly. "Best-Ever date."

Dune exhaled slowly and pretended to give it some thought. He didn't have to think very long. Sophie Saunders and the Sneaker Ball were foremost on his mind. There'd been no pretense. She was unassuming and easy to be around. She saw him as a man and not just as a sports celebrity.

Mac's smile broke. "Dude . . ." He let the sentence hang. "The bigger they are, the harder they fall."

Dune worked his jaw. "What are you getting at?" he asked.

"She's getting to you."

Mac was far too perceptive for his own good. "Drop it," Dune said.

Their exchange caught Zane's interest. "I want in."

"No, you don't," said Dune.

"I think I do," from Zane.

"Do not." That was final.

A knock on the front door brought momentary reprieve from their conversation. Zane pushed off the couch. "Pizza's here. I'll buy. Let me grab my wallet." He headed down the hallway toward the bedrooms.

Mac belched, then muttered, "Worst-Ever date. Nothing could beat tonight. Jen is everything I'm not looking for in a woman."

"Careful, son," said Frank. "She's a Cates."

Mac snorted. "Faulty DNA."

A second thump on the door and Dune rose. He didn't want to keep the delivery boy waiting. The boy turned out to be a woman. Dune's jaw dropped. There stood Tori Rollins, his brother's ex.

"Hello, Dune. I heard you were in town," she greeted him. She looked tired. "You're having late-night Sneaker Ball munchies, I'm guessing. I've been delivering pizzas to several who attended. You're my last drop."

Dune attempted a smile. Shit was about to hit the fan.

She held out three pizza boxes. "Forty-two dollars even," she said. "I tossed in a free order of cinnamon strips,

Frank's favorite. There are extra jalapeños and garlic dip, too."

Dune accepted the pizzas. "Money's coming," he said.

His brother was about to be zapped by a blue-eyed, red-headed, long-legged stun gun. There was no time to send up a smoke signal.

Across the room, Mac noticed Tori. He pushed off the papasan. The basket chair rolled and he nearly fell on his face. Recovering slowly, he hiked up his boxers and crossed to the door. All curious, charming, and under the influence. He had no idea the deliverywoman had once been married to a Cates.

"Hey, sweetheart, stick around for a slice," he invited.

"I eat pizza twice a day," she said on a yawn. "Hot, cold, burned. There's not a topping I haven't tried. It's been a long day and I'm headed home to bed."

Mac pointed down the hallway. "Shortcut to my bedroom, if you want to crash here. I'd hate to have you falling asleep at the wheel."

"I'll manage," she said. "I'm used to the graveyard shift."

Mac didn't pursue her further. He took the pizza boxes from Dune and returned to his chair. "Shot down by two women in one night," he mumbled as he cleared the empty bottles from the coffee table, then spread out the boxes. He dug in with both hands.

Tori glanced at Dune. "Poor guy."

"Trust me, he'll bounce back."

She slapped her palms against her thighs. "I hate to hurry you—"

"Sorry, I couldn't find my wallet," Zane apologized as he cut across the living room, his head down, counting bills. "How much?" he asked, looking up.

Tori saw Zane a split second before he saw her. Dune caught the flicker of pain in her eyes, followed by the flint of her anger.

Memories slammed between them, the good times shuffled beneath the bad. "What the fuck?" came from Zane. She'd definitely stunned him.

"Bastard!" Tori spun on her heel, shot across the porch, and down the steps. The lady hauled ass.

Zane colored the room with profanity, then took off after her.

Lingering animosity, thought Dune, was enough to lay a man low. "Forty-two for the pizzas," he called after Zane. "Tip big. She was family."

He swore his brother flipped him the bird from the shadowed darkness of the yard. He heard the sound of raised voices followed by the slam of a car door. He squinted. Tori was driving a yellow Volkswagen with a pizza sign on top.

The engine turned over and she hit reverse, stripping the gears. She spun the car around like a stunt driver, then floored it. The Volkswagen sped down the road.

Was that his brother chasing her taillights? Damn sure was. Zane was fast, but he wasn't *that* fast. Tori never slowed down, never even tapped the brakes.

Dune knew they had a shitload of baggage. They were both damaged from their relationship. Old wounds took a long time to heal. They needed to move beyond the dark glares and harsh words. They'd found no middle ground.

Dune held the door wide on Zane's return. His brother climbed the front steps, sweaty and breathing heavy. "Why the hell didn't you tell me she was here?" he accused. "I had no prep time. I walked straight into a nightmare."

"I was as shocked to see her as you were."

Zane backhanded the sweat off his brow and growled, "She's as stubborn as ever. She won't give me the time of day. She still drives bat-ass crazy."

"She almost ran you down."

"Pretty damn close." He looked down at his bare feet, streaked black from her fantail of dirt when he'd raced after her down the road. "She dusted me good."

Dune couldn't help himself. His smile broke. "You actually thought you could catch her?"

He patted his belly. "I'm in good shape."

"The beer slowed you down."

Zane exhaled, turned serious. "She looked good."

"She gave you her back."

"I saw her face right before she rolled up the car window on my hand."

"Did she catch your fingers?"

"Minor pinch, but I'll live." Zane rolled his wrist, then his shoulders. "She still hates me."

Dune agreed. "I got that impression, too."

"Shit," Zane muttered. "Not much more I can do tonight."

"You could send flowers tomorrow."

"Wildflowers for a wild child?" Zane thought it over and liked the idea. "I'll call the florist before I leave town. I'm assuming Tori's at the same address."

"Last I heard she was still living with her crazy kid sister and hell-raiser brother. They recently put their grandmother in a nursing home. Nana Aubrey escapes once a week."

"Her whole family was nuts, especially Grandma," Zane recalled. "All Tori ever wanted was to leave her past behind."

"Yet she stayed in town after you two divorced," Dune said. "She became the responsible parent when her mom and dad were killed in a small plane crash. That was tragic."

"I tried to contact her afterward, but she refused to take my calls. Seeing her tonight was a kick to my groin." Zane scratched his stomach. "Enough talk on Tori. I'm hungry after my run. It's pizza time."

"Mac's already eaten one and is halfway through the second," Dune said as they retreated to the living room.

Soft snoring drew his gaze to his grandfather. Frank had fallen asleep on the La-Z-Boy. The men lowered their voices and let him be.

Dune's Weimaraner made an appearance shortly thereafter, trotting in from the back porch. Ghost had sniffed out the pizza. The dog loved pizza, but pizza didn't love him. He had gastrointestinal issues. The dog passed gas when they fed him spicy food.

Mac was feeding Ghost pepperoni at that very moment. "No more, dude," Dune warned.

"Dog's hungry." Mac snuck him another bite.

"Ghost sleeps in your room tonight," Dune stated as he lowered himself onto the couch and reached for a big slice with the works.

They ate in silence, polishing off all three pizzas.

The moon had lowered behind the orange grove by the time the men crashed. The sun would rise in two hours. Dune and Zane could live on little sleep, but Mac required six hours. Less than six and he was one cranky bastard.

They cleaned up and turned off the lights. Dune gathered a quilt from the hall closet and tucked in his grandfather. He then headed to his bedroom.

He stripped down, took a quick shower, and crawled naked into the double bed. Being six foot six, his feet hung off the end and he had little room to stretch out. He'd have a crick in his neck by morning.

His last thought before sleep claimed him was of sweet, shy Sophie Saunders. The creak of his bedroom door wakened him a short time later. Dune knew without looking who had disturbed him. Mac was ditching the dog.

He stuck his head inside and muttered, "Fart-a-roni." He ducked out.

Dune heard the click of Ghost's nails on the hardwood floor before his dog hopped on the bed and took over the end. Dune shoved open the window on the wall over his head. Ghost was downwind.

Eight forty-five a.m. and Sophie Saunders breathed in the pungent scents of the boardwalk as she strolled toward the T-shirt shop. She inhaled the freshly made coffee from Brews Brothers and the sugary sweetness of oven-warm doughnuts at The Bakehouse. Outdoor vendors teased beachgoers with cinnamon churros and caramel funnel cakes.

Sophie felt at home here, far more than she did at Saunders Shores. Her heritage oftentimes smothered her. She'd spoken to her mother that very morning, and their conversation had unsettled her.

Maya so seldom dropped by unannounced, yet she'd arrived in tennis whites with a purpose. She had a standing nine-thirty lesson three days a week at the country club with the tennis pro.

Her mom was a beautiful woman, classically featured and perfectly coiffured. She was a noted philanthropist and kept her finger on the pulse of the family.

Trace could do no wrong.

Sophie was seldom right.

Her mother had made small talk while Sophie finished a slice of cinnamon raisin toast and sipped a cup of hibiscus tea. Of course, her mother had broached her favorite topic the moment Sophie finished. She recalled their conversation now.

"Your father and I were discussing your future at dinner last night," her mother said, bringing up the subject.

Sophie had inwardly cringed. Surely they could've found a more interesting topic, something less boring and bland.

"You've been spending an inordinate amount of time on the Barefoot William boardwalk," Maya noted. "We were hoping you'd give the Shores a second chance."

Her mother's suggestion gave Sophie a stomachache. "I'll give it some thought," was all she could manage to say.

Her words had appeased Maya for the moment. She'd departed shortly thereafter.

Sophie knew in her heart that she would never return to the Shores. She couldn't think of one boutique or café owner who would willingly welcome her. She'd be riding on the Saunders name alone.

More than life itself, she wanted to step outside her family's shadow and be her own person. Her niche was out there somewhere. She just had to find it.

She entered Three Shirts, leaving all thoughts of the Shores outside on the Barefoot William boardwalk. Jenna Cates waved at her from the back room. "I'm sorting board shorts," she called out. "Come talk to me."

Sophie headed toward her. The T-shirt shop was one of her favorite stores. It smelled of cotton. She liked the casual, yet hip, beach atmosphere. There was no need for overhead lighting. The morning sun shot through the front window, warming the hardwood floors.

She found Jenna with a box cutter in one hand and a pair of board shorts in the other. Colorful surfboards decorated a black background. The pattern was intricate, yet masculine. "Shorts from Dune's designer beachwear," Jen told Sophie. "They sell so fast I can't keep them in stock."

Sophie was aware of his collection for men. Beach Heat was his brand. He modeled for magazines promoting his line. His clothes were all about summer, all about looking cool on a hot day.

She'd purchased one of his California print shirts, a pale

green, short-sleeved button-down designed with a turquoise wave. The shirt was too big for her, but that didn't matter. She wore it around her house. On occasion, she slept in it.

Should Dune retire from professional volleyball, he had retail to fall back on. He also sponsored volleyball camps for kids all across the country. He traveled often, speaking on sportsmanship.

"Did you have fun at the Sneaker Ball?" Jen asked as she cut up a cardboard box.

It had been the best night of her life. Sophie touched her fingertips to her lips and smiled. She could still feel Dune's kiss. She looked forward to seeing him again. They had a bet. One of them would collect on the wager later today.

She responded with a nondescript remark. "Great music and delicious food."

Jen glanced over her shoulder and grinned. "Was my cousin a good date?"

A rush of warmth rose from her toes. Sophie felt her cheeks heat. Dating was new to her. How much should she share?

"That good, huh?" Jen teased her.

"How'd you know?"

"You're blushing. That's a dead giveaway."

"How was Mac?" Sophie asked.

Jen pulled a face that made Sophie laugh. "The worst date ever," she said. "The man's got crazy written all over him. His life never skips a beat, whereas mine often stalls and needs a jump start. I was tired last night after the ball and wanted to go straight home. Mac wanted to stop by the Blue Coconut and shoot pool. We argued."

She stacked the cardboard scraps into a neat pile, and continued with, "I told him to pull over; then I threatened to walk the rest of the way home. The ass actually stopped on the side of the road. He reached across me and opened my door."

That didn't sound good, Sophie thought. "Did you get out?" she asked.

"I started to, but Mac pulled me back." Jen's own cheeks flushed. "He had the balls to tell me to shut up. When I didn't, he kissed me. I bit his bottom lip."

Mac had kissed Jen. Sophie liked that part. Jenna's bite, not so much. "You got home okay?" She was curious.

Jen nodded. "Once I was safely out of the pickup, I informed him that I never wanted to see him again and that he was barred from the shop."

"Barred, really?" Sophie's stomach sank.

"Mac's only in town for a month," Jen said. "He should have enough shirts to last him, *if* he does laundry. I don't need his business."

Sophie wished their night had gone better.

She had a wager to win.

"I have a date tonight," Jen continued on a happier note. "Kyle Wyatt. He delivers packages for Sky Air. He dropped off several boxes this morning, then asked me to attend Twilight Bazaar at the Civic Center. The indoor flea market draws farmers, professional artists, and crafters, along with elementary school exhibits. It's very casual. It's my assistant's day off. Since store owners can set their own hours, I plan to close at six. Kyle will pick me up at seven."

"Nice," was all Sophie could manage to say. Jenna wouldn't be available if Mac showed up at the store later today. She'd moved on to someone else. Mac was no longer in the running. Sophie found that disappointing.

"What would you like me to do first?" she asked, getting down to business.

"Become familiar with the shop," Jen said. "Once you

know the layout, select a T-shirt. I wear and advertise my tees. You can change in the dressing room."

Sophie paused, looked around. Not a customer in sight.

"Mondays tend to be slow," Jen said, explaining. "I'd planned to do some rearranging. We can move the circular racks around and change out the displays. I bought crabbing nets to replace the clotheslines stretched across the ceiling. Nicole loaned me two mannequins from The Jewelry Box. I want to set them at the front of the store and dress them in beachwear.

"I'm expanding my merchandise, too," she continued. "The new inventory includes boardwalk posters, beach chairs, sand globes, and children's beach-themed coloring books, all still in boxes. They'll need to be unpacked."

Sophie faced a busy day. She was excited to get started. Selecting a T-shirt was daunting. There were so many to choose from. *If You Can't Stand the Heat, Stop Tickling the Dragon* made her smile. Her gaze widened and she pushed past *Brass Balls beneath My Mini-Skirt*.

The silly, wild, and naughty slogans weren't right for her, although Jenna wore them well. Her friend's bright yellow belly shirt imprinted with *No Tan Lines* fit her. She loved sports and the outdoors, and was evenly tanned.

Sophie finally chose a conservative navy polo scripted with *Barefoot Beach* to go with her tan slacks. Jen nodded her approval when Sophie stepped from the dressing room.

"What's next?" she asked.

"We move the circular racks," Jen said. "They're on casters with a lever brake." She set their project in motion.

Once the racks were in place, they went through every shirt, organizing them by size and brand. They set up a special display for Dune's beachwear.

"The shop's coming together." Jen stood with her hands on her hips, taking it all in. She appeared pleased. "Let's stretch the crab nets next."

"I hope you have a tall ladder," Sophie said. "We're both on the short side."

Jen nodded toward the front door. "Lucky for us, our man of height just arrived."

Sophie looked up. Her breath caught and her chest squeezed. Dune Cates stood in the doorway. He wore a plain gray T-shirt, jeans, and an easy smile. "Too early for lunch?" He held three take-out containers. "I stopped at the diner and ordered sandwiches."

"Hot or cold?" Jen asked.

"Molly's specialty peanut butter and jelly." Dune set the containers down on the front counter.

"Work first, eat second," Jenna directed her team. "I want to change out my ceiling while you're here. I'll get the step stool." She headed to the storeroom.

Sophie stared at Dune and he stared back. She lowered her gaze to his lips. She relived their kiss, so warm, so firm, so perfect. She blushed and his smile broke.

He crossed to her in three strides. "How's the volunteering?" he asked.

"It's going well." Better, now that he was here.

He leaned in and his scent embraced her: sunshine, lime, and man. "Any sign of Mac?" he whispered near her ear like a fellow conspirator.

His breath fanned her cheek, drawing goose bumps on her neck. She shivered, and he pulled back slightly. "Not yet, but it's early." She felt confident about their bet.

Dune scratched his chin. "You're aware they had a bad date."

"So I heard." She had, in detail.

"Mac's going to keep his distance."

She stood firm. "He'll show."

"You're a romantic, not a realist."

"The heart knows what the mind has yet to realize."

"Mac's already made up his mind about Jen. He'll keep the length of the boardwalk between them."

"What's Mac up to this morning?" asked Sophie, curious.

"He's nursing a hangover," Dune told her. "He was having breakfast when I left my grandfather's house. He poured coffee on his cornflakes."

"He wasn't drunk when he left the Sneaker Ball," Sophie recalled.

"Mac and Zane tied one on afterward."

"The reason?" she pressed.

"A drinking game brought out the LandShark."

A game. Men talked sports, cars, and women. Had Mac discussed Jenna? she wondered. She wanted to ask Dune, but intuitively knew he wouldn't discuss his partner further. He wouldn't give her any advantage as far as their wager.

He straightened, then shoved his hands in his jean pockets and said, "Guess I'll hang out and collect my win."

He planned to stick around. She liked that. A lot.

"Over here, Dune," Jenna called. She set the step stool near the dressing rooms. "The hooks can be twisted and pulled. Sophie and I will wrap the clothesline as it comes down."

Wrapping the line sounded easier than it was. Beside her, Jen formed the perfect lasso, while Sophie's own rope twisted around her wrist and the loops dangled at different lengths. She caught Dune watching her and wished she wasn't so clumsy.

"No lasso for you," he teased her. "Let's start over." He took the clothesline from her, shook it out, and began anew. "Hold out your hands."

She did, and he used her wrists as if wrapping yarn. They soon had a perfect circle. She sighed, relieved.

Jen hauled the rope to the back. She then patted her stomach and said, "I'm hungry."

Dune gathered the Styrofoam containers and Sophie followed him to the back room. The sun winked outside the window, casting them in silhouette. He was so tall and muscled she could fit inside his shadow.

Jenna grabbed paper plates, napkins, and canned sodas. They dined on PB&J made Molly-style. Her sandwiches were one of a kind. She took one slice of rye and one of pumpernickel, then spread crunchy peanut butter on both. She added grape jelly and strawberry preserves. The sandwich was thick and tasted great.

Dune drew back a chair and sat down across from Sophie. He opened up the snacks and offered her three different flavors of chips. He stretched out his legs, bumping Sophie's knees beneath the table.

The memory of them sitting on the counter stools at Molly's came to mind. His knee had accidentally pressed between her thighs, a jolt to her senses. They touched again now. A bit more subtly, yet equally arousing.

The rough denim of his jeans brushed the smooth linen of her slacks. He flexed his leg and her stomach fluttered. The temperature in the storeroom rose. She fanned her face with a paper plate.

"Has Zane left town?" Jen asked Dune.

"He was up and gone before my first cup of coffee," he said between bites. "He saw Tori Rollins last night."

Jen gaped. "When, where?"

"She delivered our three a.m. pizzas."

"Did it get crazy?"

"Crazy enough that he chased her Volkswagen down the dirt road in his boxers while running barefoot."

Jen nearly spewed her soda.

Sophie was confused. She could trace the Cates's history from the time William had settled the town, but she wasn't aware of any present-day involvements beyond her brother being married to Shaye.

Dune finished his own bag of sour cream and garlic chips, then stole a few of Sophie's sun-dried tomato ones. He sensed her curiosity and conveyed Zane and Tori's story.

Sophie sat there, fascinated. The two shared so much anger, so much passion. They had a great deal to settle between them.

"Opposites usually attract," said Jen, "yet Tori and Zane were so much alike, it seemed they had one mind. They agreed on everything, even finished each other's sentences."

"What happened?" asked Sophie.

Jen wiped her mouth with a napkin. "They were in total agreement until Zane chose the Air Force over her. Tori went ballistic. She never forgave him."

"How awful," Sophie said, finishing her chips.

"Zane always wanted to fly," Dune explained. "He collected model planes and helicopters as a kid. He buzzed me more than one time with his handheld-transmitter-controlled dive-bombers."

Jenna grinned. "He bombed everyone on the boardwalk."

Sophie listened intently as they continued to talk about their families. Big, happy families that came together when someone was in trouble or for the joy of celebration. Dune's and her upbringing differed greatly.

They were halfway through their meal when three young boys entered the store. They looked eleven or twelve, all sweaty and scruffy and in a hurry. "I'll see to them," Sophie said. Jenna had taught her how to use the cash register. She could ring up their sale.

She wound around the T-shirt racks and approached the boys. She'd nearly reached them when they split in three directions. She found it difficult to keep an eye on each one. "Can I help you?" she asked the kid with shaggy dark hair moving toward the dressing rooms.

He shook his head, looking uneasy.

"How about you?" she went on to ask the next boy.

"I'm looking for a pair of flip-flops for my sister," he said, drawing her attention from the front of the store.

"What color and size?"

The kid never answered.

She heard shuffling and fumbling at the main counter. She turned around just in time to see the third boy stuff several pairs of sunglasses into the pockets of his camouflage pants.

A shoplifter. Her heart nearly stopped.

Camo-boy stared at Sophie, a clear challenge in his eyes. He curled his lip, as if he *dared* her to call for backup. His two friends joined him at the door. They looked tough and hardened for kids so young.

Sophie wasn't afraid, only uncertain. She could call for Dune and Jenna or she could handle the situation herself. She wasn't a wimp. She found her voice and said, "Put the sunglasses back."

The boy in the camouflage pants smirked, then flipped her off. "Mine." He shot out the door after his friends.

"Not yours—" Her voice hitched. She was so stunned it took her several seconds to react.

Galvanized by indignation, Sophie took off after the boys. They would not get the better of her. This was Jenna Cates's store. Jen was her friend. There'd be no shoplifters on her shift.

She wasn't a runner, but she could walk fast. She caught a flash of camouflage pants several doors down. It appeared the boys had gotten cocky. They'd run a distance, then stopped and removed the price tags from their shades.

Sophie caught them outside Goody Gumdrops, Shaye's penny candy store. She figured they were headed inside for another five-finger discount. She cornered Camo-boy at the red-and-pink lollipop swirled door. She blocked his entry. She held out her hand. "Mine," she said, tossing his words back at him.

"Hers," Dune's deep voice insisted from behind her. His shadow now stretched alongside her own. A very long shadow from a very tall man.

Her backup had arrived.

Seven

Reflexively, Dune Cates placed his hand on Sophie's shoulder and squeezed. "What's the problem?" he asked, knowing full well what had gone down. He'd been watching her when she'd offered to assist the boys. He'd had a bad feeling when he recognized one of the kids. Randy Cates was a known thief.

His feet hit the pavement the moment the boy pocketed the sunglasses. Sophie was already ahead of him. She darted out the door, a woman out to right a wrong.

Randy could be difficult. He was the mayor's son. His father was a single parent and too busy with city politics to control the boy's behavior. The kid was raising himself. And not doing a very good job. He was always in trouble.

Juvenile detention was a revolving door for him. He had no business stealing sunglasses from relatives or anyone else for that matter. He'd do jail time as an adult if he didn't get his act together.

The mayor faced an upcoming election in the fall. Randy was a high-profile kid, drawing bad press. People had started to question the mayor's ability to govern a town when he couldn't keep his own son in line.

The boy's friends weren't the least bit loyal. They'd split the moment Dune showed up, afraid of the consequences.

Randy's jaw was now set, a kid of attitude and stubbornness. Dune waited for the boy to come to his senses. He didn't want to call his father or cause a scene on the boardwalk.

He felt Sophie's sigh beneath his palm. She looked more disappointed than mad. He'd nearly had a heart attack when she'd taken off after the boys. She thought to handle the problem alone. He was with her now. He had her back.

"Sophie, this is Randy, my second cousin," Dune introduced them.

She stared at the boy. "Why did you take the sunglasses?" she asked.

"My friends dared me."

"Some friends," said Dune. "They took off and left you to hang."

Heat scored Randy's cheeks. He rolled his shoulders and stood tall. He was nearly Sophie's height. The kid clutched the sunglasses so tight his knuckles turned white. Dune was certain he'd rather break them than return them.

Randy proved Dune right. He held up a pair of the West Coast Blue sunglasses, the latest hot brand sold at Three Shirts. The men's shades were expensive. Randy's father was conservative. He'd never give his son money to blow on such an item.

The boy had a mean streak. He twisted one plastic arm, and the frame nearly snapped. He then stuck his thumb on the inside of a dark blue lens and pushed. The lens held.

Randy was on a tear. What he couldn't break with his hands he now chose to stomp with his foot. He threw the sunglasses down.

Dune was about to step in, when Sophie shaded her eyes and calmly said, "The sun certainly is bright. I can see why you need sunglasses."

Randy grunted. "Duh, it's Florida."

"You have good taste," she noted. "West Coast Blue is a popular style."

"My brand," from Randy.

"You should save your allowance and buy a pair."

"Allowance? Get real." He spat on the boardwalk, within an inch of Sophie's foot. "My dad took away my spending money with my last B&E. He calls it discipline."

Breaking and entering. Dune rubbed the back of his neck. The kid had a rap sheet.

"Perhaps you could get a job," she suggested.

"Who's going to hire me?" Randy asked. "I'm twelve. Shop owners see me coming and close their doors."

"Doors shut because you shoplift," Sophie reminded him.

Randy blinked. "I've got a rep to uphold."

"I think you're better than your rep."

He shook his head. "No, I'm not."

"You've nothing to prove to your friends, but do you want adults to see you as a punk?" she asked.

Randy didn't have an immediate answer. He kicked the sunglasses between his feet like a soccer ball. Scratches showed on the lenses.

Sophie was surprisingly formidable. She didn't give an inch. Dune sensed she wouldn't give up until Randy paid restitution on the shades. She cleared her throat and kept her voice low. "It takes a man to own up to his mistakes."

"A man, huh?" Expectancy flashed in his eyes, soon replaced by cocky smugness. Dune could tell the boy had a chip on his shoulder and was mad at the world.

"Come back to the T-shirt shop, return the sunglasses, and apologize to Jenna," Sophie said.

"Don't sweat me," Randy sneered. "I'm not sorry."

"You should be," she said. "Jen doesn't steal from you and you shouldn't steal from her."

"She has more than me."

"She's earned everything she has."

"Big whoop." The kid had a smart mouth. He had no respect for adults or authority and even less for himself.

Dune listened and let it play out. Sophie was smart and sensitive and seemed to have a purpose. She wasn't put off by Randy's attitude. The kid would piss off the police.

"Square things with Jen and I'll speak to her on your behalf," she said, keeping her voice even. "I'll see if you can work with me."

She had his full attention now. Randy exhaled in a rush. "Work for money?"

"I'll pay you—"

He scooped up the sunglasses and read the price sticker. "One hundred sixty an hour?"

"Get real," Dune muttered.

Sophie shook her head. "I hired Violet's nephew Chuck last week. He works outside in the heat and earns ten bucks an hour. You'll be inside in the air conditioning. Eight bucks fits the job."

"Nine," Randy countered.

"Eight to start, with the possibility of a raise." She held firm.

Randy looked so shocked it was almost comical. Dune would never forget his face. The boy's surprise wore off quickly as he mentally calculated how many hours he'd have to work to pay off the shades. "Twenty hours," he said. "You won't cut me short, will you?"

The boy was afraid Sophie would take back her offer. Dune knew she would not. She would keep her word.

"I'll support you as long as you show up on time and don't screw me over," she said.

Screw her over? Dune almost smiled. She'd laid down the law, along with a solid groundwork for Randy to achieve a goal, however small. The boy needed to uphold his end, too.

"What time tomorrow morning?" he asked.

"You start today," Sophie informed him. "Dune will give your father a call. You're underage. We need his approval."

"My dad doesn't give a rat's ass what I do."

Dune pulled out his cell phone and had a quick chat with the mayor. "We're good to go," he told Sophie.

Dune knew the shop owners would be pleased to hear Randy Cates was off the boardwalk for the rest of the afternoon. Word would spread rapidly. Randy and his friends were sly and sticky-fingered. Inventory disappeared in the blink of an eye. Complaints brought the cops.

The Detention Center wasn't always the answer. Sophie apparently saw more in the kid than most of his relatives. It was a wait-and-see situation. Dune hoped she wouldn't get burned.

He accompanied Sophie and Randy back to the T-shirt shop. Once inside, Sophie met the boy's hard gaze with one of her own. "I have one final rule," she told him. "You empty your pockets every afternoon before you leave the store."

Randy dug in his heels, scowling and stubborn. "You got trust issues?"

"You have three pairs of stolen sunglasses in your pockets as we speak," she reminded him.

He rolled his shoulders, as if to shake a monkey off his back. He emptied his pockets, then set the shades down on the front counter. "Happy now?" he asked Sophie.

"Happier still once you stop stealing."

"Whatever." The kid's stomach growled. "I haven't had lunch," he said. "I was headed to the candy store when you stopped me."

"Sugar is not a meal," said Sophie. "You can have half my sandwich and a soda. Unfortunately the chips are all gone." She glanced at Dune. "Chip run?"

"I'll go," he agreed, "after you've spoken with Jen."

Dune made the boy wait with him while Sophie went to the storeroom. The women had a lengthy discussion. Five minutes passed, then ten. Randy shifted uneasily.

"Jen doesn't want me," the boy said.

"Sophie does," Dune said. "She can be persuasive."

Jenna didn't look all that convinced when she later faced Randy. "I've been told you're sorry," she said.

Randy looked to Sophie. "That's what I hear, too."

"You have one chance. Blow it and you're gone," Jen said flatly. "You have the afternoon to prove yourself. It's do or die, kid."

Randy's face tightened. For once, he didn't talk back.

Dune took off on his errand. He ordered two additional PB&Js from Molly Malone's Diner, then stopped at Crabby Abby's for a bag of chips. He found Sophie and Randy sharing the remains of her sandwich. Jenna had finished her lunch and was unpacking boxes, a never-ending task.

Randy spotted Dune and shot off his chair so fast he jarred the table. Manners were not on his menu. He grabbed his sandwich along with the potato chips. He ripped open the bag, stuffed a handful in his mouth, then started on his sandwich. He had no concern for anyone else.

Sophie cleared her throat. "Pass the chips, please."

Randy had tucked the bag under his arm and was slow to share. He finally set it down on the table between them. Dune noted the opening was turned away from Sophie, but she didn't seem to mind. She took a few chips and let Randy have the rest. He crunched loudly.

"Chew with your mouth closed," she told the boy.

He was slow to oblige. The kid was willful. He continued to chew openly and loudly before clamping his jaw shut. The remainder of the meal passed peacefully.

"Clean up and take out the garbage," Sophie told Randy once they finished their lunch.

Randy processed her request. "I'm a janitor?" he asked.

"Custodian, salesperson, cashier, whatever, you're building your résumé," she explained.

Randy nodded. Once his first chore was complete, Dune watched as the kid sought out Sophie. He found her setting up a display of sand globes.

"What's next?" Randy asked.

"You change clothes."

The boy's jaw set. "What wrong with what I'm wearing?"

"You're in camouflage." Dune joined them. "You look like you should be playing army, not working in a T-shirt shop."

"Who's buying? Not me."

"You'll get two work outfits," said Sophie. "Keep them clean."

"I've never used a washing machine."

"Ask your dad to help you," said Dune.

"He's never around."

"Neither are you," said Dune. "If your father knows you're at home and that you need help, I'm sure he'd be there for you."

"Believe what you want." He then turned toward a stack of youth T-shirts. He took his sweet time reading each slogan and logo. Still undecided, he moved to the adult racks.

"The kid's stalling," said Dune.

"But he's not stealing."

"That's true." Dune watched as Sophie gently shook a sand globe. Sand fluttered and the beach shifted. A tiny starfish, sea urchin, and kitten's paw shell appeared.

"These globes are amazing," she said.

"So are you," Dune told her, and meant it. "You've got a way with kids. They like you."

"They like earning money." She was realistic.

"That, too," he agreed.

He glanced around and became aware they were the only two in the store. Jenna was deep in boxes in the back

and Randy was trying on clothes. Dune assisted Sophie
with the sand globe display. The globes came in three sizes.
He smiled as she staggered them in an attractive arrange-
ment. She had flair.

The box was soon empty and ready to toss. They
reached down at the same time. They bumped shoulders,
arms, and hips. Her scent was on the air, all around him.
On his skin, his clothes. An essence of vanilla, innocence,
and sweet woman.

They straightened slowly. A mere fraction of an inch
separated them. Their cheeks brushed. His stubble rasped
her soft skin. He looked deeply into her eyes, a shadowed
forest green. Her mouth was so near, he felt her breath on
his chin.

Time had granted them a moment together. He went
with his gut and kissed her. Her reaction was an indrawn
breath followed by an involuntary sigh. She went still. He
practiced great patience. Her pleasure was paramount.

Her lips soon softened and parted beneath his. He
gently touched her with his tongue. She touched him back.

She was no longer tentative. She leaned into him, petite
and curvy, warm and womanly. She aroused him.

An age-old tension charged the air until the creak of the
dressing room door brought Dune back to his senses.

He broke their kiss, his breathing heavy.

Sophie's breath stuck in her throat. Her gaze blurred
and her heart raced. She'd been so caught up in Dune that
she'd lost sight of her purpose.

She was responsible for Randy Cates. The boy stood off
to their right, openly staring at them. He wore khaki shorts
and an *I Like Older Women* T-shirt. His beat-up sneakers
were untied.

"Do me a huge favor, man," he said to Dune. "No kissing on my time."

"Your time?" Sophie betrayed her surprise.

"You're supposed to be teaching me stuff," said Randy. "Hard to do when his mouth's on you."

"You're right," she agreed. "My first lesson: wear a shirt that is appropriate for your age."

"I like this one," he argued.

"Buy it with your own money then."

He flipped the tag, calculated, "It costs eighteen dollars. I'd have to work an additional two-and-a-half hours to pay for it. I'm only here for the sunglasses."

Dune lowered his voice near her ear. "He's all yours." He picked up the empty box and headed for the storeroom.

Sophie drew a deep breath. It seemed immature to argue with Randy. She tried logic. "There's no need to advertise your preference in ladies. If you act mature, older women will find you attractive."

"Are you into me?"

"I like men who are honest and trustworthy."

"Not kids who shoplift," Randy mimicked her voice.

Sophie was patient. "Anyone can change his life at any given moment."

"Are you changing yours?" he asked.

His question hung in the air between them. "I'm working on it," she said. "This is my summer to challenge myself and seek adventure."

"What kind of adventures?" he wanted to know.

She told him about the different jobs she'd worked on the boardwalk. His eyes went wide when she mentioned the unicycle. "I didn't have good balance," she said.

His chin came up. "I do," he bragged. "I skateboard and do tricks."

"The uni-troupe needs an extra rider," she told him. "If you're interested—"

"Don't do me any favors," he said, shooting her down.

Sophie wondered if he was afraid he'd fail or if he didn't want her interfering further in his life. She stepped back.

And he stepped forward in search of a different shirt. He held up a few for her approval.

She shook her head to reject shirts with the slogans *Numbnuts* and *Bang It,* but agreed on *I Pushed Humpty-Dumpty*—which he called lame, but still agreed to wear.

Dune returned shortly. He carried a box and a tall revolving magazine rack. He passed them both to Randy. "Jen wants you to set up the coloring books and crayons."

The boy frowned. "I thought I was working for Sophie."

"It's Jen's store," Sophie said.

"But you're the bank?" he asked.

"I'll be paying you, yes."

He nodded and got to work.

Shortly thereafter, Sophie and Dune helped Jenna hang shirts from the crab netting. The girls put the shirts on colorful plastic hangers and Dune hooked them in the nets. It was a team effort. Jenna was precise. She moved around the store, eyeing the shirts from all angles. She had Dune taking down and rearranging every other hanger. He didn't object to the extra work. He was a patient man.

Sophie kept one eye on Randy. The boy worked diligently. The coloring books were a great addition to the store. The books depicted various scenes from Barefoot William. Children could sit on the beach and color beneath an umbrella. Pictures of waves and sailboats, shells and crabs, the boardwalk and pier, would all make for a great souvenir.

"My sister would like a coloring book," Randy said.

"How old is she?" asked Sophie.

"Four," Randy told her. "She spends the week with a babysitter." He frowned slightly. "A few nights, too, depending on how late my dad works. I see her on week-ends."

"Once you buy your sunglasses, maybe you could work an extra hour and get her a coloring book," Sophie suggested. "Maybe even buy her a T-shirt."

Randy narrowed his gaze on her. "Don't try and tie me to the store for the summer," he said.

Sophie held up her hands, her palms out. "You're a free man once I ring up your sale for West Coast Blue."

"That's how I want it," the boy said. "Now what?" He'd finished putting the coloring books and crayons on the rack and was ready to move on.

"It's a slow day." Jen came to stand beside them. "We clean when we have the opportunity." She handed Randy glass cleaner and a cloth. "Six mirrors. Don't leave any streaks."

He didn't. Sophie stood off to the side, straightening a circular rack of shirts, watching Randy as he worked. The kid was conscientious. No longer influenced by his friends, he did a good job. He went over each mirror twice until the glass shone. Afterward, he and Dune did odd jobs for Jenna in the storeroom. Sophie remained on the floor, assisting a few customers.

Dune strode from the storeroom, walked over to her and said, "Four o'clock. No Mac." He strolled away, looking smug and superior.

Mac still had an hour to make an appearance.

She willed him to show.

"Four-thirty." Dune made a second pass by her.

She kept busy, sorting the latest shipment of belly chains and charm bracelets.

Dune was a clock watcher, annoyingly so. He tapped his watch the next time he walked by her. "Four-forty."

She glared at him.

He grinned back. "Not nice, Sophie," he said. "Don't be a poor loser."

She hadn't lost yet. But time wasn't waiting for Mac. Each passing minute favored Dune. Her watch read four-fifty now.

It was five till five when Randy came to her and nudged her arm. She was in a dressing room collecting T-shirts and board shorts that had been tried on, but discarded.

He looked very serious. The boy nodded toward the counter. "A shoplifter," he warned Sophie.

Her heart skipped a beat. Surely not *two* thefts in one day. She dropped the clothes and turned quickly. The man was easy to spot. He wore a black hoodie, sunglasses, and dark gray board shorts. He was barefoot. Not much of a disguise for sneaking into the shop.

Mac James. She was incredibly glad to see him.

His appearance sealed her win.

Winning made her smile. She wanted to jump for joy, to pump her arm and cheer. She tamped down her excitement. Mac looked awful. He hadn't shaved and his stubble was dark against his ashen skin. His lower lip was cut and swollen. Jenna had bitten him hard. Mac wouldn't be kissing her or anyone anytime soon. He'd learned his lesson.

"That's Mac, Dune's volleyball partner," she told Randy. "He's not a thief."

"Then why's he slinking around?"

Sophie knew why—Mac wanted to see Jenna. Yet once he'd entered her shop, he'd gotten cold feet. He wasn't certain how to approach her. It was hard for a six-foot-four man to hide among the circular racks. He stood out even with his head down and shoulders slumped.

"It's time to lock up," Jenna called out as she walked to the front of the store. Keys jingled in her hand. "You can all leave. I'm going to stay a few extra minutes and dress the mannequins."

She was nearly to the door when she caught sight of Mac. Her steps slowed and anger heated her cheeks. "What are you doing here?" she demanded.

"I was looking for Dune," Mac said sullenly. "I have a message from his grandfather."

"You can leave it with me."

"It's private."

"Dune's on the loading dock, shooting foam packing peanuts into the Dumpster," Jen said. "You can wait for him on the boardwalk."

"It looks like rain."

Sophie glanced out the window and saw it was sunny. There wasn't a cloud in the sky. She didn't contradict him, however. She'd won the bet. She couldn't wait to see Dune's face.

How much celebration was appropriate? she wondered. Should she smile, do a happy dance? Good sportsmanship was important to her. She went with a grin.

Dune's expression was priceless. He saw Mac and his eyes narrowed; his jaw set. "What's up?" he asked rather sharply.

"He's delivering a message from Frank," Jenna said.

Dune raised an eyebrow. "And the message is?"

"He wants you to pick up a dozen wheat bagels on your way home."

"My grandfather doesn't eat bagels, only white bread."

Mac shrugged. "Don't kill the messenger. Maybe he needs more fiber."

Dune ran one hand down his face, muttered, "Unbelievable."

Surprising yet plausible, thought Sophie. Frank hadn't sent Mac. He'd come on his own. He needed a reason to see Jen and had used Dune's grandfather as an excuse.

Sophie's smile widened and Dune's frown deepened.

"I'm outta here." Randy eased by Sophie. He surprised everyone by sticking his hands in his pockets and turning them inside out. "Clean," he said.

Sophie waved. "See you tomorrow."

The boy glanced at the display of sunglasses. "Fifteen hours to go." And he was gone.

"I'm leaving, too," said Sophie.

"I'm right behind you." Dune was so close she felt the heat of his body. Lime, sunshine, and man followed her out the door.

"Winner," she said once they were on the boardwalk. She then crooked her finger and led him down the boardwalk to The Dairy Godmother.

A homemade ice cream sandwich was her prize.

"Care to make another wager?" she asked after they'd placed their order. She chose strawberry ice cream between the chocolate cake bars. Dune went with vanilla.

He looked down on her. "Go again? Your win was a fluke."

"Chicken." A win was a win. She felt daring and bold.

"Feeling pretty sure of yourself, aren't you?"

"Mac used bagels as an excuse to see Jen."

"He's not thinking straight," said Dune. "That was his hangover talking."

A young girl behind the counter laid their ice cream sandwiches on two plates and passed them to Dune. They located a café table at the back of the store. Once seated, Sophie took a small bite of her ice cream sandwich and savored the taste. "The next time we see Mac and Jenna they'll be on a date," she predicted.

He blew her off. "Not a chance."

"Then wager."

"One win and you've turned gambler."

Mac hadn't been very imaginative with his bagel story,

but it had gotten him in the shop. Sophie believed he liked Jen and truly wanted to see her. Until he recognized that fact, he would strategize his way into Jen's heart.

Dune finished his ice cream sandwich. He leaned back on the café chair and stretched out his legs beneath the table. He trapped her knees and the brief pressure made her shiver. She was so distracted by his touch, she couldn't finish her ice cream sandwich, which was fine by Dune. He easily managed the last two bites.

"Any plans for tonight?" he asked her, lightly bumping her knees a second time.

She wished she did. She'd love to sound interesting and fun with places to go and people to see. Instead, she shook her head. "Jenna mentioned Twilight Bazaar."

Dune was aware of the event. "There will be food and seasonal items and lots of Christmas crafts in May. My elementary school once rented a table to display the ceramics from our art classes. I made a dozen clay giraffes, all with crooked necks."

She envisioned a tall boy with long fingers bending over a table, molding and shaping a lump of clay. "How did they sell?" she asked.

"My giraffes sold second to Zane's monkeys," he told her. "Hear No Evil, Speak No Evil, See No Evil drew everyone's attention. Parents placed orders when the trio sold out. Zane spent a summer making monkeys."

"He's younger than you?"

"By a year," he said. "He cramped my ass all through school. He was an aggressive, goal-oriented kid, always trying to top me in grades, sports, and dating. He couldn't, however, catch me in height. I was six feet when I entered high school and grew another six inches before I graduated. He was forced to look up to me then."

"I was the same height in middle school as I am now," she said ruefully.

"Five-foot-two works for you."

"I'll reach new heights when I walk on stilts."

"Still out to break a leg?" He looked concerned.

"Still out for adventure."

He nodded halfheartedly before making her an offer. "I want to teach you to swim."

His suggestion was more frightening to her than walking on stilts. Her heart raced and the ice cream sandwich she'd eaten settled heavily in her stomach. "Thanks, but no thanks. Water scares me."

He rested his elbows on the table, steepled his fingers. "Why are you so afraid?" he asked.

She shrugged. "Inborn fear, I guess. Why are people afraid of bugs, thunderstorms, clowns, sharks, and the dark? There are kids who won't go to bed until their parents check the closets and under their bed for monsters."

"Train whistles freaked me out as a kid."

"Car horns made me tremble."

He reached across the table and took her hands in his. His palms were warm and callused. He rubbed his thumb over the pulse point in her wrist. "I don't want you to be afraid of anything," he said. "You're stronger than you think. You survived the crowd at the Sneaker Ball. You took on Zane when you thought he was a troublemaker, then later tracked down Randy when he stole from Three Shirts."

"It came down to principle," she said softly. "I was defending people I care about. There's a big difference between standing up for a friend and standing in deep water."

"I'm a strong swimmer, Sophie," he said. "I wouldn't let you drown. Our first lesson: sitting on the side of your pool, dangling our feet in the water, and drinking sun tea."

She bit down on her bottom lip. "We'd sit at the shallow end?"

"Right next to the handrail by the steps."

She trusted Dune. "I'll give it some serious thought," she promised.

He nodded, seemed satisfied. "What about the bazaar?" he asked her next.

"What about it?" Was he asking her out? She was too inexperienced to be certain.

"It could be fun if you can handle the crowd."

"I made it through the Sneaker Ball."

"That you did."

He pushed to his feet and pulled her up beside him. He continued to hold her hand. People now crowded the ice cream parlor. Dune was tall, popular, and had a way of clearing a path. She followed close behind him.

Once outside, they walked down the boardwalk. It was the dinner hour and tourists sought hot dogs, pizza, nachos, and popcorn from the vendors. They'd take their food back to the beach and have a picnic.

Her eyes widened as they passed Three Shirts. She glanced in the storefront window and swore she saw Mac and Jenna off to the side, standing close and butting heads.

"Something wrong?" Dune asked when she slowed.

"Everything's fine." She suddenly had an advantage for her second win. She kept that secret to herself.

She cast a fleeting look over her shoulder. Mac and Jen were definitely arguing. She poked him in the chest and he grabbed her wrist. They scowled at each other.

Passion, Sophie thought, smiling to herself. Maybe they'd kiss and make up after their argument.

Sophie hoped Jen wouldn't bite Mac's lip tonight.

Eight

"You're not welcome in my store," Jen said as she poked Mac James in the chest. "I planned never to see you after the Sneaker Ball." She drew back, ready to jab him again.

He grabbed her wrist before she could push him further. "Feeling's mutual," he said gruffly. "You weren't a great date."

"You should never have asked me out."

"Hindsight is twenty-twenty."

They stood near the front door. It was close to the dinner hour and the evening crowd began to stroll past the windows. Jen turned off the lights, discouraging customers. Their shadows now played along the far wall, wavering with tension.

"Shop's closed," she said. "I have a date."

"Hopefully he'll show. You're such a prize."

Two T-shirts caught her eye on the circular rack. She flipped them at him, one at a time. *Have a Nice Day Somewhere Else* was quickly followed by *I Press Charges.*

He pressed his palm to his forehead. "I've got a headache. Don't shove those hangers so loudly."

Jenna slammed a couple together out of spite.

He gritted his teeth. Shrugging off the hood on his jacket, he removed his sunglasses. He widened his stance, as if seeking balance. His hair was mussed and he hadn't shaved. His eyes were red and darkly circled as if he'd drunk too much, then lain in bed unable to sleep. The cut on his lip was raw. She hadn't realized she'd bitten him so hard. He looked awful.

A third shirt caught her eye. The slogan fit him perfectly. She held up *Night of the Living Dead*. "You look like a zombie," she told him.

He pinched the bridge of his nose and admitted, "I feel like one. I blame it all on Zane."

"The man forced a beer in your hand?"

"Damn straight."

Silence stood between them until she said, "Sorry about your mouth." She tried to sound sympathetic, but failed. "You shouldn't have kissed me."

"You wouldn't shut up," he growled. "It was a kiss or duct tape."

"Tape would've been preferable."

"Next time—"

"No 'next time,' Mac," she said firmly.

"Here I was going to ask you on a date."

She couldn't help herself. She laughed in his face. The idea was absurd. He had to be joking. "We don't like each other."

"That's true," he agreed.

She cleared her throat, then said, "I owe you an apology. One I should've made before the Sneaker Ball. My friend Bree Bennett corrected my misconception of your time together."

He rested one arm on a circular rack, turning his back on the afternoon sun. "It was only two dates. We never even exchanged last names. On our second night, we went to a movie and had sex. She climaxed, we cuddled. She told me she loved me. She made mention of a church wedding—"

"And you split." Jen knew the story. "You hopped out of her apartment while pulling up your pants."

"I couldn't get out fast enough," he admitted. "I lost my lucky boxers and one Converse in my escape."

"That's what happens when you run."

"Can you blame me?" he asked.

"I see your side," she allowed. "Bree's since found someone and is very happy."

"Good to hear." Mac looked relieved. "What about you, Jen? Are you seeing anyone since me?"

"Since *you*?" Again she laughed. "We were never a couple, crazy man. The Sneaker Ball was just last weekend."

"You have a date tonight," he said easily. "Make your move."

"*My* move?" she raised.

Mac pushed off the T-shirt rack. "A man needs to know you want him."

"That goes for a woman, too."

Their conversation lagged. Mac stared at her, his blue eyes dark and searching. Jenna couldn't look away. She felt captured by his gaze. She was unexpectedly drawn to a man she'd sworn to avoid for the rest of her life. She found it so scary she shivered.

Recovering, she jingled her keys. "You need to leave so I can dress the mannequins."

He glanced at the gray cloth dummies. "No need for modesty. They're already naked."

She could have forced him out the door, but a part of her held back. She didn't want him as a permanent fixture in her life, but a few minutes more wouldn't kill her.

She gave in. "I'll put you to work if you stay."

"Roy and Joy." He named the mannies. "I want the girl."

"Not surprising."

"I'm good at taking clothes off a woman, but I've never dressed one."

"There's a first time for everything."

"Joy won't scream at me if I screw up."

"No, but I will."

His brow creased. "That's something to look forward to. Your shriek could break bricks."

She ignored him. "Go all out with the summer attire. I want head-to-toe: sunglasses, shirt, shorts, jewelry, flip-flops."

"Flip-flops?" he objected. "Joy has no feet."

"Place a pair at the base of the stand for effect."

She then crossed to men's board shorts and selected a pair in sage green. "I want colorful and hip," she told him. "The outfits need to complement each other. Follow my lead."

He hesitated and looked a little lost. It took him a moment to get started. He decided on turquoise short-shorts for Joy. Typical Mac.

"Joy's bendy." He curved the mannequin's left leg over his hip.

The man was an idiot. "Are you dressing her or humping her?"

"I'm simply pointing out her flexibility." He soon had Joy doing the splits.

"Is she more flexible than your blow-up dolls?" she asked.

"Real funny, Jen." Mac slapped Roy on the back, leaving a handprint. "He's definitely not as firm as your battery-operated boyfriends."

"How would you—" she stopped short.

His grin was slow, sinful, and knowing. "Two sex toys." He spoke as if he'd rifled through her panty drawer. "The Jack Rabbit and plastic phallic."

She gaped. The man was a vibrator psychic. "You're wrong," she lied.

Mac leaned toward her mannequin, whispered something to Roy, then pretended to listen. "Roy Boy says I'm right."

Jen flicked Mac on the forehead. "Not funny."

"Buzz-buzz."

She turned her back on him and started dressing Roy. The board shorts were too big for him. She sought a handful of paper clips to make the necessary tucks and adjustments.

Beside her, Mac straightened Joy's legs. He then tugged on her short-shorts. No judge of sizes, he'd chosen large. The shorts slid from her hips and down her legs. He caught them before they hit the floor. "She's too damn skinny."

"I'll deal with her shorts," said Jen. "Go pick out their shirts."

He scanned the shirts, slow to make a decision. Mac was always confident, oftentimes arrogant, yet at that moment, he seemed unsure of himself.

"The Beach Heat Collection for Roy," she suggested. "Let's go with the indigo shirt with the green palm trees."

Six of the short-sleeved button-downs had palms. Mac selected sunset orange. The shirt was the wrong color. "Indigo blue," she repeated.

His gaze narrowed and his lips pinched as he fingered through the shirts. He brought back black.

She shook her head. "Black's too dark. I'd prefer a summer hue."

He shifted, visibly uncomfortable. He went back to the rack and returned with three shirts. "Take your pick," he held them up for her approval.

She selected the one in the middle. "Indigo." She fanned the shirt beneath his nose. "The pale green leaves make for a great contrast."

He exhaled. "I see that now."

"You need a top for Joy," she said as she got Roy into

his shirt. "I'll paper clip her shorts in place, while you find something summery to go with turquoise."

His brow furrowed and sun lines fanned the corners of his eyes. He ran one hand through his hair and mussed it further. He looked pained.

He jammed his hands into his jacket pockets and walked slowly toward the women's shirts. He stood and stared for an inordinate length of time.

Jen had dressed Roy and secured Joy's short-shorts and now waited for Mac. "A belly shirt would work," she called to him. He'd bought one for Kami a few days ago.

Still he deliberated, drawing out his decision. He finally chose one in white with the red slogan *Rub Suntan Lotion on My Back.*

"That works fine," she said as Mac slipped the shirt over Joy's head. His hand rested on Joy's boob. "Stop fondling my mannequin," she said.

"I was straightening a wrinkle."

Yeah, right. Jenna glanced at her watch. She had one hour to wrap this up, drive home, and change clothes for her date. She needed to move things along. "I need a floppy cloth hat for Joy and a baseball cap for Roy," she directed.

She crossed the room and came back with a navy cap scripted with *Three Shirts* on the bill. It made for a great souvenir.

Mac struggled with the floppy hats. "The red-and-white striped one will pull Joy's outfit together," she told him.

He grabbed two and raised them high.

She shook her head. He'd ignored her request. Neither hat worked. Hands on her hips, she asked without thinking, "Are you hard of hearing or colorblind? Honestly, Mac—"

The look on his face would stay with her forever. Pain

flickered in his eyes, as if exposing a dark secret. He was all raw nerves and vulnerability. She heard him swallow hard and saw his chin drop to his chest. His shoulders slumped.

What had she said to hurt him? She wished she could reverse time and take it all back. He wasn't hard of hearing, but distinguishing colors was another matter. She thought back over his visits to her shop. He'd needed her assistance when matching clothes.

The man *was* colorblind.

"Mac, I had no idea." Her mouth went dry and she found it hard to speak.

A beat of silence before he sucked air, straightened. His expression was hard, angry. His blue eyes were piercing. "Dress your dummies by yourself," he said. "I'm gone."

She had to stop him and apologize. She beat him to the door and stood between him and his escape. "Can we talk?"

"I want out." He punched the door frame hard enough to split the wood and damage his hand.

She grabbed his wrist. "Don't hurt yourself before the Huntington Beach Classic."

He shook free of her hold. "I have no fight with the door."

"What about with me?"

"You bust my balls."

He rode her last nerve. "I'm truly sorry."

"Sorry for me, or sorry for what you said?"

"No pity, Mac."

Still, he appeared self-conscious. "Dune's aware I mix up colors, but no one else outside my family knows."

She now knew his secret and made him a promise. "I'd never say a word."

He didn't look convinced. "You might in anger."

"I assure you, I won't."

He pressed against her, lightly yet significantly, making her aware of him. She was stuck between the thick wooden door and a very solid man. "Let's even the playing field," he suggested. "Tell me a secret. Something that's juicy and embarrassing. Something I can hold over your head."

Her life was boring and an open book. She had so little to hide. She worked and went home to her cats. Her boyfriends came and went. She'd never dated anyone seriously. She spent most evenings with a rented movie and a bag of peanut M&Ms. She'd put on five pounds in the last two months. "I'm overweight," she finally said.

He stepped back and checked her out. "You're ready for the chubby chasers," he teased, referring to men who liked their women plump.

What an ass. She pinched his arm. Hard.

He pulled a face, then rubbed the spot. "Weight isn't good enough," he said. "Dig deeper, babe."

"I put mustard on my french fries."

"I like mayonnaise."

"I seldom clean house."

"I drop-kick my clothes." He flattened his palms on each side of her head and touched his thumbs to her temples. "You're talking habits, not secrets."

She licked her lips. "I forget to pay my bills and beg for extensions."

"Don't we all." He tipped up her chin with his finger and taunted her. "Bring a skeleton out of your closet."

She wiggled a little and he pinned her, his chest and hip bones forcing her to keep still. She felt the cut of his six-pack and the muscles in his thighs. She closed her eyes and hissed through her teeth. "My vibrators have names."

He grinned. "Is the Jack Rabbit called Mac?"

She inhaled as his words soaked in. Then the unthinkable happened. His humor made her horny. Her breasts grew heavy and her nipples poked the red nylon of her sports bra. The hot feel of him from her waist down was a turn-on.

She affected him, too. The bulge in his board shorts brushed her belly as he rested his forehead against hers. "I like a woman who calls out her vibrator's name when she comes." His voice was deep, low, and irritatingly sexy. "I'm still waiting for a secret so dark and scary that it would stop traffic if I yelled it to the world."

"I'm attracted to you."

He blinked, looked skeptical. "Don't placate me."

She crossed her heart. "It's the truth."

He eased back a little. "Are you planning to act on your attraction?"

He'd given her enough space to duck under his arm. She escaped his sexual heat. She'd been honest. He just hadn't believed her. "I shared a secret with you," she said. "A confidence to be kept, but not acted on."

"You're crushing my nuts."

"I wasn't joking."

"Prove it."

"Can't. I have a date."

"You'll be thinking of me the whole time."

"Don't bet on it."

She was back to being snippy, Mac James noted as he leaned a hip against the front counter. Lady could lie with the best of them. She was no more attracted to him than he was to her. Then why was he sporting inches? He was so hard he hurt. Shifting his stance didn't help. He wanted her.

He watched as she finished dressing the mannequins. She added the hats, then chose their flip-flops: rhinestone ones for Joy and leather for Roy.

"Nicole Archer from The Jewelry Box lent me a necklace and bracelets for Joy," she said. She moved to the front counter, where she unlocked a drawer. She removed two layered gold chains with sunburst charms along the links. The bracelets came next. She held them up for him to see. "Assorted metals inlaid with blue onyx and crystals."

He nodded, appreciating the fact she'd shared the colors. "The bracelets look expensive. Shouldn't you keep them under glass?"

"I have security on staff this week," she told him, tongue-in-cheek. "Sophie's volunteering and she hired a young boy named Randy to help out, too. The kid can be trouble."

"How much trouble?"

"He stole a pair of sunglasses during lunch and Sophie went after him. Dune then took off after Sophie. He wasn't going to let her face the situation alone."

Mac took it all in. His always calm, always collected partner had been concerned for Sophie. She'd protected Dune against Zane at the Sneaker Ball. Dune now stood beside her when dealing with a punk kid. He found this all very interesting.

"Randy's holding his own now," Jen went on to say. "Sophie brings out the best in him. He'll guard the jewelry."

"A thief to catch a thief?"

She nodded. "Exactly."

"Sophie," he said thoughtfully. "I like her."

"So does Dune."

Mac narrowed his gaze on her. "How do you know this?"

"It's pretty obvious. My cousin brought us lunch and spent half a day helping out. He's *never*," she stressed, "done more than a walk-through."

Mac grinned. "He may become a permanent fixture."

"Why are you smiling?" she asked.

"I know something Dune has yet to realize," he said. "I

like being one step ahead of the big guy. He's usually two steps ahead of me."

Jen placed the jewelry on Joy, then stood back to admire both the mannequins. "They look beach friendly," she said.

She then glanced at her watch. "I need to get going."

Mac moved toward the door. "Don't let me keep you."

"Bye, Mac."

A part of him wasn't ready to call it a day. But she was meeting up with someone and he had no excuse to stay. Grandfather Frank wanting wheat bagels wouldn't work a second time. The scheme was lame.

He was about to leave when her cell phone rang. She pulled it from the pocket of her shorts, looked at the number, and moved out of earshot. Her "Hello, Kyle," drifted back to him, faint yet discernible.

Mac assumed the caller was her date. Such a call so close to going out wasn't good. The guy was either running late or about to cancel. Mac guessed that she was about to fly solo.

He rubbed the back of his neck. This was none of his business. Why should he care? He didn't really. Yet Jenna crossed his mind when he least expected it. There was something about her that both ticked him off, yet tempted him.

Eavesdropping wasn't new to him. He was barefoot and she'd never hear him coming. He headed to the storeroom, leaned against the wall, and listened.

"I wish you'd told me about your girlfriend," he heard Jen say. A pause while Kyle spoke, then it was Jen once again. "I understand. If she wants you back, you need to work through your fight."

She sounded understanding, Mac thought. He waited for her to pitch a fit. She didn't. He hadn't realized she'd ended the call until she charged from the back room. Anger slapped her flip-flops. Her radar picked him up. She was on him in a heartbeat.

"I knew you were here," she accused. "You're like a wiretap, listening in on my private conversations."

He thought he'd been quiet. "How'd you know I was here?"

"I heard you breathing."

He'd been holding his breath and only released a short, soft *whoosh* before he turned blue. Apparently Jen had sharp hearing.

"I'm sorry," he said, the best he could do.

"Sorry that you eavesdropped, or sorry I don't have a date?" she asked.

He went with "No date."

She shrugged, sighed. "It doesn't really matter. It's been a long day and I was running short on time. I only had twenty minutes to get home and pull myself together."

"I held you up. I'm to blame."

"I may find fault with you, Mac, but not tonight," she said. "I could've shoved you out the door at any time."

Instead she'd let him stay, let him dress a mannequin. She'd recognized his insecurity in being colorblind and promised to keep his secret. He hoped she was true to her word.

"What about Twilight Bazaar?" he asked.

"I have several family members selling artwork. I need to make an appearance. I can attend alone."

"Or you could attend with me."

"Bailing me out a second time," she said more to herself than to him. "Let's learn from our past mistakes. We didn't connect at the Sneaker Ball, it's doubtful we will over art."

"I'm an art connoisseur."

She looked skeptical. "An expert on women, I could accept, but art? Not a chance."

"Art was an option if I didn't make it in volleyball," he said straight-faced. "I like to finger paint, papier-mâché, and mold peanut butter play dough. I'm a master with the glue gun and macaroni. I love to body paint and roll around on butcher paper, especially with a partner."

"You excel in sticky mediums."

"The stickier the better." Black Cherry body oil came to mind. Unexpected, but timely. The oil warmed to the touch and was lickable and tasty. He had a need to get naked and naughty. He hadn't had sex for a week. Kami had been willing and they'd fooled around. In the heat of the moment, thoughts of Jen had crossed his mind and lingered. He couldn't shake her. He'd lost interest in Kami.

All that would change tonight.

Maybe he'd cruise the Blue Coconut for a game of pool or hit happy hour at the Parrot Walk. There were always hot chicks wanting a cocktail and a hook-up. He was in the mood for rug burns and love bites.

"Mac?" Jenna snapped her fingers near his nose. "I'm leaving."

"Hang loose." He followed her out.

She locked up, then left him with a wave of her hand.

He watched her walk away. There were no mincing steps or major wiggle to the woman, he noted. She moved with purpose. She smiled at everyone she passed, many being family and friends. A red light stopped her at the Center Street crosswalk. He caught her profile.

A breeze brushed her hair off her face. Her cheekbones were high and the tilt of her chin was stubborn. She was petite and fit. No way was she packing five extra pounds. She was too damn firm. She looked hot in her belly shirt and shorts. She had a light golden tan, which he found prettier than the beach babes who baked a dark brown.

She waited and waited at the long light. She glanced at her watch, then swung her arms at her sides. A pedicab approached and she flagged it down. She climbed in the three-wheeled rickshaw. The driver took off, cutting the corner sharply.

She was gone. He experienced a sense of emptiness. He neither liked nor understood the feeling.

The bar scene suddenly lost appeal.

He felt left behind.

Jenna Cates was worth pursing.

He ran in front of the next pedicab, forcing the driver to slam on the brakes. The driver said something rude, which Mac ignored. He was at fault. He could've caused an accident on the boardwalk.

He pointed east. "A pedicab just rounded the corner," he said. "Can you catch it?"

The driver looked college age. His name badge read JOE. He eyed Mac as if he were crazy. "Give chase in this heat?"

"It's only ninety-two." Mac had played volleyball in three-digit temps. "I need speed."

"I'm a cruiser."

"I'll triple your fare."

"Add a big tip?"

Mac nodded. "Send the bill to Dune Cates."

"Get in," Joe said.

Mac settled on the narrow cushioned seat. The driver took off, pumping his legs like a superhero.

They rounded the corner at Center Street. Joe pedaled so fast that the back tires left skid marks. Mac squinted against the sun. He'd lost another pair of sunglasses. That made two pairs this week. He needed to be more careful.

He slapped his hands on the back of Joe's seat. "That's them, two blocks ahead."

It felt like a car chase scene from a movie, Mac thought, as the driver left the wide sidewalk and took to the street. This wasn't *Bullitt, Ronin,* or *Mad Max,* but a chase was a chase.

A car swerved and pedestrians scattered. Joe was hell on wheels. He beeped his horn at a flock of crows and shouted at a jogger. He was pedaling full-out and bridging the gap. Less than half a block separated them now.

Joe's commotion caught the attention of Jen's driver. The man gestured and she glanced over her shoulder. Mac was close enough now to see her face. Her gaze widened and her lips parted. She said something to her cabbie, which caused him to pick up speed.

Joe heaved a breath. He was growing winded. They quickly lost ground. The pedicab moved beyond the hustle of the boardwalk and pier and crossed into Olde Barefoot William, where the majority of the Cateses lived. The streets were quiet and the old Florida-style cottages were quaint. The homes were shingled and shuttered with wide porches. They'd withstood hurricanes and time. The homes were handed down through generations. Here lay the inner circle.

Enormous evergreens lined the narrow two-lane road. Ancient moss hung from the branches. The sun cast shadows and the scent of hibiscus and plumeria was heavy on the air. Sprinklers whirred as homeowners watered their lawns.

Mac craned his neck. His pedicab had stalled out. Joe was sweating and swearing under his breath. Mac leaned back on the seat and took a moment to plan his next move. He'd been so intent on reaching Jen that he'd yet to come up with an excuse for chasing her down. He had nothing.

He usually thought fast on his feet.

But Jen was smart. She would see through him.

He could only fake it for so long.

Jen's pedicab soon turned left onto Sand Dollar Way. Joe got a second wind. He was pedaling for a big tip. He pulled behind the first rickshaw just as Jen exited.

"Thanks, Dude." Mac slapped Joe on the back and hopped out.

Joe pedaled off and the second pedicab followed.

Jenna climbed onto the curb and he remained in the street. She stood very still and stared at him. Only craziness drove a man into a pedicab chase. He shifted several times, uncertain and feeling foolish. What to say?

She spoke first. "What the hell?"

"I stopped by for a visit." Not his best opening line.

"We saw each other ten minutes ago."

He shrugged. "It seemed longer than that."

"Trust me, it wasn't."

"I thought we were bonding back at your shop."

"Sorry, I didn't get that same feeling."

He kept at it. "I'm here, you're here."

She sighed heavily. "I don't understand you."

He didn't understand himself most days. This was not going well. "Are you going to invite me in?" he asked.

She closed her eyes and appeared to count to ten. "Better to let you in the front door than have you break a back window."

"I'd never do that."

She blinked him a look. She didn't believe him for a second. She turned and started up the stone sidewalk. The lawn swept wide and the grass was tall. Dandelions grew wild. The cottage sat back off the road. It was built on higher ground, which protected it from a storm surge.

A white picket fence bordered her property. Mac had never known anyone with a picket fence. He ran from women who wanted a house with a fenced-in yard, a two-car garage, and three children.

Damn, Jen already had the fence.

His stomach squeezed, but he didn't get nauseous, a good sign for him. He could hold it together if he tried.

He followed her. The stones were sun-warmed and smooth beneath his bare feet. He was so busy checking out her place, he stubbed his toe twice.

He'd nearly reached the cottage when the grass wavered, parted, and her cats appeared. He saw one, two—a total of four. They came after him, all big, sneaky, and slinking.

He was more of a dog than cat person. These four didn't seem crazy about him, either. They circled him. He swore one hissed. Were they feral?

"They're Savannahs," Jen said from the porch. "A pairing of the African Serval and a domestic cat."

Their wild African genes were visible to Mac; their domestic side, not so apparent.

"The cats have spots on their coats," Jen told him. "They will fluff out the base of their tails in a greeting gesture."

No fluff, Mac noted. He wasn't welcome.

A darkly furred male brushed his calf in a footrace to the steps. The cat won. He stopped on the top stair, claimed it. Mac watched the cat watch him. The Savannah was long and lean with boomerang-shaped eyes and a hooded brow. Cheetah-tear markings ran from the corner of his eyes down the side of his nose to his whiskers.

A second cat passed him. This one could leap. The Savannah made it from the sidewalk to the porch in a single bound. The cat should wear a cape. In a matter of seconds, all four surrounded Jen. Mac faced a gauntlet.

"Attack cats?" he asked.

"It takes them a while to warm to strangers."

How much time? he wondered. The Savannahs were shifty and suspicious, with a pack mentality.

"Do you plan to introduce us?" he asked.

"You're a passing acquaintance and won't be around long enough to know them well."

"Good manners, Jen," he persisted. "Their names?"

Her sigh was heavy; her expression exasperated. "They have African names. There are three males." She pointed to each one. "Jengo, Neo, and Chike."

Chike, Mac noted, was the black Savannah guarding the stairs. The cat gave him the evil eye.

"The female is Aba." She reached down and scratched the ear on a light-colored tabby. "Care to come in?" she challenged.

He had two options: walk back to the boardwalk or survive her cats. His decision came when Aba fanned her tail. Perhaps there was hope for him yet. He could charm most females.

Mac took a chance. He climbed the steps, keeping one eye on Chike. He didn't want his toes mauled or his calf used as a scratching post. He moved slowly.

Jen held the door for him. He entered, expecting cat paws on his heels. The Savannahs surprised him. One leaped onto the glider. The remaining three sought window boxes.

"No flowers for you," he said to Jen.

"The cats claimed the boxes years ago. Cool spots on a hot day."

"Do they come inside?" he asked.

"There's a cat door in the back," she said. "They come and go, but never leave the yard. They're loyal and territorial."

"You have *four*." He couldn't get over the number.

"They're my kids."

"No diapers, midnight feedings, or college funds."

"They also don't talk back and are more trustworthy

than the men I date." She flipped on the ceiling fan and an overhead light.

He'd expected a cat smell, but the air was clean and fresh. He believed a home fit a person's personality, yet the cottage was in contrast to the woman. He took in her space. The inside shutters on the windows were open. The interior was bright and pleasant. Cozy.

Her furniture was overstuffed and comfortable. Bamboo runners ran throughout. What had he expected, straight-back wooden chairs and sharp-edged tables? Perhaps photos of her with the Wicked Witch of the West and her Flying Monkeys?

There were clusters of pictures, some taken of her family and others of her cats. How she'd gotten all four to pose around the base of a Christmas tree was beyond him, yet they'd stretched out, patient and alert. Mac could never have sat still that long.

His condominium was ten times the size of her cottage. Dune had helped him invest in the beachfront property. Size mattered. His place had entertainment value.

His condo had pitched ceilings, wide glass walls, and an open staircase that led to a loft. His furniture was made for his body. He'd let a designer pick the color scheme. She'd recommended pewter, sand, and sage. Chairs-and-a-half along with ten-foot couches were spread throughout.

He had an open-door policy to friends and fans. Company came and crashed at all hours. The more the merrier.

Jenna rested her hip against an armless chair. "What now?" she asked.

He glanced at her, then over her shoulder. Her backside was reflected in an oval mirror. She stood relaxed, her left hip jutting. The smooth tapering of her spine and sexy curve of her hips gave her body symmetry and flow. She had a sweet ass.

"Stop checking out my butt," she said sharply.

Busted. He met her gaze and smiled. "I thought we'd attend the bazaar, unless you'd rather have sex."

She didn't return his smile. Instead she arched a brow. "Have you seen yourself today?" she asked. "You're a moving mess."

He crossed to the mirror. He'd had better days. He was rough around the edges with his weed-whacker hair, dark circles under his eyes, and heavy stubble.

He'd grabbed the cleanest clothes in his pile of dirty laundry. His hoodie had paw prints near one pocket where Ghost had jumped on him after digging in the sand. He wore a white T-shirt underneath, soiled by a grease stain. He'd been eating french fries and used his shirt as a napkin. His board shorts hung just fine, low on his hips and a little wrinkled, but clean enough to wear a third day. He was barefoot and would need a pair of flip-flops or sandals to get into the Civic Center.

He glanced at Jen's feet. Small. He could wear a pair of her flip-flops if necessary. It didn't matter if his heels hung over the back.

"I've looked better and I've looked worse." He was honest. "Let's hit the bazaar for an hour, then part ways."

"Brush your hair first."

"I'd also like to shave."

Her gaze narrowed. "You want to borrow my brush and razor?"

"Like we were roommates."

"Which we're not." She looked inordinately pale.

"Where's your bathroom?" he asked.

"Down the hall, second door on the left."

He found it easily. He cleaned up the best he could. He shaved with her pink Lady Schick and wet down his hair. He liked her boar-bristle brush. He then added toothpaste

to his finger and brushed his teeth. He gargled with a cap-
ful of her mouthwash.

He was soon as good as she was going to get.

He shrugged off his hoodie and tugged his shirt over his
head on his way back to the living room. Jen stood in the
same spot he'd left her. Her eyes widened when she saw
him.

"Something wrong?" he asked.

"You're undressing."

"Just down to my boards. I need something clean. Any
chance you have an extra shirt, size large?"

"You're imposing, Mac."

"One shirt, one hour. That's hardly an imposition."

Her sigh was long-suffering. "My nightshirt might fit
you."

She slept in an oversized shirt. He liked that. He wondered if she wore panties. "No flowers, baby animals, or
rainbows, I hope."

"It's solid black."

He could pull off black. "I need something for my feet"
came out of his mouth next.

She pursed her lips. "My uncle left a pair of gardening
boots in my garage. You're welcome to those."

She led him to the waterproof boots. They were brown,
worn, and snug. His toes curled under. The fleece lining
made his feet sweat. It seemed like he was standing in hell.

"You ready to go?" he asked.

She looked down on her belly shirt and shorts. "Quick
change," she told him. He followed her from the garage.

"Care to introduce me to your vibrators?"

Her steps faltered. "Wait for me by the door."

He preferred her living room. He checked the bottom
of his boots to make sure he wasn't tracking in mud or ma-
nure. The rubber bottoms were clean.

He walked around, biding his time. He opened and closed the shutters, sat in her antique rocking chair, and set her wall clock five minutes fast so she'd never be late.

She soon returned in a sundress and sandals. He stared. The light color set off her tan and the gauzy fabric was nearly see-through. He wondered if she wore underwear.

He was so into her, he almost dropped the T-shirt she tossed his way. He made a mad grab. He pulled it on and noticed her nipple imprints. He patted his hands down his chest. The cotton flattened.

He then sniffed his sleeve. "I smell like cake."

"Frosted Cupcake body lotion," she told him. "The scent is vanilla bean and butter cream."

Great, he smelled like dessert. He'd have to skip the main crowd at the Civic Center and walk the perimeters of the exhibits. He hated smelling edible.

Nine

"You smell sweet," Dune Cates heard Sophie Saunders say. His back was to her, and he turned to see who she was sniffing.

"Let me rub my sugar on you."

Mac James stood a foot away. Sophie blushed when he hugged her. Dune counted to ten. "You can let go of her now."

Mac kissed Sophie on the forehead, then released her. It was a brotherly kiss, Dune noted, and not one to provoke or piss him off. Mac was a flirt and laid his charm on thick. Not so tonight. His partner appeared friendly, but reserved. Dune wondered what had triggered the change.

"What brings you to the Civic Center?" asked Sophie.

"Jenna brought me," Mac said easily.

Ah, crap, Dune thought. He didn't like the fact that Jen and Mac were together. He'd lost a second bet to Sophie.

Sophie glanced up. Her eyes were bright and her smile triumphant. *I told you so* was written all over her face. She was gracious. She didn't whoop, victory dance, or call attention to herself. Instead, she stood very still. She didn't want Mac aware of their wager.

Dune inhaled and caught a whiff of sugar and vanilla. He eyed Mac. "Your shirt smells like a bakery," he said.

"It's my nightshirt," Jen said, joining them. She carried

a small terra-cotta planter painted with purple pansies. "The scent of Frosted Cupcake body lotion never fully washes out."

Dune raised a brow. "How'd Mac get hold of your nightshirt?" he asked.

The moment turned awkward. "He followed me home," Jen finally said.

"Followed her after her date canceled at the last minute," Mac was quick to say.

"His hoodie and shirt were dirty, so I lent him a replacement," Jen continued. "Mac likes art and wanted to attend Twilight Bazaar."

"Mac and art?" *That* surprised Dune.

"So he says."

"He says a lot."

Mac rolled his shoulders. "Have you met her cats?" he asked Dune.

Dune nodded. He'd cat-sat for Jen on a weekend when he was home and Jen needed to go out of town. "Chike was distant, but he kept an eye on me the whole time."

"No male bonding with me, either," Mac admitted.

"Chike is cautious," Jenna said. "He chooses his friends wisely."

"Next visit and we'll be tight," Mac predicted.

"No more visits," Jen said firmly.

Dune saw the look Mac gave Jen when she wasn't watching. It was an anxious, yet purposeful stare. Dune had never known Mac to be nervous around a woman. This was a first for him.

Mac had somehow finagled a date to the bazaar. The night was young and Mac and Jen had yet to face off. Dune sensed their evening would end badly. They were two very different people. Common ground wasn't in their future.

He happened to glance down. "Nice boots, dude." He grinned at Mac.

"Gardening boots," said Mac. He stepped from one foot to the other and winced. "Tight and itchy. Fire and brimstone."

"Beggars can't be choosers," Jen reminded him.

"I'm begging off shortly."

"Feel free to leave anytime," she said sweetly.

Underlying sarcasm? Dune heard it and so had Mac. Her tone set Mac off. A muscle jerked in his jaw. "Hard to believe she's attracted to me," he said.

"She is?" Sophie came alive at Dune's side.

"So she claims."

Jenna glared at Mac. "I can't believe you said that."

"I can't believe you're so upset."

"Believe it." She clutched the flowerpot so tightly, Dune expected her to crack it over Mac's skull. Instead, she turned on her heel and disappeared into the crowd. Her anger lingered. They all felt it.

Mac stared after her. "What the hell just happened?"

"Jen left you for dead," said Dune.

"I can't win for losing."

"What, exactly, are you trying to win?" Dune wanted to know.

"Or *who*?" inserted Sophie.

Mac didn't answer. It wasn't like him to close down. He always had a smartass remark. Not so tonight, thought Dune. Mac was quiet and introspective. He was oblivious to the women who passed by, smiled at him, brushed against him, and gave him the sexual eye.

Sophie patted Mac on the arm. "You can walk around with us," she offered.

"Or you can walk home," suggested Dune.

"Thanks, Soph, you always look out for me." Mac put

his arm around her shoulders. She was the perfect leaning post for his height. "I'll hang for a few more minutes," he said.

"No more than ten," said Dune.

The three of them moved with the crowd. They eventually stopped at a booth with framed pastels. "The paintings are soft and soothing," Sophie observed. "The hammocks and bedrooms make me sleepy."

"Bet the artist was tired," said Mac.

Mac released Sophie long enough to pick up a small painting of a vintage wooden rocker. The wicker was intricately painted. The back curved like a spine. "Looks similar to the one in Jenna's cottage," he said.

"A nice gift," Dune noted, "especially if a guy screwed up and wanted to make amends."

Mac continued to look at the painting. He stared so long that Dune made the decision for him. Something had gone down between Mac and Jenna that only Mac could fix. He gave his partner the benefit of the doubt. He slipped his wallet from his back pocket and passed him a fifty.

"Resolve" was all he said. He left the rest to Mac.

Mac bought the painting and pocketed the change. The Civic Center was packed and people pushed around them; a few cut between them. Mac wasn't fazed until someone stepped on his toe.

"Time to kick these boots," he grunted. "Take care of our Sophie," he said to Dune. "I'm out of here." He and his painting moved toward the main door.

"Poor Mac," Sophie sighed. "He and Jen didn't last long. They don't do well on dates."

"Poor me," said Dune. "They arrived together. That's all you needed to collect on our second bet."

"There are lots of choices at the bazaar."

She took his hand as she was apt to do. Jostled by the

crowd, they bumped arms, hips, legs. She stepped on his foot twice. He didn't mind. There was something oddly comforting in knowing she walked beside him.

They weren't an official couple, although each time he was with her, he liked her more. He found it harder and harder to remember that he was an injured volleyball player without a future. Hanging out with Sophie gave him a sense of purpose. He liked waking up to her latest adventure.

It took them two hours to view every booth and table inside the Civic Center. The vendors smiled when Sophie approached. She wanted to support every artist and merchant. She was a guaranteed sale.

She swatted his hand when he offered to cover her purchases. Still, he was fast with the cash. He watched as she bought items for everyone but herself. She was a giver.

His arms were soon filled with a handmade quilt for his sister Shaye, a pale driftwood wreath for Nicole Archer, a terrarium for Jenna, and a small stained glass window for Molly Malone. She had yet to decide who would get the button and coin necklaces.

"Need help?" Young Chuck from the diner found them in the crowd. The kid had been working with Sophie's gardener and, from what Dune had heard from Violet, was doing a great job. The boy had a green thumb, according to Luis. The gardener was happy to have a helper for the summer.

"I need to make a trip to the SUV," Dune told Chuck. He was still driving his parents' Tahoe and glad for the cargo space. "Stick with Sophie. Carry whatever she buys."

Chuck flexed his arm. "I'm strong."

Dune returned moments later to find Sophie in the children's aisle. Chuck was buried beneath arts and crafts. His vision was limited. He squinted between an amber mason jar filled with dark hot chocolate—the recipe attached—and a decoupage paperweight featuring the map of Florida.

Sophie held up a container of pink, yellow, and blue bath salts. "Aren't these pretty?" she asked.

"Your bathwater will look like a rainbow," said Chuck. Sophie took two.

Dune experienced a purely male moment as he looked at her. She was soft and sweetly curved. Somewhere between the Sneaker Ball and the Civic Center, he'd begun to picture her naked. He could see her wet, soapy, and slick. The image forced him to shift his stance. Damn erection.

He handed Chuck the keys to the SUV. "Go out the front door, third lane on the left, fifth car down, a blue Tahoe."

"Load 'em up," the boy said as he squeezed through the crowd.

There were so many children's creations, and Sophie wanted one of each. Dune watched as she fell in love with an origami swan. Next, she couldn't pass up an Empire State Building built with root beer bottle caps. Someone had drunk a lot of soda.

She bought an angel made from a paper towel roll. The roll was wrapped in wide lace ribbon and the wings were bent copper. It had a tinfoil halo.

Sophie praised the third grade girl who'd crafted the angel. Her words caused the girl to cover her face and blush. Sophie went on to order a dozen additional angels for Christmas.

"I'm going to hang them on my tree," she told Dune.

He nodded. "They'll make nice ornaments."

"I have tanks," a young boy called from the next table. "They're made of tire tread."

Cool toys, Dune thought. Made from thick, durable belted rubber, the tanks would tough it out for a lot of years. One tank had a Michelin stripe and another said DUNLOP. He bought the Dunlop for his four-year-old cousin.

A ceramic giraffe caught his eye, one similar to the one he'd made as a kid. It was far better crafted, he noted. He laid out two dollars.

It took him a moment to realize Sophie had left his side. Where had she gone? He turned and found her standing near the pet station. Dwarf hamsters in clear plastic run-about balls had caught her attention. She remained perfectly still as the balls lightly bumped her feet and rolled off. The hamsters were exercising and getting quite a workout.

Sophie went down on her hands and knees for a better look. Dune leaned against the doorframe and watched her watch them. Her soft brow creased and her green eyes were narrowed. Her curiosity was piqued.

She gently put her hand on one ball, stopping its progress. "Why are there two hamsters inside?" she asked the vendor seated on a chair in the corner.

"Small females, six weeks old," the man replied. "Each weighs less than an ounce. It takes both of them to move the ball."

Dune knew what was coming; he could feel it in his bones. It would be great for Sophie to have a pet. Hamsters, however, didn't live very long.

"Life span?" he asked the seller.

The man shrugged. "One to four years."

Sophie pushed to her feet. She cradled the plastic ball with the two females to her chest. She carefully stepped around those still running a marathon. She came to him and gave him a small smile. "I'm collecting my bet."

The vendor stood so fast his chair fell over. "Twenty dollars," he told Dune. "Do you need a cage? Food? I'm full-service."

The supplies were stored in a custodial closet. The man had a selection to pamper and spoil any hamster. Dune held the plastic ball, while Sophie chose her items. The Dwarfs were pocket pets. The tiny females huddled together, their noses twitching.

The vendor pulled a cage from the top shelf. "This is a nice starter home," he told Sophie.

She shook her head. "Too small."

She preferred the Habitat Plaza. The picture on the box showed a multi-level, high-rise manufactured with twisting tube tunnels, platforms, and two running wheels. Dune would help her put it together.

Further necessities included a water bottle, earthenware feeding dish, a chewing stick, and small bag of seeds and pellets. The vendor tossed in the clear plastic ball as a bonus item.

"Wow, Dwarfies," Chuck said when he located them again. He tossed Dune his keys. "My teacher kept a gerbil and two white mice in class last year. We took turns taking them home on the weekends."

"You can watch my girls if I ever go out of town," Sophie told him.

Chuck puffed up, proud she trusted him. "Do you need help with the rest of this stuff?" he asked.

Dune handed Chuck the plastic ball. "Handle them with care," he said.

"I'll guard them with my life."

Sophie smiled her approval.

Dune paid the vendor. The man nodded toward Sophie, who waited with Chuck by the door. "She'll treat my hamsters like family."

That she would. They were her kids now, Dune realized as he drove her home. She held the plastic ball on her lap with the protective fierceness of motherhood. She told him twice to slow down when going over speed bumps. He did his best not to laugh, but his smile soon broke out.

"What's so funny?" she asked.

"You're funny," he said. "You're such a mom."

She frowned slightly. "That's a bad thing?"

"It's all good," he assured her. He'd never discourage her from getting attached to her pets. Sophie was a natural nurturer. These were two very lucky hamsters.

They pulled into her driveway moments later. He helped her out of the Tahoe and into her house. She settled in the library and sat cross-legged on the floor. She watched the plastic ball circle the room while he unloaded the SUV.

He placed her purchases in the living room. Sophie had supported the community. She would gift wrap and hand out her presents. It would be Christmas in May for her friends.

He lugged the Habitat Plaza down the hall. "Where shall I set this up?" he asked her.

"In here." She was quick to make up her mind. "This is my favorite room. I spend so much time here reading."

She could read and watch the hamsters run. Sophie was a homebody. The Dwarfs would keep her company.

He hunkered down beside her and tore open the box. The pieces spilled out. The ventilated wire top was a bright yellow and the lower plastic levels were pink and orange. It was a simple task to put the parts together. He could've done it in five minutes flat. Instead, he took his time.

He liked being here with Sophie. She helped him fit the tube tunnels and attach the cylinders to the side panels. The running wheels came next, followed by the water bottle. She filled their food dish.

"Do you have an empty can? A toilet paper roll?" he asked her. "They need a place to sleep."

Sophie was up and searching before he could finish his sentence. She returned with a Kalamata olive can and a roll of paper towels. She ripped off one sheet and shredded a narrow strip for their bedding. She then stuffed it inside the can.

She took a deep breath. "I'm ready to hold them now."

Dune retrieved the ball from near his foot. The hamsters looked tired. They'd run several miles tonight. He twisted the top and reached inside. They were small and light as air. They sniffed his hand. The darker of the two nibbled on his finger. He gently scooped up the hungry one and set her on Sophie's palm.

Dune got to know the lighter-colored hamster, while Sophie became acquainted with the darker one. His Dwarf was so small, it could get lost between his fingers. "Do you have names picked out?" he asked her.

"I will in a day or two," she said. "I want to learn their personalities first."

"Are you ready to introduce them to their home?"

She nodded and he unlatched the cage door. He lowered his hand and the hamster ran off his fingers and into the habitat. Sophie released her pet, too. Immediately curious, the hamsters explored.

"I want to put the cage on a card table next to the sofa," she said. "My grandparents left one behind. It's in the hall closet."

Dune went for the table and the hamsters were soon set for the night. They'd disappeared into the olive can and never reappeared. He glanced down and found Sophie staring up at him.

"Thank you for my girls," she said.

"You won our bet."

"It must seem childish to get so excited, but I've never

had a pet. Trace wanted a Golden Retriever when he was a boy. My parents felt a dog would be too much work and cause too much of a mess."

"The hamsters will be easy to care for," he said. "Enjoy them."

"You don't think I'm acting like a kid then?"

Sweet, sensitive Sophie needed his reassurance. He was honest with her. "I like the way you look at life, excited and expectant. It's a great way to live."

She nodded, smiled, pleased by his answer. "Mac's never grown up," she said. "Unless he's got everyone fooled."

"What you see is what you get with Mac," Dune told her. "There's no hidden agenda."

"I'm easy to read, too," she said. "I can't hide my feelings. I frown when my heart hurts and smile when it warms."

She smiled as often as she blushed. Dune was glad to be a part of her life. Their age difference no longer mattered. Sophie had him seeing life through fresh eyes. He hoped she'd never lose her exuberance.

It was easy to become disillusioned. Life had pushed him down at the height of his career. He'd become a bit of a cynic after falling and hurting his wrist at the South Beach Open. Somehow Sophie soothed him.

He glanced at his watch. Eleven-thirty. It was getting late, yet he wasn't ready to leave. "Decaf by the pool?" he asked, hoping she'd let him stay a while longer.

She welcomed him, but on her terms. "Coffee at the kitchen table," she countered.

"It's time for you to get your feet wet."

"You only mentioned my swimming lesson today," she said. "I thought we were taking it slow."

"Slow starts with a full moon and splashing your feet."

"I'm afraid."

"I'll be with you all the way."

He took her hand and felt her shiver. She *was* scared. He wouldn't push her hard, only a nudge to get her out by the pool. They rose and he followed her down the hall to the kitchen. He dropped onto a chair while she made the coffee. The scent was dark, rich, and earthy.

"Marisole's Rainforest," she told him. "Our chef grinds an assortment of beans into a special blend. I add Italian sweet cream."

She poured two cups and crossed to him. He nodded toward the sliding doors and she sighed heavily, knowing his intent. They proceeded poolside. The full moon turned the water silver. The deck was natural blue stone. The patio furniture was stacked against the house.

Dune kicked off his sandals and rolled his jeans to his knees. He settled on the side of the pool. He sipped his coffee and waited for Sophie to join him.

She was slow to cuff her pants and slower still to sit. She was anxious as she perched on the edge. She extended her legs, stiff and straight, long before lowering her feet into the pool. The water was warm and soothing. He watched her wiggle her toes.

"Not so bad?" Dune asked.

"Not so good." She peered down on the water. "It looks deep."

"Three, maybe four feet," he said. "You could easily stand."

She took a sip of her coffee. "I prefer to sit."

They sat and talked. "What would you be doing if I wasn't here?" He didn't want to keep her from anything important.

"I often read until ten, then watch a movie," she told him. "My life's more boring than yours."

"I've watched my fair share of movies," he admitted. He often camped on the couch with Ghost, preferring a quiet night over the bar crowd. His dog didn't expect small talk or run up a bar tab.

"A little movie trivia," she challenged him. " 'Of all the gin joints in all the towns in all the world, she walks into mine.' "

He recognized the quote. "Bogart in *Casablanca*. Do you like the classics?"

"I have very eclectic tastes." She surprised him with " 'Toga! Toga!' "

He grinned. "Bluto from *National Lampoon's Animal House*." He swirled his coffee in his cup and tried to stump her. " 'Cinderella story,' " he recited the dialogue. " 'A former greenkeeper, about to become the Master's champion. It looks like a mirac . . . it's in the hole! It's in the hole! It's in the hole!' "

She rolled her eyes. "Is that the best you've got?" she asked. "Bill Murray, *Caddyshack*."

He came back with " 'Do, or do not. There is no try.' "

"Yoda, *The Empire Strikes Back*."

"Your turn," he said.

" 'No wire hangers, ever!' "

She stumped him. He didn't have a clue. He shrugged. "Sounds like a slogan for a dry cleaning commercial."

"It's *Mommie Dearest* with Faye Dunaway as Joan Crawford."

"You're good, Sophie."

"Books and movies are my escape." She snapped her fingers. "I have a quote you'll know: 'Where is it? Where's the thump-thump?' "

"That's Jack Sparrow, *Pirates of the Caribbean, Dead Man's Chest*."

She leaned into him. "Such a smart man."

Her body fit against his side, soft, warm and distracting. He had one further piece of dialogue for her. " 'Y'know, this was supposed to be my weekend off. But nooo. You got me out here, draggin' your heavy ass through the burnin' desert with your dreadlocks sticking—' "

" '—out the back of my parachute,' " she finished for him. "The alien smelled bad, too. That was Will Smith as Captain Steven Hiller. He could've been at a barbecue instead of tracking aliens on *Independence Day*."

"You have an amazing memory."

"For trivia," she said with a hint of defeat. "I'm book smart, but life-challenged."

Sophie knew her limitations. She was shy, uncoordinated, and inordinately fearful. Most people had been around the block at least once by her age. She'd just started down the driveway.

He nudged her shoulder. "Your favorite heroes and villains?"

She didn't have to think long. "*Silence of the Lambs* would be the scariest pairing with Clarice and Hannibal Lecter. Animation: the 101 Dalmatians were all heroes. Cruella de Vil scared me as a kid. Christopher Reeve as Superman and Sally Field in *Norma Rae* were heroic. Jack Nicholson in *The Shining* and Kathy Bates in *Misery* gave me nightmares."

"That's quite a list," Dune said, impressed.

She caught her breath and blushed. "Sorry to run on," she apologized.

He turned slightly and dropped a light kiss on her forehead. "I'm going with Han Solo and Darth Vadar, although Jabba the Hutt qualified as a villain, too."

She looked at him for a long moment, as if summing him up. "I bet you have a shelf of Western DVDs."

"I bet you're right." He'd only mentioned cowboys to her once, when he admired her antique pearl-handled six-shooter. Yet she'd remembered. He liked that about her.

She focused on what he had to say. "I admire the morality of the Old West and gunslinger justice."

"Spaghetti Westerns or legends?"

He grinned. "*The Good, The Bad, and The Ugly* ranks up there with *Butch Cassidy and the Sundance Kid.*"

"I enjoyed *The Man Who Shot Liberty Valance,*" she said. "It was the first instance John Wayne called someone Pilgrim."

"What's your all-time favorite movie?" he asked.

She pursed her lips. "There are so many to choose from. Movies I've watched over and over. I could go with *Wuthering Heights, Titanic,* or *Funny Girl,* but I'm going to say *Jerry Maguire.*"

" 'Show me the money!' " said Dune.

" 'You had me at 'hello.' "

"You're a romantic, Sophie Saunders."

"Romantic but realist." She leaned back on her palms and swung her feet in the water. The side of her foot brushed his and their ankles bumped.

He looked down in the water. She had small feet and slender calves. Every part of her body was compact.

"Up for a midnight swim?" he asked.

"Up for more coffee?" she countered.

"Half a cup."

She scooted back several feet before standing. Distance was her safety net from falling in the pool. She picked up his cup, then crossed to the kitchen.

"You're going in the water," he called after her.

"Later rather than sooner," she said from the sliding door.

He'd keep after her. She had a pool in her backyard and a canal beyond. She had easy access to the beach. Knowing how to swim was a safety precaution at any age.

He heard the pad of her bare feet as she came to stand

behind him. She bent over and set his cup down near his hip. She went on to rest her hands on his shoulders. He felt the bump of her knees at his back.

What was going on?

The evening was about to shock him. His jaw dropped when Sophie gave him a solid shove. There was no resistance on his part. He was so relaxed he slid into the pool.

Her laughter followed him in. He'd been ambushed. She'd barely gotten her feet wet, yet she had no regrets soaking him to the bone.

Two could play her game. He sank to the bottom in the shallow end and held his breath for a good long time.

What he thought was a joke wasn't funny to Sophie.

"Dune?" Her voice wavered slightly. "Don't make me come after you."

He wished she would jump in. He counted to ten and was about to surface when she entered the pool. He saw her clutch the handrail as she came down the stairs. Her wild, panicky splashing caused waves. She lost sight of him, yet she was so close she stepped on his stomach.

"Dune!" Her voice was now shrill from worry.

He shot up. The water swirled about his waist, but reached high on her chest. She was pale in the moonlight; bobbing and tearful.

Her tears cut him deep. He mentally kicked himself for playing such a prank. He hadn't meant to scare her. He pulled her close and rubbed her back.

She punched his arm hard. "Never frighten me like that again."

He wiped the tears off her cheeks with his thumbs. "You started it. You pushed me in the pool."

"You pretended to drown." She collapsed against him. "My heart nearly stopped when you didn't surface."

"You tried to save me." That affected him most. She'd

been scared to death, yet braved the pool for him. She was amazing.

He rested his forehead against hers. "For future reference, when you play a prank on someone, chances are good they'll prank you back."

"Like you just did to me?"

He nodded. "You didn't have a lot of playmates as a kid, whereas I grew up with three brothers and a sister. They specialized in practical jokes, stupid stunts, and getting back at each other. Had I faked drowning with Zane, he would've dropped an anchor on my chest."

She sighed against him, her relief evident.

Awareness next came into play. The surface of the pool was smooth as glass and the night still around them. Clouds crossed the moon and darkness allowed them privacy.

Time alone was good.

He lowered his hands to her bottom and cupped her butt cheeks. They fit small in his palms. Her breasts pressed against his chest and her legs wrapped around his hips. Their wet clothes stuck together. Their position was one of intimacy and arousal. It was time for him to make a move, or get out of the pool and call it a night.

He hadn't finished his coffee.

He wanted to start something with Sophie.

That something began with a kiss.

Ten

Sophie Saunders was about to be kissed. She sensed the
sexual shift in Dune the moment he clutched her bottom and fit her to him. Her arms now wrapped his neck,
with her legs around his waist. She breathed in his scent,
male and midnight. She felt the solidness of his chest and
flatness of his abdomen. His breath hitched when she settled against his groin. His erection was impressive.

Holding her tight, he walked her to the side of the pool
and set her near the handrail. He stepped between her
thighs. The bottom of the pool was sloped. Their difference in height no longer mattered. They connected in all
the right places.

His body excited her as much as his kiss. He caught her
hair in his hands and angled her face to his. He claimed her
mouth with gentle reserve. Her response was tentative yet
instinctive.

He initiated and she imitated, wanting to please him.
He groaned deep in his throat when she nipped the corners of his mouth. She flicked her tongue along his upper
lip and he sucked on her lower. When she bit his jaw, he
bit her back. He grew so taut, his muscles bunched.

He didn't rush her. He was a man of slow kisses and
slower hands. She felt flushed and tingly. Sensation height-
ened when he slipped his tongue between her lips. His

mouth was warm and moist and he tasted of sweet cream. Slow then fast, he built a mating rhythm with his tongue that left her heart pounding at an amazing rate.

Dune pushed and rubbed against her. The intimate introduction of his body left her breasts heavy and swollen and intensified the sexual ache between her thighs. She melted a little.

Years of longing compelled her to stroke his neck and shoulders; to run her hands down his sides and under his T-shirt. The heat of his skin inspired her to break their kiss just long enough to work his shirt up and over his head. Dune tossed it aside.

Sophie flattened her palms on his broad chest patterned with light brown hair. He was both rough and smooth. His heart beat steadily beneath her fingers, giving a significant skip when she brushed her thumb over his male nipple.

He was hard everywhere—the muscles along his shoulders, his biceps, his six-pack, his penis. Even his back was riveting.

Dune let her kiss him until she was dazed and her lips felt numb. He then unbuttoned her blouse and unhooked her bra in two smooth moves. She was now bare to him. A light breeze blew on her breasts and she shivered.

He warmed her with his breath. "So soft," he said. Desire roughened his voice as he kissed the hollow where her neck and shoulder met. He nipped the sensitive skin above her right breast, then took her nipple into his mouth and tugged lightly. Sensation shot to her belly. Arousal settled between her thighs. She grew restless. Female instinct rocked her hips.

Slowly, slowly, he grazed her ribs and goose bumps rose. He traced the sensitive flesh at her belly and she trembled. He squeezed her thighs and she nearly came out of her skin.

He watched her so closely, so intently, that the skin

pulled tightly over his cheekbones. The hollows in his cheeks deepened. His nostrils flared and she heard the depth of his breath.

Impatience played between them.

She clutched his arms so tight that her nails left crescent moons on his skin. Her scalp tingled and her palms itched. Her stomach fluttered. The widespread position of her legs left her vulnerable. She found it difficult to sit still.

He drew out their foreplay, running his hands up and down her back, then over her bottom and down her thighs. When his hands again settled on her hips, he lowered the side zipper on her slacks and folded back the waistband, exposing her bikini panties.

Her body flushed. Not from embarrassment, but from need. She wanted this man. His touch assured her that he wanted her, too. His long fingers splayed low on her stomach. She worried her tummy wasn't flat, that it was slightly rounded. Now was not the moment to suck it in.

Dune didn't seem to notice. Her worries faded when he caressed the crease of her sex through the pale blue nylon.

She was wet in seconds.

Passion pushed her against his palm. He delved beneath the elastic. She gasped, then stiffened as he separated her. He stroked and coaxed, creating a physical ache so strong that everything around them blurred. Her breath became short, hot pants. She felt very female, very sexual. She was close, *so* close to coming . . .

Her neck arched and stars danced behind her eyes. The feeling was indescribable. A final thrust of his finger and raw sensation overtook her. The orgasm shook her. She felt mindless, boneless, and liquid. The aftershocks curled her toes.

She forced air into her lungs and slowly focused. The sight of Dune standing bone hard before her returned her to reality. She blushed, then clutched the front of her blouse together. "I came, you didn't." Her voice sounded breathy.

"No condom, Sophie."

"You bought a box at Crabby Abby's." She'd rung up his sale.

His jaw worked. "The box is at my grandfather's. I wasn't prepared for tonight."

She clasped her hands in her lap. "Anything I can do?"

He shook his head. "To be continued."

She sensed his struggle and knew the immense amount of willpower it took for him to step back. He moved into deeper water, where he fell facedown and went into the dead man's float.

His body drifted in the moonlight. Every so often he lifted his head and drew air. He eventually flipped onto his back. His face was cut in shadow. His bare chest rose and fell; his breathing was now even.

She hooked her bra and buttoned her blouse, then slowly kicked her feet. The surface rippled. The motion caught his attention. He stood up in the middle of the shallow end. He shook his head and rolled his shoulders. Water sluiced down his body. He was still hard, but not nearly the size of moments ago.

She wasn't certain what to say. "More coffee?" she asked.

His expression was half-amused, half-painful. "Let's call it a night," he said.

He didn't use the steps or support rail. Instead he flattened his hands on the side of the pool and hoisted himself out of the water. Rivulets ran off him and onto her. She sat in a puddle.

He bent down and offered her his hand. She took it. He drew her to him. She dipped her head. They stood toe-to-toe, not touching but embraced by the same space.

"Look at me, Sophie," he said, his tone gentle. "Never be embarrassed around me."

She met his gaze. "Are we okay?"

"We're fine," he assured her. He scooped up his wet T-shirt and sandals. "Walk me out?"

She gathered two fluffy blue towels from the outside cabana cabinet and passed him one. He made a few quick swipes to his face and across his chest, then tossed it over one shoulder. He picked up his T-shirt and sandals.

They left a watery trail across the pool deck, through the kitchen, and down the marble entrance hall. "This isn't great timing," he told her at the door. "I leave tomorrow for Tampa. I sponsor several volleyball camps throughout the summer and I always make at least one appearance. While I'd rather spend time with you, my activities coordinator Will Stacy is expecting me."

"How long will you be gone?" she asked.

"Two days max."

She nodded, not wanting him to leave, but knowing he had a commitment.

He gave her a kiss at the front door, one that was light and left her wanting.

"See you soon." Then he slipped out.

Two days ran into three, and Dune had yet to return. Sophie couldn't help noticing that Mac James came around. It was hard not to miss him. He hadn't officially set foot in the T-shirt shop, but he did a lot of pacing on the boardwalk. She'd seen him eating ice cream, chocolate churros, and pizza through the front window. He hung out so often he'd become a fixture.

Jen gave no sign of seeing him. She still held a grudge against him from Twilight Bazaar. No matter how many times Sophie rehashed their conversation, she couldn't pinpoint what Mac had said that ticked Jen off. Yet something definitely had.

Funny, sarcastic Jenna appeared both serious and sad, which made Sophie feel bad, too. She didn't know how to fix what Mac had broken. Jen went into hiding. She spent most of her time in the storeroom. She let Sophie handle the customers.

Business was good. She rang up sales for six shirts to a biologist in town for a symposium on beach erosion. Young Randy proved an asset. The older man had three sons and Randy helped him select the perfect souvenir tees. Randy then persuaded him to take a sand globe home to his wife and a Frisbee for the family dog. The boy had retail in his blood.

Randy crossed to Sophie during a break in customers. His arms were filled with rolled posters. "Tomorrow's payday," he reminded her.

She smiled at him. "You'll be paid, maybe even get a bonus."

"A bonus big enough to buy my sister a T-shirt?"

"I'm sure it will cover the cost."

He pumped his arm. "Glad it's you and not Dune who's paying me," he said. "The big guy hasn't been around. I'd hate to get stiffed."

"No worry, the sunglasses will be yours," she assured him. "However, my time at Three Shirts ends today. I'm off to my next adventure. That will leave Jenna short-handed. Care to stick around and help out?"

He shrugged. "Do I get a raise?"

"That can be negotiated with Jen."

"I've grown on her."

"You'll stay in her good graces as long as you don't steal."

"My days of crime are over." He sounded older than twelve. He set the posters on the front counter, then asked, "Help me set up a display?"

She nodded. She needed to concentrate on the shop and not on Dune. Yet each time the door opened, she looked up, hoping to see him. He never showed.

Maybe she'd read more into their evening together than was actually there. He'd kissed and touched her everywhere; made her palms sweat and her heart race. She'd climaxed and he'd lain facedown in her pool. Not an equal exchange of sexual favors.

He'd been her hero for so many years. Then she'd gone and fallen in love with him. That scared her more than all her fears combined. Her insecurities surfaced.

What if he never loved her back?

What if he broke her heart?

What if—?

Randy nudged her elbow to get her attention. "You're daydreaming, Sophie."

He then passed her a poster, which she slowly unrolled. The matted photo was awesome, she thought. Six boardwalk shops were depicted in black-and-white; only Three Shirts was in color. The burnished orange storefront and tangerine door contrasted sharply with the muted shades of gray. The poster would sell like hot cakes.

"What are your future plans?" Randy asked as he carefully tacked a poster to the wall.

She grew thoughtful as she cleared a shelf for the remaining matted photos. Dune wasn't around to discourage her from jumping on a pogo stick, so that was an option. As was walking on stilts. She could start low and go high. However, a part of her was leaning toward the pedicab tours. She could handle a three-wheeled rickshaw.

Carting tourists from one end of the boardwalk to the other appealed to her. She wouldn't have to wear a helmet or body padding like she would on stilts or a pogo stick. Plus, there was no chance of falling. No bruising. No broken bones.

She knew the town's history like the back of her hand.

Giving pedicab tours would be great exercise. She needed to firm up. Dune was solid as a wall.

"The pedicabs," she decided on the spot.

"Good choice and good luck."

She'd send her sister-in-law Shaye a text. Shaye would schedule her training. There was a historical pamphlet to memorize. Sophie planned to ad-lib a little, too.

The remainder of the morning crawled by. She dusted, swept, and cleaned the mirrors until the lunch hour rolled around. She wasn't hungry, so she decided to take a walk. The sun was not her friend. She borrowed a nylon Windbreaker and floppy hat from Jen.

She stepped onto the boardwalk and immediately bumped into Mac James. "Sweet Sophie," he greeted, giving her a hug. "Good to see you."

"I've been watching you all morning."

"I've been running errands."

"You've done nothing but eat."

"So you say."

"So I know." She brushed powdered sugar from his cheek.

"Doughnuts," he said, before asking her what was really on his mind. "Anyone else see me?"

"Like who? Randy?"

He blew out a breath. "Don't make me beg, Soph."

She took pity on him. "Jenna's been working in the storeroom."

His face fell. "Shit, I've walked my ass off for nothing."

"You could've come inside."

"She would've swept me out with a broom."

"A distinct possibility." Or maybe not. Sophie glanced at the front window of the shop and saw Jen peering out. Fearing she'd been caught, she pulled back before Mac could see her.

He ran his hand through his hair, spiked one side. "Dune called a few minutes ago," he told her. "There are a couple of glitches at camp. He won't get back until tomorrow."

Good to know. She slowly exhaled the breath it felt like she'd been holding the entire time he'd been gone.

"He asked me to keep you company," Mac informed her. "So, what's up?"

"I'm going for a walk."

"I have a few more steps in me."

"Good. Let's head to the pier."

"I thought you were afraid of the Gulf."

"I like looking at the water," she confessed. "I'm just not ready to get my feet wet."

She'd gotten plenty wet the night she'd jumped in her pool to save Dune. Yet the ocean was another matter entirely. It didn't have cement sides or a handrail.

They took off down the boardwalk. Several female sunbathers stopped Mac for his autograph. He charmed each one, but he didn't plan to hook up. That spoke volumes to Sophie. Whether he'd admit it or not, he was into Jen.

Dodging fishermen and tourists, they soon reached the pier. Sophie relaxed and enjoyed the sights. The merry-go-round circled to a lively Hop-Scotch Polka. Those on the roller coaster raised their arms high on the downward slant of the track. The bumper cars beeped with each knock. The arcade amusements drew kids of all ages. Scents of cotton candy, candied apples, and fried Oreos sweetened the air.

Mac slowed beside a metal cart selling hot dogs. "Weenie?" he asked her.

Sophie laughed. She couldn't help herself.

He grinned. "Your mind's in the gutter."

"My thoughts are pure."

"Hang around me," he warned, "and you'll step off the

curb." He then ordered three hot dogs. "Dune Cates's account," he told the vendor.

They moved beyond the line of hungry customers. He broke off a piece of hot dog and fed her a bite. She wasn't hungry, but he insisted that she eat something. The bun was steamed and the hot dog juicy.

Food drew her thoughts to Marisole, her family's gourmet chef. Mari was amazing in the kitchen, but it was time Sophie tried her own hand at cooking. "I'm going to make dinner tonight," she said, more to herself than to Mac.

"I can cook," Mac surprised her by saying.

"You mean cook beyond opening a can of soup and heating it?"

He put his hand over his heart. "You wound me, babe. No one makes meat loaf better than I do. And I memorized my grandma's peanut butter cookie recipe when I was ten."

"I can't picture you puttering around the kitchen."

"I can putter with the best of them." He looked down at her. "Invite me to dinner."

"You're invited." She paused. "What can I make?"

"Mashed potatoes are easy."

Sophie nodded. She'd do her best. She glanced around and noticed they'd reached the end of the pier. She crossed to the railing and looked out over the Gulf. The waves were high. Small fishing boats bobbed in the distance. Local surfers claimed the shoreline. The sky had darkened, and only a smattering of sunbathers remained. It would soon rain.

"Shall we head back?" Mac asked once he'd finished the last bite of his bun.

She peeked at her watch. "I took over an hour for lunch."

"Get a move on." He hustled her long. "You could get fired."

"I'm volunteering, silly man."

They parted ways at Crabby Abby's General Store. "See you at five," he called after her.

The man apparently liked to eat early.

The atmosphere in Three Shirts had turned quiet on Sophie's return. She hung up her windbreaker and floppy hat, then looked in the mirror above the storeroom sink. She'd forgotten to apply sunscreen. Her nose was red.

A new shipment had arrived while she was out. Jenna unpacked, while Sophie stacked the shirts. Randy broke down the corrugated boxes, then tossed them in the Dumpster.

"How was your walk?" Jen asked, finally breaking the silence.

"I had company."

"So I noticed."

Sophie raised an eyebrow. So she was right. Jen had seen Mac through the window. "We walked the length of the pier."

"Lucky for you it was overcast and not too hot."

Clearing her throat, Sophie said, "Dune's out of town. He asked Mac to keep me company. We're cooking dinner together."

"Mac cooks?" Jen was doubtful. "He looks more like a take-out or deli man to me."

"His specialty is meat loaf."

"Hamburger in Corning Ware is easy enough."

"Want to make it a dinner party?" Sophie offered, hoping Jen would join them.

Jenna gave it some thought. "Thanks for the invite, but I'm quitting Mac. He makes me crazy."

"He's definitely an acquired taste."

"Bittersweet," Jen said beneath her breath.

Sophie heard her nonetheless. She wished for a way to

bring Mac and Jenna together. There was something between them. They only needed to talk it out.

By four o'clock, it had rained and the skies cleared.
Steam rose off the boardwalk. All browsers left the shop.
"Go home, Sophie," Jen encouraged. "Get ready for your
evening with Mac."

"It's not a date," she stressed.

"It's meat loaf." A sigh escaped from Jen. "I'd eat dirt
with the right man."

Sophie's limo driver picked her up at the corner of
Center Street and Blue Crab Way. He respectfully opened
her door and made certain she was comfortably seated. In
that moment, she wished she was riding home on the back
of Dune's Harley.

On her arrival, she found Mac camped by her front
door. He'd dressed simply. White T-shirt and jeans. A
rusty pickup truck was parked near the flower beds. She
was surprised the guard at the gate had let him pass
through, although Mac was the type to charge a barricade.

"I stopped for groceries." He collected all three bags.
"Hope you like wine. I bought a bottle of Naked Grape."

She'd learned about wine from her parents, but she seldom swirled and sipped. She preferred iced tea or club
soda with lime. She was naturally clumsy and didn't need
wine to make her tipsy.

"Cool house," Mac said when he entered. He took in
her medieval weaponry. "Highland Games are calling my
name."

She left him wielding a samurai sword and went straight
to the library to check on her Dwarf hamsters. Mac showed
up moments later. He peered into their cage. "Tiny little
shits," he said.

She rolled her eyes. "Not shits, but girls." She unlatched
their cage. "It's exercise time." She placed them both inside the clear plastic sphere.

"They have fast feet," Mac said, sidestepping the ball. He whistled and patted his thigh, expecting them to follow him like a dog down the hall. Surprisingly, they did.

Sophie brought up the rear. "They need names," she said.

"Itsy and Bitsy," he suggested.

"I don't want to minimize their size."

He set the grocery bags on the gray slate granite counter. "How about Dumbo and Jumbo?"

"They're not elephants."

"You're a hard sell, babe."

"You're not really helping me."

He unpacked the sacks. The ingredients soon stretched from one end of the counter to the other. Mac liked to spread out, Sophie noted. She bet he'd use every pan in her kitchen before the meal was served.

"You've got *Dwarf* hamsters," he emphasized. "Why not go with Dopey and Doc from *Snow White*?"

"Those are boy names."

"Like they're going to know."

"*I'd* know, Mac."

He narrowed his gaze on the hamsters. "Happy and Crappy?"

"*Crappy?*" She was offended.

"One of them had an accident."

She did a quick cleanup, then washed her hands. She crossed to his side. "How can I help?"

"Can you follow a recipe?"

How hard could it be? "Sure."

He slipped a piece of paper from his jeans pocket. "I jotted down my grandma's cookie recipe. Keep it secret."

She had no one to tell.

"I'll fix the meat loaf while the cookies bake," he said. "You can make the mashers and a salad."

He'd given her a lot to do. She located an apron along with the necessary mixing bowl, measuring cups, and spoons. Next, she selected the ingredients from the array on the counter. Her hands shook as she cracked eggs into the bowl, specks of shell included. She sloshed milk. Spilled the sugar. Whitened her hands with flour. She incorrectly measured the peanut butter.

Mac glanced her way and noted, "The batter is really thick."

She hoped the cookies would thin out when they baked.

"Don't forget to grease the cookie sheet." He'd caught her just in time. "I'll preheat the oven."

She breathed a sigh of relief once the batter was evenly divided onto the cookie sheet. She baked the cookies for twelve minutes. She noticed they hadn't flattened when she removed them from the oven. They remained doughy peanut butter balls.

Mac frowned. "Not quite like grandma used to make." He popped one in his mouth. "Chewy." He ate two more.

She managed to make a salad, which consisted of chopped lettuce and diced carrots. Her mashed potatoes were undercooked and had lumps. She set the table while the meat loaf cooked. She laid out linen and crystal. She lighted a single candle, then dimmed the lights.

Mac glanced her way. "Planning to make a move on me?"

She stood with her hands on her hips. "What do you think?"

"Love the one you're with."

She knew he was joking. He was more like a brother than a lover. "This is a special occasion," she said. "I helped cook dinner, a first for me."

He cracked open the oven door. "The meat loaf's almost done." The aroma of garlic and onion escaped along with a little smoke. She was glad Marisole kept a small fire extinguisher under the kitchen sink.

Mac opened the wine and poured himself a glass. She went with iced tea. They sat down to eat. He toasted her. "We did good, Soph."

Good, but not great, she had to admit, although the food was edible. The fact she'd taken part in the preparation delighted her the most. She went so far as to have a second piece of Mac's meat loaf, though it was burned on the top and pink in the middle. She had to admit it was nicely seasoned.

Mac ate her potatoes without complaint.

He gave her a fist bump across the table. "We'll have to do this again. Next time Dune goes out of town."

"Does he travel often?" she asked.

"He sponsors twenty sports camps throughout the country, all geared toward volleyball. The kids love when he makes an appearance. He and hot Willow—*damn*—" He cut Sophie a guilty look.

"Hot Willow?" Her stomach gave a jolt.

Mac looked uncomfortable. "Will runs the Tampa camp," he said slowly, measuring his words. "She played on the pro tour for many years. She and Dune are old friends."

Sophie set down her fork. Emotion settled in her heart. She felt vulnerable and a little jealous. Her relationship with Dune was precarious and new and not exclusive. She was living for the moment, not the future.

He was Beach Heat, handsome and popular. There'd been women long before her. There'd be women long after. The thought depressed her. She dabbed her mouth with a linen napkin.

"I'm sorry, Sophie," Mac apologized.

"Let's change topics," she suggested.

Mac agreed. His attempt to distract her worked. He ran commentary on his favorite music and video games, then told her about his childhood and family. They talked about everything but volleyball.

"I cook, but I don't clean up," he said with his second glass of wine.

She stared at their mess. "I'm not doing this alone."

"I'm too full to move."

She'd wait him out. Cooking had tired her, too.

"Where are the kids?" he asked.

She craned her neck and located the plastic ball near the refrigerator. Both hamsters were asleep. She pushed to her feet, then settled them in their cage. She rolled her shoulders, suddenly sleepy.

It had been a long day mentally. Her thoughts had lingered on Dune. She was confused and somewhat anxious. He hadn't tried to call. She was too shy to contact him.

The clank of dishes and running water brought her back to the kitchen. She found Mac at the sink, scrubbing the pots and loading the silverware, bowls, plates, and cookie sheets in the dishwasher. He left two pans to soak.

He drank more wine and she yawned. "Am I boring you?" he asked. "I'm usually the life of the party."

"We're a party of two."

He dried his hands on a dish towel and gave her a hug. "Time to fly," he said. "I'll let myself out."

Sophie headed to bed.

"Your kitchen is a mess." Maya Saunders took one step into the room and stopped. She cut her gaze to Sophie. "Did a bag of flour explode in here?"

There was flour on the counter and cupboards near the sink, Sophie noted in the light of day. Mac had cleared away the dishes, but hadn't wiped down the granite. She'd been too tired to care.

She glanced at her mother, who looked beautiful as always. Maya wore a cream skirt suit with a pale peach blouse and pearls, while Sophie had rolled out of bed in her red cotton nightshirt and baggy boy shorts. She tightened the drawstring.

Her mother was always collected and dauntingly calm, yet this morning she appeared unsettled. She narrowed her gaze and her smooth brow creased. "What's going on, Sophie?"

"I had a friend over and we cooked dinner." She explained the puffs of flour while standing over the stove, attempting to make scrambled eggs. A bit of yolk splattered and ran. She grabbed for a dishcloth and blotted it up.

"Where's Marisole?" Maya sharply asked. "Why isn't she preparing your breakfast?"

"I prefer to do it myself."

"You don't cook."

She hadn't, until last night. "A new venture for me," she said. "I might even take a cooking class."

Her mother moved toward the stove. She hit a sticky spot on the floor and what looked like peanut butter stuck to the bottom of her pumps. She shook her foot, then frowned.

"I came by to invite you to Garden Club."

Sophie cringed. Garden Club was an excuse for eating finger sandwiches and petits fours and exchanging the latest gossip. Flowers and plants were never discussed.

She passed. "I start pedicab tours this morning," she informed her mother. She'd texted Shaye late last night and been given the thumbs-up. She was set to report to the rickshaw hut at ten.

"You don't even know how to ride a bike," Maya pointed out. "You lacked balance as a child."

She was still a klutz. "The pedicabs have three wheels."

"You'll exhaust yourself."

"It's great exercise."

Her mother threw up her hands and paced the length of the counter. She was so upset, she didn't notice the specks of flour that stuck to her sleeve.

"Watch out for the hamsters," Sophie warned. The girls were in their plastic ball, racing in circles around the table.

"Rodents?" Her mother placed one hand over her heart. "We need to call an exterminator."

"They're my pets."

Her mother paled. "Where did you get them?"

"From Dune Cates."

"Shaye's brother." Maya's lips pinched. "The beach bum."

Sophie stiffened. "He's a professional volleyball player. I like him." A lot.

She so seldom stood up to her mother, Maya looked both confused and annoyed. The eggs sizzled in the skillet and Sophie turned off the burner. They looked crispy.

"How serious are you, Sophie?"

"I plan to marry him," she said perversely, speaking the first words she could think of to shock her mother.

Her mother looked faint. "Surely you wouldn't make the same mistake as Trace. Marrying a Cates is beneath you."

"A walk down the aisle?" Sophie heard a male voice say from behind her, deep and amused. *Dune.* "Will ours be a church wedding or a ceremony on the beach?"

Eleven

Sophie Saunders jerked so violently, the whisk flew out of her hand and added more splatters to the already speckled cupboards. Dune leaned against the kitchen wall, bemused by what he'd heard.

The lady had mentioned marriage.

That was the last thing he'd expected to hear when he'd loaded up his parents' Tahoe at the crack of dawn and driven down from Tampa.

He'd been anxious to see Sophie.

She'd recently rolled out of bed, he guessed, taking in her loose-fitting nightshirt and oversized shorts. Her hair was mussed. He noticed her toenails were painted purple, which made him smile.

She stood by the stove in a face-off with her mother. He figured her "marriage" comment was meant to get Maya off her back, nothing more. Sophie hadn't planned on him hearing her bold words. Her blush was cute.

"Your front door was unlocked." He pushed off the wall and crossed to her. "I didn't have to use my key," he said, conspiring with her.

"You're not living here, are you?" asked Maya, her eyes widening.

"I'm not fully moved in, but I soon will be." He met Maya's sharp gaze. "Good morning to you, too."

The older woman massaged her temple. "Dune," she said, acknowledging him with a brief nod.

The families had met, but there'd been little bonding. Time had yet to heal the rift between them. Maya had lost Trace to his sister Shaye. The thought of a second pairing obviously gave her a migraine. She stood stiff, silent, and antagonistic.

Dune curved his arm about Sophie's shoulders and gave her a reassuring squeeze. "How are the fur balls?" he asked.

She pointed down the hallway past the sliding glass doors. The plastic ball bounced off one wall and banked the other. "They exercise, sleep, and eat. Not always in that order."

"Their names?" he wanted to know.

"Still pending." She glanced at her mother. "Any thoughts?"

Naming the hamsters was beneath Maya, but she couldn't resist one final jab. She moved at the sliders and cut Sophie a hard look. "I like Good-bye and Gone."

The hamsters would stay, and Maya would get on with her day. Dune saw that something brown and sticky traveled with her. It looked like peanut butter on the heel of her right pump. Peanut butter and suede were not a good match.

He bent down and kissed Sophie's brow. "Balls to the wall before breakfast?" he asked.

"I'm strengthening my spine."

"Your mom's a workout."

She covered her face with both hands. "I didn't mean for you to hear—"

"That we're getting married?" He raised a brow.

"I used you as a buffer and I apologize for that."

"You can use me any way you like, Sophie."

He eased her around to face him fully. She lowered her hands. She was fresh-faced, flushed, and uncertain. She

hung her head. He sensed something had changed between them; something that went beyond her confrontation with her mother.

Where did her apprehension stem from? He'd been
gone only a couple days. He'd left town feeling good about
their relationship. He'd wanted her to jump into his arms,
excited to see him on his return. Instead she stood stiffly,
unable to look at him.

"I missed you," he said.

"Thank you."

Thank you? Not the comment he'd expected from her.
She was suddenly shy, polite, and distant. She appeared
afraid that he would rebuff her.

He rested both hands on her shoulders, looked down at
her and said, "I hear you and Mac made dinner last night."
His partner had left him a message on his cell phone.

"I'm learning to cook."

"Mac burns meat loaf."

"We cleaned our plates."

"I ate with Will—"

She glanced up, her eyes wide. "*Hot* Willow?"

He nodded. "That was her tag on the tour."

Sophie hesitated. "What do you call her now?"

"Willow Stacy-Grant."

Sophie blinked. "She's married?"

"To one of my biggest rivals, Dean Grant."

She seemed relieved. "You never—"

"No, I never." He understood her concern. "Who told
you about Willow?" Only his family was aware of his
youth volleyball camps and his out-of-town connections.

"Mac might have mentioned her."

Dune rubbed the back of his neck. His partner often
spoke without thinking. Mac needed a filter. While Dune
had nothing to hide, Sophie wasn't prepared to hear his
name linked to another woman. Apparently Mac hadn't

mentioned that Willow had a husband. She and Dean were happily married.

Had Sophie been jealous? he wondered. It fed his ego to think so. He lifted her chin with a finger, then brushed the edge of his thumb over her bottom lip. "I'm seeing you and only you," he told her. "Let's see where it goes."

"I like that idea."

He drew her close, only to have her pull back. She tilted her head and listened. "I don't hear the plastic ball."

A mother's instinct. Sophie was worried about her girls.

He glanced around the kitchen; there was no sign of them. She shot down the hallway toward the bedrooms, while he checked the library and living room. They were nowhere to be found.

"Dune!" She screamed his name, panic in her voice.

He hurried back to the kitchen. The sliding glass doors were shoved wide. Immediately, he saw the plastic ball floating in the deep end of the pool. The ball was rapidly filling with water.

His heart slammed when Sophie jumped in. She couldn't swim, but she was out to save her hamsters. Dune dove in right behind her. He quickly reached her. She was bobbing and instinctively treading water. She held the plastic ball over her head.

"Don't let them drown," she sputtered. The water in the ball was dangerously high. The hamsters were swimming for their lives. The slightly larger of the two climbed on the back of the smaller one, holding her down. The air pocket in the ball was a few short breaths from disappearing.

Dune grabbed Sophie under her arm and did the side-stroke until they reached the edge of the pool. He boosted her and her hamsters onto the side. He then hoisted himself up.

In frenzy, she struggled with the top of the ball. It

wouldn't twist off. He took the ball from her. The cap was definitely stuck. The hamsters had little time left. They were wet and frantic.

He took off for the kitchen. He set the ball down in the sink, jammed the stopper in the drain, then pulled a paring knife from the slotted cutlery block. Next, he inserted the tip of the knife into the leaky seal. The plastic cracked open and water spilled out.

Sophie grabbed a dish towel. Tears streamed down her cheeks as she carefully picked the Dwarfs up and patted them dry. There was nothing more pathetic than a damp hamster.

"Do you know CPR?" She choked back tears.

Dune was worried. He could perform the lifesaving procedure on humans, but he had no experience with small creatures. Fortunately, their tiny chests began heaving up and down as they took in air. "They're coming around," he noted with relief.

Sophie was beside herself. "What if they'd died?"

"They didn't," he was quick to say.

"What if they catch colds?"

"Then we'll take them to a veterinarian."

"Maybe we should take them right now as a precaution."

We, she said. He'd helped save them, and she now included him in the hamsters' care. He'd never been a "dad" to Dwarf hamsters. He rather liked the idea.

"I think they'll be fine, Sophie," he assured her. "Do you have a hair dryer?"

She nodded, then hurried down the hall and returned with one. He plugged it in and gently blew warm air on the Dwarfies. He'd never pictured himself blow-drying hamsters, yet he was doing so now. Both girls perked up. "Why don't you feed them?" he suggested.

Clutching them in the towel, Sophie took them to their

cage. She filled their bowl so high, it would take a week for them to consume all the seeds and pellets.

The ordeal buckled Sophie's knees. Her skin had air-dried, but her clothes still clung to her, wet and droopy. Apparently, she didn't care. Dropping onto the sofa, she stared at the hamsters for a long, long time. So long, Dune joined her.

Forgetting about her soggy clothes and wet hair, he drew her across his lap. She was soft and shaking. He absorbed her sigh. Her breath warmed his neck. He felt the race of her heart against his chest. He gently rubbed her back, then massaged the nape of her neck.

"My mother didn't completely close the sliding doors when she left," Sophie softly surmised. "That's how the girls escaped."

"It was an accident," Dune assured her. "They're safe now."

"I went after the hamsters and you came after me. You saved our lives." Her appreciation came with a kiss. "Thank you."

He held her close until all the tension had left her body. When she'd completely relaxed, she requested, "Teach me to swim?"

"We'll begin tonight." After her morning leap, he'd been about to suggest she drain her pool or buy a fiberglass cover until she learned to dog-paddle. Treading water didn't count. Learning freestyle swimming and the breast-stroke would benefit her greatly.

She glanced toward the wall clock designed as a medieval castle. "I'm going to be late for work."

"I can give you a ride to the T-shirt shop."

"Change of plans." She grinned, her excitement evident. "I'm headed to the rickshaw hut. I start my pedicab tours after a two-hour training session."

"Pedaling can be strenuous and hard work." He didn't

want to burst her bubble, but fact was fact. Sophie was small and her passengers would outweigh her. She'd gotten sore from riding on the back of his motorcycle. Hauling tourists up and down the boardwalk for several hours at a stretch would leave her stiff and hurting.

He could always give her a massage. He liked touching her. Intimacy appealed to him. He was good with his hands.

She slipped off his lap and he followed her back to the kitchen. Their body heat had nearly dried their clothes. His shirt had stretched out and Sophie's baggy shorts hung loose on her hips. She tightened the drawstring.

She moved to the stove and scrunched her nose. "So much for my scrambled eggs."

Her eggs were charred and stuck to the skillet.

"Cereal makes for an easy breakfast," he suggested.

"I'll pick some up later today."

"Buy Wheaties," he advised on his way out. "The breakfast of champions."

Two hours later, Dune stood on the boardwalk and took in the sights. There were a lot of people milling about for a Wednesday. Most of them carried purchases. Business was good.

He loved being home. Southwest Florida was paradise. He appreciated the clear skies and crystal blue water. A hint of a breeze broke the humidity. Seagulls screeched overhead and several pelicans toddled down the pier. The countless footprints in the sugar sand indicated the tourist trade here was alive and well.

Vacations were expensive for most folks, but the Cateses were personable and welcoming. Barefoot William came recommended as a destination of choice. No one could resist the gift shops and amusements. Children and adults alike got a thrill riding the roller coaster or carousel at midnight. A moonlit beach invited romance. Sleep came in second to the nightlife.

A tap of fingernails on his shoulder turned him to the left. A blonde in a skimpy black bikini stood beside him. The curve of her hip bumped his thigh. She smiled, he nodded, but he didn't encourage conversation. He wasn't interested in anyone but Sophie. The blonde eventually moved on.

No strings attached had been his motto for many years, yet Sophie had gotten under his skin. He'd never met anyone so sweet and kind. She was overcoming her shyness and fears. Her blushes made her special. He wanted to protect her.

Their relationship had been born of a pro/am volleyball tournament. Strange, he often felt he'd known her longer than a year. Something about her took him back to his youth. He never could pinpoint the time or place. It remained a mystery to him.

Still, she brightened his days. They were friends and would soon be lovers. They'd already had a heated encounter the night she'd pushed him into her pool. His groin tightened at the memory. The feel of her skin against his had been slick and wet. Her body had responded to his touch. Tonight he'd bring condoms.

Dune subconsciously rubbed his wrist. He and Mac had scheduled volleyball practice for one o'clock that afternoon in the high school gym. The Huntington Beach Classic was ten days away. He hated it when his joints ached before his first serve. He'd play through the pain. He'd done it before and he would do so again.

He forced himself to stay positive. Shifting his stance, he transferred the take-out container he carried from one hand to the other. He'd stopped at Molly Malone's for breakfast. Word had spread fast that Sophie was giving pedicab tours. Everyone would be on the lookout for her.

They'd cheer her on.

His aunt had put together a survival kit for Sophie packed with bottled water, an apple, a banana, and several nutrition bars, all designed to hydrate and energize her.

His relatives wanted her to be successful.

So did Dune, in whatever she chose to do.

He'd texted Shaye twice, asking if Sophie had left the rickshaw hut. He thought about being her first customer, but decided against it. He was a big man. He didn't want her expending all her energy on him. He also couldn't guarantee he could keep his hands off her. He didn't want to prove a distraction. She had a long day ahead of her.

Shaye took her sweet time messaging him back. She indicated Sophie had pedaled off a half hour ago. Barring any problems, she should've reached Dune's location by now.

He squinted down the boardwalk. There was no sign of her. Where the hell was she? The ticket booth for the pedicab tours stood beside Old Tyme Portraits. The drivers waited in the nearby parking lot for their fares. The entire excursion lasted thirty minutes, sometimes less.

He started to pace up and down. Maybe she had a flat tire. Maybe she'd worn herself out after the first block. Maybe she'd gotten an ornery tourist. Maybe—

"Are you waiting for Sophie?" Mayor James Cates asked as he approached Dune. His uncle gave him a knowing, amused look.

Dune nodded, not the least embarrassed. "She started a new venture today. I thought I'd look out for her."

"She won't be here for quite some time," James said. "I saw her earlier when I stopped by the ticket booth to thank her for taking my son under her wing. Randy's a new kid since she took an interest in him. He's even helping out around the house."

The mayor took a moment to greet several beachgoers.

He promoted the town with a good word and strong handshake. "I hung around the parking lot for a while to see how Sophie handled the tour," he went on to tell Dune. "She'd gathered quite a crowd before I left."

"What happened?" Dune had to know.

The mayor unbuttoned his suit jacket and loosened his tie. He dabbed his handkerchief to his brow. "Once Sophie was assigned her first fare, she began her tour right there in the parking lot. She didn't wait until she was halfway down the boardwalk, like so many of the drivers tend to do. She caught everyone's attention right off the bat, relaying facts about the corner shop and how it was the original store built by William Cates."

James looked at Dune. "Did you know it took three weeks to have the concrete and lumber shipped by boat from Tampa?" he asked. "The shop first opened as a fruit and vegetable stand. A few fishermen sold their catch in the back."

This was all new information to Dune.

The mayor shielded his eyes, then pointed north. "Here comes Sophie now."

Dune looked hard, but he couldn't find her in the crowd. It took several seconds for him to locate her. She pedaled slowly but steadily in the middle of a throng. An elderly lady rode in her rickshaw, while the others walked alongside her. It was eerily quiet as people listened to her every word. Everyone within earshot was getting a detailed history lesson. Dune caught the next part of Sophie's presentation as she drew nearer to where he waited for her.

"How would you like to live your life without shoes?" she asked those around her. The tourists nodded, smiled. A few raised their hands. "William Cates did just that. He was a farmer from Frostbite, Minnesota, who suffered the worst of winters. Just after the turn of the century, he sold his farm, then hand-cranked his Model T and traveled south until he reached this isolated stretch of beach. He removed his boots and walked knee-deep in the Gulf. Waves slapped his legs and the sun warmed him. He waded in the water until his face got sunburned. He immediately called Florida home. He swore never to wear shoes again."

"Never?" The woman in the rickshaw sounded skeptical.

"Only on Sundays when he and his wife Lily Doreen went to church," Sophie amended. "He noted in his journal that the moment he left God's house he immediately shucked his shoes. The soles on those oxfords never wore out. He put them on once a week for sixty years."

The tourists chuckled and Sophie smiled. The closer she got to Dune, the clearer her voice became. She was in her element and enjoying herself.

"William Cates had six children," she continued. "His hound dog Buddy was his constant companion. William went out on his fishing boat in the morning and governed the city from the one-room courthouse in the afternoon. He was the first elected mayor." She paused for effect, then said, "Twelve votes were cast. It was unanimous."

Dune took it all in. He knew so little about his ancestors. Sophie was a human history lesson.

"William was prone to late afternoon naps," she went on to say. "No one disturbed him. He rested in a hammock strung between two palms in his backyard. His wife woke him for dinner. His favorite meal was stone crab claws."

She was ten feet from Dune now. She gave him a small wave as she slowed down beside him. He noticed she wasn't huffing and puffing. She could handle the pedaling.

She didn't wear the usual driver's uniform consisting of a tan polo shirt and khaki shorts. Instead, she'd covered up with a floppy white hat, long-sleeve blouse, slacks, and tennis shoes. Sunblock whitened her nose.

"Meet Dune Cates, everyone," she said by way of an introduction to all those gathered around her. "He's a fifth generation Cates. Dune's a professional beach volleyball player, for anyone who doesn't recognize him. He's the number one seed on the circuit."

Excited murmurs flew around him as tourists took his picture. Dune smiled, then signed autographs on the back of the city tour pamphlets.

"Standing beside Dune is Mayor James Cates," she said. More cameras flashed. "In spite of tough economic times, our illustrious mayor has managed to control the town's growth and uphold William's vision."

"She's good," the mayor said to Dune, praising Sophie after she'd pedaled on.

Dune was too stunned to speak. Shy, sweet Sophie had hit her stride. She wasn't afraid of public speaking. Not by a long shot. She was a natural born tour guide.

"She's found her niche." Dune had no doubt what he said was true.

"I hope you're right," his uncle said. "I want to run something by you, Dune, if you have a few minutes."

Dune took the time. He leaned back against the blue pipe railing and listened. He was interested in what the mayor had to say.

"Dog-eared Pages, the used book store around the corner from Molly's diner, is going out of business," James began. "Clinton Cates wants to retire. I'd prefer the shop didn't stand empty long. I want to try something new. Barefoot William deserves its own museum. I'd like to offer Sophie the position of curator. She knows more about us than we know about ourselves. She'd be perfect for the job."

The idea appealed to Dune, yet there was a catch. "She's a Saunders."

"Not a problem for me or anyone else," his uncle assured him. "Everyone on the boardwalk likes her. Your sister married Sophie's brother Trace. In a roundabout way, that makes her family."

Dune nodded. This could be her dream job. He felt a surge of excitement for her.

The mayor glanced at his watch. "I need to get back to the office," he said, straightening his tie. "Run the idea by Sophie and see if she's interested. If so, have her stop by my office and we'll talk further."

His uncle departed and Dune went after Sophie. He planned to save his conversation about the mayor's proposal for later that evening. It was more important that he deliver her survival kit.

Her forty-minute tour had stretched to ninety minutes. He located her near the pier. The crowd swelled despite the heat. Sophie suffocated at its center.

Dune made his way over to her. People frowned, but let him pass. They didn't want to lose their places. Sophie wasn't nearly as wilted as he'd expected. Her blouse was slightly wrinkled and her face was flushed. She fanned herself with the floppy brim of her hat.

He opened the take-out container and passed her a bottle of water. She was grateful. He then slipped the kit under her seat.

"How are you holding up?" he asked.

She took a long sip of water before answering him. "I'm ready to head back to the rickshaw hut," she said. "I hope Shaye won't be angry." Her concern for her job was evident on her face. "I got carried away and went over the allotted time."

Dune glanced around. No one had moved. All eyes were on Sophie. "You have an appreciative audience."

She smiled. "I'm having fun."

"Are you sore?"

She rubbed her thigh. "A little." She didn't complain further. She poured a few drops of water onto her palm and blotted her face. The droplets immediately dried. "I'd better go," she told him.

She cut the front wheel sharply and made a U-turn. Fortunately, she didn't run over anyone. Dune fell in with the crowd, keeping to the rear. He wanted to hear what Sophie had to say as much as anyone.

Along the way, he learned that William's younger brother had established the first local newspaper in town. The *Sun* was printed once a week and was a one-page news sheet. William's eldest son was instrumental in the construction and extension of the First Southern Railroad. The one-rail line brought a slow stream of commerce to town. William's youngest daughter ran a bakery out of her home kitchen. She baked the best apple pies in the county.

He also discovered that his great-great-grandfather had had polio and his great-aunt had died of scarlet fever. They had no town doctor for many years. The local women applied stitches and used home remedies to treat the common cold and pneumonia.

The crowd grew bigger and Dune fell farther behind. He came across Mac outside the T-shirt shop and stopped to talk to his partner. Mac held a large soda and two corn dogs.

Something was definitely wrong, Dune thought. Mac had a cast-iron stomach and went through food as if life was an eating contest. Yet at that moment, both drink and dog went untouched. They had one hour before volleyball practice. Dune hoped he wasn't sick.

"You standing or stalking?" he asked Mac.

Mac pointed to a fissure in the foundation. "I'm holding up the wall."

"Three Shirts isn't falling down," Dune informed him. "The crack's been there for fifty years."

"I'm here in case it caves in."

Dune narrowed his gaze. "That's an interesting way to spend your morning. Is Jen aware of your Herculean strength?"

"She looked out the door and scowled at me," Mac said. "A few minutes later that boy Randy delivered a glass of *warm* tap water." Mac liked his drinks packed with ice.

Dune shook his head and smiled.

"What are you smiling about?" Mac demanded.

"The fact that we've stood here for five minutes and you haven't made one comment on women's waxing." Beautiful women strolled the boardwalk. Most wore tiny bikinis. They flashed a lot of smiles and skin.

Mac cut his glance to the next three sunbathers coming their way. "Brazilian, bikini, bikini," he said half-heartedly.

"Nice jersey, Ace-hole," one of the two bikini babes said to Mac as she passed.

Mac nodded. "It's one of my favorites."

"Mine, too," Dune stated, eyeing the familiar jersey. Mac often raided his closet when they were on tour or vacation. He'd paid a sizeable amount for the vintage 1925 Packers football jersey. He should've framed and preserved the shirt, but he enjoyed wearing it when Mac didn't confiscate it.

Mac rolled his shoulders. "I ran out of clothes."

"Ever hear of a washing machine?"

"I put out my laundry, but Frank has yet to run a load."

"You're his guest," Dune reminded him. "Be considerate of my grandfather."

"I'm family," Mac said. "Frank calls me 'son.' "

"Son of a bitch when you're out of earshot."

"I've heard that, too."

Dune glanced at his watch. "Jen or the gym?" he asked.

Mac considered his options. "Jenna hates my guts and

won't speak to me. I can work off my frustration at practice."

Dune turned serious. He seldom poked his nose into Mac's personal business, but Jen was family. "Are you into my cousin?"

"Who wants to know?"

"I'm asking, you're answering."

"True confession?" Mac asked.

"Be honest with me. I don't want to see her hurt."

"She's the one being shitty to me," Mac said.

"You bring out the worst in people."

"I'm a freakin' nice guy," he defended. "I want—"

"Someone you can't have," Dune said flatly. He went on to remind Mac, "We're leaving town shortly. My family is close. We look out for each other. Don't do something so stupid you get banned from our community."

"What do you consider stupid?"

"Don't mess with Jenna's mind."

"What if she screws with me?"

"You'd deserve it."

Mac said a bad word.

Dune motioned to him. "Enough said. Let's walk."

Mac had finished one corn dog and half his soda by the time they reached the Tahoe. He dumped the remainder of the food in a trash receptacle; then Dune drove them to the high school gym. He knew the coaches well and had reserved the facility for two hours.

Dune shouldered an athletic bag inside. He'd brought them each a change of clothes. Dressed in gray tank tops and athletic shorts, they took to the indoor court. He'd have preferred to practice on the beach, but they'd draw a crowd there. He didn't want media publicizing his injury. He slipped on his brace.

They each took a side to practice their serves. Dune

soon realized that Mac's mind wasn't on the court. Ace-hole was in his own world. His serves were unfocused, his placement sloppy. Dune needed to jar his ass back to reality.

Dune strained his wrist, but he got his message across. He aimed an overhand slam at Mac's head. Strong and accurate, it served his purpose.

"What the fuck?" Mac jumped, ducked, and was forced to chase the ball down. "I'm your partner, for Christ's sake. You nearly took off an ear. I don't want to be the Vincent van Gogh of volleyball."

"Concentrate," Dune shouted over the net. "We need to be ready for Huntington."

Mac narrowed his eyes and set his jaw. His return serve blew Dune away, landing beyond his reach.

"Nice," Dune admired.

"How's your wrist?" Mac asked. "Am I going to have to carry you in two weeks?"

Dune hoped not, but he was afraid Mac might. "Be ready for anything."

"I've got your back."

They went through a series of two-man drills. Hot and sweaty, they called it quits at the end of ninety minutes. Dune bought them each an apple juice from the vending machine. He tossed Mac a towel from his athletic bag. They sat on the bleachers and cooled off.

"I may be leaving town earlier than I planned," Dune confided in Mac. "My orthopedist called. He has a treatment for my tendonitis he wants to try, one that could strengthen my wrist."

"Solid," said Mac. "What's the procedure?"

Dune rubbed the towel across the back of his neck. "I get shots of platelet-rich plasma created by my own blood injected in the ruptured tendons."

Mac winced. "How long does it take to work?"

Dune rolled his wrist. "I'm a speed healer. I should see results within a day."

"Yeah?" Mac asked, curious.

"I should have more flexibility in my wrist and less inflammation," Dune said. "I'll stay on for observation and additional therapy. If all goes well, I'll be in top shape for the tournament."

Mac exhaled slowly. "You'd no longer face retirement. We could continue on the tour."

"That would be the best scenario."

They both knew the worst, but neither wanted to go there.

"What about Ghost?" Mac asked.

"He'll stay with my grandfather until I return. Frank could use the company."

"I'll take him for walks and give him snacks."

"No pepperoni, potato chips, or peanut butter. Otherwise—"

"He farts," Mac finished for him.

Dune cut Mac a look. "No more tricks, either. You taught him how to play dead. He lay like roadkill on our last walk. I had to carry him home. I also don't like the fact he can twist doorknobs with his mouth. He occasionally sneaks in and sleeps on the floor in Frank's bedroom. My grandfather trips over him in the morning. I don't want Frank hurt."

"No more tricks," Mac promised.

Dune knew he lied.

Mac nudged him with an elbow. "Does Sophie know about your injections?"

"Not yet, but I plan to tell her before I leave." He rubbed his brow. "She'll feel worse than I will if the treatment doesn't work."

"She cares for you."

"She's cute when she blushes."

Mac grinned one of his more annoying grins.

Dune's neck heated. "What now?" he asked.

"You're crazy about her. C'mon, admit it."

He kept his feelings to himself.

"She's going to miss you," said Mac.

"She won't even know I'm gone." Dune then told Mac about his chat with the mayor. "Sophie knows the town better than anyone. I'm sure she'll accept the challenge."

"There'll be no more adventures." Mac sounded disappointed. "I truly thought she'd make a great mime."

"I'm relieved she's out of harm's way," Dune admitted.

"You've been concerned about her."

"Yeah," Dune admitted. "Sophie's special."

Mac finished off his juice and stood up. "I'd ask her out if you weren't seeing her," he said. "I still might once you leave town."

"You're such an ass." Dune pushed to his feet, then stepped off the bleachers. "You need to fix things with Jen."

"I will eventually," Mac conceded.

"I need your A-game at Huntington."

"Don't worry. I'll bring it."

Sophie Saunders brought a pair of goggles, a nose clip, hand paddles, flippers, a snorkel, a kickboard, and a waist strap with foam blocks to her first swim lesson.

She answered the door in her blue tankini and full aquatic gear. Dune couldn't help staring. "You've been shopping," he noted.

"I got outfitted at Diver Dan's."

She'd gotten the works. He was surprised the salesclerk hadn't sold her a wet suit, air tank, and speargun. "All you need is me, Sophie."

She deflated. "Think I overdid it?"

He didn't want to hurt her feelings. "Maybe just a little," he said. "The items you purchased are for swimming in the Gulf. We'll be in the shallow end of your pool, where you can stand."

"I'm scared," she confessed.

"You jumped in twice."

"Both times without thinking."

Dune evaluated their situation. She'd been excited about her swim lesson earlier in the day, yet she'd had hours to dwell on her decision. She'd worked herself up and he needed to calm her down.

He dropped his athletic bag on the aqua marble floor and drew her close. He wanted to feel her against him. Six inches of foam block kept them apart. The lifebelt dug into his groin. He sucked air. Shifted his stance.

Despite their separation, Sophie stretched and wrapped her arms about his waist. She slapped him on the back with her hand paddles. Her flippers tromped his bare feet. Her eyes looked twice their size behind the goggles. The nose clip forced her to breathe through her mouth. She puffed air.

Dune gently set her back. "Let's strip down to the basics," he suggested. "Swimsuits only."

He helped her remove her goggles. She blinked up at him. Her expression reflected her every emotion. She was self-conscious in her swimsuit and deathly afraid of the pool. Color drained from her face. She needed reassurance.

He brushed her hair out of her eyes.

She leaned her cheek into his palm.

He kissed her lightly.

She managed a small smile.

He wanted her relaxed. He soothed her further. He skimmed his hands over her shoulders and down her arms. Her skin was as soft as living silk. "It's going to be fine, Sophie, trust me."

She nodded, and he removed her nose clip. She inhaled deeply and tried to rub her nostrils. She nearly poked her eye out with the end of a hand paddle. Dune massaged the bridge of her nose until the red marks faded.

Off came the foam block belt and paddles. He then knelt down and helped her remove the flippers. They fit her feet tightly. Her toes were pinched. He noticed she'd changed the color of her toenail polish from purple to a glossy red. He smiled to himself. She was going for sexy.

She stood before him now in only her suit. He could sense her apprehension as she fought her nerves. Dune had never been afraid of anything in his entire life. He wanted to infuse that kind of confidence into Sophie.

He took her by the hand and led her down the hallway. She dragged her feet. He caught sight of the hamsters. Sophie had purchased them a new plastic ball. They cornered the kitchen and rolled straight toward them. The girls appeared to have grown overnight.

Sophie perked up. "I named the darker of the two Scarlett," she said, "as in Scarlett O'Hara. I love *Gone with the Wind* and think Scarlett is a brave name."

Dune agreed. "She looks like a Scarlett."

"I want you to name the other."

The honor carried a huge responsibility. He gave it some thought. "How about Glinda," he said, "after the Good Witch of the North in *The Wizard of Oz*." He figured the movie would appeal to her.

And it did. "Glinda is perfect!" She seemed pleased.

The Dwarfies did a U-turn and followed them all the way to the sliding glass doors. Their little legs were churning fast. Dune and Sophie slipped out before the girls could follow them. He then secured the sliders. The hamsters reversed their direction. There'd be no repeat of the ball in the pool incident.

He drew Sophie across the pool deck to the shallow end. The night was quiet, the air calm. The inside lights reflected outward. The glow was both intimate and private.

Dune tugged on her hand, hoping she'd take the stairs down into the water alongside him. Instead, she held back. He scooped a handful of water and splashed her.

She glared at him.

He laughed at her.

"Ease up, Sophie," he teased. "The pool is as warm as bathwater."

She gripped his hand tightly. He was her lifeline. One step down and an inch of water covered her ankles. He was sure she'd hyperventilate.

"Take deep breaths," he instructed her.

Her eyes were wide. She trembled.

He continued down the stairs ahead of her. He now stood on the floor of the pool. Their clutched hands and outstretched arms connected them. He squeezed her fingers.

"I want to kiss you," he enticed her.

"Come back to the steps."

"No, you come to me."

Her expression nearly did him in. She wanted him, would do anything for him, yet fear paralyzed her.

"Three steps, Sophie," he encouraged her. "You can do this."

She blinked and a tear escaped.

He felt awful.

She probably felt worse.

Her breathing deepened as she gathered her courage. The stairs were forgotten as she took a wild leap. She landed in his arms. He collected her to him. She buried her face in his neck and her heartbeat raced against his chest. Her thighs tightened like a vise at his waist. She wasn't ready to be kissed. Her full concentration was centered on not drowning.

He ran his hands down her back and cupped her bottom. He needed to distract her. He shifted the conversation from the pool to her pedicab tours. He rested his forehead against hers and asked, "Any soreness from pedaling?"

She leaned back slightly. "Shaye limited my tours. I only did three. She mentioned buying a trolley so I could ride easily and reach more tourists."

"That's my sister, the businesswoman. She's always thinking of ways to benefit our town," he said as he eased the two of them beyond the stairs. He hoped Sophie wouldn't notice. She didn't. Not yet anyway.

"I made sixty dollars in tips," Sophie said. "I plan to give the money to the animal shelter."

"They'll appreciate every dime."

"I stopped by Three Shirts and paid Randy before I left the boardwalk. He bought his sunglasses and a T-shirt for his sister. He plans to purchase something for his father with his next paycheck."

"Speaking of his dad," Dune began. She'd given him the perfect opening to convey his conversation with the mayor. "My uncle wanted me to pass on a message." He laid out James's plans for the museum.

Sophie had loosened her death grip on him by the time he finished. She was wide-eyed and interested. "Barefoot William deserves a museum," she agreed. "I'm honored James thought of me for the curator."

"Stop by his office for the details," Dune said.

"I will tomorrow."

Water sloshed between them. She looked around. "No deeper, Dune."

Busted. He kissed her at that moment to take her mind off the depth of the water. Her breath was sweet and moist. For all her fears, Sophie liked kissing. She slipped him her tongue. Dune let her tease and taste. She took pleasure in his mouth.

He slowly broke their kiss. "Back to your swimming lesson," he said. "It's time for you to stand on your own."

"How deep are we?"

"The water will reach your chest."

She glanced down on her breasts. "I'm not feeling very buoyant."

Dune chuckled. Sophie had a quirky sense of humor. She'd begun to relax. He released her, and she slid down his body. The slide was pure torment. Every inch of her brushed and bumped and he became as hard as her kickboard. He pushed back a step.

Panic flashed in her eyes. "Don't leave me, Dune."

"I won't," he assured her. "It's time for you to bounce a little, get a feel for the water."

Her bounces were controlled. He figured most of the ripples were caused by the shakiness of her body. It was slow going, but Dune had all night. He'd stick it out until Sophie learned the basics and she could survive in the pool on her own.

She was receptive and did her best to follow his instructions. Dune credited her for all she attempted. He taught her breathing techniques and how to float. She struggled through the arm strokes and kicking and developed her own style of swimming.

He finally stood off to the side and let her go it alone. Sophie couldn't swim a straight line. She zigzagged back and forth across the shallow end. She kicked like a champion, but she had little momentum.

She wore herself out. She clung to the side of the pool, hung her head, and exhaled. "I'm tired," she said.

He'd grown weary just watching her. "Let's call it a night."

She scooted her hands along the edge toward the handrail. She was halfway there when he saw her face contort. She hunched over as if she were in pain. What had happened?

He made a mad splash through the water to reach her. "Sophie, are you okay?" He didn't wait for her to answer. He circled her waist and lifted her up onto the side of the pool. "Where does it hurt?" he asked.

"A cramp. My left calf." Her voice shook.

He ran his hands from her knee to her ankle, kneading, palming, and seeking the knot. He made several attempts to find it, but he felt nothing but her smooth skin.

"Flex your foot up, then straighten it."

She did. "It hurts." She closed her eyes, moaned.

Dune studied her. Something was off. Her moan didn't sound real. It seemed forced and robotic. What the hell? He caught her squint and knew instantly she was playing him.

He ran one hand down his face. "You got me good," was all he could say.

She bent her knee, placed her foot on his chest, and shoved. He flopped back and flailed his arms for effect. She grinned. "When you prank someone, chances are good they'll prank you back." She tossed his words back in his face.

He'd started it and she'd finished it. He'd fooled her when he'd pretended to drown, but Sweet Sophie now pulled her own practical joke. He liked this side of her. She seemed quite pleased with herself, too.

She inched toward the handrail and started up the steps. Dune caught her from behind and dragged her back into the pool. She slipped underwater. She came up sputtering. He tucked her into his body. She squirmed, then settled against his chest, her legs wrapped around his hips. He shifted his stance and she went suddenly still.

"You poked me," she said.

"No, I didn't."

Then he realized he had. Sophie turned him on and his dick was rigid. The head of his penis now bumped her sex. She was fascinated by their fit in the water. It wouldn't take much to slip off her bikini bottoms, drop his board shorts, and slip inside her.

That would be too quick.

He wanted their first time to be as close to perfect as he could make it. She deserved a lot of foreplay.

"That's just the nature of the beast," he said ruefully. "I want you, and my body gives me away."

He'd expected her to blush, but she surprised him. "I like a sure sign in a man," she said softly. "There's no mistaking your need."

He looked down on her. Her pulse quickened at the base of her throat and her nipples puckered. Female instinct rocked her hips. She was as ready for him as he was for her.

The time was now.

"Your bedroom?" he asked.

"Follow the hamster ball," she said. "I just saw their shadows pass the sliders."

Twelve

Sophie Saunders was going to have sex with Dune Cates, a man she'd been crazy about since she was seven. Her pulse raced as he lifted her out of the water and held her high against his chest. She circled his neck with her arms. Water droplets glistened on his slicked-back hair. Their wet bodies were warm and slippery.

He climbed the pool steps and carried her easily across the deck. He twisted slightly so she could open, then close, the sliding doors.

Awareness came in a look, a touch, a softly spoken word. Dune told her she was beautiful and special and that he was so stiff he could barely walk.

He made it to the front door and found his athletic bag. He scooted it along with his foot. He was over a head taller than Sophie and his shoulders were twice as wide. She rested her cheek against the solid wall of his damp chest and heard the steady beat of his heart. His forearm secured her bottom. She looked up as he glanced down. He stopped in the hallway and kissed her.

His kisses started light as air. Still, she shivered. He kissed her cheek and behind her ear, just barely teasing her. Sophie followed his lead and did what came naturally to her. She kissed his chin and neck, then flicked her tongue to the pulse point at the base of his throat. His scent hinted of chlorine, lime, and man. Clean and masculine. His groan rose from deep in his chest. A guttural, turned-on sound.

His kisses grew deeper. He was patient yet insistent. He drew her beyond what she expected or had ever known. She was naïve, but not shy. She'd grown up afraid of crowds, the Gulf, and her shadow. She'd never feared Dune Cates. And she'd never feared sex.

He was as into her as she was into him. He broadened his stance and braced his back against the wall long before they reached her bedroom. He positioned her so her legs wrapped his waist. He ran his fingers down her rib cage, at first with infinite care, then with male craving.

His hands clutched her hips and his thumbs teased her belly. He touched the sensitive back of her thighs, then stroked the crease behind each knee.

He squeezed her bottom.

Flush against him, she felt every inch of his maleness. He was stiff and substantial; a man in his prime.

She wasn't tentative. She trusted him. She touched him instinctively. She ran her hands through his hair, then drew her thumbs across his cheekbones. She traced the powerful set of his shoulders. He was all warm skin and seductive muscle. She feathered her fingers over his chest hair, scraped a nail across his abdomen. He inhaled sharply.

She tightened her thighs and melted against him.

He eventually pushed off the wall and continued down the hall. He shoved the athletic bag ahead of them with his foot. He walked slowly and they continued to kiss.

He lifted his head slightly as they neared the end of the hallway. "Your bedroom?" he asked.

"Last room on the right."

He kissed her all the way to the master suite. They slowly broke apart when they entered the room. Dune went very still as he took in the surroundings. Sophie looked at the large room as she imagined he saw it. History rose from the floor to the ceiling. It was a bit intimidating, even to a confident man.

"Damn, Sophie." He set her down and took her hand. "You're a Renaissance woman." His voice was low and amazed. "That's one massive bed."

She understood his astonishment. She was far from frivolous, but she valued a good night's sleep. She'd invested in a luxurious antique bedroom set, which included a grand four-poster of dark wood and marble overlay. Thick Corinthian columns with fluted tops stood at each end. The headboard was wide and intricately carved. The top of the board arched nearly to the ceiling. She'd chosen sconces over lamps and overhead lighting. Two sconces were attached to the headboard.

She'd made her bed with earth tones: taupe sheets and a brown satin comforter. Decorative and European sham pillows in green and gold were propped against the headboard. A plush, leather-padded bench with scroll arms banked the foot of the bed. Oriental runners covered the chocolate marble floors.

Two polished burl armoires bordered her blue brocade fainting couch along the far wall. A swinging floor mirror in a wide wooden frame was positioned near a window with eastern exposure. Sophie often laid in bed and watched the sun rise. She looked over at Dune. He was someone worth waking up beside in the morning. She hoped he would stay the night.

"Take a minute to look around," she offered. She needed to catch her breath after all their kissing.

He shook his head and turned back to her. His eyes warmed and his smile spread. "I'd rather look at you."

He fixed his gaze on her and he never looked away. Action, then reaction. He wanted to see how his touch affected her. Her emotions were easily read. She'd never been able to hide her feelings.

He bent down and lightly kissed her brow, the curve of her chin, then her breastbone. His hand found its way under her tankini top. He stroked upward and palmed her breast. She went soft inside. He rolled her nipple between his thumb and forefinger. Her heart beat faster.

His long fingers next stretched to her shoulders. The thin straps on her swimsuit gave way. The top was damp, yet loose and easy to slide. It tipped on one nipple and the point of her hip on its way down, pooling at her feet.

She stood before Dune in her bikini bottom.

She felt overly exposed.

He comforted and supported her. "You're beautiful, Sophie." His voice was as deep and strong as an embrace.

He lowered to one knee and ran his forefinger between her breasts. He bent his head, licked a nipple, and the tip puckered. She blushed when he kissed his way down the center of her body. Dampness gathered between her thighs.

"So soft, so sexy," Dune breathed against her belly.

He gently removed her swimsuit bottom. She stood naked before him. A sparkling water droplet rolled down her breast and caught on her nipple. Another one glided down to her belly. A third glistened like a diamond in her triangle of curls. Dune removed the droplets with the edge of his thumb.

Shyness dipped her head and she tried to cover herself with her hands.

He nipped her inner thigh. "No hiding, Sophie."

Her hands fell to her sides. "I want to see you, too," she said.

He pushed to his feet and let her take over.

They communicated through their chemistry. He was hot for her and she felt lit up from the inside out. She'd waited her entire life for him to find her and make love to her.

Touching Dune seemed right somehow. She wasn't tentative or clumsy. She was straightforward and curious as she explored his big body.

She loved the texture of his skin; the underlying flex of his muscles. She rose on tiptoe to bite his shoulder, then tongue his male nipples. She fanned her hands over his abdomen. Her fingers shook as she removed his board shorts. She stared at him then. She couldn't help herself. Sculpted and symmetrical, he stood tall and firm; magnificent in her eyes and larger than life.

She caught her breath and gave his erection the attention it deserved. She held him with great care. She stroked and his hips rocked. His penis heated between her palms. His low groan pleased her.

Sophie knew her limitations. She could never be a temptress; never hold sexual power over any man. But she would give her last breath to satisfy Dune. She wanted him that badly. She felt sexy and a little reckless with this man.

She could no longer show restraint or hold back her increasing urges. Neither could he.

Dune tossed his athletic bag toward the bed, then took her in his arms. He walked her across the floor until her calves bumped the wooden sidebar. He guided her down until she lay on her back. He settled beside her.

His mouth sealed with hers, again and again. His teeth teased her lower lip. Her eyelids fluttered closed. His kiss was sensual and molten, stirring her soul and heightening her arousal.

He made her feel special.

His hand slid down the length of her body. His long fingers stretched and searched, his palm pressing hotly into her abdomen. He stroked her wetness, then inserted the tip of one finger. She tensed until his knuckle hit a spot that made her moan. She lifted her hips instinctively, a wave of intense pleasure reaching deep down inside her.

Aroused and anxious, she clutched his bare shoulders, needing stability. The hair on her nape and on her arms tingled as if she were about to be struck by lightening.

"Let me know if I'm hurting you." His voice was strained. Hesitation creased his brow. The corners of his eyes and mouth were drawn with concern.

"You won't," she breathed against his mouth

Her words relaxed him. He managed to exhale.

He left her for only a moment, rolling over and scoring a condom from his sports bag. Once sheathed, he covered her with his body. He entwined their fingers and drew her arms over her head. Her entire body seemed stretched. Her breasts rose firm and high and her stomach flattened. Her hips came slightly off the mattress.

He appreciated her nudity. His gaze seared her.

He parted her with his knee and eased into her with one slow stroke. A heartbeat of pain made her stiffen; then it was over. Her body accepted him.

He pulsed inside her.

Her stomach quivered.

Dune went perfectly still. She sensed he wouldn't continue without a sign from her. A sigh of longing broke on her lips. She was completely his.

His eyes dilated and his nostrils flared. "It only gets better," he breathed near her ear.

The best came with a shift of his hips. He rocked gently, thrust slowly. He soon found a rhythm she could accept.

She inched toward an elusive sensation; an emotion that would fulfill her. Her heart warmed and her soul soared. She now understood what it meant to crave a man with her entire being.

Any loneliness she'd felt in her life disappeared. As if it never existed. She belonged to him.

She was close to coming and so was he.

Sharp pants of pleasure escaped her lips.

Dune's own breathing was ragged and rose from his gut.

She surrendered.

And his control broke.

Color flushed in her cheeks and she cried out, a sound that came from her core.

The very air around them seemed to explode.

A hard, racking shudder convulsed her.

One last stroke and Dune gave himself up to his climax. He followed her to the end.

Spent, he collapsed on his side and held himself up on one elbow. He drew her to face him. Their heartbeats slowed. She felt in sync with him.

He stared down on her, gently brushing strands of damp hair off her face and neck. "Are you okay?" he asked.

"Never been better," she said, honestly.

Her words seemed to please him. One corner of his mouth curved. "We have great chemistry together."

"Isn't sex the same for you every time?" she had to ask. Dune was experienced. He'd been with other women. She needed a basis for comparison.

He cupped her chin, stroked her cheek. "I'll quote Mac," he said. " 'Sometimes it's good, other times it's bad. A few nights you wish you'd just stayed home.' "

"I'm satisfied." She kissed his palm.

"You wore me out, woman." He rose, then walked into the master bath and disposed of his condom. "Shower, Sophie?" he asked from the doorway.

She nodded. The warm water would soothe her soreness. She'd had an active day between the pedicab tours, her swim, and sex with Dune. Of the three, making love had strained her muscles the most and left her tender.

Bold in her nakedness, Sophie crossed to him. He drew her into the shower and tucked her close. He set the spray on hot and pulsing. He poured her Sweet Pea shower gel onto his palm and told her to relax.

Sophie leaned back against the tiles and smiled to herself. There was something to be said for a man with soapy hands who knew his way around a soft-bristle, long-handled bath brush.

Spectacular and orgasmic came to mind.

She was appreciative.

Seven-thirty a.m. and Sophie Saunders contemplated sex etiquette. The morning after seemed a bit awkward. Did she make Dune coffee? Fix him breakfast? Offer him privacy? This was all new to her.

She lay naked, sprawled across him, her breasts bared, her bottom covered only by a sheet. A slight turn of her head and she noticed how the satin caressed her ass. She blushed, remembering how Dune had cupped her bottom when she'd knelt astride his hips, cowgirl-style. She liked feeling in control. She'd held the power twice last night.

She wondered if she was able to walk. Sex with Dune was both thrilling and strenuous. Her lower body ached as if she'd exercised for a solid month.

She'd gotten up several times during the night, needing to stretch and move around. She'd returned the hamsters to their cage, then later risen to comb her hair and brush her teeth. Afterward, she'd walked around her bedroom in hopes of relieving her soreness. She felt bow-legged.

She wasn't used to having a man in her bed, especially someone as big as Dune. While they fit together perfectly during lovemaking, they'd compromised in sleep. She smiled over their differences.

She liked fluffy pillows stacked behind her head, while he preferred only one, and a flat one at that.

He slept best with the room temperature below seventy; she liked it above.

She preferred the comforter pulled up to her chin. He wanted nothing on him, not even a sheet.

Classical music put her to sleep. She'd put Arthur Rubinstein's Chopin Nocturnes into her DVD and closed her eyes. Dune turned it off the moment he thought she was asleep. Sneaky man.

She could live without her music.

She couldn't live without the man.

His arms now wrapped her waist, securing her to him. His body radiated heat. He was far warmer than a blanket. She shifted slightly and encountered his erection. Morning sex would be amazing, she thought, just not at that moment. She hurt too much. If she had sex again, she would need a walker or a cane to get around today.

She cautiously wiggled her toes and tried to straighten her legs. Her first pedicab tour was at ten. She planned to stop by the mayor's office later that afternoon. She was very interested in the curator position.

She didn't know Dune's schedule. He continued to sleep, which gave her the opportunity to study him. She held her breath, then lifted herself up on one elbow, afraid she would waken him. Her heart squeezed in appreciation of his male beauty. She understood why women mobbed him. The tag Beach Heat served him well. He was one hot volleyball player.

His blond hair was now mussed, his brow smooth. His eyelashes were light brown. He had a small scar at the corner of his left eye. She lightly traced it with the tip of one finger, then went on to cup his jaw. His morning scruff appealed to her. She didn't care if he ever shaved again.

She found a second scar just under his chin. She softly kissed it. She then admired his suntanned shoulders and the strength of his chest. His upper arms were ripped. His abdomen was defined. She wanted to look lower, to peek beneath the sheet, but she knew her movement would disturb him.

He surprised her by clearing his throat and saying, "The scar by my eye happened when my brother Zane hit me with a rock. Scar under my chin was caused by Shaye. She took karate and kicked me."

Sophie tried not to laugh, but she couldn't help herself. "Your family is dangerous."

"We took each other down as kids, but as adults we're united. Barefoot William means everything to us."

"Your town means a lot to me, too," she said.

"We're glad you're a part of it."

That was good to hear. She never wanted to impose on anyone, but she felt comfortable with the Cateses.

"Today will be a busy day on the beach," she said. "A number of activities are scheduled for the tourists: stand-up paddleboard racing, sandcastle building, and kite flying."

"It's fun to watch the action from the boardwalk if you're not participating," he told her. "The unicyclists will be performing as well as the stilt walkers."

She sighed. "I wanted to ride with the uni-troupe."

"Backward?" he teased.

"I could've turned myself around."

"Trust me, you're better off at the museum. It's safer. I want you protected."

His concern pleased her. "I'm looking forward to speaking with the mayor."

"You want me to join you for moral support?" he asked. "I could meet you on the boardwalk and drive you to the courthouse."

"That works for me," she agreed.

"Mac and I have volleyball practice at eleven. I should be done by three. I'll meet you near the rickshaw hut."

Dune shifted on the bed then. He pushed back against the headboard and sat up. He eased her across his groin.

She winced and he worried.

"You're sore," he said, reading her expression. "I'm sorry, Sophie."

"I'll be fine," she assured him.

He held up his hands, wide palms and long fingers. "I give a good massage," he said with a smile.

She lay on her stomach and let him work his magic. His hands were therapeutic. There was nothing sexual in his strokes, only healing. He kneaded the kinks from her neck to her toes. Her body went liquid under his touch.

He gave her a forty-minute rubdown. "Better?" he asked.

"Between you and an aspirin, I'll recover."

He stroked a finger down her spine, his gaze hot on her bare skin. "More sex means less soreness. You'll get used to me."

She rose on her knees. "You'll prove your theory to me later?"

He trailed a finger down her cheek and his gaze roamed over her appreciatively. "I'll give you lots of proof."

She hesitated, uncertain. "What's the best way to start our day?"

"You cook a gourmet breakfast and serve me in bed."

She went wide eyed until one corner of his mouth twitched. She poked him in the chest. "It's toast and coffee."

She slid off the bed and went in search of her bathrobe. She found it on a hanger behind her bathroom door. She secured the tie, then backed into Dune as he came in. He wore black boxer briefs and carried a shaving kit. He walked a little stiffly himself; the bulge in his briefs was evident. She couldn't help but do a double take at the sight of his muscular chest. She loved his strength and size.

He looked down on her and blocked her from leaving.

He was suddenly serious. "My stubble scraped your chin. I'll shave more often when we're together."

She didn't mind. The raspberry marks would fade with her face cream. "I'm going to feed the hamsters first, then I'll fix your toast," she told him.

"Glinda and Scarlett come before me?"

"Priorities." She grinned. "They're little and helpless and you're self-sufficient."

He swatted her on the bottom before she left.

Seeds and thin slices of apple went to the Dwarfs. The hamsters scurried around in excitement.

She returned to the kitchen and started the coffee. Breakfast for Dune soon grew into a tall stack of burned toast.

"I'm not that hungry, Sophie," he said when he entered the kitchen. He'd taken a shower and his hair was finger-combed. He wore a *Spike It* white T-shirt and khaki shorts. He was barefoot.

"I was going for the perfect piece of toast," she said over her shoulder.

"You've gone through an entire loaf."

"I'll get it right yet."

He came to stand behind her. His arms curved around her waist and he pulled her back against him. He kissed the top of her head. "You're wasting bread."

He stepped to the side and tossed the bread wrapper into the trash can. He looked the stack over and selected two slices from the middle. The least burned of the bunch. "Butter?" he asked.

"In the refrigerator," she said.

Dune swung open the door. He chose peanut butter and jelly, too. He took out a pitcher of orange juice, then set the table for her. He moved around the kitchen without difficulty, as if he'd lived with her forever.

In those moments, Sophie realized how easily he fit into her life. She was shy where he was secure. Somehow his assuredness was rubbing off on her. She was slowly coming into her own. She liked the new, emerging Sophie. Liked her a lot.

They'd just settled at the table when her mother arrived. She knocked on the glass, then shoved back the sliders as though the house belonged to her and not to Sophie.

Maya's timing couldn't have been worse. The sight of Dune and her daughter having breakfast together stopped her mother cold. Maya was impeccably attired, as always, in a charcoal gray suit and matching pumps.

Her outfit was the exact color of Scarlett's fur, Sophie thought.

Maya's face pinched. "I see you have a visitor."

"Sophie invited me to breakfast," Dune said. "I just arrived."

Sophie was grateful for his white lie.

Maya looked skeptical. After all, Dune had blurted out that he was moving in with Sophie, though Sophie doubted her mother had believed him. This was different.

There was no mistaking Sophie's tousled hair. Whisker burn marred her chin. The tie on her robe had loosened and the top and bottom satin panels lay open, exposing her cleavage and thighs. She quickly covered herself.

Dead silence was followed by a long-suffering sigh from her mother. "Be sure to make your bed," she said.

Maya still told her what to do. Sophie felt like she was five years old again.

"What can I do for you, Mother?" she asked.

Maya stood stiffly. "I asked you a month ago what you wanted for your birthday and you never responded," she said. "Your birthday is on Saturday. What have you decided?"

Dune nudged her, then suggested, "How about a pool party?"

Maya shook her head. "Sophie's afraid of water. She doesn't swim."

"I do now," Sophie said. "Dune taught me."

Her mother surprised her. Instead of a caustic remark, her face relaxed. She nodded. "How nice of him. Your grandmother always hoped you'd learn. She tried to teach you, but you cried so hard you vomited in the pool."

Dune poked her. "You puked?"

The memory had stuck with Sophie. "I was six and I'd just eaten breakfast. Waffles and maple syrup. It wasn't a pretty sight."

Dune rubbed her back. "You were a kid. You got scared. No big deal. A nervous stomach can be nasty. I've seen professional volleyball players let nerves get the better of them before a tournament. It happens."

He was kind, Sophie thought, always building her up and never tearing her down. She was grateful. "A small party might be nice," she said. She had a few friends now. She could invite Shaye and Trace, Mac and Jenna, as well as the women from her volleyball team.

Her mother frowned. "You're not a good hostess," she stated flatly. "You're too shy. People don't want to attend a party where the birthday girl stands in the corner."

"I think she's outgrown the corner," said Dune. "I've recently seen Sophie as the center of attention."

Maya raised an eyebrow in disbelief.

Sophie blinked. "When was that?" she asked him.

Dune smiled down on her. "When you spoke to the mayor at the Sneaker Ball, and later when you gave the pedicab tours. You had a captive audience."

He was right. People had flocked around her. They'd listened to what she had to say. She'd been interesting and entertaining.

"We'll throw a party here poolside late Saturday afternoon," Sophie decided with confidence. "Works for me."

Her mother huffed. "That doesn't give Marisole enough time to plan a menu."

"I won't need Mari," Sophie said. "I can fix hamburgers, hot dogs, potato salad—"

"Let's make it potluck," Dune offered. "Less work for the birthday girl. Everyone will bring a dish."

Maya was stunned. "You're asking guests to bring their own food?"

"That's how it's done in Barefoot William," said Dune.

"But this is Saunders Shores," her mother argued.

"You're welcome to join us." Dune was polite, but firm. "Can I put you down for a container of coleslaw? Or corn on the cob? Better yet, a cake?"

Maya looked at him as if he'd lost his mind. She moved to the sliding glass doors, keeping her back to them. "Your gift, Sophie?" she pressed without turning around.

Sophie's throat tightened. "Come to my party, Mother."

Maya didn't miss a beat. "Your father and I have plans for Saturday," she said without remorse. "He's playing in a charity golf tournament at Royal Palm Country Club. I'll be joining him afterward for dinner, drinks, and the silent auction. It's an all-day event and will run quite late."

Disappointing yet typical, Sophie thought. Her parents so seldom came around, especially when she needed them most. This was her birthday. She'd reached a quarter century, a personal milestone with so few memories of doing things as a family. She tried not to let the hurt show on her face. She would celebrate with her friends, thanks to Dune.

Her mother tapped her fingernails on the glass slider. She appeared anxious to leave. "I'll have a present selected and delivered to you," she said, then slipped out.

Sophie's heart sank.

Dune tried to lighten her mood. "At least she's picking out your gift. That's something to celebrate."

"My mother doesn't run errands." She knew that for a fact. "Her personal shopper will pick up the phone and call a trendy boutique. A dress will be delivered, probably tea length and in basic black. The dress will hang in my armoire beside the dozen other dresses she's sent to me over the years."

Dune took a bite of cold toast, then followed it with a sip of lukewarm coffee. Sophie admired his willingness to work through the breakfast she'd prepared for him.

"We'll find an occasion to wear this year's dress," he said. "I'm good for a fancy dinner."

"And dancing?"

"Have you improved since the Sneaker Ball?"

She'd stepped all over his feet when they'd slow danced. "We'll only dance fast."

"I'll suffer the bruises," he said. "Holding you close is better."

He stretched his arms over his head, then rolled his shoulders. "I'll talk with Shaye before volleyball practice," he said. "We'll put your party together."

Her heart warmed. It had been years since anyone threw her a party. Her mother had given up on her by her ninth birthday. She was still a kid at heart.

Dune glanced at the stove clock. "It's after nine," he said. "Mac and I have volleyball practice and you need to get to work."

Sophie scooted off her chair. "I'd hate to be late and have Shaye fire me."

"She'll never fire you," he guaranteed. "You're her top driver."

"You're planning a party for Sophie?" Mac James asked Dune. They stood side by side before the volleyball net, practicing drills. "You've missed your calling, dude. I could see you as a party planner. This could be a second career for you when you retire."

Dune cut him a look. "You're not invited."

"Bullshit." Mac set the ball and Dune spiked it. "I'll be there." He paused. "You can put me in charge of fun and games."

"Shaye suggested pool volleyball."

"Cool. We can have chicken fights, too," said Mac. "I call Sophie as my partner."

Dune tossed up the volleyball and made Mac dive for it. "She's not sitting on your shoulders."

Mac recovered the ball and set up the next play. Dune slammed it to the far right corner, just inside the line. Mac grinned.

"What are you smiling about?" asked Dune.

"You know why."

" 'Cause my game's so good?"

" 'Cause Sophie's so good for you."

She was good for him, Dune silently agreed. "I'm inviting Jen," he forewarned Mac. "No bickering."

"No guarantees."

"Have you been by her shop?"

Mac shook his head. "Not for two days now."

"Are you hoping she'll miss you?"

"I'm keeping her guessing."

"Don't keep her guessing too long. I've told her she can bring a date."

Mac powered the ball into Dune's chest. "What the fuck?"

Dune had provoked and gotten a reaction. Mac needed to wake up. Being in limbo distracted him and made him crazy. He needed to straighten things out with Jen or move on. "You can bring a date, too, if you like."

"I don't like," Mac said irritably.

A mad Mac made for a strong practice session. His partner took out his frustration on the ball. Mac slammed it so hard, Dune waited for it to deflate.

Four hours passed and they called it a day.

"I'm meeting Sophie shortly," Dune said. "We're headed to city hall to see the mayor, then stopping by the shop he's designated for the museum."

"Togetherness, how sweet."

"Get a life," Dune said as he headed to take a shower.

Dune caught up with Sophie at the northern end of the boardwalk near the rickshaw hut. She leaned against the blue pipe railing, looking out on the beach. She wore her floppy hat and body-covering clothes. She still avoided the sun.

His shadow fell over her, stretching long. She smiled at him over her shoulder. "Hello, Dune." He liked the way she said his name.

His stance widened as he drew her back against him. Her shoulders pressed against his chest. Her bottom settled against his groin. He bent and kissed her neck. Her blush rose. He kissed her again, enjoying the pink in her cheeks.

"The stand-up paddleboard race is about to start," she told him.

Dune checked out the beach. A hundred participants stood ready, their boards held over their heads. Single paddles were raised, carried alongside the boards. Everyone wore personal flotation devices. Life preservers ranged in color from hot orange to bright pink. The foam waist straps were basic beige.

Lifeguards patrolled the beach. Two manned speedboats waited nearby, ready to help if needed.

Dune knew many of the competitors. Some were

novices; others were veterans. The water was so warm, T-shirts and shorts or swimsuits were worn instead of wet suits.

They listened as the starter's voice echoed through a megaphone: three, two, one, go! There was a mad dash for the water. The majority of the paddleboarders mounted their boards with ease. Several beginners knelt, tipped, and lost their balance. They scrambled to recover their paddles.

Sophie pointed to a young girl, a preteen, in a one-piece swimsuit and arm floaters. "She's having trouble getting into position," she worried. "Someone needs to help her."

"She'll be disqualified if anyone assists her," he said.

The girl fell off her board ten times before she centered her feet between the rails. She managed to keep her knees bent and her back straight. Her strokes were short and alongside the board. She was finally headed in the right direction.

"The course is a figure eight," Dune said. "There will be rough water at the middle crossover point as participants enter and exit. A competitor is eliminated if he touches another board with his paddle."

"The girl is last." Her concern grew. "Do you think she can catch the others?"

"She has a lot of water to make up." Nearly half a mile, Dune figured.

Sophie crossed her fingers. "Last place is fine, as long as she finishes."

The lead athlete paddled with a precise, sure stroke. He appeared to skim the Gulf. He was soon headed back to the beach. A crowd had gathered and people cheered him on. It seemed every participant had a friend waiting.

One of the lifeguards passed out trophies for first through tenth place. The beach started to thin out by the time the last of the competitors hopped off their boards. The young girl stalled yards offshore, visibly struggling.

Sophie looked up at Dune. "She deserves a prize for perseverance. We must encourage her."

We. Again Sophie included him in her life. He found he liked that more and more. "How about giving her paddleboard lessons?" he suggested.

Her smile broke. "Perfect," she agreed.

He took her hand. "The Chamber of Commerce sells gift cards for all the boardwalk shops and fishing excursions. Visitors can also get certificates for surfing, snorkeling, and paddleboard classes, all taught by the local lifeguards."

The city building was four doors down. They walked fast. Once inside, he reached for his wallet, only to have Sophie put her hand over his. "I want to do this for her."

She reached into her pants pocket and pulled out a handful of bills. "More pedicab tips going to a good cause," she said. She counted out fifty dollars. "Paddleboard lessons," she told the clerk behind the counter.

"Good for five hours." The woman quickly processed the certificate and stuck it in a gift envelope.

Sophie thanked her and they took off again. Dune watched her, amazed once more by her generosity. Sophie had a big heart and was about to perform a random act of kindness. He admired her greatly.

She reminded him of his sister Shaye. Shaye owned Goody Gumdrops and was always handing out free bags of penny candy to kids with little money. She felt everyone deserved a treat.

Side by side they took the stairs down to the beach. The finish line was nearly deserted now. The girl was still a good distance from the shore. She appeared tired, Dune thought. Her shoulders were slumped and her board wobbled. He hoped she didn't fall off before she made it back to the beach. He was certain Sophie would dive in and try to save her.

Dune stood back as Sophie approached the lifeguard who handed out the trophies. Her voice rose softly over the slap of the surf. "Be sure the girl on the paddleboard gets this certificate," she said. "She doesn't need to know the gift is from me. Tell her that she may be the last to finish today, but she'll be the first tomorrow."

The lifeguard nodded. "Got it. Thanks, will do."

Sophie returned to Dune. "Can we stay and see her finish?" she asked.

"I'd say she deserves a round of applause."

They both clapped loudly when the girl came ashore. She dragged her board and paddle and staggered up to the lifeguard. She dipped her head and smiled when he patted her on the back and praised her with, "Way to go!" He presented her with the gift certificate.

"We can go now," Sophie whispered.

"You don't want to see her open the envelope?" Dune asked.

Sophie put her hand over her heart. "I feel her excitement. That's all I need."

Dune curved his arm over her shoulders. "You're a good person, Sophie Saunders." She would be a nurturing, compassionate mother, he realized. She drew his thoughts to family and settling down.

She jarred him a moment later when she said, "I might enter the paddleboard competition next year. I could take lessons, too. What do you think?"

"You'd need to strengthen your arms, practice balance, and become a stronger swimmer," he said, being honest with her. "Then you'd be fine."

"Thanks, Dune."

"For what?"

"For understanding my need for adventure."

He would always worry about her, but Sophie had been confined for too long. She needed to feel free. He hoped many of her experiences would include him.

They returned to the boardwalk, where the unicycle troupe was gathering to perform. His cousin Rick was already mounted and doing tricks. Rick circled Sophie on his "giraffe," riding forward then backward, and finally bouncing on one tire.

"You're amazing," she called to him.

Rick saluted her, then motioned to the troupe. They rolled on, riding single file down the boardwalk.

Sophie turned to Dune. "Can we walk for a few minutes? I'd like to see the sandcastle building and kite flying contest."

Dune obliged. He kept her close as they worked their way through the crowd. Everyone was enjoying the hot day. Florida residents recognized a change in seasons. Today truly felt like summer to him. The sun refused to hide behind the clouds and what little breeze there was tickled the back of his neck.

People viewed the sandcastle contest from both the boardwalk and beach. Each entry was roped off. A couple scooted over and Dune and Sophie squeezed in along the railing. Sophie took off her floppy hat and fanned herself.

Dune bent down and blew in her ear.

"You're not cooling me off." She swatted him with her hat.

He was feeling the heat himself. She was so close they continued to touch. Each brush of her body forced him to shift his stance and make a discreet adjustment.

"Look at that medieval castle and moat." She pointed left. "That giant sand crab is true-to-life. The pincers look real."

"I like the sailboat." He squinted down the beach. "Someone's attempting to build the Empire State Building."

"The mermaid is cool, too," she added. "But the Most Original Award should go to those two boys closest to the pier. They've constructed a person buried in the sand."

"What would you like to build, Sophie?" he asked, curious.

She pursed her lips. "Moby-Dick."

"That's a very big whale. He'd take a lot of sand."

She nudged him with her elbow. "I'd enlist helpers."

He'd gladly take part.

She sighed. "It's a shame the sand creations aren't permanent. They'd make amazing beach art."

"Wind, rain, and high tide will take them down," he said, "along with some human destroyers."

She looked at the sky and Dune followed her gaze. Several kites flew in the distance. Enthusiasts ran along the shoreline, slowly releasing the tethers. There was no wind, and as many kites came down as stayed up.

Sophie patted her cheeks. She was slightly sunburned. "I'm ready to see the mayor," she said.

They drove to James Cates's office. Dune's uncle welcomed Sophie with open arms. Dune liked the fact his family embraced her. She'd slipped into their lives with a shy smile and a big heart.

The mayor offered them coffee or a cold drink. Sophie went with iced coffee and Dune chose bottled water. Once they were comfortably seated, James laid out his vision for the town museum. He then asked Sophie for her thoughts and suggestions.

She didn't hesitate; she spoke with foresight and enthusiasm. James was impressed. Dune was amazed. Sophie was definitely in her element.

The mayor told Sophie that Kai Cates would be her

contractor. Dune liked Kai. His cousin was an amazing carpenter. He'd get the museum in shape in no time.

James then asked if Sophie was familiar with a fiscal budget. She shook her head. He went on to assign her an office assistant to guide her through the process, which she readily accepted.

The curator position was officially hers by the end of their conversation. The mayor gave her a set of keys so she could check out the store. Sophie could barely contain her excitement. Her smile was broad, and her steps were light, fast, and fluid. Dune loved seeing her happy.

Twenty minutes later, he found a parking space near the empty shop. He parallel parked the Tahoe. He felt Sophie's eyes on him. He turned and raised a brow. "Is something on your mind?"

She rested her hand on the dashboard, pensive yet determined. "I want to learn how to drive," she said. "I don't want to depend on other people for my transportation."

"No one minds driving you places," he assured her.

She pursed her lips. "I mind. Roger chauffeurs me to the boardwalk and Shaye takes me home after volleyball practice. I no longer want to be an imposition."

"Roger is employed by your family and Shaye values your time together," he said. "People like doing things for you. You're sweet and appreciative."

"Nevertheless, it's time," she stated. "I've thought about buying a car. I like the TV commercial for Nash's New and Used Cars. The man looks honest."

Dune could debate Hal Nash's honesty with her, but he kept his comments to himself. He'd steer Sophie to the right car when the time came. "We can check out the dealership once you get your license," he agreed, "maybe other car lots, too."

They stepped from the Tahoe and crossed the street. The windows of the shop were dirty, making it difficult to see inside. Sophie put the key in the door and they entered. The scent of leather, paper, and a hint of amber incense hung on the air. Dust bunnies clung to the corners. A few yellowed paperbacks were left on the floor. Clinton Cates was not a tidy man. The two connecting rooms and small office needed a good scrubbing, followed by a coat of fresh paint.

Sophie took it all in. "It's fabulous," she said with a sigh.

"The store requires cleaning," said Dune. "You can hire—"

She stopped him. "No," she said. "I want to do everything myself."

"Have you ever scoured walls and scrubbed floors?" he gently asked. "This place needs elbow grease."

"I'll manage." She sounded positive. "The prospect of opening a museum so near the boardwalk will draw people. I'll have lots of volunteers."

He hoped so. He tucked her close to him. "I'm leaving town right after your birthday," he said. He went on to explain the medical procedure he would undergo prior to his participation in the Huntington Beach Classic.

"These injections could cure your tendonitis?" She was hopeful.

"Maybe, maybe not," he said honestly. "It's a procedure I have to try."

"I know it will work."

He wished he was half as optimistic as Sophie. He tightened his hold on her. "I don't want you to feel alone while I'm gone."

She looked up at him. Her gaze was as soft as her smile. "Never alone, never again. I have a lot of friends."

They stood in the middle of the room and kissed for a very long time, until the front door opened and closed with a loud bang.

Mac James made his presence known. "Get a room," he grunted.

"Get lost," Dune growled.

Sophie was kinder. She slipped from Dune's arms and went over to hug his partner. She swung her arms wide and spun around in a slow circle. "You've caught the 'before.' " She used air quotes. "The 'after' will astonish you."

"I'm sure it will," said Mac. "You've got powers, Sophie Saunders."

"I use my powers only for good."

"Damn, you're cute." Mac chucked her on the chin. "Run away with me."

"I'm not a good runner," she said.

"She's running nowhere with you," Dune said. He nodded toward the door. "You were headed where?"

Mac took the hint. "To Crabby Abby's, Dairy Godmother, and Three Shirts to the Wind." He held up the small rectangular box he was carrying. "I'm giving Jen the painting of the antique rocking chair."

"She'll love it," said Sophie.

"Go for it, dude," Dune encouraged.

"There are no guarantees this will work," Mac said.

"Play it from all angles," Dune said. "It's overtime and you're going for match point."

Thirteen

"Play it from all angles." Mac repeated Dune's advice as he entered the T-shirt shop. Match point. His heart gave a significant kick. He felt like he was going into overtime.

He hated overtime.

There were no customers in the store. Everyone was on the boardwalk and beach. The sandcastle and kite flying contests would end at five. Judging followed, and then trophies would be awarded. Mac hoped the twenty-foot sea serpent took first place. It was a legendary beast and a scary sight to kids. Children took their parents' hands when they skirted the monster's humped body and tall, arched neck.

He glanced at his watch. Where the hell was Jen?

"Jenna's in the back," Randy told him after Mac had stood at the front counter for five whole minutes.

Randy was sweeping up the shop. He had a smirk on his face, as if he'd planned to make Mac suffer. Sneaky little shit.

Mac wondered if he looked as foolish as he felt.

The boy and his broom were headed Mac's way. Mac was certain Jen had told her employees that he wasn't welcome. Randy didn't look the least bit happy to see him. The last thing he wanted was to argue with the kid.

Mac rounded a rack of shirts and walked toward the back. He kept one eye on Randy. The kid's reflection was visible in the two big mirrors on the wall.

"Workers only in the storeroom," Randy called after him.

Screw that rule.

Mac jerked open the door and walked in. He found Jenna leaning over and shoulder-deep in a cardboard box. Her butt was up in the air. Her sexy bottom was small, tight, and encased in a pair of skinny jeans. Mac recognized the denim by its texture. He wasn't certain what color her top was.

He'd always favored statuesque women with slim hips and model-long legs. His attraction to Jen was a fluke. He had no sane reason to pursue her, yet whenever they were together he found himself distracted by her no matter who else was in the room.

He tried not to look at her, but he was aware of her every move out of the corner of his eye. He continually thought about what it would be like with her when they eventually made love.

Sex with Jen was a given.

The only question was the time and place.

She was driving him nuts now. Leaning over the edge of the big box, she wiggled her ass in the air as she stretched downward. Her full concentration was on the contents. She'd yet to come up for air or notice him.

Her butt cheeks became a prime target.

Mac slapped her on the ass.

The *pop* sounded loud in the room.

She rose with such force that she stumbled backward and right into him. He caught her shoulders and steadied her. She turned on him, her lips parted, her eyes wide. She held a sharp box cutter in her left hand.

He didn't trust her.

He stepped back.

Her face was red, flushed and hot as much from hanging upside down as from her embarrassment. Her *All Stressed Out and No One to Choke* T-shirt was untucked and wrinkled. She looked ready to kill him.

"What part of 'stay away from my shop' didn't you understand?" she hissed.

He held up his hands. "I'm a guy who lives dangerously."

Randy took that moment to poke his head in the door. "Everything okay, Jen?" he asked.

Mac expected her to tell the boy to call the police. She surprised him by saying, "I'm fine. Thanks for checking."

"I'll leave the door cracked," Randy offered, then wandered off.

Mac figured the boy would stay within earshot. He appeared protective of Jen. Mac clutched her gift behind his back. "I stopped to see if you were still mad at me," he said. "You left me stranded at the bazaar. When you took off on your broom, I had to hitchhike home."

"Hitchhike?" She raised a brow. "Michele Chambers offered you a ride in the parking lot, which you accepted."

So, she knew about Michele. Word spread fast in Barefoot William. The Cateses had a hotline. Michele had come on to him the moment he'd left the Civic Center. He hadn't known her before that night. She'd introduced herself with a want-you, got-to-have-you smile. She had a dimple in her chin and deep cleavage. A man could get lost between her breasts. He'd resisted, even after she took the long way home.

"Nothing happened," he told Jen.

"That's not what she said."

He said, she said. Mac hated verbal volleyball. "What did she say?" He was curious.

"That you checked into a motel."

He scratched his jaw. "Was the register signed Dune Cates? I take his name wherever I go."

"I'd forgotten that fact." She released a breath. Mac swore she looked relieved.

"Your friend Bree Bennett once stretched the truth about me," he reminded her. "You later apologized. Same will happen with Michele. You can say you're sorry now or later."

"You're so full of yourself."

"I can't help the fact women want me. In Michele's case, I didn't want her back."

"My mistake," she said so softly he barely heard her.

She eased around him, then snuck a glance over her shoulder.

A glance that he caught. "Were you checking me out?" he asked. He was certain she had been.

"I was looking for the box cutter."

"It's in your hand."

Flustered, she set the cutter down on the café table. Her color was high, her expression anxious. She slapped her thighs. "You make me crazy."

"Good crazy?" He could only hope.

"Bat-shit crazy," she said in frustration. "I like order and peace in my life. You breathe chaos."

"It's who I am, Jen."

Her shoulders slumped. "I know."

He was who he was. Women had asked him to change over the years. Change into what? A fireman, airline pilot, professor, or superman? Priest was not an option. He was a big kid who made a lot of money playing beach volleyball. Many wished they were him. He lived in a cool glass house, had a bad-ass Corvette, and enough money to retire today if he chose to hang up his board shorts.

Then there was Jen with her cottage, cats, and snarky attitude. Attraction was a fickle bitch, he decided. He'd have to talk himself out of liking her, if he could figure out what drew him to her in the first place. It was complicated.

He'd yet to learn why she was mad at him. That troubled him the most. "Why are you still angry?" he asked.

"You honestly don't know?" Disbelief darkened her eyes.

He shook his head. He hadn't a clue.

"We'll discuss it when you figure it out."

Shit, she was going to make him work for it.

Reconciliation was beyond his reach, but maybe his gift would smooth things over a little. He passed her the box. "I brought you a present."

Her stunned expression was priceless. She recovered quickly. "You can't buy your way out of our argument."

"I wouldn't think of it."

"You're used to manipulating women."

She knew him too well. "Decompress, Jen. Open the box."

She did so, very slowly and cautiously, as if she expected a spring-loaded surprise. Her face softened when she saw the painting. "I love rocking chairs." She traced the intricately curved lines with her finger. "This looks just like the one in my living room. Very thoughtful, Mac. Thank you."

"I'm glad you like it."

She propped the painting on her desk next to a color photo of her cats. "Rockers are so soothing," she said. "I relax in mine whenever I've had a bad day."

"The chairs are great for sex, too," he said before he could stop himself. It just slipped out. "Nice motion."

Her jaw clenched. "Way to spoil the moment."

Damn, another strike against him. "I was making conversation."

"Change the subject," she said. "This time, don't let your penis pick the topic."

Lady was harsh. He finally came up with news he could share with her that had nothing to do with sex. "I just saw Dune and Sophie coming from the mayor's office. She's the new curator for the Barefoot William Museum."

Jen was pleased. "That's excellent news. The project will keep her busy while Dune's away."

"We'll *both* be away," he stressed.

"I'll miss *one* of you."

"I won't tell Dune," Mac said. "He'd feel bad."

She rolled her eyes. "Are you ever serious?"

"Only during volleyball and sex."

"Otherwise life is a joke?"

"I don't find *you* funny," he said. "You're on my case most days. You should be nicer to me."

"Nicer?" She opened her mouth, then closed it. Her silence spoke for her. *He made her bat-shit crazy.*

Seconds later, Randy pushed through the door. "I'm clocking out," he told Jen. He handed her a list with five projects neatly checked off. "All done."

Jenna smiled. "You worked extra hard today, Randy, especially on the loading dock. You immediately got the dolly when you saw the deliveryman's arm was in a sling and helped unload his truck. Nice going."

The kid looked down and shuffled his feet. Compliments appeared to be new to him. He wasn't quite sure how to handle them.

"Bonus day," Jen added. "Pick out something to take home. Anything you'd like."

Randy startled. "Anything?"

She nodded. "Let me know what you're taking so I can cross it off the inventory."

Randy spun on his heel so fast he nearly ran into the wall. The kid went shopping.

"You never give me free stuff," Mac complained.

"You don't work for me."

"I could volunteer like Sophie did."

"You'd only get in my way."

"Watch me." He moved toward a stack of beach towels tossed on a table. "I can fold." He took up the task.

Jen crossed her arms over her chest and watched. "Retail is not your calling," she eventually said.

The corners of his towels didn't meet and the stack tilted left. The pile could not be displayed. He needed folding lessons.

Randy returned with his freebie in hand. The kid could've selected designer sunglasses, a surfer's braided-leather bracelet, or a shirt from the Beach Heat collection. Instead, he'd chosen a small sand globe.

"For my sister," he said.

Jen smiled. "She'll love it. Wrap the globe in tissue paper and put it in a gift bag."

"A gift bag?" His eyes widened.

They were seldom given out, and only to special customers who spent more than one hundred dollars. "The metallic blue bag is exceptionally pretty," Jen said. "It sparkles."

"Thanks." He turned to Mac on his way out and gave him some advice. "Man, you need to work on your moves." Then he was gone.

"I don't see him with a girlfriend," said Mac.

"I don't see you with one, either."

"That hurt my feelings."

She laughed in his face.

The shop was dead quiet, though Mac could see a steady flow of traffic outside the front window. People were coming off the beach and strolling along the boardwalk. Those passing by carried the excitement of the day's activities with them.

"Now what?" Mac posed the question he couldn't get off his mind. "It's just you and me—"

"And my six o'clock customers."

He watched Jen tuck in her shirt and smooth the wrinkles with her hand. She slid open her desk drawer, drew out a comb and ran it through her short blond hair before adding a little gel. Next, she glossed her lips with cherry balm, then switched out her pink rubber flip-flops for a sexy rhinestone pair.

"I'm going to stand at the door, smile, and flag down customers," she told him.

He raised a brow. "A little red-light retail?"

"Only you would see it that way," she said. "The sand-castle and kite flying contests are over. Tourists are deciding on dinner and souvenirs. Some shop owners will hand out discount coupons; others will give away free samples. I need to catch the crowd's attention, too."

"I'm a big draw."

She considered him. "You're the poster child for fun in the sun."

"I give good fun."

Jenna Cates stared at Mac James. The man had a point. Retail was slow, and if he could stir up business, she would be grateful.

But Mac needed boundaries for this to be successful. A free-for-all was out of the question, so she set down rules. "You can't slice prices," she said firmly. "There'll be no coercing or forcing people inside. No bribing, either."

He winked at her. "It's all about charm."

He changed his T-shirt before taking his place by the door. He went from basic navy to one that read *My Body's an Amusement Park. No Tickets Necessary.*

He drew a crowd in less than ten minutes. Jenna stood and watched, amazed. People recognized him immediately. He was a sports celebrity. Men congratulated him and women cornered him. Mac signed autographs and smiled for pictures.

He captivated everyone he met, Jen noted. He stole a woman's good sense with his smile. His blue gaze teased and seduced. People wanted to share his space and breathe his air. He appreciated their business and told them so. He expressed his gratitude to one sexy sunbather twice.

Jen kept count.

The store was soon filled to capacity. A waiting line formed outside. All merchandise moved fast. She stood behind the front counter and rang up a month's worth of sales in a single night.

She caught Mac's eye. He sent her a cocky smile. Her stomach warmed. Her panties dampened. She was lost in the lusty thoughts of him when—

"My change, please?" A middle-aged man held out his hand.

Damn, she'd let Mac distract her. She hated when that happened. She quickly returned to business. Mac had suggested the Beach Heat Collection to her customer. The man had bought two button-downs. She slipped his shirts into a green plastic bag with the store logo. She counted back his three dollars and wished him a nice evening.

Jen kept the shop open until the crowd thinned.

Mac stood at the door and saw everyone out. He'd created a party atmosphere and been a great host. She was grateful for the income.

"Keys?" he asked.

She tossed him the ring of keys and he locked up.

"We moved a lot of inventory tonight," she said with a sigh. She scanned the shop, noting the significant gaps between hangers, the dwindling piles of shorts, and the reduction in flip-flops. She stifled a yawn. "I need to straighten up and replenish the stock."

He set her keys on the countertop and eyed her with

concern. "You're tired," he said. "The stock can wait. Go home, recharge."

He was right. Her lower back ached from standing and bending all day. A relaxing bubble bath called to her, as did her freshly made bed. "Home sounds good," she agreed. "Sleep even better."

"Care for a bedtime story?" he asked. "I can crawl in beside you and recite a short version of *The Indian in the Cupboard.*"

"I'll pass."

He came around the counter and closed the space between them. They were barely a breath apart. He tipped up her chin with his finger and forced her to hold his gaze.

Her cheeks grew warm beneath his stare. Her chest rose, her breasts felt heavy. He leaned in, and his dick nudged her belly. His scent was a mix of all the people who'd mingled in her shop.

Mac had greeted everyone personally. Surfers had thumped him on the back. Traces of salt water and sea air now blended with the sugary sweetness of a four-year-old's cotton candy. Mac had held the little girl while her mother selected a sun visor. The child wiped her sticky hands on his shirt.

Women's fragrances marked him as a desirable mate. Lovely, Light Blue, and Juicy drifted to her. Juicy belonged to the hot sunbather. Someone had splashed him with a fruit smoothie. Orange juice stained his athletic shorts.

Beneath the distracting scents of his fans, Jen found Mac James. He was earthy and sinful; all energy and challenge. No man was sexier.

"Dune invited me to Sophie's birthday party," he breathed against her mouth.

"He invited me, too."

"Want to go together?"

She shook her head. "Sorry, but no."

He looked confused. "Why not?"

She traced the lettering on his T-shirt. "You're exciting and fun, like a carnival ride. But all rides come to an end."

"Some make you puke."

"I'm not sick of you, Mac."

"You're still mad and you refuse to tell me why."

"You need to figure it out."

"I'm not good with mind games."

"Yet you play them all the time." She pushed past him, collected her keys, and let him out. " 'Night, Mac," she said at the door.

"You and the sandman sleep tight." He took off down the boardwalk.

Mac James had never watched a woman sleep. Jenna Cates looked good doing it. All hell would break loose if she woke up and found him standing by her bed. She could call the cops and have him arrested for breaking and entering. He didn't want to spend the remainder of his vacation in jail.

Still, he'd taken a chance. He'd made several attempts to speak to her that evening, yet she didn't want to talk about *them*.

He'd jimmied a back window to get inside her place. Once he had the window open, he'd heaved himself over the ledge and hit the floor with a thud. He'd drawn the attention of two of her Savannahs, Jango and Neo. They'd circled and checked him out. There'd been no biting or scratching. They'd let him off easy.

The cats stalked him down the hallway. The cottage had two bedrooms; the master was closer to the kitchen. Moonlight slanted through the bamboo shades and spread across the bed. Jen lay on her back; wisps of her hair feathered her cheek. No telltale dark roots. She was a natural blonde.

Her face was relaxed. Her lips were slightly parted. The

sheet slipped to her waist. She wore her black nightshirt. Frosted Cupcake body lotion scented her skin. The rise and fall of her chest was slow and even. Her nipples peaked beneath the cotton. She appeared peaceful.

Chike, the largest of the Savannahs, lay by her pillow, all stretched out and giving Mac the evil eye. Mac glared back. He'd never had a staring contest with a cat. Chike won.

He debated climbing into bed with Jen. Not for sex, just to be near her. Maybe hold her. A first for him. He didn't understand his need to see her. He'd fought the urge and lost.

He'd liked women for as long as he could remember. He sneaked kisses as far back as the fourth grade. He'd felt his first budding breast in middle school and worked his way into a girl's panties by his freshman year in high school. He'd had regular sex in college.

He'd had a few relationships and his fair share of fuck buddies. Expectations beyond a night together were few in his mind. Pleasure and minimal conversation worked for him.

Until Jen.

He never felt lonely, but he had tonight. The feeling was new to him. He didn't like it. He'd grown antsy after leaving the T-shirt shop. His restlessness only increased when Dune took off to see Sophie. Mac invited himself along only to have Dune un-invite him.

His partner wanted to be alone with her, which Mac understood. Sophie was one in a million. Sweet, shy, and sensitive, she'd gotten under Dune's skin. Mac couldn't figure out why his own attraction ran to snippy, sarcastic, and bitchy.

Somehow Jenna Cates did it for him. For now anyway. She challenged him; made him crazy. He couldn't predict tomorrow or next week. Tonight, he couldn't get her out of his head.

With Dune gone, Mac sought out Frank to keep him company. He'd needed a distraction. He'd challenged the older man to a game of cribbage. Lost. Next, they played gin. Frank won all five hands. Mac had no more challenge in him. Frank blew him off and went to bed.

Mac next turned to the TV. After ninety minutes of *M.A.S.H.* reruns, he took Ghost for a walk in the orange grove. He strolled aimlessly and soon realized he was lost. There were trees everywhere and no sign of the house. Fortunately, the dog knew his way back. Mac rewarded him with a Pup-Peroni stick.

Now at Jen's, he wished he had catnip to entice Chike off her bed. The Savannah was territorial and unmoving. Mac rethought his plan to see her. Perhaps it was a stupid idea. He debated leaving. Sneaking out the way he'd come in would be easy. She would never know he'd been there. He wondered if the cats were tattletales.

He took one step back when Chike did the unthinkable. The Savannah pawed Jenna's arm. Pawed her *twice*. Mac swore it was deliberate. Jen shifted and wakened slowly.

Seeing him, she looked startled as hell. She pushed up on one elbow and turned on the bedside lamp. The room was cast in a soft glow.

"Home invasion," she muttered, her voice hoarse from sleep.

"You have bed head," he said without thinking. "And pillow creases on your cheek."

"You're scruffy and dressed like a slob."

There was nothing wrong with his T-shirt and jeans. They were the cleanest of his dirty clothes.

"Got a minute?" he asked.

She glanced at her alarm clock. "It's two a.m."

Time mattered little to Mac. At least she hadn't screamed

and brought the neighbors down on him. He lowered himself beside her. The queen-size mattress dipped and she tipped toward him. She caught herself before they touched.

Chike arched his back and climbed over Jen. The big cat sat on his haunches and showed his front claws. He hissed, a low guttural, attack sound. He mirrored Jenna's mood.

They both hated him.

Mac doubted he and the cat would ever be friends. The best he could hope for was to make it to the door without scratches, teeth marks, and flying fur.

"Chike doesn't like me," he said, stating the obvious.

"Neither do I." She met his gaze, her expression hostile. "How'd you get in here?" she asked.

"I have superpowers. I walk through walls."

"Why did you wake me up?"

"Technically, Chike woke you," he said. "Insomnia loves company."

"You're unbelievable. Go home."

"Not before I apologize," he said forcefully. "I've run our conversation at the Civic Center through my head a hundred times. I still have no idea what I said to tick you off. Whatever it was, I wish I could take it back."

She stared, her expression tired but thoughtful. She gathered herself together and said, "You told everyone at the bazaar that I was attracted to you."

"It was a *joke*," he defended.

"It was our secret."

He shrugged. "No one believed me."

"The fact that you told anyone at all makes you untrustworthy."

"Truth is, you don't like me, babe, so what does it matter?"

There was a long pause during which she looked surprisingly unhappy and vulnerable. He was at a loss for words. She licked her lips and swallowed. The pulse at the base of her throat was visible. It raced.

Mac knew a heartbeat could quicken from anger, physical activity, or attraction. Jen was pissed at him, but something more beat beneath the surface. He looked deep into her eyes and saw her desire. "You do care," he said, amazed.

"Not a chance."

"You would never have been upset by my comment otherwise."

She frowned, then flopped onto her back and stared at the ceiling. "There's a big difference between liking someone and lusting after them."

"You want my body?" he asked.

"That's yet to be determined."

She had the hots for him. Her attraction was real. He now understood why she'd gotten upset and put him through hell. He had thought she was punking him at her shop when she'd shared her secret. He now knew she'd been serious. Surprise, surprise.

Smiling wasn't appropriate, especially since Jen was despondent. She'd told him the truth and now expected him to use the information against her. She drew her forearm over her eyes and hid from him.

There'd be no hiding tonight.

He leaned closer, keeping one eye on Chike. He was going after the girl and didn't want the cat coming after him.

"I came to hang out with you," he said, "to hold you, to talk."

"You came for sex."

That, too. "Introduce me to your vibrators."

"They're tucked in for the night."

"Then don't wake them up. I give better buzz."

She rolled her eyes. "You're bad for me, Mac."

"I'm good in bed."

"Arrogance isn't sexy."

"Confidence is."

She exhaled so sharply her body went flat. She lowered her arm and patted the mattress. "I'll regret this in the morning."

"I won't."

He would've been all over her had it not been for Chike. The Savannah was a thirty-pound barrier. The cat's ears flattened and his pupils constricted. His lips drew back. He arched and puffed up his hair, appearing bigger than he was. His tail lashed out and he gave a low, throaty yowl.

The cat's warning was not lost on Mac. He wasn't a wuss, but an attack cat gave him pause. He saw Chike as a challenge. He needed to get around the Savannah to get to Jen. She was enjoying his predicament and not helping him in the least, just taking it all in. He had no idea what to do. He had no experience around cats, especially ones with wild eyes.

He went on gut instinct. He would've given his left nut for a pair of thick, leather gloves, but all he had was skin. Having his arm ripped to shreds before the Huntington Beach Classic wasn't a good idea. He couldn't play with his hand bandaged.

Wanting Jen won out. He'd brave the cat.

Son of a bitch.

Slowly, cautiously, he let Chike appraise his hand. Mac felt the twitch of the cat's whiskers right before Chike bared his teeth and head-butted Mac's palm. *Butted him twice.* The big boy swatted Mac's wrist with one paw, then purred. Purred like a motorboat. A long jump and he cleared the bed, landing on the floor.

Mac's jaw dropped. He watched the cat leave the bedroom. The Savannah had swagger. The other cats collected in the hallway, then disappeared into the darkness.

Mac slid off the bed and closed the door. He didn't need Chike and his crew sneaking back in and scaring him soft in the middle of sex. He leaned against the doorjamb and caught his breath.

Jenna sent him a slow, sly smile. "You passed the Chike test," she said, impressed. "He intimidates, but never bites. He's a teddy bear at heart."

A teddy bear with very sharp teeth.

His jaw worked. "You made me jump through cat hoops to get in your pants?"

"I'm not wearing panties."

Her words stroked his dick. A twist of her hips and her nightshirt slid up to her abdomen. The sheet now wrapped her thighs and dipped between her legs. The cotton creased her sex. He was hard in a heartbeat.

He dragged his T-shirt over his head and tossed it aside. He toe-heeled his Converse. Then unsnapped, unzipped, and dropped his jeans.

Her eyes went wide. "No underwear?"

"Easy access."

He retrieved six condoms from his wallet and returned to her bed. He dropped the Black Ice packets on her nightstand, one at a time. The sound of the silver foil wrappers against the unfinished grain of the wood was loud in the silence.

"You're ambitious," she said.

"I'm bred for stamina."

She rolled her eyes. "We'll see about that."

He eased onto her bed and sank deep. The mattress was as soft as a goose down comforter. There was no immediate touching, only deep staring. He felt her heat. She was a woman of fire and passion and a royal pain in his ass. Still, he wanted her.

There'd be no sarcasm tonight. He'd kiss her until she didn't have a thought in her head; much less the ability to speak. She had a kissable mouth. Lush, moist, and inviting. He nipped her lower lip and sucked gently.

She was his lightning strike. They sparked and sizzled from their first kiss. She closed her eyes and moaned. A woman's moan, low with longing.

Arousal clutched his cock.

Anticipation jacked him even harder.

He made love to her with his mouth; his kisses were deep, thorough, and insistent. His tongue thrust between her lips, curled, tasted, seduced. She kissed him back, giving, taking, needing him.

He believed in the exchange of sexual favors.

He favored Jen. He wanted her satisfied.

He slid his hands beneath her nightshirt and felt her up. His thumb brushed her high, firm breast. He circled her nipple, then her navel with his forefinger. Sensation overtook her. She squirmed, shivered, and dug her nails into his shoulder.

Her nightshirt came off easily. The neck hole was wider than he remembered. No doubt he'd stretched the shirt when he wore it to the bazaar.

They were both naked now. He admired her bikini wax.

A brush of an arm, a turn of a leg, and friction rubbed their bodies together.

He took her way down deep into the mattress and covered her with his body. He buried his face in her neck and breathed in the cupcake scent of her lotion. Every part of his body sought its sexual mate. His chest pressed her breasts as his dick nestled between her thighs.

More kisses, more touching. More moans.

He embraced her and her soft sighs.

She wasn't a woman to be held down long. She was strong for someone so small. Determined, too. She wiggled and squirmed. He let her escape. She pushed him onto his back. He willingly changed positions.

He hitched himself up against the headboard until he was sitting up. She then knelt between his legs, leaning up and into him. Her breath bathed his neck, his chest, his hip bones. Blood flowed to his groin when she breathed against his belly, then puffed warm air on his penis.

She took him in her mouth and his entire body twitched. The swirl of her tongue promised release.

His muscles bunched and his body burned.

His back arched and his hips came off the bed.

He clutched the sheet, strained, swelled, and went sexually insane. He was so hard he hurt.

Restraint nearly killed him. His willpower lost to his need to be inside her. He caught her by the upper arms and drew her up over his body. Her legs spread as she settled over his hips. He snagged a condom off the nightstand, stripped the wrapper, and sheathed himself.

She rocked forward then back, teasing his dick, yet refusing to take him fully. He curved his hands over her hips and squeezed her. His gut tightened. His urgency was raw, rushing, and intense.

His orgasm was dangerously close and he wanted her as wild and blind with passion as he was. Even more so, if that was humanly possible.

She looked down on him and one corner of her mouth curved. She wore a woman's smile, one sly with intent. She went on to frustrate him further. She stroked his dick, holding him between her palms and rubbing her hands together. Friction and heat; slow, then fast. Air exploded in his lungs. Damn, he was about to die.

He refused to come without her. He ran his hands along her thighs until he reached her sex. He parted her and traced tiny circles around her clit.

She was wet, slick, and ready for him when he palmed her mound and penetrated her with two fingers. She threw back her head and let him take her higher still. Pleasure flushed her body.

He withdrew his hand and slipped inside her, a slow streamlined motion of man into woman. Her ragged sigh ripped along his nerve endings where their bodies linked.

Jenna Cates was lost to this man. Mac was sex personified. She'd grown up at the beach and spent her life swimming, surfing, and sailing. She'd seen a lot of hot guys with buff bodies. No one came close to him. He was lean, ripped, and hotwired. He was charged with electricity. His sparks licked down her spine like a hot tongue.

She ran her hands up and down his back, feeling the flow and flex of his muscles. Her legs tightened around him. She thrust her fingers into his hair, pulling his face down for a kiss. He penetrated her mouth with his tongue.

They rolled their hips, and he pumped up into her as she rocked back and forth. He groaned deep in his throat when she rose up and down, releasing his cock, then drawing him inside her once again. She took him deeply.

He touched her everywhere, palming, squeezing, stroking. Her breasts grew heavy and her clitoris tingled.

He raised his head and locked gazes with her. His blue eyes darkened; possessive and searing. His breathing became desperate.

A craving took hold of her and she began to unravel.

Time went away and her orgasm stretched to the breaking point. She moaned, stiffened. Shattered.

He came a second after her, his expression going from pain to pleasure. His ripping-hard climax drove her to a second orgasm. The aftershocks shook them both. They lay tangled and spent. The scent of sex lingered on the rumpled sheets.

Silence followed their sexual high. Neither one moved, neither one spoke. Neither chose to break their intimate truce.

He held her for a long, long time. She closed her eyes and rested her forehead against his shoulder. They shared space. Breathed the same air.

It was then she realized her best friend Bree had been right. Every woman deserved a lover like Mac in her life.

Even for one night.

Fourteen

Everyone deserved a birthday party like Sophie Saunders's, Dune thought as he leaned against the sliding glass doors that separated the kitchen from the pool deck. The day was golden. Bright and sparkling. The sky was as tropical blue as the water in the pool. The air vibrated with excitement and celebration.

He'd kept one eye on Sophie throughout the afternoon. He liked knowing where she was and what she was doing at any given time. She presently sat on the side of the pool, talking to Nicole Archer from The Jewelry Box. Sophie was animated and happy. So were all the people around her.

The crowd continued to grow as the afternoon wore on. His initial plans for her party had been intimate and low-key, but word soon spread, going viral. His friends and relatives crossed Center Street to make her day memorable. No one mentioned the century-old feud. The Cateses loved Sophie and wanted to take part in her special day.

Sophie wasn't shy today. She was comfortable with his family. She greeted her guests with smiles and hugs. Dune frowned when Mac kissed her on the mouth. His partner pushed his buttons. He could be a prick sometimes.

He glanced at all those gathered around the pool. Many lounged on the patio furniture and a few sat in the Jacuzzi.

Several couples floated on double-wide air mattresses. Jenna Cates stretched out on a floating green sea turtle.

The young boys, Randy and Chuck, jumped off the diving board. Their cannonballs sprayed like geysers. No one cared. Everyone was in swimsuits.

Soon they had so many partiers, Dune and the other men set up buffet tables around the perimeters of the pool to accommodate everyone. Food in abundance was spread out everywhere, from picnic basics to gourmet dishes.

The Cates family grilled hamburgers and hot dogs. They'd brought baked beans, macaroni and cheese, corn on the cob, a variety of salads, and three-fruit Jell-O molds. Someone had sliced an enormous watermelon into triangles.

The Saunders family's chef contributed as well. Marisole refused to sit idle at Sophie's party. She'd arrived with a team of servers from the Sandcastle Hotel. They carted in trays of artichoke and prosciutto, crabmeat-stuffed deviled eggs, and shrimp linguini. The team loaded platters with cold fried chicken and beef kabobs. There were at least ten desserts. That didn't include the three-tiered birthday cake.

Sophie would send everyone home with a plate of leftovers. Mac would pack a cooler.

The scent of grilled burgers drifted over to Dune, making him hungry. Everything tasted better in the open air. He was about to help himself to the buffet when Mac James sauntered over to him.

Mac nodded toward the pool. "I see you taught Sophie how to swim," he said. "She has her own style."

Dune agreed. A most unique style. She'd slipped into the pool and was making waves. Her arms slapped the water and her legs kicked up a storm. His sister Shaye and her husband Trace moved out of Sophie's way as she reached the cement side.

Her hand now on the edge, Sophie bounced up and down

to get her footing, then wiped the water from her eyes. She tilted her head and tried to clear her ears. Through it all, she smiled. Dune's heart warmed just looking at her.

Beside him, Mac twitched a grin. Dune knew what was coming. He set his back teeth. "What are you smiling about?" he asked.

Mac eyed Sophie. "You know what, big guy."

Dune knew without a doubt. Sophie had become an important part of his life in a very short time. Somehow he felt as if he'd known her forever. That was impossible. They hadn't crossed paths before the previous summer, but they had a strong bond nonetheless.

The two men watched as she bobbed and took a deep breath, ready to cut back across the pool. "I don't see synchronized swimming or an Olympic gold medal in her future," Mac said when Sophie collided with Jenna's float. "But she swims better than Ghost."

Dune glared at him.

"What?" Mac shrugged. "C'mon, it was a compliment."

"She's a beginner, but she'll improve," Dune said with confidence.

Every day she got stronger in the water. She wasn't secure in the pool alone, so she called Dune when she was ready to practice. He was there for her, sitting on the side for an hour, his feet in the water, and watching her do short laps.

He was in need of exercise as well. He'd skipped volleyball practice to set up Sophie's party. He felt the need to swim, jog . . . have sex.

Sex would be best.

He stretched out his arms and shifted his stance on the natural blue stone pool deck. The sun was brutal and the soles of his bare feet burned. Sophie had very fair skin. She needed to seek the shade.

"I hope she doesn't get sunburned." Mac also showed concern for her.

"She's covered in sunscreen," Dune told him.

"Nice use of your hands, bro."

Dune had slathered sunblock over every exposed inch of her body. He'd taken his time spreading the lotion evenly on her skin. Even then, a few rays snuck through. Soft pink spots stained her otherwise perfect complexion. Most likely, she'd have worked up an appetite after all her swimming.

Dune caught her eye and motioned for her to get out of the pool. She held up five fingers, indicating she would take a few more minutes. He nodded his understanding. She did another lap.

"When are you going to put a ring on her finger?" asked Mac.

Dune refused to give him a direct answer. Instead he said, "The same day you get engaged to Jenna." Sophie had once wagered that Mac and Jen would commit to each other by the end of the summer. He wondered if Sophie had an inside track on their romance.

He glanced at Jen on the green turtle float. Her eyes were closed and her lips were tipped up at the corners. She looked content. "You've stayed away from her today. What's up?" Dune asked Mac.

"I'm giving her space," Mac said easily.

"At her request?" asked Dune.

"A mutual agreement." His partner appeared very relaxed and confident in their decision. "She needs time to think about us."

"Us?" What the hell? When had Mac become an us?

"We worked through our issues," Mac said. "I'll keep my distance until after Huntington. Then we'll discuss our future."

"Your future?" Dune was stunned. He'd been so involved with Sophie, he'd lost track of his partner's pursuits.

Mac's smile was wide. "Jen and I found common ground."

They were sleeping together, Dune thought. At least they weren't at each other's throats, although a fading bruise on Mac's neck indicated there'd been biting.

"Here comes your girl," Mac said as Sophie gripped the handrail and took the steps, climbing out of the pool.

My woman. Dune openly admired Sophie. She looked hot in her new swimsuit. It was a birthday gift from Shaye. His sister had convinced Sophie that her blue tankini was outdated. Shaye had helped her select a one-piece black racer with crisscross straps in the back. Sophie looked sleek, slick, and sexy.

Dune nudged Mac when Mac stared too long.

Mac looked back at him. "Did you see the mountain of presents in her living room?" he asked. "I shook a few boxes and peeked into several gift cards. Lady's made a haul."

"What did you get her?"

"I bought her a beginner's cookbook at The Kitchen Sink," he said. "The information is very basic. It starts out by telling the cook the difference between the stove and refrigerator."

Dune rolled his eyes. "I think Sophie can skip the introduction."

"The cookbook also explains how long to prepare a three-minute egg," Mac said, enjoying his joke. "The recipes are easy. I've made One-Step Lasagna and Busy-Day Beef Kabobs."

"It's a great gift," said Dune. He raised a brow. "Did you charge it to me?" Not that he minded. Mac always paid him back; it just took a while.

"You didn't have an account there, so I paid cash," Mac said. "The Kitchen Sink is a nice store. The owner is friendly and she looks like Paula Deen."

Dune knew the store. It was one of a dozen small shops located on the street behind the boardwalk. The Cates family owned the property, but the shops were rented to outside entrepreneurs. The stores weren't competitive with those businesses already standing.

"Hey, babe," Mac said to Sophie when she joined them. "Are you hungry? Care to share a plate with me?"

"I'm starving," she admitted. "But there'd be no going halves with you. I'd get one bite and you'd eat the rest."

"You're probably right," he agreed. He caught sight of Marisole replenishing the shrimp linguini. "Will your chef chase me away like she did at the Sneaker Ball if I have seconds or thirds?" he asked.

Sophie patted him on the arm. "Eat until you're full."

Mac rubbed his hands together, then took off for the buffet.

Dune shook his head. "We'd better eat now, while there's still food available."

They each filled a plate, then looked around for a place to sit. Trace and Shaye were finishing up their meal at a table near the diving board. Dune and Sophie slid into their seats after they'd collected their dishes and left.

Sophie ate two bites before people stopped by to chat with them. Dune's relatives wanted to discuss the Barefoot William museum with her. They had suggestions and sought out her opinion. Sophie listened, evaluated, and assured everyone the museum would honor William and all his family. She planned to include every Cates in her vision. His family applauded her efforts.

Dune leaned back in his chair. He recalled how he'd been the one surrounded at the Sneaker Ball and how Sophie had quietly looked on. Today their situations were reversed.

Gone was the shy, fearful Sophie. She was now the center of attention. She'd evolved into a resilient, respected woman. She had her own sense of purpose. Dune was proud of her.

"This is a good time to open your presents, Sophie," said Shaye, returning to their table. "Everyone's eaten. Let's digest our food before we play games in the pool."

Sophie nodded in agreement.

Shaye then asked Trace, Dune, and the boys to help cart Sophie's presents out to the pool. She didn't want the guests dripping water into the house. Dune agreed with her. They went to retrieve the gifts.

The boxes came in all shapes and sizes. The wrapping paper ranged from fancy foil to Sunday funnies. Sophie took an entire hour to unwrap her presents. She admired each gift and passed it around. She wanted each of her guests to know how much she appreciated the present.

Dune smiled along with Sophie when she opened Jenna's gift. It was a digital frame, perfect to load up with photos of her hamsters.

Chuck and Randy had pooled their money together to buy her gift. They'd also considered Scarlett and Glinda in their purchase. They presented Sophie with a ten-dollar gift card from Pet Outfitters so she could buy food and toys for her girls.

The gifts went on and on. Dune realized that his family knew her well. Each present represented something important in her life. His second cousin Rick had bought a small, framed metal-crafted unicycle.

Nicole Archer had made a high-heeled sneaker brooch from black opals. The jewelry held precious memories of the Sneaker Ball for Sophie.

His Aunt Molly from the diner had put together a breakfast kit, including her special waffle mix. Sophie loved waffles.

Violet had selected tiny volleyball-style earrings for her. Vi claimed Sophie was a competitor now.

Sophie sighed when she opened Dune's gift. It was a leather journal along with a slender gold ink pen. The historical family journals had guided her to where she was today. He wanted her to document her life from this point onward.

Sophie Saunders would have many memories to enter into the journal if he had anything to do with it.

Sophie was as overwhelmed as she was appreciative of the outpouring of love from the Cates family. She put her hand over her heart once she'd set aside the last gift and looked out over the crowd. Tears glistened in her eyes and she could barely express her gratitude. "I'm at a loss for words," she began, "I don't know how to tell—" Her voice broke before she could finish.

"Tell everyone that I gave you the best gift?" Mac finished for her.

Sophie gave Mac a small smile. "I'll challenge you to a meat loaf cook-off someday soon." She took a deep breath and managed to continue. "I'm so glad you've adopted me. You've given me a home away from home." A tear escaped from her eye and traveled down her cheek. No one moved. It was a touching moment.

Dune crossed to her. He curved his arm around her shoulders and tucked her close, offering comfort.

He heard Molly, Violet, and several others clear emotion from their throats.

"Who's ready for a game of chicken?" Mac called out, lightening the mood. He held a drumstick in his hand. "Teams consist of one guy and one girl. The girl sits on the guy's shoulders and each team tries to unseat the competition. No poking in the face. No pulling anyone's hair. Winners are the last two standing. I call dibs on Sophie."

"Do you mind?" Sophie asked Dune, laying her hand on his arm.

Dune would have liked to have had her all to himself, but since she was the guest of honor, he shared her with family and friends. "Lean forward," he told her, giving her pointers on how to play the game. "It's all about balance."

Mac took Sophie's hand in his, then looked at Dune. His voice was low; his taunt meant for his partner alone. "I've waited a long time to have Sophie's legs wrapped around my neck."

Dune shook his head. What an asshole.

He stood back and allowed them to have their fun. The first round consisted of a lot of splashing, laughing, pushing, and tugging. Dune moved closer to the side of the pool and coached Sophie.

The final three couples now battled it out. The teams included Trace and Shaye, Randy and Violet, and Mac and Sophie. Mac took on Trace and Shaye first.

Shaye had grown up with brothers and was highly competitive. She'd played chicken all her life, and was tricky and sneaky. Shaye would never let Sophie win without a fight, even on her birthday.

Sophie was having the time of her life. She slapped the water and shrieked like a young girl. It was a silly kid moment for her, yet one Sophie had never experienced. She laughed so hard she nearly fell off Mac's shoulders.

"Don't laugh so hard that you pee in the pool," Mac said to her over his shoulder.

Sophie tried to keep a straight face, but couldn't. She could barely catch her breath.

"Don't cover my eyes," Mac told her when she clasped her hands around his head to keep her balance. She quickly released him. "We need to fight them from the front, not from the side. Roll your hips forward and concentrate, Soph. We're going in for the kill."

Mac played dirty. He hip-checked Trace, then stepped on his foot. Trace faltered and nearly lost his balance. Mac circled left and positioned Sophie so she could grab Shaye by the shoulders and unseat her. Shaye tumbled back and fell into the water. She came up sputtering.

"Nice move." Shaye gave both Mac and Sophie a high five. Trace bumped their fists.

The final round of chicken came down to Sophie and Mac and Violet and Randy. Randy was a head shorter than Mac, but he had the footwork of a prizefighter. He danced around and trash-talked his opponents. Only once did Violet bop him on the head for swearing. Otherwise it was all said in fun.

Dune watched as Mac again pulled a fast one. Kid or not, Mac took advantage of Randy's weakness. Mac backed him toward the deep end. Randy was so busy taunting and showing off, he misstepped. He tipped over and Violet flipped backward into the water.

Mac pulled Sophie from his shoulders and hugged her. "Winners!" He pumped his arm in the air.

Mac delivered Sophie to the shallow end. She climbed from the pool, shook out her hair, and stomped her feet. She stood by Dune and slipped her arm around his waist. Her happiness meant more to him than any hug she could've given.

"Warrior woman," he praised her.

She flashed a smile. "We kicked ass."

Kicked ass. She was sounding more and more like Mac.

Sophie's guests applauded her win. The clapping soon faded when the south pool gate opened and Maya and Brandt Saunders joined the party. They were formally dressed, their expressions pained. It was obvious they'd rather be anywhere else but there.

Dune sensed Sophie's surprise and uncertainty. She hesitantly left his side and approached her parents, looking pale beneath her sunburn. He swore he heard her knees knock together.

Trace took a step forward, only to have Shaye touch his arm in a silent request to let Sophie handle this alone. Dune wanted to stand beside her, too, but he thought better of it. He believed in Sophie. She'd manage on her own. No Cates would interfere. This was a Saunders matter. Sophie met her parents on the pool deck near the diving board. She straightened her shoulders, clasped her hands over her stomach. Her words were softly spoken. "I'm glad you came to my party," she managed to say.

Her mother's gaze touched on everyone there. "We'd hardly be missed if we hadn't shown up." Her tone was dry. "You appear to have adopted the entire Cates clan as your family."

Sophie cleared her throat. "They came to my party when you refused," she said.

"They came en masse," her mother observed. "They parked their vehicles wherever they could find a spot on our private cul-de-sac. There are tire marks in our front yard where someone made a U-turn."

"That U-turn was mine." Mac raised his hand and confessed. "I also owe you a rosebush."

Maya glared at Mac. "You need to be more careful, young man."

"I'll have Luis take a look at your yard on Monday," Sophie said to appease her mother. "He'll fix the damage."

"Your mother has a right to be concerned, Sophie, but that's not what we came for. Here is your gift," her father said, moving things along. He withdrew an envelope from the inner pocket of his suit coat and handed it to her. "Happy Birthday, Daughter."

No smiles, no hugs, no sign of affection, Dune noted. They were a repressed couple. The dead silence became more strained as Sophie stared at the envelope.

No black dress this year. Dune hoped her parents hadn't

gone with a gift certificate to a high-end boutique. Or worse yet, written her a check.

Slowly, her hands shaking, Sophie opened the envelope. Her face softened when she saw what was inside. "Two tickets to the Andrea Bocelli concert in Miami in the fall," she said loud enough for everyone to hear.

"The tickets aren't on sale yet," her mother said. "Your father called in a favor to get them."

Men in high places pulled strings, Dune thought. Sophie loved the opera. He was pleased that her parents had put some thought into her gift this year. Or maybe Trace was behind their initiative. Either way, Sophie was pleased. That was all that mattered.

"Thank you," she said, clutching the tickets to her chest. She glanced toward the dessert table where Marisole and the servers were now slicing pies, cutting up the brownies, and scooping the peach cobbler onto blue plastic plates. "Would you like a piece of my birthday cake before you leave?" she offered. "It's my favorite. Red velvet with cream cheese icing."

Dune knew she held her breath as she waited for their answer. He was not surprised when her mother said in a condescending voice, "Sugar doesn't sit well on an empty stomach. Besides, we're headed to a charity event at the country club; drinks, dinner, and the silent auction."

Her mother cast a final look around and shook her head in disgust. "Such a mess you've all made," she said. "I'll call Platinum Sparkle first thing in the morning. They work Sundays."

A cleaning team, Dune thought. They would sanitize all Sophie's memories and leave her nothing but the scent of bleach. He couldn't allow that to happen. He stepped forward and said to Maya, "That won't be necessary. We'll clean up before we leave."

Her mother's smile was tight. "How nice of you."

"We can haul garbage to the curb with the best of them," said Mac, unfiltered.

"Have a nice evening," Sophie wished her parents on their way. There was no reason for them to stay.

Maya flicked her wrist. "Do get back to your fun."

Fun was all young Randy needed to hear. The kid had been quiet while the adults talked, but he couldn't wait to get back into the pool. He stood on the diving board and bounced up and down, going higher each time.

It was a moment etched in time that no one would ever forget. Maya and Brandt turned toward the south gate at the exact moment Randy jumped off the board. He was tucked to cannonball. He landed the biggest splash of the afternoon.

Those standing on the pool deck near the deep end got soaked to the bone, including Sophie's parents. Maya and Brandt stood as still as statues caught in a sudden rainstorm, dripping wet from head to toe.

They would have to change into dry clothes before they could attend their charity event. Maya was in need of a hairstylist. Water filled Brandt's polished wingtips.

No one moved. Trace was the first to recover. He grabbed two towels from the cabana cabinet and approached his parents with a few mumbled words of apology. Dune could only stare. The damage was done. Trace escorted his parents out.

"Monumental," Dune heard Mac say.

Randy got out of the pool to everyone's stares. He freaked a little. "Did I do something wrong?" he asked, worried.

"Everything's fine," Sophie assured him. "It's a pool party. You're allowed to splash."

"Splashing is not for amateurs," Mac said. "You've gone pro, kid."

Randy looked relieved.

"Dessert, then volleyball," Mac said, taking over the

role of social director. "I hear a piece of birthday cake calling my name."

The mayor crossed to Dune. James was in his element cooking at the grill. "Mac's going to want more hamburgers," he said. "I'm low on charcoal. Sophie mentioned there was another bag in the garage."

"I'm on it," Dune said, going for the briquettes. He was happy to keep the party going after the splashing incident. He'd never forget the shocked look on Maya's face if he lived to be a hundred.

He walked through the kitchen and out the side door. The breezeway connected the house to the garage. Mature vines climbed the trellises and tiny pink flowers bloomed. He ducked a bumblebee. The air smelled sweet.

He found several storage areas inside the garage and opened the door to each one. Sophie kept her youthful memories packed away in closets. He found a girl's Huffy bicycle, a dollhouse, and a few stuffed animals. One plush lion had a bright reddish mane, as if he'd been fed spaghetti.

Behind door number three, he located the bag of charcoal. He pulled out the bag and noticed a stack of sports magazines along with a canvas carrier on the floor. A sense of déjà vu made his skin prickle, as if he *had* to check it out. He crouched down.

It was a backpack, well-worn, and with a crooked zipper. He stared and stared, his chest giving an unfamiliar squeeze. Oddly nervous, he flexed his fingers.

He tugged on the metal tab and the zipper gave way. He lifted one of the flaps and, in that instant, he had the strangest sensation he had turned back time.

His breathing deepened as a jumble of images hit him all at once. He caught flashes of a young, brown-haired girl wearing glasses and looking panicky. She was alone and vulnerable. He saw a fallen bicycle near an elementary school. Cars passed and honked, yet no one stopped to help her. Not even the other schoolkids.

He'd gone to her rescue. He recalled parking his Harley and picking up the books scattered across the roadway. He'd fixed the zipper on her backpack so she could get home, then shielded her from the traffic as she applied one of his superhero Band-Aids to her chin.

Had that girl been Sophie?

He looked inside the backpack. *Sophie Saunders, Second Grade* was written in indelible ink on the inside. He ran his thumb over her name. His gut tightened as he delved deeper into her past. A dozen children's books spilled out. An old Superman Band-Aid was folded in half. He fingered the pair of crooked eye glasses. There was a pack of number-two pencils, a 24-count box of crayons, and a wooden ruler. A green spiral notebook caught his eye. He opened it to the first page.

He saw a few math problems and an old homework assignment. Then he came to his name and his heart slowed. *Dun, Dome, Doone* was neatly printed near the bottom. He didn't recall giving her his name, yet apparently he had. She hadn't known how to spell it.

He remembered riding off with one eye in the rearview mirror. It had taken her two tries to get back on her bike. He'd hoped she would be safe. The fact that she'd kept her backpack spoke volumes to him about what had happened that day.

Her little girl's heart had never forgotten him.

He'd wanted to protect her then as much as he did now.

He set the canvas bag aside and turned to the sports magazines. He was featured in each one. The dates catalogued every tournament from his rookie year to the day he became top seed. No one had ever followed his career so closely. Not even his parents. But Sophie had.

He pushed to his feet and let the moment fully sink in.

Emotion settled heavily in his chest. His mind raced. He had several questions for her. Had she had a crush on him from the age of seven? Had she idolized him in her teens? Had she fantasized about him when she became a woman? Did she see him as the man in the magazines? Or could she see the real man behind the hype and publicity?

Only she had the answers.

Hero worship was lost on him. He didn't want that from her. But did he have the right to ask for more, especially when his future remained uncertain? He didn't want to fail or disappoint her. Could he live up to her expectations of him?

He rubbed the back of his neck. He felt his throat close. He needed to think things through. He wondered how long he could remain in the garage before someone came after him and the bag of briquettes. Who would miss him first?

Sophie Saunders felt Dune Cates's absence even before she consciously realized he was gone. The day felt cooler, as if the sun had slipped behind a cloud. She looked around, not seeing him anywhere.

Her brow pleated, a shiver of worry slipping through her as she went looking for him. The mayor mentioned that Dune had gone to the garage for charcoal. She entered through the breezeway and spotted him immediately. He gave her butterflies. He was a handsome man. She took a moment to admire his bare chest and muscled legs. He looked good in his teal green board shorts. A pair of his Suncats was hooked in his waistband. The sporty sunglasses were oval with navy lenses and a flexible wire frame.

She held up a piece of birthday cake on a blue plastic plate. She smiled as she crossed to him. "I saved you a slice," she said. "Mac's eaten the top tier and is working his way down."

"Thanks for thinking of me." His voice sounded odd to Sophie's ears.

She angled her head, puzzling over his tone. "You're always on my mind," she said.

"You're on mine, too."

Her steps faltered when she saw the open storage room door and her childhood on display. She brushed her damp hair out of her eyes and looked at him. "Is something wrong?" she asked.

"James sent me for charcoal," Dune told her. "I found your backpack under the briquettes."

She released a sigh. "That backpack holds a lot of memories from elementary school."

"So I see." He hung her canvas bag on a hook on the back of the door. "Tell me about the day you fell off your bike."

"That was the day I met you."

"I remember now. Your backpack jarred my memory." He looked confused. "Why didn't you tell me that we'd met?"

She shrugged and the cake on the plate tipped. She pushed it back with her thumb. "I was embarrassed," she confessed. "I was an impressionable young girl. You were an older boy with shaggy blond hair and Lion King eyes who rode a motorcycle. As I grew older, there were times I couldn't see your face clearly, but I always remembered your kindness. That mattered most to me."

She looked over at the sports magazines scattered on the floor. "I first learned your last name in *Sports Illustrated*. Trace had a copy on the desk in his home office. I flipped through it one day while I was waiting for him to take me to the dentist. I saw your photo and decided then and there to follow your career. I admired your strength and drive. I imagined you were a good man."

She paused, continuing with, "I watched your tournaments on TV. You were surrounded by women after every match, yet you took time to talk to the kids, too. You're a great role model, Dune. You challenge life, something I've wanted to do but never had the courage to try. This summer you supported me and my adventures. I'll always be grateful to you for that."

"No hero worship?" His brow creased and his jaw clenched. The question appeared important to him.

She shook her head. "I know your faults."

That took him back. "Name one?"

"You don't pick up after yourself in the bathroom, you can't seem to find the dishwasher, you drink the last of the sun tea without making a new batch, and you have yet to clean the hamster cage."

"I get the picture." He exhaled slowly, as if relieved. "I don't want you to see me as more than I am."

"I promise to see you as a whole lot less."

He rolled his eyes, smiled. "Mac's humor is rubbing off on you. Stay away from him the rest of the day."

"Can't," she said. "He already picked me for his pool volleyball team."

"You're playing in the shallow end, right?"

"We may have to rotate sides."

"New rules," said Dune, bending them to her favor. "One side, ten points wins."

"You're bossy."

"I'm saving you from treading water."

She'd sink like a stone.

He took the cake plate from her then. He ate several bites and said, "I'd like to lick cream cheese icing off your nipples tonight."

Her knees went weak.

Dune gave frosting a whole new meaning.

Fifteen

Monday morning and Sophie Saunders sat alone at her kitchen table. She ate a piece of birthday cake for breakfast. Red velvet was her favorite. She liked breaking the breakfast rules. No eggs, no cereal, no fresh fruit, only dessert. Sugar was her new wake-up call.

She'd never look at cream cheese icing in quite the same way. It was pure decadence, so thick, sweet, and smooth. She'd enjoyed licking the icing off Dune's inner thigh. He'd reciprocated and tasted her twice. She now had a frosting fetish.

It had been the best weekend of her life, both fun and sexual. Dune had thrown her an amazing party. She would always be grateful. He also knew how to keep a woman up all night and make her very happy. She'd be smiling to herself all day.

He'd left her house at first light. Sophie had offered to go with him to the airport and see him off, but he'd insisted she stay in bed. Exhausted, she kissed him good-bye, then fell back asleep clutching the pillow still warm with his body heat. She'd slept another two hours.

She faced a busy day ahead. The museum was her first stop. There she'd meet with both her contractor Kai Cates and her fiscal advisor from the courthouse. She was so excited, she could barely sit still. Her vision of the museum would soon be a reality.

A flash of the hamster ball alerted her that her girls were getting their morning exercise. She'd let them out of their cage before she'd made her coffee and cut her piece of cake. Their feet now churned as they looked for new places to explore. They reminded her that life was an adventure. Already, she'd experienced many great moments.

The kitchen clock read eight-thirty. It was time to get dressed and start her day. She caught up with Glinda and Scarlett in the library and returned them to their cage. They went right for the wheel. Spinning was a big part of their lives.

Sophie headed to her bedroom. She opened an armoire and carefully chose her outfit. Today she would be cleaning the museum. She'd be scrubbing walls and floors and didn't care if her clothes got dirty. She was capable of doing laundry.

She was feeling strong and good about herself when she selected a brand-new blue T-shirt embellished with a rhinestone butterfly and a pair of skinny jeans with the price tag hanging from the belt loop. She cut off the tag.

Next, she sat on the edge of the bed and slipped on a pair of Keds. Her bed resembled a sea of tangled sheets and spent desire. Her cheeks grew warm. The comforter was disheveled and two corners of the bottom fitted sheet had come undone. Pillows lay scattered everywhere, on the bed and on the floor.

The room temperature was cooler than she was used to at night. Dune had set the thermostat at sixty-eight degrees. She'd shivered, then warmed with his touch. Sex with him had been hot and nonstop. She missed his body heat. Sighing, she raised the thermostat several degrees on her way out.

She would change the sheets later, but not the pillowcases. Dune's scent lingered on the fine-threaded cotton. She'd take his male scent to bed with her tonight.

She called her limo driver and Roger pulled into her driveway within ten minutes. After a short hop across town, she arrived at Center Street. She scheduled an eight p.m. pickup before he drove away. With Dune out of town, she needed to stay busy. She planned to put in long hours getting the museum ready to open to the public.

Once on the sidewalk, Sophie stared at the shop about to undergo a major transformation. The museum was around the corner from Molly Malone's diner, making it a location with a lot of foot traffic.

Behind her, the morning sun made its climb upward, casting deep shadows along the street and between the buildings. A glare off the storefront window made her blink.

Sophie shielded her eyes and smiled to herself. Here was where she wanted to be. She could think of no better career than that of curator of the Barefoot William Museum.

She was about to relive history.

She would make the Cateses proud.

She took the keys from her hobo bag and opened the door. Dust fluttered about her and made her sneeze. She needed to start a list of cleaning supplies. Air freshener was a must.

"Hey, Sophie," Kai Cates gave her a shout as he came in behind her. He was a tall man with dark blond hair. His body was solid and lean. He wore carpenter's pants and a T-shirt scripted with *Nail It*. A twined leather bracelet circled his wrist. Nicole Archer from The Jewelry Box had created the masculine piece of jewelry. Kai never took it off.

Sophie smiled at the man who would breathe life into her vision of the museum. "What do we do first?" she asked. She was open to his direction.

He looked around. "The place needs to be cleaned, but that can come later. Let's talk about the renovation. I need to know where you're headed."

She motioned him into the second room toward the back of the shop. She knew what she wanted. She had the room laid out in her mind. She shared her vision. "I want an enormous mural drawn on the west wall, one depicting the Cates family tree. William will be at the top," she said. "His family and relatives will branch out below him. Beside each name, I want to document something special about the person."

She knew William well from his journals, and she'd already researched many of the family members. She had a good grasp on everyone's background and how they had contributed to the growth of the town.

"Go on," Kai said, impressed.

"The artist will paint snowfall and sunshine by William's name, portraying both Minnesota and Florida," she said. "Perhaps a hammock and a hound dog, too. His wife Lily Doreen loved to knit. She made wool scarves for her family long after they moved to Florida. Perhaps the muralist could depict knitting needles and yarn." She glanced at Kai. "What do you think so far?"

"It sounds wonderful," Shaye Cates answered for her cousin Kai. She stood in the doorway, listening intently. Violet, Randy, and Chuck came in behind her. "I like the sense of warmth you've created and the closeness of generations. Please continue," she encouraged Sophie.

Sophie picked up where she'd left off. "One of William's brothers, Walt, owned a trawler called the *Breakwater*. A fishing boat fits him best. Another younger brother, Harold, ran the weekly chronicle. A newspaper would work for him. A steamy apple pie goes to William's youngest daughter, Helen." She then skipped several generations and returned to the present. "Your Grandfather Frank was the local cribbage champion for decades. His wife Emma played an upright piano."

She smiled at Shaye. "A beach chair and a computer on the shoreline by the pier describe you best."

Shaye threw back her head and laughed. "You know me so well."

"How about a tool belt for me?" asked Kai.

"Done, unless you'd rather be known as the owner of Hook It, Cook It," Sophie said. Hook It sold bait and tackle on the pier. Cook It stood next door, a small chef's kitchen where fishermen could have their daily catch cleaned and filleted for a fee, then baked or fried for dinner or lunch.

"Let's go with the hammer and nails," said Kai, pleased with his choice.

Violet raised her hand. "What about me?" she asked. "I love working at Molly Malone's, but I won't be there forever."

"No drawing on the mural will be a fixed testament of who you are," Sophie promised her. "We can modify the design at any given time."

"What about your boyfriend Dune?" came from Randy.

Her boyfriend. Sophie blushed. They were friends and lovers, but there'd been no mention of commitment. Randy assumed that because she and Dune spent time together they were a couple. She wouldn't embarrass him by correcting his misconception.

"A volleyball and board shorts for Dune," she said.

"How can I get in the mural?" Mac James asked as he strolled into the shop. He carried a big box of cleaning supplies.

"You marry a Cates," said Shaye.

That stopped him short. "No other options, huh?"

"It's the Barefoot William Museum," Sophie reminded him. "It's all about their family."

"Have you chosen anyone to paint the enormous tree?" asked Violet. "There are several professional artists in the area."

"I like to paint," Chuck spoke up. "I could do the outline."

"I'll make the branches," came from Randy.

They were so young, Sophie thought. In the back of her mind, she'd envisioned a seasoned artist for the job. However, she couldn't dash the hope in the boys' eyes.

There was something to be said for youthful exuberance. They were the next generation of the Cates family and needed to make their mark on the boardwalk.

"You two boys can work together," she suggested to Randy and Chuck. "Submit a few sketches to me and we'll go from there. I'm open to seeing your designs."

"Tonight, my house, we'll get started," Randy said to Chuck, punching him on the arm. Chuck was all grins.

Shaye stood beside Sophie and hugged her. "Thanks for taking care of our boys," she said, keeping her voice low.

Our boys. Shaye made her feel like family.

"The mural will be an awesome attraction in the back room," Shaye continued. "What do you have planned for the front?"

"Lots of photos, along with any antiques the Cateses wish to donate to the museum," Sophie said. "Anything valuable can be set behind glass. Kai can install a security system. I plan to display the journals, too."

"You've got your work cut out for you," said Violet, rolling up her sleeves. "Let's get the shop cleaned up so you can get down to business."

"I've enlisted Mr. Clean for the job," Mac said, holding up the cleaning solution and a scrub brush.

Sophie looked at everyone, surprised. "You're all here to help me?"

"I didn't show up on my own," Mac admitted. "I got a text from Dune threatening my life if I didn't lend you a hand."

"I got the same text," said Violet.

"So did we," Randy and Chuck said at the same time. "Dune knew it was our day off."

"Apparently my brother made the rounds during his layover in Atlanta," said Shaye, laughing. She looked over her shoulder and a small sigh escaped. "Oh, my, I don't believe it. Here comes Grandfather Frank."

Sophie had met Frank only once at Shaye and Trace's wedding. Shaye had introduced them after the wedding ceremony on the beach. Frank had been brusque toward her. He hadn't offered his hand or spoken a word. His nod had been brief. She found him intimidating.

He stood before her now, a man with a full head of white hair, a sharp, challenging gaze, and a stern expression. Age bent his shoulders ever-so-slightly. He wore a faded gray shirt, white shorts, and Dearfoam house slippers.

Mac eyed Frank's feet. "Dude, slippers?"

"My feet hurt," Frank said, his tone gruff. "I wore work boots in the orchard yesterday and got two blisters."

"Did you wear socks with your boots?" Again from Mac.

Frank narrowed his gaze. "I can dress myself, son," he said.

"How'd you get here, Grandpa?" Shaye asked, concerned. "Your license expired a month ago and you haven't been to the DMV to renew it. You know I'm available whenever you need a ride."

"Trace picked me up. My coming here was his idea,"

Frank said, stunning them with his explanation. "He drove out to the house and offered me a lift. He thought I'd be interested in the renovation. I damn sure am."

Shaye smiled. "My husband is full of surprises. Where is he now?"

Trace appeared seconds later. "I'm bringing up the rear." He walked straight over to Shaye and kissed her with a husband's pleasure in seeing his wife. He was dressed for the office in a dark business suit and polished wingtips.

Sophie was glad to see her brother. Trace was formidable, but he had a big heart. He understood his wife's closeness to her family. Shaye had been heartbroken when her grandfather disowned her following their wedding the previous summer. Resolution between them was coming slowly.

For his wife's sake, Trace had put the past behind him and was making an effort to heal old wounds. He'd taken time out of his busy day to drop off mops, brooms, sponges, and several buckets.

Trace's idea of drawing Frank into the renovation was brilliant, Sophie thought. Shaye and her granddad were once again together, working toward a common goal.

"Frank, you've met my sister Sophie," Trace said by way of introduction. "I think she'll make a great curator of the museum."

Frank pursed his lips and looked her over with an inquisitive eye. Sophie sensed his mental debate. She wasn't certain he liked her. The fact that she cared so much for Dune had her holding her breath while she waited for him to say something. She hoped Frank would accept her.

He came around, but on his own terms. "I don't cotton much to any Saunders." He was a man of strong opinions. "I find you far too young for this position. You're fortunate that I have some time on my hands, young lady. You need a consultant."

"Historical accuracy is important to me," said Sophie. "I would appreciate your assistance."

"I'll be here every day," he assured her. He seemed pleased to have a purpose for getting up in the morning. "I'll get my driver's license renewed later today."

Sophie found herself staring at Frank. At his wide brow, the awareness in his light brown eyes, the solidness of his jaw. He remained a good-looking man even in his golden years.

"Dune looks a lot like you," she said without thinking. Her cheeks warmed.

"You've got a keen eye," the older man said. "The family notices our similarity, but you're the first outsider to do so."

Outsider. That was how he saw her. His attitude might never change. She inhaled deeply, trying not to let her hurt feelings show. If she was going to make the museum a success, she had to get organized.

She looked around the room, at its cracked walls and scuffed floors. She'd never cleaned beyond wiping down her kitchen counter. How hard could it be? Still, she hesitated to get started.

"I have to get back to the office," Trace said, breaking the silence. He kissed Shaye a second time, then crossed to Sophie. He gave her a quick hug, lowering his voice near her ear. "You can do this, Sophie. I'm very proud of you."

He left the shop, his words giving her confidence. She needed it. Everyone was watching her, waiting for instructions. She said the first thing that came to mind. "Pick a spot and scrub."

That was all the direction they needed. Her helpers began to sweep, scrub walls, and do windows.

Sophie got busy, too. She discussed shelving and glass-front displays with Kai, listening to his suggestions and adding her own ideas. He took the measurements for shelving additions, while she checked to see how the clean-up work was progressing.

By noon, the morning shift had departed, all but Mac. He stuck it out. The afternoon crew, consisting of Jenna, Eden, and Nicole, showed up at one. Mac glanced at Jen and Jen returned his stare. Sophie saw the heat in Mac's eyes and the longing in Jen's own before Jen looked away. They were definitely into each other, she thought.

Molly delivered a late lunch from the diner. They ate picnic-style. Everyone sat on the floor and enjoyed grilled cheese sandwiches and double-chocolate fudge brownies.

Sophie found Frank watching her throughout the day. He caught her at the worst moments. Like when she was carrying a cleaning bucket and backed into a wall. The water spilled out and soaked her T-shirt.

Mac was Mac. He let out a low whistle, his eyes wandering to her breasts. "Wet T-shirt contest," he called, encouraging the other women to participate.

Damp sponges flew at Mac from every direction. Eden had the best aim. She caught Mac in the face. He inhaled lemon soap and blew a bubble. The man had talent.

Sophie tugged on the hem of her shirt, drawing the cotton away from her chest. She wished she'd brought a change of clothes.

Jenna saved her from further embarrassment. She went to Three Shirts and returned with a dry yellow tee. *Heigh Ho, Heigh Ho, It's Off To Work I Go* was scripted on the front.

Shortly after that, Sophie tripped over a broom. She couldn't help it. Her thoughts were on Dune and she ran into Eden, who was sweeping up the floor. Eden was apologetic, but it wasn't her fault. Moments later, Sophie stepped on a full dustpan and the contents spilled on the clean floor. She felt bad, making extra work for Eden.

Her friends knew she was clumsy, but Frank didn't.

She'd wanted to make a good impression. She hadn't succeeded. She found that disappointing.

She rolled her shoulders, then twisted left. That's when she saw Frank rubbing his lower back. She realized he'd been standing all day. He'd grown uncomfortable. She immediately sent Mac to Molly's diner to borrow a chair. Frank needed to get off his feet.

"Pop a squat," Mac told Frank when he returned with the chair.

Frank sat down heavily. He took off his slippers and rubbed his feet. Sophie noticed his blisters were red and raw. Poor man. She hurt for him. She carried Band-Aids in her hobo bag. She offered him two.

Frank's expression was stern but melancholy when he accepted the adhesive strips. "You remind me of my Emma." His voice was low and gravelly. "She was"—he paused for a moment, deciding what to say—"what you might call awkward at times. But she had a big heart and always had a smile for me, even on the worst of days."

He looked toward the front window. Sophie sensed his stare went beyond the glass and to another time. "Do you play the piano?" he asked her.

Sophie shook her head. "I'm musically challenged."

"Come to my home sometime," Frank said, meaning it. "I'll teach you how to play 'Chopsticks.'"

"I'd like that," Sophie said.

The day advanced according to plan. Three o'clock and her fiscal advisor, Ted Donahue, arrived right on time. He was a man of medium height with a slight build and a pleasant face. He wore a white shirt tucked into brown pants and sported a tie designed with colorful M&Ms.

"My daughter's favorite candy," he said when he saw Sophie smile. "Mandy's five, and her life's all about plain and peanut M&Ms."

Sophie had loved Snickers as a kid.

Ted tapped his hand on his briefcase. "The mayor assigned me to work with you. Is there a quiet place where we can talk?" he asked, noting the cleaning and scraping going on in the front room. "I want to go over your fiscal budget and employment contract."

"My office is in the back," she offered.

Kai had set up a temporary desk for her, consisting of two sawhorses with a board in between. They remained standing since there were no chairs. Ted popped open his briefcase and produced the necessary paperwork.

Sophie scanned the computer-generated budget. It was all Greek to her. She excelled in history and literature, but math was not her strongest skill.

After thirty minutes, her eyes crossed. Ted was a very patient man. He answered her questions and went over the graphs with her until she grasped the basics.

"It's not that tough, Sophie," Ted assured her. He removed his glasses and rubbed the bridge of his nose. "Think of the museum budget like a household budget. You have so much money to spend each month. The most important thing to remember is not to overdraw your checking account."

She nodded. That made sense to her.

He rummaged through his briefcase and located a thick manila envelope, which he handed to her. "Your employee contract." He pointed out several important paragraphs and explained each one in detail. "Read it over carefully and sign on the lines with the Xs. I'll pick it up later this week."

He packed up his briefcase and, on his way out, he said, "I encourage you to accept donations to the museum."

Sophie walked him to the door. He shook her hand politely. "I'm not a Cates by birth," he told her, "but I love history. The museum will be a nice addition to the town."

Ted cleared the door just as Mac shouted, "Make way

everyone, garbage to the Dumpster." He hefted two large bags of trash and headed for the loading dock.

Sophie noticed her volunteers were diligent throughout the remainder of the day. No one had taken a break. They kept a steady pace. It was long past six when they began to slow down, backs aching, knees sore. Sophie glanced around her museum and let out a relieved sigh. Gone were the dust, dirt, and moldy scent. A fresh aroma of lemon filled the air. The walls were scrubbed free of grime. The front window sparkled.

Kai Cates crossed to her. He hooked his thumbs in his tool belt, then said, "Nicole and I are headed out, if that's okay with you. We have plans."

"Every night is date night for us," Nicole said, joining them. She winked at Sophie. "It keeps the romance alive."

Definitely alive, Sophie agreed. Kai and Nicole raised the temperature in any room. His gaze was hot and his smile was sexy. Nicole licked her lips, tempting him. Their heat made Sophie's skin prickle.

"I'll see you in the morning, Sophie," said Kai.

"I'll be here after eight," she told him.

Eden came up behind her and gave her a hug. "I'm all worn out," she said, wiping her face with a paper towel. "By the way, I ordered several new vintage cut-outs for Old Tyme Portraits. Stop by and I'll take your picture."

"I'd like that. Thanks, Eden." Sophie watched her helpers leave one by one. Trace picked up Shaye and Frank minutes later.

Frank turned to Sophie at the door. "You have a long way to go, young lady, but the end result will be worthy of your efforts," he said, nodding his approval.

His compliment pleased Sophie.

"I'll see you bright and early in the morning." He followed Shaye out.

Sophie leaned back against the sandpapered wood of the

front door. She was tired, but happy. Frank was the biggest surprise of all. She'd bet the older gentleman would beat her to work each morning.

He'd been enthusiastic, sitting in his chair all afternoon, watching the museum take shape, his sharp eyes missing nothing, scolding Mac when he fooled around.

Frank's presence pleased Sophie greatly. She hoped he would become a permanent fixture. It occurred to her he would need his own key. She'd have an extra one made for him.

Her thoughts turned to the work she'd planned for Tuesday. She and Kai would select paint for the front room. Once the painting was completed, Kai would buff the hardwood floors, which were scuffed and marred from customer traffic.

The bookstore had been a popular spot for tourists and had seen a lot of sandy bare feet and flip-flops in its day. Sunbathers had purchased their favorite novels to read on the beach.

It would soon be history buffs pouring through the doors, she thought, visitors who were as interested in the past as they were in the present. She had fascinating tales to tell them. She knew the Cateses better than she knew her own family.

Her good friend Jenna bumped Sophie's elbow as she came to stand beside her. "I have to take off, too," she said. "I left my assistant in charge for the afternoon. Jamie is competent, but I need to cash out."

"I appreciate your help," Sophie said.

Mac hung around a moment longer. He stood by Sophie and stared at Jen until she cleared the door. He craned his neck to catch a look at her on the sidewalk.

"Why don't you go after her?" Sophie asked.

"Can't," he said. "I 'overwhelm her.' " He used air

quotes. "She expects me to play nice and give her space until after the Huntington Beach Classic."

Sophie pursed her lips. "Since when do you do what's expected?"

"I never have until Jen," he admitted.

She was hesitant. "So, you'll be back?" It was important for her to know the answer. If Mac returned, so might Dune.

"I'll be back so fast Jen won't know what hit her," he said. "I plan to hop a plane following our final match point."

"You're predicting a victory?" she asked.

Mac grew serious. "I believe in Dune. He's the best player in the game," he said. "Study his face the next time you watch us play on TV. No one has more mental control than he does. He *wills* us to win."

Sophie understood. She knew Dune's expression well. His steely-eyed stare was so intense it made her shiver. His game was powerful and precise. Dune became the game of volleyball with his first serve. "The two of you are unbeatable when—" She broke off her sentence, biting down on her lip.

"When we're both healthy," he finished for her. "Don't worry, Sophie. Somehow we'll pull off Huntington. Then we'll evaluate our situation." Mac rubbed the back of his neck. "Dune has his treatment tomorrow. If the medical procedure works, the Hermosa Beach Open will be the next stop on our tour."

"Hopefully he'll have options," she softly agreed.

"Volleyball is his life," said Mac. "That's all he's ever known."

Sophie had to face the truth. There was a distinct possibility Dune might not return to Barefoot William. Not for some time, anyway. Should his tendonitis improve, he was going to be very busy traveling. According to the information she'd found on the Internet, the schedule for the upcoming professional beach volleyball tour ran through October.

She sighed deeply. It could be a long five months.

Her stomach clutched at the thought of not seeing him for so long, but she had to live with that. She would never ask him to choose between her and his sport. There'd be no contest.

He'd pick volleyball.

"I'm off, Soph." Mac dropped a light, brotherly kiss on her forehead. "I told Frank I'd bring home dinner. We're having Mexican tonight. He likes beef tacos and I'm having supersized burritos. Maybe I'll buy him a sombrero so he can eat in style." He paused, grew thoughtful. "Want to join us? We could do the Mexican Hat Dance."

Sophie grinned, knowing Mac would liven up her evening, but she'd rather be alone. "Not tonight, Mac. I'll be here for another couple hours, then I'm headed home to my girls," she told him. "It's popcorn and a movie for me."

"Sounds good. Bye, babe." He gave her a wave, and then he was gone.

The door closed, and Sophie walked around the shop. She took a good look at the two rooms that would make up the museum, then her office. She could see the family mural, the black-and-white photographs, and display cases on the walls. A living history of the boardwalk she loved. Finally, she sat down on the chair Frank had vacated. She hadn't realized how mentally exhausted she was until now. She closed her eyes and massaged her brow.

"Hello, anyone here?" a woman called from the front room.

Sophie startled at her mother's voice. "Back here," she said.

Maya appeared in the doorway looking as elegant as if

she'd stepped from a fashion magazine. Sophie wondered what special occasion had prompted her to bring out her formal attire. Her mother looked stunning in a tea-length black satin dress and black leather pumps. She carried a silver evening bag. Diamonds sparkled at her ears and on her wrist. Her makeup was light but effective, giving her a polished look. Her hair was loosely tied back with a black velvet ribbon. She looked younger than her fifty-seven years.

"You look lovely, Mother," Sophie said, meaning it.

"Thank you" was all Maya said. Nothing more, no mother-daughter conversation about the designer or where she'd bought the dress.

Instead, she looked around the room, her gaze landing on the buckets and mops. She sniffed, and the corners of her eyes and mouth pinched slightly. The strong smell of cleaning products was not to her liking.

"I'm surprised to see you," Sophie initiated.

"Trace mentioned you've been hired as the curator of the Barefoot William Museum," her mother said.

Sophie felt a momentary sense of relief. Leave it to her big brother to help her out by breaking the news to her parents. She appreciated his sharing the information with them. Trace had saved her from the brunt of their caustic remarks.

"I've read William Cates's journals and I admire the man," Sophie said with great care. "He embraced the town as if it were family. All he ever wanted was to provide for those he loved and to live in peace." She met her mother's gaze. "Our ancestors treated him poorly. Evan Saunders was a capitalist. He bullied William. He kicked sand in William's face. Evan took land that belonged to the Cates family without asking. Any alliance that might have formed between the two families turned into a bitter feud."

Maya pursed her lips. "Do you wish you'd been born a Cates?" she asked.

Sophie shook her head. "No, I'm happy with who I am." She had a question for her mother, one that had weighed heavily on her mind for many years. Somehow, she found the courage to ask her, "Are you glad I'm your daughter?"

"Why would you ask me that?" Maya lips parted. She appeared genuinely surprised.

Sophie's mouth was dry and her throat closed. She took a deep breath, then managed to say, "I feel like I'm a disappointment to you."

Maya glanced aside, refusing to meet her eyes. She drew a tight breath as she brushed imaginary lint from her sleeve. Sophie realized she'd made her mother uncomfortable.

"I'm sorry you feel that way," Maya finally said.

"It's more than a feeling, Mother. It's a fact." Sophie's heart squeezed tighter yet. "In your eyes, I seldom do anything right."

Maya stiffened. "I've never meant to make you feel unwanted or less of a person."

"Perhaps that wasn't your intent," Sophie said, allowing her that concession. "But I've never felt good enough around you."

A heavy pause hung in the air before Maya said, "I don't know how to say this, Sophie, but I see myself in you and that frightens me."

Sophie's eyes rounded. "You see me in you?"

"We are very similar in many ways," Maya confessed to her. She glanced at the ceiling, then around the room, stalling for time. Her words came slowly and when they did, Sophie was taken aback. "I was plump, unpopular, and insecure when I was younger," her mother began. "I never dated in high school. Then I went to college. That's when your father fell in love with me.

"Unfortunately, Brandt's parents found me lacking as a future daughter-in-law," she continued, her voice turning brittle as she spoke. "I wasn't good enough for their son, they said in no uncertain terms. They didn't approve of our engagement because I wasn't a socialite with an old-money pedigree. His mother, Juliana, had chosen another woman for Brandt and did everything in her power to push us apart."

Sophie considered her Grandmother Juli. The woman was stylish and refined. She had reserved parking places around town and she'd donated a pew to her church so family members could sit together. But her expression was stiff, her manner disengaged, and her smile never reached her eyes. As a young girl, Sophie had been as afraid of her grandmother as she'd been of the boogeyman.

Maya paced the length of the front windows and back. Her sigh was self-deprecating, more of a shudder. "I can recall Juliana inviting me to a boat show at Saunders Harbor. She wanted Brandt to see how poorly I fit in with their elite crowd. We had to cross ramps between the yachts, not easy for me to do carrying a peach mimosa in a long-stemmed glass. I nearly died when the sole of my pump scuffed the rubber walkway and I tripped. Brandt grabbed my elbow, but I jerked forward and lost my balance." Maya stopped, her eyes widening as she remembered the embarrassing moment. "The mimosa drink flew straight into Juli's face."

"Oh, Mom," Sophie exclaimed, her voice sympathetic. "I'm so sorry."

"So was I." Maya sighed heavily. "Juliana upped her campaign against me and continued to point out my faults. Like the time I wore a white dress to a house party after

Labor Day, a major fashion faux pas in her eyes. Nobody else noticed, but she did. She criticized my choice of dress to anyone who would listen to her. That included everyone who wanted to be invited to her next afternoon tea."

Maya walked to the window and looked out, staring at the passersby on the boardwalk. "Juliana threatened to disinherit Brandt if he married me. Imagine how I felt when I discovered Brandt was more materialistic than I'd realized. He caved in to her demands."

Maya glanced back at Sophie. Her brow wrinkled ever so slightly and the hollows in her cheeks deepened as she drew in a long breath.

Her lips twisted together when she said, "I loved him and refused to let him go. How could I? He'd been the only man to pursue me and, as I saw it, my only hope for marriage."

She clutched her evening bag so tight her hands shook. Sophie had never seen her mother so anxious. "Trace is not aware of what I'm about to tell you, Sophie," her mother said. "I must ask you to keep my confidence."

"Your secret is safe with me, Mother."

"Throughout our relationship, Brandt was never shy about wanting . . . sex." She said the word as if it were distasteful. "To keep him, I did what I had to do." She paused. "I got pregnant."

Sophie's jaw dropped. Her beautiful, sophisticated mother had carried a baby to keep her man. "Did Grandma accept you once Trace was born?" she asked.

"We came to an understanding," she confessed. "I gave her an heir in exchange for the Saunders name. Sadly, I discovered I wasn't the maternal type. I hired a nanny to care for my baby. Juli held that against me, too."

"Trace turned out just fine," Sophie was quick to say.

"Your father doted on him. Brandt saw Trace as the perfect son, and he was. Interestingly, my life took on a drastic change after that. To my surprise, Brandt stood up for me and his mother backed off. Even more surprising, as the years went by, Juliana took me on as her pet project. She delighted in molding me to the Saunders image. In the end, she won." Maya lifted her chin. "Here I stand today, well dressed, well mannered, and well off."

"Trace was meant to be an only child," Sophie assumed.

"That was our plan until your father and I spent a long holiday in Costa Rica," Maya said. Her eyes shone and her cheeks pinkened. "That's where we renewed our wedding vows. On our flight home, Brandt got amorous. Private jet, too much champagne, high altitude . . ."

Sophie's eyes went wide. "I was conceived at thirty thousand feet?"

Her mother actually smiled. "We almost named you Skye."

Sophie was so stunned she couldn't speak.

"You were a beautiful baby with a sweet disposition," Maya said with warmth in her voice that Sophie had never heard before. "I tried to be a good mother, but as you grew older, I saw myself in you. There you were, tripping over your own feet and with a nervous stomach, just like me when I was a kid. I was always afraid you'd vomit in public. I'd take you shopping and you'd hide in the dressing room away from people. I was so embarrassed for you. When you began seeking solace in books, I left you to your reading. I was happy you'd found a place where you felt comfortable, but I admit, Sophie, it also gave me an excuse to avoid my responsibility as a parent. That I regret more than you'll ever know, but I've always loved you."

Sophie nodded, taking it all in. "I'm no longer that awkward little girl with her nose in a book, Mother. I've grown up. This was my summer of adventure," she said with conviction. "I've outgrown my shyness and I don't have so many fears. I think I've found my niche here in the museum. This could be the start of a promising career."

"Ah, yes, the museum," Maya said, a different light coming into her eyes. She was holding something back, but what? "That was the original purpose of my visit." She unfastened the clasp on her evening bag and fingered through the contents before drawing out two tattered leather journals.

"I gather those are not your diaries," Sophie said, smiling, trying to put her mother at ease.

"These are a lot more interesting and I assure you, they're authentic." She handed them to Sophie. "Evan Saunders was a cutthroat capitalist, but there was a side to the man few people ever knew. Read his final account of what happened between William and him. Your opinion of Evan may change."

Sophie stared at the journals, afraid to breathe. The leather looked ancient and she had no reason to doubt her mother's word. It must have taken a lot of courage for her to come to the shop and admit her mistakes. And to give her daughter the daybooks.

Sophie turned to the first page; the paper was creased and crackly and yellowed with age. The ink had smeared over several words, but the majority of sentences were legible. Her heart gave a squeeze when she saw Evan Saunders's name scrawled at the top of the first page. She was holding a man's private thoughts in the palms of her hands.

What would she find? Secrets? Memories? She'd read the earlier chronicles of Evan's life written through nineteen forty-five. From what she could see at first glance, these pages spanned his later years.

"Why are you giving me the journals now?" She wondered at her mother's motive.

"Despite appearances, I never minded the feud," Maya

admitted. "The Cateses always seemed beneath us. There was no reason for them to cross Center Street. Then Trace married Shaye and you became interested in the beach boy. Times changed, so here I am."

Beach boy. Sophie let that pass. For now. She looked at her mother, not knowing what to say. "Thank you," she managed, holding the journals tight to her chest. "I'll take good care of them."

"I know you will, Sophie. I trust you," Maya said. She walked to the door, then turned around before she left. She had something else on her mind. "Trace mentioned that Dune Cates was out of town. I thought we could have breakfast together this week."

"I'd like that," Sophie said. "I have a new cookbook. I'll make you French toast."

Maya made an attempt to dissuade her daughter from cooking. "We could eat at the Sandcastle," Maya offered as an alternative. "The hotel serves a sumptuous brunch."

Sophie was firm. "I'd rather cook."

Maya had one hand on the door handle when she glanced back at Sophie. A corner of her mouth lifted. "Yes, you do have my stubbornness." She seemed pleased by that fact as she slipped out the door.

By the time the limo driver came for Sophie, she had everything locked up. With the journals tucked safely in her purse, she headed home. Roger dropped her off at her front door.

Once inside, she checked on her hamsters. She took Glinda and Scarlett out of their cage and put them in their plastic ball, then gave them the run of her house.

She changed into her favorite silk lounging pajamas. A bowl of popcorn and glass of chai iced tea accompanied her to the library. There she curled up on the couch and opened the journals.

She read the entries slowly. Evan had documented his

business dealings, commented on his family, and written scathing passages on the Florida heat. He was not a warm-weather person.

Sophie felt little affinity toward Evan until the final pages of the second journal. The ink was faint, smudged, and difficult to read. His posts were sporadic, yet his words touched her heart . . .

August 15, 1950
    William Cates called me a swindler. He swears I stole a parcel of land out from under him. The acre sits south of Barefoot William. He's wrong, but he won't admit it. He's got more pride than I do. There are no county records of ownership. I bought it fair and square.

March 3, 1951
    The fish were running tonight and I caught two snook off the shoreline. The water was rough. William baited a hook right before twilight and we both waited. We stood fifty feet apart. Someone on the beach took our photograph with a Kodak Brownie.

September 9, 1951
    Hurricane Abigail destroyed both the Barefoot William and Saunders piers. William and I came together to discuss building a central pier, one that would benefit us both. An argument ensued. William wanted the pier for fishing and amusement. My vision was for a yacht harbor. Nothing was finalized. A second discussion is scheduled for next week.

November 21, 1951
    William and I continue to argue over the pier. We have agreed on a central courthouse for both cities. That will give us access to land documentation and recorded deeds. No more finagling over who owns what.

We've decided not to approach our families with the joint venture until after the first of the year. We don't want the holidays disrupted. We plan to start construction on the public facility as early as next March.

December 15, 1951
    I've been told William has fallen ill. I have not yet heard his diagnosis. I hope it is not serious.

January 5, 1952
    One of my business associates informed me that William's health is failing. I went to his home, but was told he couldn't have visitors. I left him a fishing lure. He will understand my message.

January 26, 1952
    William's family buried him today. His heart failed him. I stood within the shelter of a pine tree and watched as his casket was lowered into the ground. His widow was inconsolable. Death seems so final. I've lost an adversary, yet also a formidable friend. We had come to an understanding by the end of his life. We'd planned several projects together that would have ended the feud between our families. With William's death, I fear those ventures will no longer be realized. William's legacy will be one of beloved father and fine fisherman.
    I will miss him.

Evan's last words touched Sophie deeply. Tears escaped her. She ran her fingertips over the final post at the back of the journal. The script was in a different handwriting.

It said: *Evan Saunders. Deceased. May 31, 1954.*

He'd passed away within two years of William Cates.

Sophie closed the journals and cried. She went through a box of Kleenex. Life was unpredictable. It held promises and secrets and was far too short.

She thought about William and Evan. The two men were from different backgrounds. They were business rivals. They bickered and fought their entire lives, yet in the silence of twilight, with fishing poles in hand, they shared moments of peace. And of friendship.

An olive branch had been extended late in their lives.

In truth, the peace offering was still there, stretching through time, waiting to be recognized.

Sophie would find a way to acknowledge their alliance.

It had been kept a secret for too long.

She needed to speak to Frank Cates.

Sixteen

Sophie arrived at the museum at eight a.m. sharp. Mac James dropped off Frank Cates at five minutes after eight. Frank entered the shop in a huff.

"The boy made me late." Frank pointed a finger at Mac. "I was ready to leave when he decided to change clothes. Again. He was as fussy as a girl this morning."

Heat reddened Mac's neck.

Sophie noticed he'd cleaned up his act. No T-shirt or board shorts today. Instead, he wore a white polo shirt, khaki Dockers, and loafers without socks. His hair was still damp from his morning shower. He'd taken the time to shave. He looked good.

"What's the occasion?" Sophie asked him, curious.

Mac shifted his weight. He seemed unable to stand still. "Jenna agreed to have breakfast with me before I leave," he said. "My flight's scheduled for eleven. This will be my last chance to see her until after the tournament."

His expression was torn. She knew he had to leave town, but sensed that a big part of him wanted to stay. Volleyball would win out in the end. The sand was where he made his living. He owed it to Dune.

She wondered if he'd heard from his partner. She bit down on her bottom lip, unable to hide her feelings.

Mac read her expression and said, "Not a word from

him, Sophie. I'm certain he'll contact you once he knows the status of the procedure."

"I'm hoping for good news."

"Healed or not, I know Dune. He'll play this weekend," Mac said. "He won't forfeit."

"Jen and I plan to watch the match at my house," Sophie said. She turned to Frank. "You're welcome to join us, too. I have a large plasma television."

"By large, she means one hundred and fifty-two inches." Mac encouraged him to watch the match with the girls. "You'd feel like you were sitting in the stands."

Frank scratched his jaw. "I'll have my driver's license by Saturday. I just may join you."

"You'll have the best seat in the house," Sophie promised him.

Mac left then, to meet up with Jenna.

With his departure, Sophie found herself alone with Frank. What she'd read in Evan's journal weighed heavily on her mind. It was as if she had the key to unlock the door to a new future for Barefoot William.

She motioned him toward the lone chair in the shop. "Take a seat, Frank. I have something to show you."

Frank cast her a wary glance, but did her bidding. He narrowed his eyes. "Are you delivering bad news?" he asked.

"Bad or good, I'm not certain how you'll feel," she said with a sigh.

Sophie reached inside her purse and produced the leather journals. She'd wrapped them in a soft cloth for safekeeping. She removed them now and handed them to Frank. "Here are Evan Saunders's daybooks."

Frank was taken aback. "Where'd you get these?"

"My mother gave them to me yesterday. They chronicle his last years with William. Read his entries carefully and without prejudice. I assure you, they will alter the history of Barefoot William as you know it."

Frank held the journals on his lap for several minutes, as if he was hesitant to read them. He was stalling, Sophie thought, but she gave him the space he needed.

"I'm going to Brews Brothers for coffee," she decided. A walk down the boardwalk and back would give him plenty of time to process the entries. "Would you like a cup?"

Frank nodded, but didn't look up. "Make mine white."

Sophie understood. He wanted cream added.

"A cinnamon bun would be nice, too," he said.

Frank had a sweet tooth, Sophie noted. There was an easy recipe for scones in her new cookbook. She could make them for him sometime. How difficult could that be?

Stepping outside the shop, she walked slowly along the sidewalk toward the boardwalk, a half-block away. She glanced in the window at Molly Malone's and saw Jen and Mac seated together in a booth. Mac held Jenna's hand and she allowed it. They had publicly become a couple.

Sophie couldn't help but smile. Should they continue as they were, she would collect on her final bet with Dune. There was an engagement in their future. She could feel it in her bones. The wild man of volleyball was about to settle down. His female fans would weep.

After a quick stop at the coffee shop, Sophie headed back to the museum. A seagull circled overhead, sweeping low, then diving for bread crumbs left on the boardwalk from someone's breakfast sandwich. Sophie managed to juggle the coffee and cinnamon buns without mishap. Her coordination had improved and so had her confidence.

On her return, she found Frank standing before the front window. His shoulders slumped. His eyes were red-rimmed. He caught her staring at him and stuffed a crumpled handkerchief into his pants pocket. He looked sad.

She crossed the room and set down their coffee cups and cinnamon buns on the chair, then stood beside him.

Frank clutched the journals to his chest. "So much hate over so many years. A man gets old fast with that much hatred inside him," he said, his voice hoarse. "Grudges and bad blood lasted a century. Maya sure took her time in delivering the truth."

"My mother saw no reason to smooth the waters," said Sophie. "Not until I was appointed curator of the museum. She thought I'd portray Evan Saunders in a bad light and tell his story only as the Cateses saw him. She felt the journals would give me a new perspective on their relationship."

"Have they helped you?" he asked.

Sophie nodded. She felt strong and secure in her heritage. "Had William lived, their joint projects might have unified the two towns."

"We'll never know," said Frank.

He grew quiet, looking out the window toward the Gulf. The sun glinted off the water. Vendors pushed their carts along the boardwalk, selling cotton candy and churros to tourists.

What was he thinking? Sophie wondered. That it was too late to undue years of feuding? Or that the two families could come together after all these years?

Frank took a deep breath, pulled his hand down his chin, and turned back to her. "William and Evan were both stubborn, opinionated men. They needed two lifetimes, maybe even three, to settle all their differences."

He passed the journals back to her. "What do you plan to do with them?" he asked.

"I'm going to photocopy the final entries that Evan wrote about his friendship with William," she told him. "With your permission, I'd like to read the entries at the dedication ceremony. Once the museum opens, I want to put them on permanent display."

Frank sat down and thought about the journals for a good long time. His head was bowed as he took the lid off the coffee cup marked with a "C" for cream. He took a sip, then ate two bites of his cinnamon bun before saying, "What happened between our families couldn't be changed then, but it can be now. Shaye is important to me. It's time I accept Trace."

He looked up at Sophie over the rim of his cup. "Whatever their reasons, my family has already accepted you. You snuck in when I wasn't looking."

"I love your grandson," she said before she could stop herself. She blushed.

"He has feelings for you, too, girl," said Frank, "but first things first with Dune. He faces a big weekend ahead. His career is on the line."

Sophie swallowed hard, hoping for the best.

"Man, Sophie, your TV is bigger than the one at the Blue Coconut," Kai Cates said when he and Nicole stopped by on Saturday afternoon. "Hope you don't mind if we watch the tournament with you."

"You two are always welcome." She was glad to see them both. And everyone else who just happened to be in the neighborhood.

Twenty members of the Cates family now gathered in Sophie's den, a few stretched out on the marble floor. Dune and Mac had climbed the leader board and would soon face cousins Scott and Sean Taylor in the final match.

The doorbell rang again. This time it was Shaye and Trace arriving with blue and red tortilla chips and spicy avocado dip. Jenna was behind them. She'd packed a cooler with icy cold sodas and beer. Everyone wore either a Beach Heat or Ace-hole T-shirt.

Sophie went into the kitchen and made popcorn in the microwave. She burned the first bag. Frank pronounced the second one edible, although he picked out the black kernels.

She settled on the sofa between Frank and Jen. She leaned forward as the sports announcer relayed both professional and personal facts on the world-class players. This was a match between the first and third seeds. The Taylors were out to dethrone Cates and James.

The camera panned the beach, showcasing the crisp Huntington Beach shoreline from the pier to the sand court. Aqua Gold sponsored the sanctioned tournament. Long billowing banners caught the brisk wind blowing south of the pier. The hostesses' tents were set up around the perimeters of the bleachers. Bikini-clad beauties passed out samples of the suntan oil.

The sun was high, and the sky was clear. Beachcombers walked the compact sand at low tide. Bicyclists checked out the action as they cruised along nearby asphalt paths. Onlookers peered down at the beach through coin-operated telescopes mounted on the pier. Volleyball fans had turned out in droves. Swimsuits were the attire. It was standing room only.

The camera swung over to Dune and Mac as they appeared on the court. They wore white tanks, black board shorts, and sunglasses. The fans went crazy. Men admired their athletic ability. Women wanted their bodies.

Sophie studied Dune as he prepared for what she knew was the most important match of his life. Wanting so bad for him to do well, she squeezed her fists together so tight, her nails dug into her palms. She couldn't take her eyes off him. He swung his arms, rolled his shoulders, warming up. He rotated his wrists. He looked in good shape, she thought, but he'd yet to serve, had yet to spike the ball.

Most matches lasted forty minutes, give or take. It would be nail-biting for her. Jenna looked just as nervous as Sophie felt.

Sophie did have one thing to keep her grounded. She'd spoken to Dune the previous evening. It had been good to hear his voice. They'd talked about the museum, the hamsters, and her newfound friendship with Frank. But when she'd asked about his medical procedure, he'd skirted the issue, saying only that he was okay. She had no idea if the injections were successful or how he would play today.

She heard the referee blow the starting whistle and the first set began. Sophie's heart was in her throat when Dune got into position. He stood behind the backline, ready to serve. His expression was fierce, his body taut. He rose up and—

"Ace! He spiked the shit out of the ball," Kai shouted, pumping his arm in the air. "Sorry, ladies, but that was one hell of an ace."

"Damn fine," Frank agreed. "Dune's making a statement."

He definitely was, Sophie thought, cheering him on in her heart. He set the mood for the match, going with a fast offense. Sean Tyler was next to serve.

"Sean's sporadic at best," Shaye told Sophie in a calm voice. She knew the players' weaknesses. "On a good day, he's solid. On a bad one, he'll serve out of bounds."

Sean started out strong. He hammered his serve.

Dune met the ball at the net. Scott came back, setting the ball while Sean hooked it down. Mac couldn't reach it in time. The score was tied one-one. Mac would now serve.

Sophie bit down on her bottom lip, leaving her bowl of popcorn untouched. She watched as the score climbed. At seven-seven they changed sides. A short time later, the score was Cates and James 20, the Taylors 19. Mac was at the serving line. He and Dune needed the point to win by two and claim the set.

"Mac feeds off the pressure," Jenna said with confidence. She squeezed her soda can so tight she dented the aluminum.

"Dune and Mac are bringing the energy," said Kai. "They're both jacked."

Seconds later and Mac rose up for his serve. He pounded the ball to the far left corner. Scott Taylor was fast. He made the save, tipping the ball for Sean's return.

Dune was a big blocker at the net.

Mac dropped back and played deep.

Sean tapped the ball. Dune was ready when it clipped the net. He jumped up and stuffed one down. The point went to Cates and James.

Sophie fell back into the soft leather, relieved. They'd won the first set.

"Dune's an intuitive blocker," said Shaye. "He sees a play even before it happens."

Both teams took a short break between sets. The camera followed Dune and Mac to the sidelines, going in for a close-up.

Sophie wasn't particularly happy when she saw the bikini-clad Aqua Gold hostesses offer the players towels and bottles of water. Dune accepted a towel, wiping off his neck and shoulders. His expression was serious and unreadable. Mac drank deeply from his bottled water. The women lingered way too long for Sophie's liking. Jen's, too. The bikini babes were nearly draped over their men.

Both women breathed a sigh of relief when the next set was ready to start.

Kai was seated on the marble floor beside Nicole. He looked up at Sophie. "Notice how Dune and Mac pick up the pace when it's necessary," he said. "They make big plays when it counts."

"The Taylors have tunnel vision. They don't recognize the big picture," said Shaye. "Dune is a visionary. He's always one play ahead of his opponents."

The set progressed and the score remained close. Cates and James were ahead by two points, then the game shifted. They missed opportunities. Dune slammed the ball cross-court and it went out of bounds. Then Mac dove face-first into the sand, but he couldn't make the save. Their next rally ended in the net. Three bad plays and they suddenly fell behind by one and had to earn back their lead.

Sophie became worried when Dune shook out his wrist. She wondered if it was hurting him, but he gave no sign that he was experiencing pain. His expression was pure focus.

Cates and James battled back. Their plays were impressive. Dune swung high and hard and put the ball away, time and again. Mac served aces.

Shaye pointed to Sean Taylor. "He's got an eye twitch," she noted. "Players only get nervous when they struggle. The Taylors are out of sync. No nerves for our boys, they're in the zone."

"It's hard to believe Dune was ever injured," said Jenna. The score reached 21-21.

"Come on, guys," Shaye shouted at the TV. "Break the tie!"

Jen could no longer sit still. She pushed off the couch and circled behind it. She wrapped her arms across her chest and breathed deeply.

Sophie's heart was beating so hard, she was certain everyone in the room could hear it. She swore it thundered even louder when Scott Tyler served and Cates and James went up by one when Mac smacked the ball into no-man's-land between the players.

Sophie bounced on the sofa and clapped so hard she spilled her bowl of popcorn all over Frank. "Don't move," she said, apologetic. "I'll scoop it up."

"Don't worry about me," he said. "It's just as easy to eat popcorn off my shirt as it is from the bowl."

"One more point." Jen was breathless.

Everyone in the room held their collective breaths, only to release it in a whoosh when Dune next served and the Taylors powered back.

The score was again tied.

Sean Taylor was up to serve. The ball came across the net at an odd angle. Dune managed to scoop it up, and Mac made the jump. Then something happened that no one saw coming. He twisted in the air and landed on his ankle at an awkward angle. They scored the point, but Mac was down.

A time-out was called.

"He's sprained his ankle," Jen said, upset.

"Or broken it," came from Kai. He frowned at the screen, his hand fisted on his knee. "Dune helped him up, but Mac's not putting any weight on his foot."

"Oh . . . no." Sophie sighed. Dune was already hurt before they started; now Mac was injured. She shook her head, her gaze locked on the TV.

"The Taylors are looking smug." Trace scowled. He set down his beer on an end table with a loud thud.

The camera shifted to the two cousins. They were elbowing each other, looking cocky and not the least bit concerned for their opponent's welfare.

Sophie watched as Mac walked around the court, testing his ankle. "He has to be hurting," she said.

"Even if he is, he won't show it," Shaye said matter-of-factly. She leaned back in her chair and crossed her arms.

"Looks like they're not stopping the set," Trace said, surprised at their decision. He glanced around at the others, then returned to the television.

Play continued.

"One more point," Shaye said anxiously.

Mac's next serve tipped the net. Scott Taylor dumped it back on Dune. Both teams kept the point alive. The rally went on and on. It took a long rout to terminate the point.

Time seemed to slow when Dune handset the ball and Mac chopped it between Scott's feet. By intent or accident, Sophie couldn't tell which, the volleyball bounced up and hit Scott in the balls. He bent, coughed, and couldn't recover the save.

Cates and James had won the match.

The Taylors threw down their baseball caps, two very angry men with unsportsmanlike attitudes.

Everyone gathered in Sophie's den screamed as loudly as the fans on television. It was a moment she would never forget. Dune's family jumped up and down and hugged each other as if they'd won the set themselves. Even Frank got into the spirit of the win. He toasted the boys on TV with his beer.

"Never underestimate the heart of a champion," said Frank with pride. "They powered through adversity."

"Look, they're being interviewed," Shaye indicated, quieting them. Everyone sat back down.

Sportscaster Ty Kemp praised the players' consistency, accuracy, and effort. He then asked Mac about his ankle.

"I'll live," he said. He was hunched over with two gorgeous beach babes tucked beneath each of his arms, like big-breasted crutches. They supported him during the interview. He couldn't stop grinning.

Dune stood tall beside Mac. He wasn't alone for long. Sophie watched along with the entire TV audience as a hostess from Aqua Gold brought him a fresh towel. Dune removed his sunglasses and she blotted his brow, then patted down his shoulders and chest. Dune smiled his appreciation. Sophie frowned.

The sportscaster pulled Dune back to the interview. Ty Kemp relived the match, detailing each play. Dune added to the sportscaster's commentary, promoting their strengths, but never mentioning their weaknesses. He commended the Taylors for a good match, calling them tough competitors.

The interview wound down with Kemp's final question.

"What are your upcoming plans, Dune?" the sportscaster asked him. "Will you be at Hermosa Beach in two weeks?"

"A lot depends on Mac's ankle," Dune said without hesitation. "After he gets it checked out, we'll make our decision."

"Good luck to you both," Kemp said, ending the interview.

The cameraman made one last sweep of the court. The crowd was going crazy, cheering and whistling. The celebration had begun. Dune and Mac were surrounded by women, all sexy and beautiful, and all wanting to share in their win. It was party time in Surf City.

Silence settled in the den, each of them with their own thoughts until Shaye said, "It's been a long day for our guys. They need to relax."

"Mac requires medical attention." Jen was clearly agitated. Her tone was anything but subtle when she said, "His human crutches need to get him to the emergency room."

Jenna glanced at Sophie, the bummed-out look on her face saying it all. Her uncertainty was evident. Sophie returned her look. They were both thinking the same thing. The men they knew and loved were on the opposite coast at the center of an enormous party bash. They were the honored guests. Women would do just about anything for their attention.

Sophie's stomach sank and insecurity gripped her.

What could she do? Or Jen? Dune and Mac were in their element. They were warriors on the beach, and victorious in their match. Fans wanted a piece of each man. Groupies could be persistent. Sophie sat down when the last sweep of the camera showed five hot blondes hanging onto Dune. One woman had her hand tucked into the back waistband on his board shorts.

That wasn't anything new to Sophie. She had witnessed the same scene on TV every time she watched Dune play. Up until now, she'd accepted his popularity. He was a red-blooded male. He liked women and they liked him. He worked hard at his sport. He needed to cut loose after his match. It hadn't mattered to her how many women came on to him.

Sophie couldn't deny to herself that wasn't true anymore. Tonight, it mattered greatly to her. She'd thought they had something special.

She wasn't so sure now.

She stared at the television screen long after the sporting event came to an end. Long after the list of credits went by and the beach and volleyball net faded. She was vaguely aware of Shaye and Nicole picking up empty bags of chips and soda cans.

Jenna rose from the sofa first. Sophie noticed how pale she looked. As if she, too, had lost something tonight. "I'm off," she said with tightness in her voice. Then she was gone.

Shaye, Trace, and Frank stayed behind.

Shaye tried to comfort her. "Hang in there, Sophie," she said. "The celebration comes with the win. The after-party will soon fizzle. Mac's injury will take top priority. He's hurt and will spend most of the evening in the emergency room. Dune will stick by him."

"There are so many women," Sophie's voice was no more than a whisper.

"They come and they go," Shaye told her with confidence. "Women love athletes. Volleyball draws a lot of female fans in skimpy bikinis." She patted Sophie on the arm, trying to reassure her. "That doesn't take anything away from you and Dune."

Sophie's heart squeezed. His wrist had appeared healed. He had options now. Volleyball was his life. She wasn't sure he'd return to Barefoot William.

"We'll let ourselves out," said Shaye. She and Trace both gave Sophie a hug, then left.

Only Frank remained, and that wasn't for long.

A commercial for dog food came on the TV, prompting Frank to say, "That reminds me, I need to stop at the grocery store on my way home and pick up food for Ghost. Dune wouldn't be happy that we split a Swiss steak TV dinner last night. Ghost refused the mashed potatoes and vegetable medley. He only wanted the meat and dessert. He sure likes vanilla ice cream."

"You need to take care of Ghost," Sophie said as she walked Frank to the door. "It's time for me to put my hamsters in their plastic ball so they can run. They're big enough to each have their own ball, but when I separate them, they don't go far. They prefer to be together."

"Familiarity is important," Frank agreed. He gazed down, giving her a grandfatherly smile. "Never judge by appearances, Sophie. Trust in your heart."

Seventeen

Sophie's heart hurt for several days.

Everywhere she went, the pain went with her. Shopping, fixing up the museum, reading a book, the ache never left her.

It was still there this morning when she found Frank waiting for her at the museum with a box of assorted doughnuts and hot coffee.

"Any word from our boy?" Frank referred to Dune.

"Nothing, sorry," she said, disappointed.

Relationships were new to her. Maybe she was expecting too much from him. He'd called from the hospital, informing her that Mac had fractured his ankle. Mac didn't need surgery, he said, but his partner would be in a medical boot for six to eight weeks. Mac planned to recover at his beach condo in Malibu before heading back to Barefoot William.

Dune also mentioned checking on his volleyball camps while he was out on the West Coast. The summer sessions were about to start. He wanted to be sure each site was well staffed with the ratio of attendees to coaches three to one. The kids mattered most, he told her. The benefits of their experience could produce a top seed someday.

Dune made no reference to when he might return and Sophie didn't press him. He texted her once a day, but kept the tone light and easy, as if she were only a friend and he was ruffling her hair. Sophie's stomach sank at the end of each impersonal message.

"I watched the morning news," Frank said, settling onto his chair and grabbing a glazed blueberry cake doughnut. "The CNN sports anchor reported that Dune is actively seeking a new partner for the Hermosa Beach Open. The newscaster dropped names, but nothing has been finalized." The older man frowned. "That doesn't sound like Dune. He's loyal to Mac."

Sophie had no idea what was happening on the West Coast. She could only concentrate on her own here and now. She dedicated herself to her job as curator. She spent long hours at the museum. Frank didn't miss a day and often arrived ahead of her. She had given him a key. He greeted her every morning with hot coffee, baked goods, and a weathered smile.

They'd grown close, Sophie realized. They spent a great deal of time talking. The older man told her stories of his father and grandfather, and had her laughing over his own childhood. He liked soapbox derbies, but he had never won a race. He collected Lionel trains and brought the train set out every Christmas. He and his adolescent friends played tag in the cow pasture, only to have the bull chase them. He was good for a game of gin or cribbage at any hour of the day or night.

There was also another side of Frank she'd never dreamed existed. The soldier. He was a loyal man, she learned. He'd served in Korea. He shaved his head bald when one of his Army buddies was diagnosed with cancer and went through chemotherapy. He was a pallbearer at the man's funeral. He marched in the Veterans Day parade each year.

This morning, Frank had something else on his mind

than telling stories, and he wasn't shy about saying it either.

"I don't know what's wrong with that grandson of mine," he said, finishing his coffee. "He's always been considerate of others. I'm sorry he hasn't been more communicative, Sophie."

"I'm sure he has a lot on his mind right now," she said. Her hands were cold, her heart colder. "He needs to make the right decision for his future, Frank."

"I remember how it was when I met my wife. Emma Loraine Halverson was the prettiest thing a man could see on a summer day," Frank began. "She'd ridden the train into town with her family. They were on vacation. I fell in love with her when I saw her at Milford's Soda Shop sipping a strawberry shake topped with whipped cream and a cherry. She reminded me of sunshine with her honey blond hair, blue eyes, and warm smile."

"What'd you do next, Frank?" Sophie wanted to know.

"I introduced myself," Frank continued, "then I asked her if I could sit at her table. She lowered her eyes and nodded. I could barely eat my double-dip vanilla ice cream cone, I was so nervous. I kept wiping my face with my handkerchief." He sighed. "I'll never forget that day. Ever."

His smile was wistful. "I asked her to marry me after two dates. She agreed. We married on a Sunday. Emma's parents returned to Ohio and their daughter remained in Barefoot William. We had four children. Their children gave us eighteen grandchildren. I'm waiting on Shaye and Trace to give me a great-grandbaby."

She could've listened to Frank tell stories all morning, but she had work to do. People came and went throughout the day as they had all week. Randy and Chuck showed up at the museum with their sketchpads in hand.

Sophie discovered the boys were quite talented. She decided to give them a chance to draw the Cates family tree.

The rest of the week followed the same pattern. Shaye and Trace stopped in to check on Sophie at noon on Wednesday. Shaye had tears in her eyes when Frank and Trace shook hands and agreed to work together in the future. Frank had a parcel of land that Trace wanted to acquire for a public park. Frank was ready to negotiate.

Late Friday afternoon, Jenna Cates arrived at the museum in a pedicab. She asked the driver to wait for her at the curb. She then pushed through the door. "How are you doing, Sophie?" she asked, leaning back against the doorjamb.

"I could ask you the same thing," Sophie returned, eyeing her friend. "You've lost weight."

"Six pounds," Jen said with a weariness in her voice Sophie hadn't heard before. She pinched the bridge of her nose. "I have dark circles under my eyes." She ran her fingers through her hair. "Uncombed and no gel."

Her gaze was flat, too, Sophie noticed. Jen had pretty brown eyes, but they weren't nearly as bright or fiery as when Mac was in town.

"I'm a mess," Jen admitted, jamming her hands in the pockets of her denim shorts. "I've never allowed any man to walk into my life and steal my heart." She sighed. "Not until Mac James sauntered into Three Shirts. He broke my rules and I fell in love. Not my smartest move."

"Mac is a charmer," Sophie agreed.

"A charmer who hasn't called me," said Jen. She released a breath, then gently asked, "Any word from Dune?"

"Nothing recent," Sophie told her. "I'm assuming he's busy, between his volleyball camps and dealing with Mac. Mac needs to rest. Without supervision, he'll be up and walking on the beach—"

"Using hot, gorgeous women for crutches," Jenna said, flinching. "I can't get that image out of my mind."

"Me, either," Sophie said, remembering the TV news coverage of the celebration. She could still picture Dune surrounded by tanned, toned, and adoring female fans. He'd been the center of their crush, appearing pleased by their attention.

She understood an athlete's popularity. Mac and Dune wanted to give back to their fans. The crowds paid their salaries. But did there have to be so much touching? The women patted, stroked, and tugged the players to them. The image made Sophie miserable.

"We can't just sit at home and wait for Dune and Mac to return to Barefoot William," Jenna said. "We aren't even certain they'll be back."

The fear she might not see Dune for months was the worst fear Sophie had ever faced. The very thought she might see him again someday, but with another woman, would prove awkward, humiliating, and heartbreaking to her.

"We need a girls' night out," Jen said with conviction. "I've always wanted to try Barconi's bistro on Saunders Shores. It's time for me to cross Center Street. I'm in the mood for Italian food."

Jen was right. Fine dining was the perfect way to move on with her life. "I've eaten there several times," Sophie said. "The chef is from Bologna, Italy. The bruschetta and Chicken Roberto are my favorite dishes. I'd love to have dinner with you."

"Cool. Shaye's organizing midnight movie madness on the pier," Jenna went on to say. "*Transformers: Fall of Cybertron* will be the first of many Sunday summer shows shown on the outer wooden wall of Cook It, Kai's chef's kitchen. Lots of families attend every year."

"Sounds like fun," Sophie said, her mood lifting. "What should I bring?"

Jen thought a moment. "Beach chairs, popcorn, candy, and soda. That's it."

Sophie dipped her head, an old fear haunting her. She said, "I always wanted to ride the merry-go-round and Ferris wheel. I was too scared as a child. My time is now."

Jen nodded. "I love all the amusements. Ever play Whac-A-Mole? Ring toss? Balloon darts?"

Sophie shook her head. "They sound entertaining."

"And addicting," Jen said, smiling. She turned to leave, then stopped. "We'll get through this, Sophie." She gave her a quick thumbs-up, then opened the door. It closed behind her.

Sophie hoped Jen was right and she would survive. She massaged her chest, right over her heart. Her feelings were bruised. Her sense of disappointment was eye-opening. She'd believed in Dune, yet once he'd returned to volleyball, his fame and fanfare claimed him again. Sophie now stood on the sidelines.

She gazed out the front window and watched as Jenna climbed into the pedicab. She leaned back on the seat; her shoulders were slumped. Sophie felt her friend's sadness. It went bone deep.

Jenna Cates missed Mac James. She hated the fact she'd allowed him to take over her life. She wanted to kick something; that something was the curb when the driver dropped her off at her cottage. Her flip-flops were flimsy. Damn if she didn't stub her toe.

She took the stone path to the steps that led to her porch. She noticed the beige paint was peeling at the corners of her cottage and along the roofline. It was time to spruce up the place.

Most of the cottages on her street were brightly colored: sunshine yellow, seashell pink, a deep lavender. In that moment, she decided on sky blue with white shutters. The paint would brighten her life and make for a nice change.

Climbing the stairs, she looked around. Where were her Savannahs? They always approached her the second she started up the path. Not so today. So, where were they? They seldom spent time in the house. They preferred lying in the grass beneath a shade tree or stretched out in the window boxes.

She stopped, listened. It was eerily quiet.

She removed her house key from her denim pocket and keyed the door. She pushed it open. Slowly. Something was wrong. She could feel it. The hair at her nape prickled, as if she were about to be ambushed.

Mac James took her by surprise. He looked right at home seated on the antique rocking chair in her living room. His walking cast was propped on the ottoman. He appeared calm and comfortable, while her heart raced and her stomach fluttered.

Her cats had betrayed her, allowing him inside their domain. Chike now curled on his lap. Jango, Neo, and Aba lay on the floor close by. Jen couldn't move. She could only stare.

She took him in. He was too handsome for his own good. It had been eleven days since she'd seen him, yet it seemed like forever. His hair was longer and curled at his shirt collar. His blue T-shirt matched his eyes. The logo read *Come and Get Me*. Oh really? She wasn't going anywhere near him. Not after that postgame display of flash and flesh that he'd put on for the TV audience. One leg on his jeans was cut off at the knee to accommodate his cast. He wore a single leather flip-flop.

"Jenna?" His voice was low and deep. He tilted his head and narrowed his gaze. Uncertainty flickered in his eyes when she kept her distance.

She clenched her fists and tamped down her excitement at seeing him. "Who let you in?" Her voice was tight and unwelcoming. "Did you jimmy the back window?"

"It was all Chike's idea," he defended himself, scratching the Savannah behind the ears. "I couldn't fit through the cat door. Chike suggested the window."

Jen could hear Chike's purring all the way to the door. The sound irritated her. A lot. Her furry protector rolled onto his back, wanting his belly rubbed. Mac obliged. Chike looked at her from his upside-down position. She swore he winked at her. Her cat was a traitor.

"How's your ankle, Mac?" she wanted to know.

"It gets sore when I stand, so I'm forced to use my crutches."

"Which ones?" She sounded snarky, but she didn't care. "Aluminum or human?"

His brow creased, as if he didn't understand her question. After a moment, he burst out laughing. His laughter was inappropriate as far as Jenna was concerned.

"I had assistance off the court after the tournament," he said. "I'm sure the camera caught the worst angles."

"I saw tits and ass."

One corner of his mouth lifted. "You're jealous."

"Maybe . . . a little." She was honest.

"Don't be, Jen. I was thinking about you the whole time."

"When exactly did you think of me?" she asked him bluntly. "When you were being kissed by the groupies or when the Aqua Gold hostess rubbed suntan oil on your shoulders?"

He pursed his lips. "Definitely during the rubbing."

"You're such an ass."

"I'm your ass, Jenna."

"What if I don't want you?"

"You do, babe." He was smiling now. "Once you calm down, you can tell me how much."

He was way too sure of himself. She crossed to him then. Gripping his arm, she tugged hard. "Out of my rocker and out of my house," she ordered him.

"You don't mean that."

"Yes, I do." Chike received her message, loud and clear. He hopped off Mac's lap and resettled on the armless chair. Mac was left on his own.

He saw through her, which irritated Jen all the more. "You're mad I didn't call you, and I understand that." He ran one hand down his face. "Following the tournament, I was psyched that we'd won. I'm not going to lie, I enjoyed the praise, the prize money, the—"

"Women?" she had to add.

"The women lasted as far as the ambulance," Mac informed her with a straight face. "Dune stayed with me at the hospital. There was no one else. The doctor was as ancient as his nursing staff."

"No sponge bath, then?"

"Nurse Granny Panties washed the sand off my foot, but that was it."

Jen forced down a smile. "Your fingers weren't broken. You could've sent me a text."

"Not in the mood I was in, Jen." He blew out a breath, then went on to say, "I left the hospital ornery, complaining, and feeling damn sorry for myself. Ask Dune, he'll tell you how crappy I felt. He and I had just come off a major win. He'd played well, and Hermosa was a definite possibility."

He paused, grew thoughtful. Jenna waited to hear what he had to say. She owed him that.

"It's funny," he said, "how life shuts a man down when he's at an all-time high."

"We've all suffered setbacks, Mac." She no longer gripped his arm, instead she found herself stroking his shoulder, offering him comfort. "We start again from where we've left off."

"A fractured ankle makes it tough for a player to return to volleyball," he said. "A few have tried, but a second bad twist, and I'm sitting on the sidelines again."

"Surely you have options."

"I plan to put in an employment application at Three Shirts," he told her. "I know the shop owner. She's aware that I can draw a crowd."

"That you do." Having Mac around full-time was more than she'd hoped for. Jen liked the idea. They'd be a good team.

His jaw worked. "I've made additional adjustments, too," he continued before she could argue with him. "I cleared out my condo in Malibu and listed it with a real estate agent. It's located on the sand in a prime spot and should sell quickly. I sold most of my furniture. The few remaining pieces I chose to keep will be delivered here in a few days."

She blinked. "Here, to my home?"

He nodded. "I didn't think you'd mind."

She pinched his shoulder. "Don't think for me, Mac."

He winced. "A husband deserves a few items of his own—"

"Husband?" She backed him up.

"I plan to marry you."

"Do I have any say?"

"Very little, actually," he said. "Your cats like me; they want me as a roommate."

Seductive warmth settled on her chest. Mac James with his sexy smile and hot body had come home to her. He wanted her as his wife. She smiled at her Savannahs. "It seems I'm outnumbered."

He reached out and drew her to him. She climbed onto his lap. He ran his hands up and down her sides. His thumbs stroked beneath her breasts. "You've lost weight," he noticed once her bottom rested on his groin. He snuck a peek down her shirt. "Did you go down a cup size?"

She slapped his hand away. "I was worried about you and couldn't eat," she admitted, sighing.

"I was worried about me, too," he admitted.

She poked him in the chest. "Never keep me in the dark again. Your problems are my problems, understood?"

"Got it," he agreed. "Never doubt I love you."

"I like you a little bit, too."

"Prove it." He rocked slowly forward, and then back, learned the feel of the chair. "I've got condoms in my wallet and you positioned on my thighs. Where do we go from here?"

She showed him where by kissing him deeply.

He had her clothes off before she even missed them.

She stroked.

He squeezed.

He growled his passion.

She moaned her pleasure.

The antique rocker creaked, groaned, and gave good motion.

The motion of the Gulf was slow and lazy, Dune Cates noticed as he leaned against the bright blue pipe railing on the Barefoot William Boardwalk. He scanned the beach, hoping to locate Sophie Saunders. He couldn't wait a moment longer to see her.

He'd arrived home an hour ago. He immediately grabbed a cab from the municipal airport to the museum on Center Street. Hopping out at the curb, he found the front door of the shop propped open. He peeked inside. The scent of paint and floor polish was strong. He'd been gone two weeks. From what he could see, Sophie had accomplished a great deal in a very short time. New paint, floors, shelves, and display cases. The place was taking shape.

"Dune, welcome home," his grandfather called out to him from the back room. He was seated on a chair, supervising Randy and Chuck as they worked on the mural.

Dune was impressed with the boys' work. Sophie had a great idea to make the Cates family tree a key part of the museum. He had an even better one. Dune was hoping his and Sophie's names could be added to the middle branches before the trunk was drawn and the paint dried.

"I'm looking for Sophie," he told Frank.

"And why might that be?" his grandfather surprised him by asking. The older man sounded protective of her.

"I want to let her know I'm home."

"She's not expecting you, son," Frank said outright. He stood then, crossed to Dune, seeming uneasy.

"I wanted to surprise her," Dune told him.

Frank's brow furrowed. "Surprises sometimes backfire." He looked at him straight on.

There was something in the older man's voice that made Dune question, "Are you telling me she won't be glad to see me?"

His granddad never minced words. He cleared his throat and said, "I can't speak for Sophie. I can only tell you what I see. She's missed you, Dune, but I don't recollect you telling her that you missed her."

"I texted her."

"Not every day, you didn't. Modern technology isn't personal, son. Words on a little screen don't go a heck of a long way in reassuring a girl you've been thinking about her, too." He paused, rubbing his chin. "She's gotten real serious, Dune, and she seldom smiles. She walks around with her hand over her heart like it hurts."

Dune had thought about her often, but he'd also needed

to get his own head on straight. Major decisions were faced and finalized during the past week. At the end of the day, he'd never meant to cause her pain.

He loved Sophie Saunders.

It was time to let her know how much.

"Where can I find her?" he asked, needing to see her now, more than ever.

"Sophie needed a break," Frank told him. "The paint fumes were getting to her. You'll find her on the beach."

Dune raised his brow. "The beach?"

Frank nodded, and Dune couldn't help but smile. Was Sophie braving the waves? He couldn't wait to find out.

He gave his grandfather a man-hug, a thump on the back, and a fist bump. He then left the shop. He jogged the half-block from the museum to the boardwalk. The sand was patterned with tourists, many now packing up after a long day at the beach. He scanned the shoreline and the wooden pilings on the pier. There was no sign of Sophie.

Growing impatient, he jammed his hands into the pockets of his jeans and began to pace. This wasn't what he'd planned. Sophie was sad and hurting inside. How could he mess up so bad? He walked from Molly Malone's Diner to Crabby Abby's General Store and back again. He looked over the rims of his Suncats and squinted against the sun. Still no sign of Sophie. Where the hell was she?

He was ready to take to the beach when he saw her. His heart stopped. She stood in profile, knee-deep in the Gulf with sunlight glistening all around her. Her focus was on a young girl taking a paddleboard lesson. He grinned. This was the same girl who'd entered the stand-up paddleboard races several weeks ago.

Dune saw the girl wave at Sophie, and caught Sophie waving back. She watched the girl's lesson with avid interest, clapping her hands and giving her encouragement. It appeared they'd met and become friends. He decided not to interrupt their moment.

Twenty minutes passed, and the lesson ended. The girl grabbed her board and approached Sophie. Together, they walked across the sand toward the Popsicle Shack. Sophie reached into the pocket of her shorts and paid for two icy treats.

Dune continued to watch as the two of them talked. Sophie was such a kind person, always thinking about others. How come it took him so damn long to make up his mind? He knew the answer. His career was on the line, too.

Once they finished with their popsicles, the girl took off. Sophie waved good-bye to her, then scuffed through the sand, coming toward the wooden ramp that led to the boardwalk.

Where was his desert nomad? Dune wondered, thinking back on when he first arrived in town. Gone were her bucket hat, rain poncho, and waterproof pants tucked into her rubber boots. There'd been a time she'd tripped over her own feet and nearly taken a nosedive.

Not so today. A very sexy woman replaced his nomad. Sophie looked hot. She'd pulled her brown hair into a high ponytail. Red sunglasses shaded her eyes. The sun had lightly kissed her exposed skin. She glowed.

He'd never seen Sophie in a tank top, yet she wore one today. It was royal blue. Her navy walking shorts fit loosely. He liked her barefoot. One of the lifeguards called out to her, and Sophie smiled back. Dune swore the guy was flirting with her, but the guard's words didn't distract her. She didn't stumble or blush.

The closer she came, the harder it was for Dune to breathe. Simply put, she was a stunner. Men stared and admired her. Dune hoped he hadn't screwed up and she'd moved on. The thought kicked him in the gut.

She was nearly to the steps now. The breeze blew in his direction, picking up her soft, powdery, vanilla scent.

Anticipation squeezed his chest.

Attraction tightened his groin.

Sophie's hand was on the weathered, wooden railing when she looked up and noticed him. Her breath hitched, but she didn't run up the stairs and hug him. Instead she slowly removed her sunglasses and stared at him. There was apprehension in her gaze and banked sadness. She tilted her head, waiting quietly for him to speak first.

"You have yellow lips," were the first words out of his mouth.

Her smile was small. "I love banana popsicles."

"I like grape."

"So does Melissa, the girl on the paddleboard."

"I see you've met her."

"I've caught a few of her lessons," Sophie said, her voice as soft and faint as the breeze. "She introduced herself. Apparently the lifeguard let it slip that I'd given her the gift certificate."

Dune hoped she'd join him on the boardwalk, yet she remained at the bottom of the ramp. He curved his hands over the pipe railing. He squeezed so hard his knuckles whitened. Both wrists felt strong. He'd healed well. He had so much to share with Sophie, yet words failed him at that moment.

A first for him.

A seagull flew between them, squawking and mocking their silence. Smartass bird.

He noticed an empty cement bench a few feet away, one situated between the Denim Dolphin and Goody Gumdrops. Two large potted plants stood as sentries, giving the spot privacy. A store awning provided the shade. "Come sit with me," he requested.

"Dune, I—" she began, hesitating.

"Please, Sophie?"

She nodded, then came up the ramp slowly. Once on the boardwalk, she didn't take his hand as she was apt to do. Instead, she clasped her hands behind her back.

He sensed her vulnerability. Her uncertainty.

She doubted his sincerity.

Her hesitation scared the hell out of him.

He motioned for her to take a seat. They settled beneath the awning. A foot of empty space separated them. Late afternoon shadows played across their knees and ankles. He couldn't stop looking at her. She was sun-warmed with flecks of sugar sand on her feet. Her toenails were painted a dark blue.

"The museum looks great," he started out by saying, hoping he'd chosen a safe topic.

"I can't take all the credit," she said. "It's been a group effort. The Cateses have been very supportive of my plans."

"My grandfather is quite taken with you."

"I like him, too."

Sunbathers soon came off the beach in a continuous stream, chatting about their day. Dune turned his back on them. His focus was on Sophie.

"I've missed you," he said.

She gave him no more than a nod.

Her apathy nearly killed him. He rubbed the back of his neck. "I'm sorry it took me so long to come home, Sophie."

"You're here now," she said, looking at him. Her eyes were filled with hurt. "Your family will be glad to see you."

"What about you?" he asked. "Are you happy I'm home?"

She wasn't ready to answer him. Reaching for his hand, she gently stroked his wrist. Her touch warmed him. "I watched your match on TV. You played like a true champion, Dune. You have options and can continue on the tour if you choose."

"I don't choose," he told her.

That startled her. "What changed your mind?"

"You did, Sophie." He held her hand and she didn't resist. He took that as a good sign. "I was on a high after Huntington," he admitted. "My wrist felt good and Mac and I played hard. Winning solidified our top seed."

"I was excited you'd won," she said, then lowered her head. "So were a lot of other women."

So that was it. The women bothered her. He could fix that. "Fans and groupies stroke a man's ego," he said honestly. "Their attention is fleeting and superficial. They want to share our spotlight. Trust me, had the Taylors won, the attention would've been on them and not us."

He eased Sophie closer to him. They now bumped hips and thighs. "I taped an interview with Ty Kemp that will air before the Hermosa Beach Open, announcing my retirement, but I wanted you to be the first to know my decision."

"Are you sure this is what you want?" she asked, her voice barely a whisper.

He looked her in the eyes. "Yes. The time is right. I can retire on my own terms and not be forced out of the game."

She understood. "It was a decision only you could make."

He took a chance and curved his arm about her shoulders. She rested her cheek against his chest. He kissed her forehead. Her skin was incredibly soft. "I'm sorry that I didn't call or text you as often as I should have, but you were always on my mind. I had to work through my own personal issues. There were many. Retiring from a sport I lived and breathed since I was twelve years old weighed heavily on my mind.

"Mac took up a lot of my time, too," he continued. "He's not a good patient. I had to mash his pain medication in chocolate pudding to get him to rest."

Her smile tipped. "Mac would be a handful."

"You said it. He refused to use his crutches, preferring to shuffle. I stuck around while he located a Realtor and listed his condo. I cut out when he started selling his furniture."

Her green eyes went wide. "What are his plans?" she asked, curious.

"Let's just say you won our final bet," he said, the look on his face pained. "Mac beat me back to town by two hours. He's about to ask Jenna to marry him."

She sat up straight, her excitement evident. "I won!"

"Choose anything you want."

"Anything?" she asked. "Does that include you?"

"It could," he said slowly, liking that idea. "My condo's up for sale and my volleyball camps are up and running. I'm home, sweetheart."

"Home . . ." She went so still, he thought she'd stopped breathing. A tear escaped and her face softened. She managed a smile. "I'll like having you around."

He kissed the tear off her cheek, then whispered against her ear. "I want to be here for you." He could think of no where else he'd rather be. "I love you, Sophie." The words felt right. "I'll teach you how to drive, to paddleboard, to walk on stilts, whatever adventure you want to try."

"I'll learn how to cook," she promised. She licked her lips, then asked him, "Can I interest you in dinner? I'm baking one-step lasagna for the third night in a row. The noodles have been chewy."

"I can live with chewy."

"Could you live with me forever?"

"Marriage is forever, Sophie."

"Then I choose you," she said with finality. "I like winning our bets."

His chest swelled, and his smile broke. "You've won my heart, Sophie Saunders. You helped settle the feud. Frank already thinks of you as family, but let's make it official, the sooner the better."

"How soon is soon?" she asked.

"You tell me," he said.

"It will depend on the size of our wedding."

"I'll leave that up to you."

"Your family is enormous," she said, counting on her fingers.

"They'll all want to attend."

"I'd like to involve my mother in the wedding," she told him. "Our relationship is tenuous at best, but we've gotten a bit closer. I made French toast for her the other day. It took a lot of maple syrup, but she ate every bite."

"That's great news," Dune said.

"She also made a sizeable donation to the museum," she added.

"That was generous on her part."

She sighed. "We will never have a normal mother-daughter relationship, but she's trying and I'm trying. That's all I can ask for."

Dune squeezed her shoulder, then gently rubbed her back. "You'll have a better bond with your own daughter," he assured her.

"Babies." Her cheeks pinkened.

"I want a big family, Sophie."

"I do, too." She smiled at him. "I want tall boys who ride motorcycles and play volleyball."

"And girls who love books and Dwarf hamsters," he added. "I see a lot of sex in our future. Sex with cream cheese icing and"—he pressed a kiss to her lips—"popsicles."

Sophie shivered in anticipation. Then melted against Dune.